Run Cissy *Run*

Betty J. Vaughn

TotalRecall Publications, Inc.
1103 Middlecreek
Friendswood, Texas 77546
281-992-3131 281-482-5390 Fax
www.totalrecallpress.com

ISBN: 978-1-59095-675-5
UPC: 6-43977-46753- 9

Printed in the United States of America with simultaneous printings in Australia, Canada, and United Kingdom.

Library of Congress Control Number: 2015944446

FIRST EDITION
1 2 3 4 5 6 7 8 9 10

I dedicate this book with gratitude to my uncle, Dr. Lonnie H. Blizzard, President Emeritus of Lenoir County Community College in Kinston, NC. He has been an unfailing supporter, mentor, friend, and promoter in bringing my books to fruition. His enthusiasm and knowledge of this period of history spur my own research and desire to delve more deeply into our heritage and the history of eastern North Carolina.

About the Author

Ms. Vaughn holds a BS degree in art from East Carolina University in Greenville, NC, and she studied art history and Italian at Scuola Internazionale di Grafica in Venice, Italy while supervising a study program there under the auspices of Columbia University. She currently resides in Raleigh, North Carolina.

Author's Note

Many of the characters peripheral to the story are true portraits of people who lived in New Bern, Kinston, Wilmington and other North Carolina locations during the Civil War. It is hoped that their descendants will find their characterizations acceptable and will gain some insight into the world of their ancestors. Where appropriate, actual incidents and atrocities have been incorporated in order to present both sides of the difficulties that ensued in the South during the war in a fair and historically accurate manner.

Awards

Run, Cissy, Run is the 2013 Award winner for historical fiction from the North Carolina Society of Historians. Both of the previous novels in this series: **Muddy Waters** and **Turbulent Waters** were winners in 2011 and 2012 respectively.

Judges' comments:

"The storyline, characters and settings were so real it was difficult to believe that (this book) is historical fiction. While many parts of the book are true, the well-chosen words holding these truths together take on a tone of reality and the reader becomes lost in the story and wanting more, whether truth or fiction.

It is evident that the author has done a tremendous amount of research in order to write this book and she provides a rich source of information about overlooked areas of history or those areas deemed 'less important' than others. In checking some of these areas, we have found her research to be fastidiously accurate, just as we have found her commonsense analysis of military situations to be enlightening. It is gratifying to find an astute historian whose skills far exceed that realm; someone who can take facts and weave them together with fiction and end up with a story that actually 'could have happened.'

It is that way with this book. So many emotions are felt as you ride the proverbial literary roller coaster...Ahh, it was a wonderful story...full of emotion, unexpected twists and turns, close calls and tragic moments. All of this and history, too!"

Chapter 1

Cissy LaRoque tucked her head into her shoulders as she hunkered behind the Camellia bush. Fiercely screwing her fingers into her ears and squeezing her eyes tightly shut, she ignored the strident calls of her mother to come inside. She knew she was in for a tongue lashing for staying in the sun, ruining her new dress with grass stains, unladylike behavior, and any number of other sins catalogued in her mother's daily litany of complaints. Sticking her chin out stubbornly she decided she would just stay there until night and then, under the safety of darkness, sneak into her bedroom. Later she could slip down to the kitchen where Bessie would have left her a plate of supper. Bessie was her friend and ally in the non-ending series of battles that formed her relationship with her mother.

It hurt badly that she could not make her mother love her. It frustrated her that she didn't know what she had done that was so wrong; that she could never earn a warm word, a kiss, or a hug from the woman who had borne her. Had it not been for her father, Graham LaRoque, Cissy would not have known parental love.

Just as her mother shrilled another peremptory order for Cissy to come inside, her father rode into the yard behind their waterfront home that graced a bluff overlooking the Neuse River in New Berne, North Carolina. The raised voice of his wife, Monique, skittered gratingly across his nerves. He couldn't blame his only child for ignoring the summons. His wife's imperious demands never came to anything but pain for either him or Cissy. He supposed he was partly to blame for the constant invective cast on the child from the malicious tongue of a jealous woman. Cissy was his one true love and Monique knew it. Looking back he could only wonder what momentary foolishness had led him into matrimony with such a harridan.

Yes, she had been breathtakingly beautiful to look upon, but even before they wed he had recognized her self-centered ambitions and the willfulness that allowed no room for anyone else. Sighing softly, he acknowledged that it was her icy aloofness that had inflamed his passions and challenged him to conquest. In hindsight, he rued that he had not sought a more complacent woman. There had certainly been others to choose from. But hindsight could not help either him or Cissy now.

Swinging down from his horse, Graham saw the soft robin's egg blue of his daughter's dress peeping from behind the camellia. "Cissy, darling, come to Papa."

"No. I don't want to. I'm playing doodle bug." Quickly Cecily, called Cissy since birth, grabbed a twig and began to energetically stir the conical depression in the sandy soil near the foundations of their house that announced the presence of that small gray insect. Chanting, she sang, "Doodle bug, doodle bug, come get your coffee."

Rounding the bush, Graham smiled down at his daughter. Even with her curls disheveled and her checks smudged with dirt, she was an angelic vision: radiant emerald green eyes, a small slightly retroussé nose, full lips, thick blond curls, and an elegantly slim form promising a stunningly beautiful maturity. At six, she was a cheerful but stubborn hoyden. "Did that doodle bug show up yet?"

"I don't think so. I'll just keep stirring." With a determined set to her mouth, Cissy dared her father to order her to desist and go to her mother.

"Come inside with me, darling. Let's see what Mama wants before she becomes angry with us both. Will you do that for me, sweet little girl?" Graham wheedled gently.

"I can't Papa. My dress is all dirty and Mama's going to be really angry. I think I'll just wait for a while."

Graham laughed, "Do you think it's going to become clean all by itself if you wait?"

"Of course not, Papa. That's silly. I'm just waiting until she forgets about me and gets mad about something else." Cissy looked at her father with a sardonic quirk to her mouth denoting a cynicism beyond her years.

"I think I'm tempted to play doodle bug with you, but I'd better go see what I can do to placate your mother. When she calms down, you go to your room and clean up, then join us for supper. All right, darling?"

"*If* she calms down?" A wry frown flickered across her face.

"You'll come on in then, Cissy. That's a good girl." Graham ruffled her hair before walking toward the veranda, squaring his shoulders for battle as he went. Graham was a handsome man in the prime of his years, an accomplished businessman, educated, affable and thoroughly miserable. Fleetingly he envisioned himself and his daughter ensconced in one of the ships that came into New Berne's port and safely on their way to Europe, before his wife awakened the following morning. He had not seen his cousins in San Remy du Provençe in many years and they had never met his daughter. If only it could be, he breathed before walking through the door to face a woman he had come to detest but still lusted after.

"Monique, my dear, what has you in such a foul mood this afternoon? I could hear you shouting all the way down the lane. It's a little unseemly for the servants to hear you show such temper." His unaccustomed criticism of her conduct should bring the lightening from his child's head to his own, he thought with satisfaction.

"How dare you imply that my conduct is uncouth! I'm quite sure you will recall that I am the one descended from the French aristocracy. I've dealt with servants all of my life."

He could have recited her diatribe by heart: her family name was the distinguished one, but who had ever heard of the LaRoques? Had it not been for an unforeseen decline in the de Guibert family fortune, she would never have married so beneath her station and been saddle with life in such a backwater town. She spewed the oft-repeated litany in French, knowing he would understand every spiteful word.

"Thank you, my dear. I appreciate this belated assessment of my merits. However, I don't believe you expressed any reluctance to marry beneath your station at the time." Graham was coldly furious at his wife and even more furious for allowing himself to be angered by her. Repetition should have dulled the edge so it no longer rankled, but it did. "I certainly recall the Comte and Comtesse's delight when I proposed, especially after they requested and received a detailing of my financial particulars. They seemed to think I was quite a bargain. I'm beginning to think they got the better of it."

"How dare you!" Monique whirled on him, intending to slap him until she caught the steely glint in his eyes. Changing tactics, she suddenly smiled and softly pleaded, "Graham, let's not be difficult. There's something I've been waiting to discuss with you for sometime and such unpleasantness between us is unnecessary anyway."

Monique flounced across the parlor floor to stand by the long window that overlooked the front garden. Graham waited, nonplused by the sudden change of tenor. He watched her work her mouth as she fidgeted, obviously wondering how to begin. Refusing to make it any easier, he calmly walked over to the table that held a decanter and poured a glass of sherry. "While you work out how to drop this discussion on me, would you care for some sherry?"

"What? Oh, yes, please," she granted distractedly.

Calmly he poured a glass for her as well, and then seated himself on the divan where he slowly sipped his sherry. Crossing his legs nonchalantly, he studied her through narrowed eyes as she paced back and forth across the richly colored Turkish carpet that glowed in the striped sunlight pouring through the louvered shutters that covered the floor length windows of the parlor. The nine years that had passed since their wedding had done nothing to dim the twenty-eight year old woman's looks. If anything, maturity had brought her a greater beauty and a more sultry awareness of the power it gave her. He felt a stirring in his groin as he watched her and recognized it for what it was, a physical response to her external appearance that had nothing to do with his heart and emotions. Belatedly, he realized that she had caught his appraisal and gloatingly knew it for what it was.

Jutting her breasts provocatively, she leaned back against the bombé chest that filled the space between the front windows. Her eyes lowered seductively as she purred, "Graham, we have become much too confrontational. It seems my nerves are constantly frayed from the rigors of living here. I think I'm just a wee bit lonely for Paris and Maman. Perhaps, it would be good for us if we had some time apart. Maman wrote that Papa is not doing well and asked that we come for a visit. He very much wants to see Cissy before he dies. I know you cannot leave just now until you resolve some things business-wise. I thought Cissy and I might go ahead to Paris and you could join us later in the year."

Graham commented obliquely, "I confess I was thinking just now of going to France myself. I haven't seen my cousins there since our wedding."

Monique beamed victoriously, "Marvelous. I'll have Cissy's things packed and we will be away as soon as you can arrange passage for the two of us."

Graham shook his head. "You misunderstand me; you're not taking Cissy with you. I'll bring her with me when I come."

"You cannot be serious? A child belongs with the mother. What would you do with her here? She would be left to the lackadaisical whims of the servants. Heaven only knows she is impossible as it is. What on earth would she be if I left her here with no discipline and structure? That's impossible. She would become even more intractable. If she continues like this, she'll never make a good marriage with anyone of any note."

"Monique, forgive me the bluntness of this observation, but you and Cissy are not on very good terms. She does little to please you and she suffers from feelings of failure and inadequacy when she's around you. Rarely does the child get any commendation from you; rather, there is a constant barrage of censure for one failing or another. I do not intend for her to be subjected to months of harsh and unfeeling criticism for everything she does. Further more, there is nothing wrong with her that a little loving tolerance from you and time will not cure. She'll stay with me and I will see to it that she is properly cared for. You go on your own and have your visit. As soon as I can leave, we will follow." Graham raised an eyebrow and continued; "I doubt that she will have aged so much by that point that she no longer has a chance in the marriage market. I confess I don't know many men that are going to be chasing a six-year old to propose. Furthermore, this is 1850 and America, not France. I will not stand for an arranged marriage for our daughter, not now and not later."

"Your precious little girl can do no wrong, of course," Monique stopped herself from continuing. "I think I just explained my reasons for taking her now. Who knows if my father will still be alive when you get around to coming."

"You forget I also read the letter from your mother. She mentioned that Rene is complaining a bit about the indignities of age, but she certainly gave no indication that he is on his deathbed. I fail to see the urgency of this visit, although I share with you an inclination to return to France, not only to see your family, but my cousins, as well. If you wish to leave immediately, I will arrange it, but Cissy will be traveling with me, not with you."

You catch more flies with honey that vinegar, she reminded herself as she rubbed the fabric over her breast with her hand. Graham watched as the nipple peaked and despised himself for the eager response that stirred in his loins. She still held him in sexual thrall and well she knew it. Lifting one perfectly arched brow, Monique shifted her eyes to his crotch in blatant invitation.

Cissy was crouched in the bushes beneath the parlor window listening to her parents' rising voices as they launched into yet another battle of wills. When she realized that she was once again at the center of the verbal maelstrom, she edged away from the window and ran pell-mell from the yard into the woods behind her home where the trees were just beginning to bedeck themselves in the colors of autumn. Not content at the too close proximity to the battle that raged in her wake, she continued into the trees finally emerging in the garden of their widowed neighbor, Evangeline Forrest. Cissy crossed the grassy lawn using shrubbery that dotted the green expanse to screen herself from watching eyes. Reaching the far side of the lawn, she sat down on the bank of the river and stared out at the wide expanse of sparkling water.

She could not help but remember her mother's words. The most awful thing Cissy could imagine would be to go away with her mother, no father to protect her from her mother's vicious tongue. Her father rarely won in arguments with his wife, preferring to accede to her wishes rather than create greater strife. If he lost this one, she would have to go to France with her mother. Thinking of having to leave without him, made fat tears roll down her cheeks leaving grimy trails in their wake. Her shoulders shook with silent sobs. So wrapped was she in misery, that she failed to hear the quiet footsteps that approached her.

"What's wrong, child?" a soft, cultured voice inquired.

Startled, Cissy sprang to her feet and would have dashed off, but a gentle restraining hand on her shoulder held her there. Cissy looked up into the kind eyes that were peering at her with concern. Studying the halo-like aura of golden hair that tumbled about the woman's face, Cissy blurted, "Are you an angel?"

"Well, you're the first to ever mistake me for one of those." The woman chuckled merrily. "No, my dear, I'm not an angel. Now, tell me what has made you so sad?"

"My mama hates me and now she wants to take me away from Papa and go all the way to France to find me a husband. I'm just a little girl and I don't want to get married, not ever. I'm not going. If she tries to make me, I'll run away. Papa is the only one that loves me. I'm staying with my papa forever and ever." New tears followed the muddy paths of the old ones.

"Sweetheart, I'm sure your mother loves you. How could she not?" Evangeline smiled at the little girl. "I don't have a child," she bit back the words 'not anymore,' before continuing. "But if I had, I would want her to be just like you."

Cissy looked at the women in surprise, "You would?

"I would," Evangeline smiled her assurance. "Now you come to the house with me and have a nice cool glass of something to drink. I think I heard Beulah say she made some teacakes and lemonade. I think that would just be perfect, don't you?"

Cissy wanted that lemonade and cookie more than anything. She wanted it so badly it made her mouth water. But if she stayed away any longer and her mother found out, she would be in terrible trouble, worse trouble than she was already in. Her mother did not like for her to socialize with the neighbors, either child or adult. If she knew that Cissy had criticized her to others, she would be even more incensed. Cissy bit her lower lip in concentration, considering whether or not she dared. Finally she looked up with an impish smile, "You won't tell on me, will you, if I stay just for a minute?"

"Of course, I won't child. It will be our secret and we will gobble those cookies up quick, quick, so you can run home." Evangeline smiled down at the little girl, feeling her heart break at the sadness in those emerald eyes. "My name is Miss Evangeline. What's yours?"

"I'm Cecily LaRoque, but everyone calls me Cissy." Skipping along at the woman's side, Cissy felt her heart lift. She had a friend, a nice lady who must know how much Cissy loved teacakes.

When Evangeline looked down at the bedraggled child at her side she felt her heart contract. Her only child, Lorena, had died of diphtheria at the age of six. Surely this lively little girl must be of much the same age as her daughter when she had died. A sudden fierce longing for Lorena gripped her heart like a physical pain. Momentarily staggered, Evangeline struggled to regain her composure as she led the child to the solarium for the promised treats. Intent on the plate of cookies, Cissy was oblivious to the woman's inner agony as they entered the house.

"Oh, it's nice here. It looks happy." Cissy twirled in a circle noting the brightly colored furnishings and paintings that filled Evangeline's home.

I'm glad you think so, Cissy. These are my paintings. I make them happy because they've become my friends and companions. It's good to have pleasant company, I think." Evangeline paused to look at the paintings that filled the entry hall. They were all washed in sunlight whether floral, landscape or portrait. "I try to keep the sunshine in my life. Dark days are always lit by these paintings you see here."

"I wish I could paint, but Maman doesn't like me to do

messy things. I may only draw," Cissy commented.

"You're welcome to come paint with me. Perhaps we should ask your parents permission for you to do so?" the woman offered.

"I don't think so. I'm not supposed to even visit. I'm sure she would not like me to visit *and* paint," Cissy smiled sadly.

"We'll just wait a bit then. Since your mother is leaving for France, after she has gone we could ask your father if you'd like?" Evangeline surprised herself by suggesting the child defy her mother's wishes.

"Yes, please." Cissy beamed with pleasure. Her day had just brightened with the promise of good things to come. As though pushing the thought of France from her mind, Cissy stood and solemnly extended a sticky little hand. In her most grownup voice she intoned the memorized response, "Thank you very much, Miss Evangeline. You have been most hospitable. Good day."

Evangeline watched as the enigmatic little girl, who seemed far too sad and mature for her years, ran across the lawn towards the shadowy trees along the rim of her property. As Cissy slipped beneath the branches of a large longleaf pine tree, she felt as though her heartstrings were attached to the little girl---stretching as she disappeared from sight, yet still firmly anchored to her. Tears gathered behind her closed eyelids as she remembered holding her own child to her breast, her husband watching with paternal pride. Charles had adored becoming a father and his kindly eyes had lit with love whenever he gazed at either his wife or child. Those last days of his life had been filled with unquenchable mourning for their lost child, and then he too was gone, the victim of a ruptured appendix. Evangeline knew if she allowed herself to dwell on her losses, she would sink back into the despondency that had consumed two of the three years since their deaths. She had fought to regain her life and find small moments of joy in days that were now devoid of those she had loved and forever lost. She had fought too hard to emerge from the depths of depression to allow it to consume her once again.

Gently closing the door beneath the fanlight that scattered patterned brightness on the polished foyer floor, Evangeline walked to the back of the house and the sun-washed room that she had converted into a studio. Soon she was seated at her worktable grinding the pigments she would mix with oil to create the paint she needed for the canvas that waited on an easel by the window. It had become her refuge from a world that had proven too hurtful. She should not have spoken to the child and she chided herself for it. To do so had only reminded her of her losses. As she worked grinding the pigments into powder, she fought the tears that threatened to blind her, that would over-whelm her once again with renewed grief if she allowed.

Cissy fought her own battle with sadness. As she neared the rear of her home, her steps slowed unconsciously. She knew she must find a way to reach her room unimpeded by any voice that might call attention to her current state of disrepair. Creeping past her parent's bedroom, she heard her mother's low moaning and the deep rumble of her father's voice. She did not know what it was that caused the furtive sounds but recognized it as an adult thing that she dared not question. At least they were in their room and unlikely to catch their grimy child as she sneaked her way to her room and the waiting washbasin.

Graham rolled off his wife and onto his back. Looking at the ceiling, he rued that once again lust had conquered him. He heard Cissy walking softly down the hall to her room and was at least grateful that she had managed to elude her mother's critical eye. Hopefully Tizzia would see to it that the child appeared well cleaned and freshly dressed when she slipped into her seat in the dining room. He could not help the sardonic smile that flitted across his face when he heard the sexually contented purr of his wife. Perhaps her mood would translate into a tranquil supper hour for the three of them. However, had he been privy to her thoughts he would have been immediately disabused of the notion.

Monique relished the idea of months without an observant husband, months when elderly parents would prove no deterrent to her enjoyment of the pleasures of the round of balls and parties that marked the annual coming-out season. If she left soon, she would be there just in time for the first ball. Idly she allowed her thoughts to drift to her former suitor, handsome Marcel Lambert, scoundrel, wastrel and charmer. She'd loved him to distraction and nearly lost her virginity to him in their neighbor's garden during her first ball. Her parents had firmly disabused her of any future with a man who had limited finances and nothing to recommend himself besides an old and distinguished lineage. Perhaps, if he were still in Paris, she might enjoy more than innocent flirtation now that she was a married woman. With Graham's money and her marital status, she would be free to do as she chose. If only she were a widow, she thought. Resentment of a husband she did not want and a life she hated, brought a frown to her face.

"Please, have fresh water sent up. I feel the need for a bath." Monique ordered as she stood and wrapped a diaphanous dressing gown around her body. "It wouldn't hurt you to freshen up either. You smell like that mare you were riding."

"Which *mare* are you referring to, my dear?" Graham could not resist the pun.

"I suppose you think that's humorous? I can assure you I do not," she snapped with glacial venom.

"I'll send for water," Graham glowered as he rose from her bed and walked into his adjoining bedroom. Once again, he damned himself for succumbing to her seduction. In the deep recesses of his heart he wondered if he would ever be free of the harridan he had married. As a devout Catholic, he could only leave his fate in God's hands.

Not so, Monique. For her, she would forge her own way to a future, with divine blessing or without made no difference to her. Staring out the window at the river that led to the sea, she waited for her bath water. Sneering with contempt for the man she had married, she dreamt of adventures awaiting her across the Atlantic.

While the maid entered and completed preparing the bath, Monique turned to admire herself in the full-length mirror. With calm deliberation, she loosened the peignoir and studied her nude body, smiling in full confidence that she could bend any man to her will by using her physical assets. Just as Graham was gullible in his lust for her body, so would others be. She fully intended to use what advantages she had to procure a life away from this small town, a town so different from the Paris where she had carelessly flirted away her young adulthood. True, she could no longer be the belle of debutante balls, but now she would not be subjected to the same constrictions placed on young ladies by calculating parents determined to procure advantageous husbands in exchange for their nubile daughters' fragile hymens.

Dinner was relatively peaceful as Monique was so lost in schemes for the future that she forgot her earlier anger at her daughter. Looking across at Cissy, she realized she would be glad to be free of the encumbrance of a child while she plied her wares in the drawing rooms of Paris.

Not trusting her mother's mood, Cissy studiously avoided returning the cold stare her mother focused on her and instead, toyed with the peas she hated, pushing them, one by one, from one side of the plate then to the other. Judging from her parents' comments, a beneficent God had spared her the ordeal of months alone with her mother in a strange country. Under lowered lashes, Cissy glanced towards her father. Catching the look, Graham winked in understanding and grinned at her. Lowering her head further, Cissy hid her own smile from her mother.

Graham smiled at the warm glow the candles cast on Cissy's golden curls. He was as happy as his daughter to soon be free of the constant invective that had become their daily fare from his wife. Somehow, he promised himself, he would make these months with his daughter good ones, giving her the assurance and security that knowing you are loved and treasured brings to anyone, young or old.

Chapter 2

Cissy stood at the railing of the ship watching the river shores slide smoothly past as they rounded the turn into the port of New Berne. The unseasonably mild late February sun was warm on her back as a steady breeze softly lifted her curls into the air. Her father smiled down at her with gentle sadness. Even so, she suspected he was as glad to be returning home from the trip abroad as she. The winter in Paris had not been a happy one for him. She knew he was both angry and saddened that her mother had decided to remain behind in Paris. Cissy was not. She knew she would not miss her mother. A small sigh of contentment escaped her lips, before she quickly clamped them shut to keep her thoughts securely inside. She knew it was wrong to rejoice that she would be free of her mother for some time longer. Years of avoiding censure had taught her to keep silent, but her mind was as free as a scampering rabbit and she could not help which burrow it chose to explore.

"Was that a sigh I heard, sweetheart? You're not sad to be coming home are you?" Graham worried for his child. His wife's defection offended his pride and dignity as she had been blatant in her flirtations during their visit, making no secret that she preferred the company of the arrogant rakes that circled her like hounds after a bitch in heat. But the fact that she had ignored the child, except when some small moment of irritability at Cissy's childish enthusiasm reminded her mother that she was near, told Graham just how remote from the both of them the woman had become. He did not mind as much for himself as the fact that his child was deprived of a mother's presence and guidance.

Her maternal grandparents, while admiring Cissy's beauty, were best served by silence from this child that they had only just met. Their routine had no place in it for an eagerly curious and active child, even one as well behaved as Cissy. As for Graham, they were more interested in the prosperity of his business ventures than any real concern for him as their son-in-law. In amused tolerance, he had reassured them of his continued successes and they had ended their interest at that. The fact that he provided generously for his wife's comfort and needs on his departure was ample requirement as far as Monique and her family were concerned. He could only make futile conjectures as to when, or if, she might choose to return home.

Cissy and her father stood in companionable silence as the ship was brought to dock. On the shore, her father had spotted his man, Toby, come to collect them for the short journey home. "It won't be long now, Cissy. And I'm glad of it. I don't like long confinement onboard ships."

"That steamboat that brought us to New York was nice, papa, and it went fast, too. I liked that one."

"For sure it's faster than going across the Atlantic by sail, but I do get tired of the engine noise. For me, the old sail powered boats are much more peaceful even if they're slower. It will be interesting to see what boats are plying the waters between the continents when you are an old lady. You'll have to remember this very first voyage so you'll have something to compare to."

"I'm not going again unless you go to." Cissy paused and looked up at her father, "Papa, do you think maman will stay long with grandpère and grandmère in Paris?" She held her breath as she waited for his reply.

"Sweetheart, I can't read the future. Your mother has decided for now that she needs to stay on in Paris. When she'll want to come back to us, I don't know. But, don't worry, I'm sure she loves you and misses you, so she won't be too long." Graham hastened to reassure his daughter, mistaking her question for anxiety about her mother's absence.

"I think she should stay with my grandparents. She likes it there better than here, and besides, you can take good care of me all by yourself." Cissy looked up into his startled eyes. "I love you better anyway."

"Ah, Cissy, you know I love you more than the oceans could hold. You are feeling a little sad towards your mother just now, I need you to understand that your mother's decision to stay on has nothing to do with you. It's more a grown-up matter between your mother and me. You know that, don't you?"

"Papa, I may be just a little girl but I'm not stupid. Maman just doesn't like children and she doesn't like me. If she did she wouldn't always fuss at me so. She never says she loves me and she criticizes me for everything I do and say." Cissy stated it so factually it left no room for argument. For once Graham was nonplussed by his daughter's comments. Cissy glanced up at her father with concern, "Don't worry, Papa. We're going to be just fine, just us two."

It was Graham's turn to sigh, "Yes, Cissy, we are."

Graham was suddenly aware of the responsibility that raising Cissy without a woman's help would place on him. He could only hope that his love would be enough to replace that of her missing mother and his guidance would be sufficient to rear her into the kind of woman he aspired for her to be. But of course, Cissy was a wise and determined child. He chuckled softly; aware that about the best he could do was guide with gentle reins and let her have her head the way he had always done.

"Oh, Papa, look there on the wharf. I see Miss Evangeline. I wonder what she is doing. Do you think she came to meet me?" Cissy waved eagerly at the distant figure.

"I don't think so, sweetheart. I only wrote Toby and Bessie that we would be arriving today." Graham remarked. Considering how the Forest woman had pretty much isolated herself following her husband's death, he added with some surprise, "I was unaware that you knew Mrs. Forrest."

"She's very nice. We're good friends."

Hiding his surprise, Graham responded, "Well, good. I'm glad you have a new friend."

Soon Graham and Toby were busily occupied loading the carriage with the more fragile belongings that Graham had purchased in France. Their trunks would follow in the wagon that Toby had arranged to transport them. As Cissy waited in the carriage for her father and Toby to sort the remainder of the packages, she studied the crowd on the wharf to see if she could catch another glimpse of Evangeline. Frustrated at her inability to see over the tall people and taller hats in the milling throng, she at last resorted to standing in the seat. Evangeline had just emerged from the warehouse beside the wharf holding a box, when Cissy spotted her. Waving excitedly she jumped up and down on the seat, calling to the woman. Unexpectedly the horse lurched, jerking the carriage and pitching Cissy onto the floor, just as Evangeline saw her.

Graham alerted by his daughter's scream, found himself colliding with Evangeline as she, too, dashed to the rescue. "Please excuse me, Mrs. Forrest. It seems my daughter has taken a tumble. I hope I have not injured you in my precipitous rush?"

"No, no please. I was rushing myself to see if she's hurt." Evangeline smiled past him into Cissy's beaming face as the child clambered once more into the seat. "Hello, Little Miss Cecily, are you alright?"

"Oh, I'm fine. I was just looking for you. What do you have in the box? Is it a surprise that came on our ship?"

"You must forgive her curiosity, Mrs. Forrest." Graham

could not help but notice how the woman's jaunty hat enhanced her coloring.

"Not at all. This box is very special. It contains some pigments that I ordered all the way from Paris."

"Oh, my. They're for your paintings. I want to paint, too. May I come paint with you? My maman is living in Paris now, so she won't mind if I paint. Right, Papa?" Cissy beamed expectantly at her father.

"We don't invite ourselves, sweetheart. Remember your manners, please." Graham was embarrassed to have his wife's absence remarked on in such a public place, and before he had determined how best to deal with it.

Seeing his obvious discomfort, Evangeline patted Cissy on the hand. "You are more than welcome to come paint with me anytime your father will permit. Now, you must excuse me as my carriage is waiting. Leroy hates dealing with that skittish horse of mine when there are hoards of people around. Mr. LaRoque, good day to you."

"And to you, Mrs. Forrest." Graham bowed to her as she departed, but he could no more stop his eyes following her than he could those of his daughter.

Evangeline knew he watched and momentarily rejoiced. Her stomach had fluttered, there by the carriage, when she first looked into his eyes, surprising her that a man could stir her after so long alone. Following the loss of her husband and child, she never wanted to chance that kind of pain again with another man, a man who would want to make love to her and spill his seed in her begetting another child that could die. She held the memory of her lost family close. It was all she had left to warm the lonely nights that stretched ahead of her until she aged and died, withered and dry from long years of cold hours. Squaring her shoulders, she put her head up as she pushed the gloom into the recesses of her mind. She would not wallow in self-pity. Rejecting the vanity that made her glad a handsome man found her attractive, she reminded herself to think about the pleasures of her painting and her home. There was safety in that.

"She's so very nice, Papa. Is it all right for me to go to her house and paint? She invited me to a long time ago. I know she doesn't mind." Watching her father's eyes on Evangeline's retreating back, she slyly added, "She surely is a pretty lady."

Graham murmured an absent-minded agreement, as they turned away to begin the drive home. It was with a heavily preoccupied mind, that he began this phase of his life without his wife. The first order of business would be to find a suitable housekeeper to maintain the daily running of his home and to see to his daughter's immediate needs. At the moment he had no clue as to whom he could employ. Surely someone in his acquaintance would know a gentle woman, perhaps an elderly widow of reduced circumstances, who would be willing to work for him. He heaved a breath of frustration and settled his head against the leather of the carriage seat, allowing the warmth of the sun to tease the weariness and frustration from his face. Slowly the crease between his eyes began to soften as he relaxed. The realization that his wife was dallying with her former lover and preferred life in Paris to life with him and their daughter had eaten at his insides like a cancer, until he acknowledged that what rankled more than the fickleness of Monique's shallow affections was the blow to his male pride. Perhaps, he had to admit to himself, he had ceased to love her long before, if ever he had. True, he had enjoyed marriage to a woman that other men envied him for possessing, but his heart had never been as warmed by her as his body had been.

The image of Evangeline Forrest kept playing across the screen of his closed lids. He silently chortled at his own ready turn of interest to another woman, and one with whom he could entertain no thought of anything beyond friendship. As a Catholic, he was not free to remarry and as a woman of quality and refinement, Evangeline was not one to use as a mistress. The thought of visiting a bordello for lustful companionship held little appeal, yet he suspected he was ill suited for a life of chaste denial.

The rhythmic clopping of the horse's hooves quickened tempo as they turned into the drive leading to his home. Silently Cissy slid her hand into his and gave a gentle squeeze. "Wake up, Papa. We're almost home."

"I'm not sleeping, sweetheart. I was just pondering the possibility of a governess for you since your mama is going to be away for awhile."

"What's a governess? Is that like a mama?" Cissy was instantly suspicious. Unconsciously sticking her lower lip forward, she pouted for a moment before declaring, "If it is, I don't want any old governess."

"Now, now. Don't go getting your dander up. A governess is just an older lady who teaches you various school subjects along with proper manners for a young lady. Wouldn't it be fun to have a nice lady as a companion?"

"I have one. Miss Evangeline is a friend and she is going to teach me to paint like her. Besides, I have you. I don't want a governess." Her lips pouting, she pleaded, "Please, Papa?"

"We'll talk about it later, Cissy. Right now, wave at Bessie before she wears her arm off."

"You're silly. Bessie can't wear her arm off from waving." Cissy giggled in restored good humor.

With luggage settled and things stowed, Graham joined his daughter at the table for supper. After elaborate French fare during those months away, he hungered for a simple southern meal. However his appetite was quickly ruined when Bessie walked in with her special treat for his return. He watched his daughter's eyes widen in astonished dismay as she stared at the offering. Curled yellowish chicken claws protruded from the bowl where shreds of meat and tatters of skin stuck to gelatinous pale gray pastry. Bessie proudly sat it on the table before him.

"I done fixed y'all a special dinner, suh." Bessie beamed proudly as she indicated the dish.

"Exactly what is this, Bessie? I don't recall you serving it before." Graham caught Cissy's eye, warning her to mind her manners.

"That my chicken and pastry. I never cooked it for y'all before because I knowed the mistress wouldn't be liking it. I figured you going to be missing good old plain cooking after all that fancy stuff over yonder. "

"That's true, Bessie. That's true." He watched as the smiling Bessie left the room before beckoning to Cissy. "Let's be naughty. I'll put a little on your plate and some on mine and then we'll dump it out of the dining room window. Bessie's feelings won't be hurt that way."

"Good, because I don't want to eat that with those old chicken feet poking out." Cissy wrinkled her nose and then giggled as they cautiously crept to the window and pitched the contents of their plates below the Camellia bush that stood there. Plaintively Cissy stated, "I *am hungry*, Papa."

"We'll just eat the green beans and cornbread. I'm sure Bessie will have made a special dessert treat as well."

"I surely hope Bessie doesn't make this chicken and pastry thing anymore," Cissy exclaimed with a worried look on her face.

"That's why I didn't dish out too much. When she sees we didn't eat a lot, she'll know it isn't a favorite. I think that's a nicer way to handle it than telling her we don't like it. Don't you?"

"I do, Papa. I don't want to hurt Bessie's feelings. She's always nice to me."

"I know. She sneaked supper to you when your mother sent you to bed without any." Graham grinned at her.

"You knew?" Cissy stared at him in surprise.

"I did. It'll be our secret." Graham reached over and tussled his daughter's hair. For the first time in months, dinner was free of tension. He could enjoy his daughter's company without wondering what the next snide comment from his wife would be regarding either his failings or those of their daughter. He knew that Cissy had also suffered under the barrage of orders and complaints from her mother. Even though she had been critical at home, in France it was as though each of their perceived faults had been magnified in Monique's eyes.

His musings were interrupted when Bessie returned to the dining room bearing the large chocolate cake that was a favorite of both father and child. "Oh!" Cissy squealed with excitement. "My very, very favorite. Thank you, Bessie."

"You're welcome, child. You eat yourself a big old piece now."

"I will," Cissy exclaimed with enthusiasm.

They had finished their dessert and Graham was sipping his wine, when a scratching noise in the garden caught their attention. Rising from the table, they crept to the window and looked down. A fat raccoon lifted a greased face and calmly looked back at them. It was apparent he enjoyed the chicken and pastry far better than they.

"Look, Papa. He's so cute. I think I'll name him Robin for Robin Hood. He's a good thief because he's eating that for us."

Graham laughed softly, "I think that makes him a very good one. Now little one, it has been a long day. Let's get you to bed and then I'll come tell you a story. Go on up now and let Tizzia get you tucked in. I'll be up in a moment."

"All right, Papa." Cissy gave a last loving glance at the raccoon before running lightly up the stairs.

During the coming weeks, Cissy cultivated a careful routine for Robin by placing hoarded scraps beneath the Camellia. In the beginning, she would wait in the shadows by the corner of the house until he began to eat and then she would creep away on silent feet. Each evening she stayed a little longer and when he seemed to be growing accustomed to her presence, she began a slow progression from the corner towards the dining room window. In the dim light of dusk, she waited and patiently moved her place of watching until she was within a few scant feet of the animal. The first time she spoke, he looked up in alarm and waited for her to move. When she did nothing, he resumed gnawing on the pork chop bone that was his feast for the evening.

The next night she again spoke. "Hello, Robin," she cooed. "Do you like your dinner?" Again he looked up and watched until, sensing nothing to cause alarm, he continued eating.

The big event came after weeks of patience when at last Cissy extended a wary hand to lightly stroke the animal's fur. Again he froze and waited. When she withdrew her hand, he went back to the bacon rind.

Soon when she brought his evening treat, she would find him waiting for her. He allowed her to pet him after he had finished his meal. Cissy was delighted. It was the first pet she had ever had, as her mother would allow no animals beyond the half feral cats that patrolled the stables for mice. And she was too afraid of the tall powerful horses to approach them.

Visiting with Robin became a nightly ritual. In time, Robin would come to her and follow her about in the late afternoon as the setting sun cast long shadows from the trees across the lawn, drawing parallel lines away from the shore of the bordering river. Cissy's days were peaceful and happy. She did not miss her mother. At night, when her father reminded her to include her mother in her evening prayers, she did so. But, she suspected God knew she didn't mean it. Each time she felt a slight tremor of fear that he would punish her for the sin in her heart.

She was also learning to paint under the tutelage of

Evangeline, who despite the longing the child evoked in her for the daughter she had lost, took Cissy under her wing. With the woman's encouragement and unstinting praise for her efforts, Cissy found a new pride in herself and a sense of accomplishment. More and more she wished that Evangeline were her mother and not the carping Monique. Few days went by the child did not make her way through the woods that separated her father's land from her new friend's. Evangeline always made Cissy feel welcome and began to enjoy the child's easy chatter and sunny disposition. On occasion Graham would walk over to fetch her home for the evening meal. Evangeline's heart skipped a beat each time she saw him standing on her porch inquiring for his daughter. She hated that she blushed and stammered in his presence and wondered what he must think of her. Had she only known that he too felt drawn to her, she would have been even more flustered.

Cissy had visited with Evangeline for most of the afternoon. With shadows lengthening and the November air growing chilly, she knew it was time to leave. "I have to go now, Miss Evangeline. I need to find Robin so he can walk me home."

"Your Robin sounds like a very nice little gentleman. Would you introduce me sometime?"

"I will, but I can't just now. He is still a bit nervous around other people. He doesn't let Papa get near yet." Cissy smiled, "He'll like you just fine when I tell him how nice you are. He'll like Papa, too. He must. My daddy is the nicest man in the whole wide world."

Evangeline could not resist asking, "Do you miss your mother, child?"

Reluctant to admit that she didn't, Cissy worried her lower lip for a moment while she thought how to avoid telling a lie. "Mama is happy in Paris. She hates it here. She was always fussing at Papa and me. She should stay with my grandparents. It's better for her, I think."

Not sure how to respond, Evangeline merely commented, "I see."

"Papa is happier, too. I think he likes you. Maybe y'all could be friends, like we are." With adoration shining in her eyes, Cissy shyly added, "You can be my mama if you want to."

"That is so sweet of you, darling. But, I can never take your mother's place. While she is away, we can pretend I'm your special mother-like friend. Will that make you happy?" Evangeline swallowed hard to restrain the emotion that welled up at the child's innocent offer.

"Thank you! I like that." Quickly Cissy hugged her goodbye before skipping down the steps. She needed to find her raccoon and get home before dark.

Cissy did not like the woods at night, not even at twilight. The swaying Spanish moss had an eerie spectral quality like the ghosts that peopled the stories Bessie sometimes told her in the kitchen. In the snug warmth from the fireplace and with the cook's stout body for defense, the tales only caused a mild frisson of fear, but that was magnified to near terror when she found herself alone in the shadowy depths of the mysterious wooded verge. A few moments of running haste, brought her into the familiar environs of her own yard. There she paused to check under the magnolia and then the camellia to see if Robin had hidden himself while he awaited her. Not finding him, she called softly, but her bright-eyed raccoon did not come.

At the table, a morose Cissy picked at her food. Normally the crispy fried chicken and roasted potatoes elicited a robust appetite. Tonight with Robin missing she could only fret. Graham watched her as she moved the same piece of chicken first to one side of her plate and then back again.

"Sweetheart, this is one of your favorite meals. What's so awful that you can't eat it?"

"I'm sorry, Papa. I'm just too worried."

"It must be terrible if my very favorite little girl can't eat

Bessie's special supper." Graham persisted, smiling inquiringly at his daughter as she continued pushing the chicken about.

"It's Robin. I don't know if he doesn't like me anymore or if maybe he is sick or something. He didn't walk me home from Miss Evangeline's tonight like he always does. I was scared in those old woods without him."

"Maybe he was off on some kind of raccoon errand. I suspect if you put some of that chicken under the bush for him, he'll come running in no time."

"Oh, that's a good idea. Would you excuse me please, Papa." Cissy was already squirming from her chair.

Reaching over, Graham laid a restraining hand on her arm, "Now, now, there is no need to worry or rush. Eat something. There will be quite enough left for Robin. I'll even save him some of mine."

Cissy tried to eat but worry superceded any appetite she might have had. At last Graham gave up, "Take your leftovers to Robin. I'm sure he'll come scampering for them in no time."

"Thank you, Papa." Cissy grabbed her plate and hastened to Robin's spot beneath the Camellia. As the night deepened and Robin still did not appear, a tear slipped from her eye and splashed into the food she had so tenderly spread out for her pet. Tired and frustrated, she heeded her father's call to come in.

"I'm sorry, Sweetheart. He's your pet but he is also a wild animal and sometimes he just needs to be like other critters. I'm sure he'll be back tomorrow, so try not to worry yourself." Graham picked her up in his arms and snuggled her neck, "Let's take you up so Tizzia can get you ready for a good sleep."

Cissy smiled gamely when he returned to kiss her goodnight and listen to her prayers, but her heart wasn't in it. She slept fitfully and by first light was down the stairs where she struggled to open the heavy front door without making a squeak that would awaken her still slumbering father.

Hurrying to Robin's bush she peered beneath the branches. The food from the previous dinner lay untouched.

Cissy's feet were wet from the morning dew that sparkled on the tender green of the lawn and the cool air chilled her. Discouraged, she skirted around the house and entered the kitchen where a surprised Bessie greeted her, "Chile, why come you out here in your nightgown and no shoes? Yo' Papa going to be mighty upset with you. You set down here by this fire and let's see if we can't get you warmed up some while I finish cooking this here breakfast."

"Thank you, Bessie," Cissy said as she obediently sat on the stool and extended the soles of her feet to the fire.

"I spect you mighty hungry this morning. You ain't et nothing to speak of last evening. I beginning to think you don't like my fried chicken no more," Bessie grumbled good-naturedly as she forked the sizzling bacon from skillet to platter.

"I love your fried chicken. I just couldn't eat anything because I was so worried about Robin. I can't find him."

"Much scraps as you been toting to that little ole critter, he bound to be back here looking for some more," Bessie said as she put Cissy's breakfast on the table. "You eat up now so you got energy to get out there and play. Fore you do though, you might better get on some shoes and something besides that nightgown."

"Thank you, Bessie. I will," Cissy could not resist the odor of the crisp bacon that was mounded atop a bowl of creamy grits. She wasted no time in applying herself to the savory food.

Dressed and well fed, Cissy renewed her search with optimism. She began at the edge of the woods and systematically began to search in all of the places she had previously seen Robin. After some thirty minutes of diligent effort, she forced herself to squelch the despair she felt welling up inside. Instead, she doggedly continued calling for Robin while brushing her hands to part tall weeds, and looking beneath bushes and under small trees. It was nearly noon when she at last spied a familiar coat of fur lying under a small sassafras tree. Hastening to her raccoon, she touched the small body and found it stiff and unyielding. Her pet was dead.

Her heart broken with its loss, Cissy rocked back on her heels and wailed. Her only pet was gone, killed by a careless hunter and left to bleed to death.

The crackling of footsteps on the carpeted floor of the forest went unheard. She jumped with surprise when a tentative hand touched her shoulder. She looked up through lashes wet with tears and met the dark, kind eyes of a lad of perhaps eight or nine. Crouching next to her, he reached out to touch the raccoon. "I guess this must have been your pet?"

She nodded unable to form words around the lump in her throat.

"I'm Logan Gwaltney. I live down the road a ways." He jerked his head to indicate the general direction.

"I'm Cissy LaRoque, Cecily actually. That's my house through the trees yonder," she hiccupped softly as she said it. "This is my pet, Robin."

"Come on, Cissy. Let's give him a funeral."

Woodenly Cissy stood and followed him as he carried the body of the raccoon to a sandy clearing. Putting the animal down, he pulled a knife from his belt and began to scoop the dirt to form a shallow grave. "While I'm doing this, would you like to look for some wild flowers? Over there are some violets that would look pretty on his grave."

Again she nodded to him, and then proceeded to pick a small nosegay of violets. When she returned to the shallow grave, Robin was already resting inside. The boy said, "I'll put my handkerchief over him and we'll fill the grave with dirt. Would you like to help?"

Cissy and the boy together pushed the small mound of freshly dug soil into the grave and then patted it firmly in place.

Cissy placed the flowers on top and then looked at her new friend, unsure what to do next. He answered her silent question, "We'll say the Twenty-third Psalms and then I'll say a prayer. Is that good for you?"

"You say it. I'll listen."

Softly he intoned the familiar and soothing words as Cissy began crying softly. When he was finished he took her hand and looked into her green eyes. He thought she was the prettiest thing he had ever seen despite disheveled hair and her face blotched from crying. He did not know what impulse caused him to lean forward and gently touch her lips with his own.

"You're mine now, Cissy, forever and ever and I'm going to marry you when we get big.

"You can't. I'm going to marry my Papa cause he's all alone now that Mama is in France. If she doesn't come home, I'm going to marry him."

"You can't do that silly goose. Girls can't marry their papas. You're going to marry me. Besides, I've done and compromised you. I heard Mama say that if a boy goes kissing on a girl he has to marry her to protect her reputation."

Cissy looked askance at this new information, unsure what to say. Logan saved her the trouble by taking her by the hand and leading her back to her house. He left her there, whistling as he walked away. After that, few days passed that Logan did not visit. Soon they were fast friends and the pain of losing her pet diminished. Although she continued to visit with Evangeline, Logan became her steady companion.

Chapter 3

Graham dropped the latest of Monique's infrequent letters onto his desk with a sigh of disgust. Once more she had asked for more money and a prolongation of the visit that had already extended over a year and a half. He resented supporting her to pursue a life of licentious abandon in the drawing rooms of Paris while she ignored the duties of wife and mother. Yet, he knew in the depths of his heart, he didn't care if she ever returned. Oh yes, he missed her voluptuous body when he retired in the evening to a cold and lonely bed. But life was so much easier and far more pleasant without her constant harping and petty spite. Cissy had blossomed in her absence as well. Graham suspected part of that was due to the unprecedented freedom Monique's absence provided the child. For the first time, in Logan, she had a playmate of similar years and she had a woman who loved and mentored her. Thinking of Evangeline, Graham reminded himself that it was time Cissy returned home for her supper.

When they had first returned from Paris, he had frequently walked over to get Cissy from Evangeline's house. Each time he had felt his attraction growing along with his need for a woman. As a well-bred woman, Evangeline was someone who would demand an honest and committed relationship. He constantly reminded himself that with a wife already he had nothing to offer her. Now it had been months since he had last seen the woman, having forced himself to stay away until the attraction he had felt at the pier subsided. Secure in the belief that the feelings that had overcome him previously were mere ephemera, today he was determined that he would fetch Cissy himself.

The sound of joyful laughter was like a magnet inexorably pulling him to its source. Graham emerged from the woods to see his daughter waving a paintbrush in the air and merrily chasing Evangeline about the piazza of her house. Both were whooping as they twisted and turned around the wicker chairs and tables that furnished the shaded expanse. When his foot landed on the lower stone step, both wheeled around in surprise, stopping in mid stride. With her hair askew, her face daubed with paint, and her bosom heaving, Evangeline was an enchanting sight. He felt his heart drumming with excitement as he looked at her.

Embarrassed by his scrutiny and aware of her dishabille, Evangeline flushed. "Oh my goodness, I must look a sight. Cissy and I were just finishing up our day's painting."

"It seems the canvases may have received less than your faces." Graham laughed at the two of them.

"I am so sorry. I'm afraid we got a bit carried away with our teasing." Evangeline turned to Cissy, "Come, darling, and I'll get your face cleaned."

"It's okay. I can do it when I get home and besides, Papa doesn't mind. He's smiling at us. Right, Papa?" Cissy grinned impishly at her father as she awaited his reply.

Graham forced his face into stern lines, "I just mind *one* thing."

Both Evangeline and Cissy worriedly held their breath as they waited for him to continue. Unable to maintain the frown, he grinned. "I'm just sorry I wasn't here earlier, so I could have had some fun, too."

"Please come in. I'll have my servant bring you some tea while I wash Cissy's face."

"I'll decline the tea, however if you have a bit of whiskey, I wouldn't say no." Graham raised his eyebrows in question.

"Of course. Please have a seat in the parlor. You'll find a decanter and some glasses on the sideboard there. I don't drink it, so it's just been sitting there since my husband died. I don't suppose it goes bad though."

He held the door for Cissy and Evangeline as they entered the spacious foyer, "I'm sure it'll be fine."

Evangeline motioned with her hand, "The parlor is just there. Excuse us. We'll only be a moment."

Graham poured a drink and then seated himself in a chair by the window where he could relish the ambiance of the room. Light filtered through the lace under-drapes casting dappled shadows on the dark cherry floor that was polished to a high sheen. The walls were filled with colorful paintings that he suspected were mostly by Evangeline's talented hand. There was an occasional landscape and portrait that seemed to be of a different style and temperament but yet fitted well with the paintings that she had authored. As he sipped his drink, he felt a peace descend on him and fill his heart. It seemed as though he had finally arrived home after a long and peril-fraught journey. He knew Cissy must have felt the same magnetic draw. How else could he explain her daily trips to this house? Here was a home filled with love and joy that had risen above the pain of loss, freed of a crushing blanket of bitter grief. How she must have mourned the loss of husband and daughter? He wondered how she had managed to put together such a seamless life under the burden fate had given her to bear.

Light steps accompanied by skipping ones announced the return of the freshly scrubbed miscreants. He noted that Evangeline had tamed her wayward tresses into a neat bun and both faces were red from a recent scrubbing. Cissy rushed into her father's arms and he gave her a quick hug. Looking up into Evangeline's eyes, he saw the naked longing that filled them and knew she was thinking of those she had lost. Graham held her gaze until she looked away in confusion. And then he allowed his gaze to hungrily delineate her form. Despite his best intentions to remain emotionally aloof, he found his body responding to her allure and his heart to the warmth of her aura.

With a hard swallow he cleared the lump that formed in his throat and forced his voice to sound normal. Masking his emotions behind cool formality, he said, "I fear I have been less than an exemplary neighbor. I have allowed my daughter to steal your hours and have not reciprocated with any hospitality at all. Do forgive me and permit me to compensate in some small measure by having you over for dinner tomorrow noon." He held his breath while he awaited her answer, fearful that she might refuse.

Her response was equally formal. "Firstly, I must disabuse you of the notion that your daughter has been anything but a more than welcome delight. It is I who must thank you for permitting her to visit me. It is the highlight of my day."

When she paused, he felt his heart sinking as he waited for her to decline his invitation. Then she continued, "However, despite the fact that you owe me nothing for her visits here, I would be delighted to have dinner with you tomorrow." He watched her closely as she responded, willing her to meet his eyes once again, however she kept them firmly focused on Cissy who was swiveling her head from first one adult to the other.

"Wonderful. We look forward to seeing you tomorrow." Graham smiled at her and taking his daughter by the hand, said, "Come, Cissy, it's way past time we were getting home. Bessie will be scolding us for sure if we keep her hot supper waiting."

"Bessie doesn't mind if I visit Miss Evangeline. She says it's good for me."

"Nevertheless, we need to go now." Turning to Evangeline, he gave a slight bow, "Until tomorrow."

Evangeline watched them walk across her piazza and down

the steps. She watched as they crossed the lawn and entered the woods. She only stopped looking when the trees finally lost them to view. Only then did she turn into her house and softly close the door behind her. She had seen the need in his eyes and knew that it did not begin to match the hunger she felt. She could only hope that she had hidden hers. Although she was thrilled that he had invited her to dinner the following day, she was fearful of where her emotions might lead her. He was fettered to another despite that woman's long absence. Evangeline found herself puzzled by a wife who could leave behind such a handsome and charming husband and such a lovely and sweet daughter. Regardless of Monique LaRoque's motivation, she had to accept that Graham was not free to give his heart or to share his life with another. And she was not sure if ever again she would willingly hazard her own heart.

The following morning, Cissy was awakened by the tinkle of pebbles falling on the gallery floor beyond the French doors that opened into her room. She threw back her covers and hastened to the door where she pulled the drape aside and peeked out. In the garden below, shielded from her father's room by a large hydrangea, stood Logan. She waved to him and he motioned to her to join him in the garden. After struggling into her clothes as best she could, Cissy slipped quietly down the hall and out to her friend.

"What are you doing here so early?"

"I wanted to take you somewhere special. If we don't go now it may be too late."

"Where are we going?" Cissy was anxious about leaving the house so early and without her breakfast. She knew that her father thought Logan was a nice boy, but she also knew she was not allowed to leave the yard without his permission. She pondered for a moment before reluctantly shaking her head, "Maybe I should have breakfast first and tell Papa. You can have breakfast, too."

"No. We have to go now, Cissy. Come on. It won't take long and you'll be back in plenty of time for breakfast." Not waiting for an objection, he seized her hand and tugged her along in his determined wake.

Cissy followed at first with reluctance and then infected by his enthusiasm, she was soon dashing after him through the thick shrubs that grew along the banks of the Neuse River. They were well out of sight of the house when he motioned her to be quiet and proceed with caution. Holding his finger to his lips, he inched forward with Cissy on his heels. Leaning forward he cattail fronds to one side to expose a nest of duck eggs. As they watched a tiny beak began to emerge from first one and then another until all six eggs shattered and six ducklings in all their new damp glory arrived into the world of air and light.

"Oh, they are so precious," Cissy cooed with delight. She reached her hand forward to take one but Logan immediately halted her.

"No. They're wild. Don't touch them. Their mother might not like it."

"Oh. I didn't think of that." She felt a momentary twinge of disappointment.

Sensitive to the nuances of her feelings, Logan smiled. "It's okay. We'll come back and see them later when they're not so tiny."

"Thank you for bringing me, Logan," Cissy said. "I'd better go home now or I'll be in trouble.

"I'll walk you. Young ladies should not walk in the woods alone," with all of the confidence of almost three years of greater maturity, he offered his arm as escort.

"Don't be silly." Cissy pushed his arm away and ran lightly ahead of him down the path. "I'm just a little girl," she shouted back at him.

Logan immediately forgot his previous maturity and chased

after her. She giggled when he caught up with her. "I almost out ran you, *Mister Gwaltney,*" she teased.

"Almost doesn't count." Logan added, "I'll come back tomorrow and we'll go see how the ducklings are doing."

Cissy slipped into the house and quickly made her way to the kitchen. Bessie smiled when she entered. "You just set yourself down there, child. Your papa done et his breakfast and gone into town for some business. He say he be back here before dinner with y'all's neighbor Miss Forrest."

Cissy did as she was told. When she had eaten, she went to her room and played with her dolls until she heard her father's horse clip-clopping his way down the drive to the barn. After positioning her dolls just so in their chairs by the little tea table, she skipped out to the stable where her father was chatting with the stable boy.

Graham turned to her, "Come, little one. We need to freshen ourselves for dinner with Mrs. Forrest."

"Oh, Papa, I'm so glad you invited her. I like her ever so much. I wish she could be my mama."

Graham bit his lip to stop himself from ready agreement with his daughter's heartfelt sentiments. "You have a mother, Cissy. We need to remember that, don't we?"

"Yes, Papa." Chagrinned by her lack of feeling for her mother, Cissy reluctantly agreed. "Still, Miss Evangeline is *sooo* nice!"

"That she is. Now scoot up to your room. I'll send Tizzia to help you into one of your better dresses."

Graham was preoccupied as he readied himself for his visitor. The town was abuzz this morning with talk of Yellow Fever. Several citizens had been stricken and died and the full heat of summer not yet upon them. Prior to Monique's defection, she and their child had spent summers in the cool of the mountains of Virginia safe from the ravages of the miasmas of the low country. Although he could not stay for the three full months of their visit, he too had gone for a month to six weeks each summer. Now, thinking about it, he added one more nail to the coffin of his affection for his wife. He could not take his child to the safety of the mountains for three months and still maintain his business interests from such a distance for that period of time. The previous summer the town had been lucky to escape the season with no widespread outbreak of deadly fevers. That would not be the case this season if these early deaths were any reliable harbinger of things to come.

It was with nervous anticipation that Evangeline Forrest walked up to Graham's door. His fidgeting exceeded hers, but she could not know that. Graham answered the door at the first knock. Through the glass beside the door, he had watched her progress from the edge of the woods, across the lawn, onto the piazza and to the door.

"Please do come in," he invited. "It's a beautiful day. I'm sure you must have enjoyed your walk. Fortunately, it is still not too hot and the breeze from the water makes the air delightful."

"Yes. It is a perfect day," Evangeline stammered. Embarrassed she reached for Cissy, hiding her face when she leaned over to give the child a hug of greeting. With her, she was on safe emotional ground.

"I'm so excited, Miss Evangeline. This is the very first time you have eaten with us. Ole Bessie is about fit to be tied. She is so anxious you won't like dinner." Cissy paused, then whispered, "Now if she cooks that ole chicken and pastry stuff again, it's okay not to like it. We don't either. But we didn't tell her."

Graham and Evangeline burst into laughter at the child's comment, at once making them both comfortable.

After that, the dinner of fried pork chops, mustard greens, mashed potatoes and gravy followed by blueberry pie was all they could have wished for from Bessie. They lingered at the table over coffee.

Graham could not help turning to the topic of greatest concern in his mind. "Have you heard about the outbreak of Yellow Fever in the area?"

"Yes, I have. My cook was telling me about it at breakfast. Typically I have removed to the mountains for the summer season by now, but the last few years I just didn't have the energy to do it..." her voice trailed off. She had not gone as she had been sunk in the depression of mourning and cared little if she lived or died.

"I confess I'm more than a little worried. Normally we also decamp for higher and cooler climes, but without my wife to accompany my daughter and since I am unable to stay for an extended period, we remained here last summer as well. Fortunately there was no epidemic then."

Cissy followed the conversation closely, as an exciting idea dawned. She waited for just the right moment, and then exclaimed, "Miss Evangeline can take me, Papa. Can't you, Miss Evangeline?"

Startled by the sudden question, Evangeline paused.

With embarrassed haste, Graham rushed to reassure, "Now, now, Cissy, I'm sure Mrs. Forrest has other plans. We do not impose ourselves on others, little one." He smiled an apology at Evangeline. Secretly he thought his daughter had arrived at the perfect solution and one he had dared not voice.

"No, please, don't apologize. It was an unexpected idea, but far from an unwelcome one. I must confess it sounds delightful." Evangeline laughed, "In fact, it's wonderful."

"That's settled then. I will immediately make arrangements for you to travel to Hot Springs, Virginia. Assuming that is acceptable with you, of course. Dr. Goode has spruced up the Homestead with a fine dining room and new decor, so it's a very pleasant place to summer. I do enjoy the hot springs when I'm there. The water seems to rejuvenate me."

"It was my custom to go to Ashville for the season, but I have always wanted to go to the Homestead Hotel. Everyone just raves about it. Apparently, it is quite the place to be in season. My late husband told me that lots of politicians and their wives vacate Washington during the summer and have made this quite a destination."

"That has been true. However, with the growing hostilities between North and South over the slavery issue, I'm not sure if the two camps will decided to summer in the same hotel this year." Graham shook his head. "I would be lying if I didn't tell you that I find the situation more and more perilous. I don't see how we can avoid a serious and open conflict with the North if tempers continue to rise."

"It is a worry, but must it mean war. Can't it be equitably resolved?"

"I suppose that will depend on how we define equitable." Graham sighed, "This is too fine a day to worry over such problems. Let's walk by the river and plan your trip with Cissy."

In a few short days, all had been packed. An excited Tizzia would go as well to serve as maid for both Evangeline and Cissy. Graham knew he would miss his daughter, but he was relieved to have her removed from the dangerous low country heat. He watched as the train chugged from the station, black plumes of smoke billowing into the sky. Cissy and Evangeline stood on the back platform waving until they disappeared from view. His summer had just grown immeasurably longer. All he could do now was hope to avoid the fever himself and wait for the cool days of autumn and their return. Graham thought it just as well he could not go. He did not trust himself to be in such intimate proximity with Evangeline as staying with them at The Homestead would entail.

Graham waited two months and could stand it no longer. He planned his surprise visit, giving no clue as to his intentions when he wrote. But, today August 12, 1852, was Cissy's eighth birthday. He wanted to be there to celebrate it with her, to be with her. And he wanted to be with the woman he could not eradicate from his mind, either awake or dreaming. He walked into the dining room after the hotel patrons were seated for dinner. Standing in the doorway, he scanned the seated diners. As though they were a lighthouse beacon guiding him to safe harbor, a lingering ray of golden sunlight formed a halo around their heads as they leaned toward one another at their table by the window. As he drank in the sight, Evangeline leaned over and patted Cissy's cheek. Both burst into merry laughter, unaware that they were watched. When he reached their table, it was apparent they thought he was merely a waiter serving them their dinner. Without so much as glancing up, they leaned back slightly to allow for the placement of plates before them. Clearing his throat, he asked, "Ladies, do you think there is room at the table for a tired traveler who has come quite a long way for a slice of birthday cake?"

"Papa!" Cissy cried as she leapt from her seat and flung herself into his welcoming arms. "You are the best birthday present of all."

"Ah, sweetheart, I could never forget your birthday. *You* were the best present I have ever had." Graham gave her a warm hug before turning to Evangeline, "I hope the two of you are enjoying your time here. I can't begin to tell you how very grateful I am that you agreed to bring Cissy."

"Please, you know I was delighted. This has all been a marvelous treat for me." Evangeline indicated the vacant chair between them, "Do be seated. This is good timing for you. They haven't yet served dinner. You must be starved after the long train ride."

"That I am," Graham acknowledged as he seated himself.

"Are things well in New Berne?" Evangeline inquired.

"Unfortunately there have been more deaths from fever,

however it seems to be abating somewhat. Nonetheless, I'm glad the two of you are here for a few weeks more."

"And we are relieved that you have avoided falling victim to the disease. I confess we have worried." Evangeline looked up into his intent gaze and then dropped her eyes in confusion.

Graham watched the blush that colored her cheeks and hoped that she welcomed his presence. Did he dare to hope that she was disconcerted by the same attraction that plagued him with restless longing? Putting that thought aside, he devoted himself to both the dinner and the conversation of his daughter and her companion as they recounted the events of their summer sojourn. Cissy's joy at her gifts and the presence of the two people she most loved, bound the three of them in a circle of warmth. Graham found himself regretting the end of the evening when he would have to bid the two of them goodnight and retreat to his lonely room.

He had been so engrossed in his conversation and witty repartee with Evangeline that he failed to notice when Cissy's eyes drooped and her head lolled in sleep against the cushioned back of her chair. Evangeline nodded to his daughter and whispered, "The little one has had a long day."

Graham gathered his daughter into his arms and tenderly carried her to the room she shared with Evangeline. There he deposited her on her bed. When he leaned forward to tuck her in, his hand brushed Evangeline's who had reacted to the same impulse. He felt a tingling jolt in his nerve endings where their skin had come into contact. He stood erect and without thought to consequences, pulled the woman to him and lightly kissed her lips. For a moment she seemed stunned into a frozen stupor, then under the warmth of his kiss, he could feel her thaw as she began to respond to his ardor. He was the first to pull away.

Shaken by the power of his body's reaction and need of her, he found himself stammering in apology, "I'm so sorry. Please forgive my impulsive behavior. I confess I have been drawn to you from the moment I saw you at the dock the day we returned from France. I wish I were free to offer you my affection as you deserve."

Evangeline smiled into his eyes and then placed a gentle finger on his lips. "Don't apologize. It was a lovely kiss. I wanted to kiss you, too. I realize you aren't free to offer me your heart. I'm just grateful for your friendship and for sharing your daughter with me. Let's leave it at that."

That summer began a pattern of summer visits to Virginia. Each summer Graham spent at least a month with them during their stay. In the relaxed and holiday like atmosphere, he found himself more and more captivated by the woman that remained beyond him. He never again tried to kiss her although he frequently yearned to. Feeling her eyes on him, lingering on his mouth when he talked, he suspected that she hungered for his kiss as well.

As the years in their familiar rhythm passed unmolested by change, he watched his child grow to adolescence and then young adulthood. He watched her become a lovely, sensitive, warm and altogether charming young woman, albeit, a stubbornly independent one. He celebrated the accomplished young daughter that had emerged under Evangeline's tutelage and loving guidance.

He had taken a mistress whom he visited from time to time. Rosalee wanted no entanglements and viewed the relationship as a purely physical one that brought the widowed woman an occasional luxury that she could not have afforded on her own. The lack of any demand on his person and emotions drew him back to her when his need for a woman became too great. Evangeline had captured his heart. Although he corresponded in a desultory fashion with Monique, he had long since abandoned the idea that she might return. It was more than apparent that she was happy to pursue a life free of Cissy and him. They were just as happy to be rid of her, although neither of them admitted it openly for fear of what the other might think.

Except for his increasing worry over the growing dissention between the northern and southern states over the issues around tariffs, slavery and state's rights, Graham viewed the passage of time with sanguine acceptance of his life. His businesses had prospered and expanded to include international trade and shipping of goods, all operated from his office on Pollock street within sight of the wharfs where his ships lay at anchor. The shipping of cotton, pitch, pine, and tobacco to Europe had brought him great wealth. The mills in England had long since grown dependent on his regular delivery of cotton. His ships returned to homeport stuffed with the goods that the south craved and did not manufacture on its own. He was amazed at the growth of his fortune during these times of prosperity.

Graham followed the New Berne newspaper and those from New York that were delivered on his ships. Since the passage of the Wilmot Proviso, he had seen the handwriting on the wall for the south. The increasingly vehement New England Whigs were determined to wipe slavery from the land and to seize some of the political power that the south had long held. With more free states admitted to the Union, the south's hold on congress was slipping. While Graham secretly chastised the north for its double standard in regards to labor...the sanctioning of child labor, penurious wages and little protection for workers while southern slaves were housed, clothed, fed and maintained in old age...he would not regret the demise of slavery. Despite little veiled animosity from some of his fellow townsmen for his actions, he had long since sold his slaves, or given them their freedom for long and dutiful service. Of the latter group, his household staff had remained and was paid wages in addition to room and board.

Chapter 4

Monique lazily rolled over in bed and reached for another of the bonbons that were always on her bedside table. She knew she should not indulge as she was beginning to put on weight. Marcel delighted in commenting on her increasing voluptuousness. It was always so slyly done that she could not tell if it were compliment or snide comment. Picking up her peignoir, she arose from the bed and pulled it around her nude body. Marcel had slipped from her room before the household arose and made his way back to his own quarters in the Rue du Renard, an easy walk from her parents' residence in the upscale Place des Vosges in the Marais quarter. He had left an agitated woman behind. Standing by the window, Monique gazed unseeingly into the elegant square, as she replayed their conversation in her mind. Did she dare accept the scheme he had proposed?

She had sat up in surprise when Marcel remarked, "I think, my dear, that this relationship has existed for long enough under the present circumstances." He paused, just long enough to frighten her into thinking that he had at last tired of her charms, before continuing, "It's time that we consider a more permanent liaison: marriage, as it were. Unfortunately, there is that small impediment of a husband that must be factored into the equation."

"But, Marcel, you know we are Catholic, as you are yourself. It's quite impossible."

"Not impossible, just complicated. However, were you widowed, not only would you be free to marry, but there is a sizeable fortune to be considered. Realizing of course that my own financial fortunes have suffered some reverses, I'm sure you would not be willing either to divorce or marry if it means a reduction of your financial circumstances."

"Ah, Marcel, have you lost at cards again?" Monique sighed with fond exasperation. "You are such a naughty boy."

"Never mind that. I'm asking if you will marry me when you are free?"

"What's the point of asking, when I'm not free, nor likely to be? Graham is a very healthy man." She shrugged her shoulders and reached for him. She purred suggestively, "It's still early and since we are awake anyway..."

"Monique, concentrate," Marcel snapped with frustration, his face growing cold with anger. "Are you so obtuse that I must spell it out to you?"

"I beg your pardon?"

"Please, darling, let's not quarrel. I did not mean to insult. It's just that it sounds most harsh when stated in bald terms. I hoped that you would understand without the necessity for that."

Monique studied his face for a moment. His affable, charming mask was back in place, revealing nothing of the emotions within. "Are you saying that you love me and want to marry me so much that you are willing to make something happen to Graham?"

Flashing that smoky lazy smile she so loved, he waved his hand nonchalantly and gave a very Gallic shrug. "If fate were to intervene and cause some unfortunate accident, it would be fortuitous I think."

Monique bit her lip and studied him trying to discern what had caused this sudden interest in marriage. "Marcel, after eleven years as we are, I'm just a little surprised that you now wish to marry. Just the other day you were scolding me about growing old and fat, and threatening to find a younger mistress.

Although you said you were just teasing, I confess I was offended after giving you the best of my youthful beauty."

"You know I was teasing, darling. There could never be another woman to compare to you." He lifted his hand to her left breast and drew lazy circles around the nipple. Her charms had long since ceased to entice him.

Removing his hand, Monique smiled archly. "Is it me; or is it Graham's money that you want?"

"Now I am the one that's offended. How can you be so cruel when you know you have always owned my heart?"

Ignoring the question, she continued, "So how do you plan to bring about this marriage you want so soon and with such fervor?"

"I think you should go home, darling. Be nice to Graham and get to know your daughter again. Then, in a month or so, I will arrive. With some careful planning on my part, I suspect we will find ourselves free of unnecessary barriers not too long after."

"Suppose Graham has left his money to our hoyden daughter and nothing to me? After all, I haven't seen him for years. He hasn't asked about my return for more than eight of them. Cissy is far more likely to inherit than I."

"Ah, sacre bleu! She's only seventeen. As her mother, you will be the guardian until she comes of age. That gives us ample time to secure the fortune for ourselves." Marcel grinned, "Then you can buy all of the things you want without needing to write for money. You'll be marvelously rich. Just think."

Monique had chafed at living on an allowance even though it was a generous one. Serious contemplation of the scope of the fortune that could be hers stirred the raw ambition and greed that simmered just below the surface. "That *would* be nice."

"Not 'would.' The word is 'will.' " Pulling her to him, he began making love.

In the rosy aftermath, Monique wasted no time beginning to plan for the money. She gloated, "We will liquidate everything there and return to Paris. My parents are old and have not been good stewards of the family fortunes. You can see just how worn they've allowed this house to become. I'll use some of the money to restore its former grandeur. Just think of the parties we can have here. We'll be the envy of all of Paris."

"It will be as you wish, my dear." Marcel rose from the bed and began to dress. "Now write to your husband and announce your return. Be sure to post it today. Then we will arrange passage."

"Do you think it's safe? The papers say a war between the northern and southern states is eminent. I most certainly don't want to find myself in the middle of that."

"It hasn't happened yet. If we manage things expeditiously, we should be there and back before anything happens on that front, hence the need for haste."

Her letter reached New Berne on April 16, 1861. Four days previously, forces of the newly formed Confederacy had launched a bombardment on Fort Sumter in Charleston harbor ending the uneasy but peaceful antagonism between the states. On the 15th of April, Lincoln's request for troops from North Carolina to assist in quelling the insurrection met with a resounding refusal from Governor John Ellis, thus propelling the reluctant Tarheel State into war on the side of her sister southern states. Graham was so preoccupied with his daily copy of the *New Berne Progress,* and it's discussion of rapidly evolving events that the letter from Paris lay on his desk most of the afternoon unopened and unremarked.

It was Cissy who found it. She had walked into his study frustrated from another outburst from Logan who was avidly pursuing her, intent on the marriage that he had determined was their destiny while they were still children. Viewing him more as friend or brother than a prospective husband, she had laughed when he proposed and chided him for being silly. He had stormed away livid with anger, leaving her uneasy at this rupture of a friendship that had been hers as long as she could remember.

"What has you so engrossed in that paper, Papa?"

"Darling, I fear we are in for a long and difficult war now that North Carolina is joining her sister southern states. It could mean serious trouble for us in New Berne, as this is an important port and a gateway into the interior of North Carolina. In the center of the state we have the major rail connection route to Virginia. Not only that, but this area is a fertile source of food for a hungry army. The north will want to deprive us of these advantages."

Graham paused and weighted his words well before he added, "I am considering sending you to your mother in Paris. Now before you explode, hear me out. I don't want you caught in the middle of a war. If you don't wish to go to your mother, perhaps Evangeline would go with you and I could rent suitable accommodations for the two of you. Go to London if you prefer."

"No, Papa. I'm not leaving and I'll just bet that Evangeline won't either. I'm not going to go away and leave you. For goodness sake, I'd worry myself sick and Evangeline would, too. Just forget that idea."

"Cissy, sometimes I despair of your independent nature. Surely you see the sense behind my suggestion?"

Cissy sat in the chair beside his desk without answering. As she sat there debating how to respond, her eyes fell on an envelope bearing writing she recognized. "Speaking of the old witch, it seems she has deigned to write us again. I wonder what she wants now?"

Graham considered remonstrating with her for the lack of respect for her mother, but merely shrugged in eloquent resignation and accepted the proffered letter. He broke the seal on the thick stationery and began to read. Suddenly he stopped in surprise. "I just do not believe it. Your mother wishes to return."

"What on earth for? You know she doesn't love us."

Graham let out a long breath. "I have no idea why she wants to return now of all times. But, *she is* my wife and your mother. I don't see what choice we have."

"I do! Just write her right back and say she isn't welcome. Think how inconvenienced she would be since we are at war. She might have to do without her precious French perfumes and silks and wines and food and whatever. I bet if you send her enough money she'll forget all about it."

"That's pretty cynical, Cissy."

"Maybe it is, but you know it's true."

"Hmm, I'll think about it."

"What's to think about? If you don't write she may just come anyway. Heaven forbid such a catastrophe."

"You know, I am sorry that you feel so vehement about your mother. You owe her something for giving you birth."

"Ha! That's not such a big thing. It's what she did, or rather didn't do, afterwards that matters." Cissy stood up and stomped to the window. Working herself into a temper, she cried, "Besides, you love Evangeline. And don't even bother to deny it. You know it. I know it. And Evangeline knows it. She loves you, too. How do you think Mama's return is going to fit into that whole scenario?"

Graham felt his heart leap at her words. So Evangeline was in love with him. The long years of denial suddenly fell away and he was happy that he could openly admit his love. "Yes, Cissy. I love her. I know you do as well. I have yearned for her love knowing that I could not claim it and that it is so unfair to her. I haven't loved your mother in ages, if I ever did. The problem is she is my wife, like it or not."

"I most decidedly *do not*!"

"Very well, I'll write and tell her not to come."

Cissy crossed to his desk and sat in his lap. With his arms around her she cuddled close like a little girl. "I'm sorry, Papa. Forgive my temper tantrums. Sometimes I forget how very hard this must have all been for you. I love you so much. You're the best Papa in the whole world."

"I love you, too, Cissy." Graham nudged her back to her feet, "My goodness, you are a lot more to hold now than when you were a little girl. Speaking of my grown-up daughter, tell me why Logan left in such a hurry. Don't tell me you two had another fight?"

"It wasn't exactly a fight. He wants to marry me and I don't want to marry him. I don't want to marry anyone. For goodness sake, I'm too young. Yes, I know lots of girls are already married and mothers by seventeen, but I don't want that for me."

"When you meet the right one, you will. I'm not sure how your old Papa will deal with that, though. We've been such a unit for so long, to have you gone from here would be a rare pain."

"One more reason not to send me to Europe," she remarked archly. "And, not to worry. There is no one I know that's going to make me want to marry."

Graham would have teased her for shortsightedness had he foreseen that in less than a week she would meet a beau that would quickly steal her heart.

That Saturday night Cissy entered the elegant Isaac Taylor house on Craven Street knowing she looked her prettiest. Catching sight of herself in the tall pier glass that stood in the entry hall, she could not help preening at her reflection. The ball gown of cream Swiss with small emerald green dots and trimmed with green satin bands and lace was one of her most becoming as it brought out the green of her eyes and the golden sheen of her hair. She turned from the glass prepared to enter the drawing room, when a restraining hand on her elbow caused her to glance over her right shoulder into the dancing eyes of a stranger. He looked to be in his early twenties, tall, elegantly slim, and far too handsome.

"Forgive me miss, but I cannot help but agree with your assessment," there was laughter in his voice when he said it.

Flustered that she had been caught in a moment of self-admiration and by the best looking man she had ever met, she could not prevent the stammer. "Ah, I... I'm sure I don't know to what you refer, mister...?" Taking a deep breath, she struggled to regain her composure. " I'm sorry I don't believe we've been properly introduced."

"My apologies for my presumption, miss. Allow me to present myself. I'm Nathaniel Pearson, nephew of the Taylor's. I'm visiting from Kinston, hoping to enjoy a few festive evenings such as this, before we are all embroiled in the coming war. I must say if New Berne has many belles as lovely as you, my visit will be a treat for my eyes, but the ruin of my heart. Alas, I will never be able to tear myself away for something as disagreeable as war."

"I'm Cecily LaRoque. My father is a friend and business acquaintance of Mr. Taylor." Still embarrassed and becoming annoyed at him for catching her unawares, she turned to leave, "Do excuse me, please."

"Only if you promise me a dance later."

"Unfortunately, I fear that all of my dances have previously been taken," she said firmly. Secretly she could only hope that he would not remark on the fact that she had just arrived and thus had not had the occasion to fill her dance card.

"Well, in case you should have a free moment, I will find you again. Otherwise, I shall spend the evening desolate for being deprived of your beauty." He bowed, but not before she caught the saucy grin on his face.

"Excuse me. I see my father is wondering what has become

of me." Cissy curtsied and made her way to her father's side, aware that Nathaniel's eyes followed her. She shrugged and put her chin up, he unsettled her with his confident insouciance but she would not allow him to see her discomfort. Her father knew her too well not to notice that she was a bit rattled.

"Is something the matter, sweetheart?"

"Nothing. Why would you ask?"

"You just seem a little discombobulated somehow. Perhaps, I'm just being a foolish and protective father."

Changing the subject quickly, Cissy inquired, "Is Evangeline here. She told me she's invited."

"I think she's planning to come. I haven't talked with her since we walked over to visit yesterday, but she said as much then," Graham looked past his daughter and spied Evangeline as she entered the drawing room. "Ah, there she is. I promised her a dance."

"If I know you, you'll have all of her dances." Cissy laughed before adding, "If you can tear yourself away, you might spare me one."

"Judging from the way that young man was watching you as you came over to me, I suspect you will have your dances well claimed yourself." Graham, patted her arm, "Now excuse me, sweetheart. I'm going to greet Evangeline. And I see Logan is on the way over here with a bit of a determined look on his face."

"Oh, my. He is *so intense,*" Cissy complained.

"That's the way men are when they lose their hearts. I think he lost his to you long ago. Logan is a fine young man, Cissy. You could certainly do worse."

"Of course. He's very nice and he's been my best friend since I was seven years old. It's simply that I can't see him as anything else."

"Not to fret, time solves many conundrums."

Logan walked up as Graham turned to leave, "Cissy." He

bowed to her and then nodded to Graham, "Mr. LaRoque, it's good to see you, sir."

"I will visit with you later, Logan. I was just on my way to greet Mrs. Forrest."

Logan waited for Graham to get beyond earshot, "I've come to claim the first dance, Cissy. I see the band is getting ready to play."

"I'll dance with you only if you'll not pester me about anything to do with the future," Cissy stated with a slight toss of her head.

Logan grinned. He could not help teasing, "Of course, my love. We have a long life ahead in which to plan for our future. Right now, I just want to lead you into this dance."

"Don't call me your love. We're *friends*."

"And I love you like a very, *very* good friend. Let's not quarrel about something that can't be helped. Let's just dance."

Logan took her elbow to lead her to the dance area, but was blocked in his progress by a man he had never met. "Excuse me, Miss LaRoque. May I have the pleasure of this dance?"

"Excuse us, sir. Miss LaRoque has just promised this dance to me," Logan was annoyed. Cissy had known him long enough to see he resented the forward way the elegant man was looking at her, and he was angered by the challenge in Nathaniel Pearson's eyes. A muscle flexed dangerously in his jaw before Logan gained control. Just as he unclenched his fists, the music began and he swung Cissy into the lively rhythm effectively cutting off the stranger as he did so.

"He's certainly presumptuous." He tried to keep the annoyance from his voice but failed, "Apparently you know him?"

"Oh, for goodness sake. He's kin of the Taylor family from Kinston. His name is Nathaniel Pearson, and I only just met him."

Logan swung her around and then back, "I don't like him.

He's too arrogant acting to suit me."

Cissy knew she shouldn't bait him, but could not help responding, "He has very nice manners and he is certainly handsome."

Logan didn't reply but the thunderous expression on his face gave her a good clue as to his thoughts. When the dance ended, he immediately held her close and led her into the next one, stopping Nathaniel's progress in their direction.

Much to Cissy's increasing annoyance, Logan stuck to her like a fly on honey. Finally in exasperation she smiled sweetly and pleaded, "I'm so thirsty. Would you mind fetching me a cup of punch, please?"

Logan looked around to see if Nathaniel were waiting in the wings before agreeing. He glanced back once he reached the refreshment ladened table to assure himself she was still there. The moment he turned away, Cissy slipped through the French doors onto the veranda.

"Ah, at last you're alone."

Cissy looked up in surprise as Nathaniel emerged from the shadows and into the light shining through the windows. "Oh, I didn't realize anyone was here."

"I've been watching you dancing and waiting for my chance. If I concentrated hard enough, I hoped I would bring you to me. Apparently I succeeded."

"Not at all. I was too warm and just stepped out for a breath of fresh air." She was flattered that he had watched her and wanted her company. "Besides, do you always get what you want?"

"Almost always."

"Then you must possess a rare talent for concentration."

"When it's worth my while. That's a lovely song they are playing. Perhaps you would consider dancing with me here?" He took her hand and swept her into his arms without waiting for a reply.

Cissy stiffened momentarily with shock. Relaxing under the practiced warmth of his gaze, she allowed her feet to follow him in the dance. His dancing was as smooth and effortless as everything else about him. She was breathless with excitement at the new feelings he aroused in her, feelings that she did not know she possessed. Never had anyone made her feel so desperately alive and so yearning for something that remained undefined and just beyond her grasp. Lost in thought, she did not at first hear his question, "I'm sorry. I fear I must ask you to repeat."

"I said that I would like to call on you, if you will permit?"

"Oh yes, please, do."

"Miss LaRoque, might I also address you a bit less formally?"

"I'm Cissy. Call me Cissy, Mr. Pearson."

"Mister? I think you might be allowed to call me Nate." He smiled down at her, "Let's see if my cousins' dinner is as good as they promised. I confess I feel a mite peckish."

Cissy felt she would choke if she tried to eat anything. Chiding herself for being flustered by Nate's nearness and interest, she took his arm as he led her to the bounteous table. From the corner of her eye, she caught a furious glare from Logan. Turning her head quickly, she pretended she had not seen him. "Tell me, Nate, how long do you plan to stay in New Berne?"

"Initially my visit was to be only a few days, however I now plan to delay departure as long as possible so I can get to know you a little better."

"I'm sure you flatter me. However, New Berne is a lovely town and I think you will enjoy being here."

"It is for sure larger than Kinston and there are the beautiful river views to commend it. But, the best feature so far has been the beauty of its ladies." Nate's eyes swept the room taking in the array of gaily-bedecked girls. Cissy was not surprised to see that several of her friends were eyeing her covetously and attempting to catch her escort's gaze as he glanced about.

Logan had watched long enough. He was annoyed with Cissy for not waiting for his return and he was furious with the handsome stranger for monopolizing her dances and time. Logan realized that in looks and suavity he was no match for the man. However, there was something about that carefully polished appearance that he didn't trust and didn't like. Maybe he was just plain jealous and that was the basis for his suspicions, but somehow he didn't think that was it. The man was just too smooth and practiced to be honest as far as Logan was concerned. And Cissy seemed much too intrigued for his hackles not to rise at another male vying for a woman he claimed as his own.

"Dammit," he muttered, not realizing he had vocalized it.

Graham was standing near enough to hear. Hoping to head off trouble, he said, "Logan, don't get your dander up. Cissy's just feeling her oats. She's not going to do anything stupid. We'll both see to that, I'm sure."

"I'm not so sure. That Pearson fellow is a sight too arrogant for my taste, and a hell of a lot too sure of himself with the ladies."

Evangeline put her hand on his arm, "Logan, would you do me the honor of the next dance? Graham was just saying it's time that he danced with his daughter and I don't want to be left standing alone like some wallflower."

Graham was grateful for the interruption. "My dear, you will never be a wallflower. You are much too beautiful for that, however, I think it *is* time I danced with Cissy."

Cissy had seen the threesome talking and knew that she was probably the topic of discussion. Before she could take Nate's arm and steer him away, her father was at their side.

"Sir, you must excuse my daughter. I'm claiming her for the next dance. However, there's a bevy of other lovely ladies here tonight that would no doubt enjoy a dance with you," Graham commented dismissively as he lead Cissy into the next dance.

"Papa, why did you do that? I was enjoying Mr. Pearson's company."

"Yes, I noticed, however, it's time you socialized with others here. To do otherwise is impolite and unladylike. I don't mean to chide you, Cissy, but you do need to be careful not to be too forward and available to strangers. You know next to nothing about this man. Just because he is of good family doesn't mean that he is the kind of gentleman I want monopolizing my daughter's time."

"Oh, botheration! You are just taking up for Logan," Cissy accused.

"Logan doesn't need my intervention. He is the kind of man that any girl here would be honored to claim as hers. If you spurn him, there will be no lack of other ladies who will not treat his attentions with disdain. So, no, I am not protecting Logan. However, before you are too cavalier with his affections in that regard, you may want to give pause and consider."

As the dance came to an end, she pondered his words. Cissy's retort was interrupted by Logan's tap on her father's shoulder, "Forgive me sir. Would you allow me the pleasure of claiming the next dance with your daughter?"

Cissy allowed Logan to lead her into the dance and under the cover of the music, hissed, "You know I just abhor, hate, and detest it when you act like you own me!"

"And I just love, adore, and cherish you when you have your temper up. You make such a darling little spitfire." Logan added mischievously, "You know, I think I'm may abandon my pursuit of you as another lady here has some decided advantages. Polly Burton has the sweetest disposition of anyone I know, unless it's Miss Evangeline. Plus, she has a lovely face, a divine form---I do apologize for mentioning this---and seems to be genuinely fond of me. Of course, when I marry her, you're going to be mighty sorry you treated me with such cruelty."

For a moment Cissy was startled. Despite her father's words, she really had not considered that Logan might take genuine notice of another girl and she wasn't sure she liked it, even if she didn't want him for herself. "Pooh! You're just trying to make me jealous and it won't work."

"Of course it won't. You're smitten with Mr. Pearson this week, and maybe next week a new gentleman. I have begun to think you're fickle. I'm not sure that's an admirable trait in a lady, certainly not in someone that I would marry. I must say Polly grows more appealing all the time."

"Logan Gwaltney, how dare you. You know full well that I have never promised myself to you, so how can you accuse me of being fickle?" Over Logan's shoulder Cissy could see Polly staring longingly at him. Perhaps, Logan wasn't teasing after all. The thought that he found Polly sweeter than her, pretty and even admirable, was not a happy one. But then, why should she care? "Perhaps, next dance you should devote yourself to her, since she is such a paragon of all virtues."

"I think that's a superb idea. I do thank you for your encouragement. I would not want to think your feelings had been hurt by my pursuit of someone else."

True to his word, Logan devoted the remainder of the evening to a glowing Polly. Although he tried to give the eager girl the attention she deserved, his eyes followed Cissy as she danced with Nate, laughed into his eyes, and smiled with delight at his every word. Logan was so angry at Nate's easy confident way and so furious that Cissy had so readily fallen for his charm, that he was barely able to respond to Polly's gentle comments and questions. Looking at the girl in his arms he could appreciate her beauty and sweet nature, but she did nothing to excite him to the passion that one glimpse, one stray thought of Cissy could bring. He chided himself for leading

Polly on. He knew he should not. But he was determined to see if Cissy was so smitten with Nate that what he did was inconsequential, or whether his attentions to another girl might inspire some twinge of unease. He ruefully surmised that so far Cissy seemed oblivious, not only to him, but all others in the room except for the man that was paying her court.

Chapter 5

"Not to worry, my love, just because he sent you money and told you not to return is no great problem. You simply go anyway. We'll just look at the bright side. You may now have an unexpected and lavish shopping expedition prior to departure. Plus, I've seen a wonderful sealskin hat and opera coat that I would very much like to own. Perhaps, your windfall will be a boon to us both until we can assure a more permanent arrangement." Marcel smiled cynically to himself as he gazed out the window at the dawn breaking over the eastern rooftops. It would be a gray day, unseasonably cold and rainy. The weather only added to his gloom.

Monique lifted herself from the mattress on one elbow, exposing her voluptuous breasts as she did so. "Graham can be most obstinate when he's thwarted. He'll be furious that I refused to obey his instructions to remain. Not only that, but there's a war on for goodness sake. I certainly don't want to be caught in the middle of it. Heavens, he says in the letter that New Berne is a likely target for Union occupation. Why not be patient, darling? We can go as soon as the war is over and it's safe to be there."

"No. If you don't wish to do this so we can marry, then I must look elsewhere for my future." His voice was coldly adamant as he continued to stare into the grayness of dawn. He couldn't afford to dawdle. He needed money soon or his debts would land him in debtors' prison. Monique was beginning to wear on his nerves. His interest faded a little more each time he saw her, but she was a tool to financial security and for that she was still useful.

Monique hated that she sounded contrite and wheedling but could not stop herself, "Please, darling, you know I love you to distraction and I want nothing more than to be your wife. Truly I do. I only ask for a bit of patience."

"Patience? For the love of God, how many years *more* must I be patient? No, Monique, either we do this now, or I have no alternative but to move on." He continued to stare out the window, refusing to turn and face her. He dared not, for he did not want her to see the cold contempt and frustration that colored his face.

Monique rose from the bed and went to the window where he stood. Wrapping her arms around him, she rubbed her cheek against his back. "Don't be angry with me. I know you're right to be tired of this. It really is frustrating to have to arise before day each morning to sneak from the house. Why don't you go on home now? It will be light soon. If you will call for me early afternoon, we can go shopping and I'll buy you those things you want."

"Very well. I'll leave; but only if we go by the booking agency while we are out shopping and obtain a ticket for you to return to New Berne." He refused to soften his voice or his resolve. She had to act soon or he would be forced to find another needy woman with a fat purse.

Monique's voice held a pout when she replied, "If you insist, I will buy the ticket this afternoon. I just don't understand the need for a sudden rush to the States in the middle of a civil war. Not only that, but the weather is going to be miserable today."

Marcel merely shrugged his shoulders in that ancient wordless Gallic response. With no need for further conversation, he pulled on his clothes and left just as the servants were beginning to stir below stairs. He confessed to himself that he was bored with the entire arrangement. Perhaps once Graham LaRoque's fortune was securely in his grasp, he would find a way to dispense with her. At the very least, he would certainly find another mistress and proceed to ignore Monique.

An ocean away, Cissy found herself as troubled by her new love as her mother was by her old one. After only a few days courtship, she was head over heels in love and eager for the proposal that she felt sure would come her way. No matter his protestations of love and admiration, when she bothered to be honest with herself, she could not help feeling that Nate was somehow less than genuine. Whenever she hinted at marriage, he shied away like a nervous horse. When they were in public, he seemed to cool to her. Most damning of all as far as she was concerned, when there were other available women around he flirted unabashedly. Even so, she was determined to have him.

"Daggum it, Cissy, pay some attention when I'm talking to you, please," Logan exclaimed angrily. "You don't know beans about that pretty popping jay you've fallen for. Rumor has it he had to leave Kinston because he has compromised a girl there and refuses to do the honorable thing. I've watched him flirt with everything in skirts. He's pretentious and a fool and if you let him, he'll break your heart."

"What do you know about him: nothing but malicious rumors? You're just jealous. You'll say anything to spoil it all for me," Cissy flung back. His accusations only aroused her own fears and insecurities, paradoxically making her angrier and more determined to defend Nate.

Logan glowered at her, "That's damned unfair and you know it."

"Don't you dare curse at me."

"That's not the half of what I'd like to say," he muttered.

Cissy shrugged her shoulders dismissively, "Nate is calling for me this afternoon. I think you should say goodbye before he arrives. You're in no temper to be pleasant to anyone today."

"I'll gladly leave to avoid seeing that arrogant fool." Logan collected his hat from the hall tree in the foyer and walked onto the front veranda. He slapped the felt bowler on his thigh before carelessly plopping it on his head.

Cissy followed behind as unsettled by his anger as she was annoyed by it. "Goodness, it is so humid. I can just feel a storm brewing. Perhaps, you should wait until it's over, after all. If it's storming, Nate will be late arriving anyway."

"At this point a good rousing storm is just what I need." A distant rumble of thunder and a quickening breeze offered assurance that he might well get his wish. His horse whickered and pulled against the hitching iron by the steps signaling his nervousness of the approaching tempest. Logan loosened the reins, and soothing the horse with his hand, swung easily into the saddle. He gave Cissy a cursory salute before tearing off down the lane to the road. Cissy glared after him as he galloped down the brick path that ran through a tunnel of live oak trees draped with Spanish moss. The gray tatters of moss swayed drunkenly in the rising wind giving a ghostly feel to the lane.

Cissy watched until he reached the road at the end of the leafy green tunnel. Usually he turned to throw her a kiss before he rode from sight. Today he merely tugged his horse hard to the right and made for his own home further down the river. There was no way he could reach shelter before the storm caught him, she thought with some satisfaction. A sudden crack of thunder followed by a jagged bolt of lightening sent her scurrying into the house.

Cissy spent the remainder of the day by the parlor window. She tried to read to distract herself, but time and again, her eyes sought the lane, willing Nate to be there. He did not come, and by supper she was thoroughly disgruntled.

Watching her at the supper table, Graham sensed her underlying anger and debated telling her what he had seen in town. He wanted to protect her and save her from what could be a terrible mistake, however he was not sure his daughter was ready for his advice. And the information he had, the suave Mr. Pearson would no doubt explain away were he confronted. Graham watched Cissy surreptitiously as she picked at her dinner. Normally the succulent baked chicken with rhubarb would have warranted a hearty appreciation from his daughter.

"You seem a mite testy tonight, sweetheart. Is something troubling you?"

"I'm fine, Papa. I guess I must have eaten too much at dinner," Cissy remarked.

Graham could not stop the words that followed, "Cissy, wasn't Mr. Pearson supposed to visit this afternoon? I seem to recall you remarking on it earlier."

"He *was*."

"I saw him in town earlier and assumed he had already been out to visit and left early."

"No. The storm must have changed his mind."

"Sweetheart, I want you to slow down just a little with this fellow. I know you think you fancy him, but he's not for you."

"I think that should be my decision, Papa."

Graham soothed, "Of course, Cissy. I'm not trying to tell you what to do. I'm only asking you to be a bit more cautious with your heart."

"What is it that you have against Nate? Is it because you're determined I marry my *friend* Logan?"

"I've said before, and I'll say again, Logan is a fine young man. If he doesn't appeal to you, he'll have no trouble finding any number of willing girls. This is not about him. My concern is how little you know about Mr. Pearson and the rumors I've heard. Were it not for his kinship to the Taylors, he would not be received in polite society due to certain recent events in Kinston that are unfit for your ears. Furthermore, I saw him in town this afternoon squiring a young lady of questionable reputation. Judging by the attention he was paying her, I suspect his affections are of the capricious and fickle variety. Constancy is rarely a long suit for the type of man that chases every pretty skirt around."

"Please don't lecture me, Papa. You aren't exactly the ideal candidate for offering advice in the romance department." The minute the words left her mouth, Cissy regretted them and hated herself for the look of pain that registered in her father's face. "I'm sorry, Papa. That was mean and hateful, and I don't mean it."

"It's alright. Perhaps, I deserve it. My only concern is for you. I love you too much to lose you to some scoundrel that will only abuse your affections."

"I love you, too, and I hate it that you cannot be with Miss Evangeline when you both love one another. Mama never deserved you." Cissy smiled at her father, "Let's change the subject shall we?"

"That's fine with me," Graham said. "Perhaps, you would rather talk about the gorgeous moiré silk fabric that came in on the ship today. I took the liberty of reserving it for you. I cannot guarantee how many more ships will be able to sail into port with such luxuries now that hostilities have been declared."

Cissy thanked him for the fabric, delighted for the new gown it would make. After a pause she remarked, "Logan thinks that we are going to be invaded along the coast any day now. He says the regiment he joined is training and as soon as they have uniforms and equipment they will be sent to war. Do you know anything about that? Nate is going to join, too. I think they are both silly. They are as excited as children about the chance to go off and get shot at."

"As I have said before, the North has no choice but to gain control of our coastal waters. It allows them supremacy over the entire eastern part of the state if they succeed. That would prove a serious blow to the South. As a man of the sea, experience tells me they will try to crush us by water from all sides: the Mississippi, the Gulf and the Atlantic coast. If they close our ports, we cannot survive." Graham blew out a long breath, "Fortunately for us, President Davis has been wise in appointing Robert Lee to head the forces in Virginia. As a wise soldier, Lee will see the need to protect our ports here. He already managed to secure the munitions at Harper's Ferry by sending Thomas Jackson there."

Graham chuckled to himself. As the new head of the Virginia Military Academy, Jackson went to see Lee about using his cadets to train recruits and instead received an officer's commission from Lee. Jackson then suggested his brother-in-law Daniel Harvey Hill, a mathematics professor at the University of North Carolina for a commission. Lee was happy to take them both. Like Lee, they had seen service in Mexico.

"It will be interesting to see what happens now with Joe Johnston and Lee both in contention for the control of the armies. I respect them both but have a partiality for Lee, I confess."

"Have you heard from your friend Lewis Armistead? Is he still in California?" Cissy could not help smiling when she thought of Armistead. His mother was from one of the oldest and most distinguished families of New Berne, his great-grandfather the renowned John Wright Stanly. General Armistead, twice a widower, called Lo for short, had acquired the nickname Lothario. There was more joke than truth to it.

Graham returned the smile, knowing where her thoughts had taken her. "Lo is on his way east. He cannot fight against his homeland anymore than Lee, Jackson, and so many others. The south is fortunate that it can claim so many good veterans of the Mexican War. It's a particularly difficult decision for poor Lo, though."

"Why is that, Papa?"

"His best friends in the world are Mira and Winfield Hancock. Win is a Union man. Despite being as close as brothers, they're now officially enemies. Unfortunately, in a civil war that is often the case: friend against friend, father against son, and on and on. I hate the thought of the pain and suffering that will come to us all as a result of this mad rush into war."

"Nate says it will be over in just a few weeks and all will be fine."

"Then your young man is a bigger fool than I thought. With what does he propose we do battle? Ego alone will not suffice. Almost everything we use is imported. We manufacture next to nothing. We most certainly do not have the factories that can be converted to making the weapons and machines of war. No, this will not end quickly and it will not end well. Mark my words, Cissy. That is why I want you and Evangeline away from here."

"I talked to Evangeline, Papa. She knows you want us to leave, but we are not going to leave you here."

"If I could leave, I would. I have too much at stake to simply abandon everything. Not only that, but the ships I have retained are vital if we hope to bring the goods we need from Europe. I'll probably relocate their homeport to Wilmington if I see that we are in danger here. It is more defensible geographically. Right now I'm just biding my time and trying to figure out which way the dice are going to roll. Men like me are going to be a critical element in the coming struggle, just as much so as the men that march into battle."

"I don't understand everything that is going on, Papa, but I'm sure you're right. You always seem to foresee things and act wisely. I just hope you are wrong about this war lasting a long time."

"I wish it, too. But, once the scent of blood is in the air it takes a strong wind to carry it away. A lot of good men will die before this madness is over."

"You don't think we should have stayed in the Union, do you, Papa?"

"I wish that we could have my dear. I fear Lincoln's election, the tariffs that are now imposed on imported goods, the outcry from the abolitionists, and the arguments for state's rights have left us no wiggle room. Once Lincoln ordered North Carolina to send troops to fight against fellow southerners, we had no choice but to secede."

Cissy tossed on her bed that night, unable to sleep and unable to forget the warnings of Logan and her father about Nate. In the morning, she had made up her mind to be cool and aloof the next time he came calling.

She did not have long to wait. Nate arrived in early afternoon to find Cissy pulling weeds in the flower garden and studiously ignoring him. The more he talked, the more laconic she became. Finally, even Nate, who rarely noticed others except as a mirror to reflect himself, could see that something was decidedly amiss with the girl who had seemed smitten by his charms on previous visits.

"Cissy, are you upset that I did not call yesterday as promised? You do realize the weather was quite inclement?"

"Good heavens. Of course I know what the weather was. As for your not calling, I must confess I have completely forgotten that you were even planning to come. I don't recall you mentioning it."

"But you must. Remember we were sitting on the veranda and I told you I would be back yesterday?"

"No. I can't say as I do." Cissy continued pulling weeds, refusing to look up.

Nate was not pleased with the turn of events. He was well aware that Cecily LaRoque was a prime catch. Not only was she beautiful and intelligent, but she also was the only heir of a doting father. Nate's own financial prospects were dismal since his father's loses in tobacco speculation. He had not bothered to educate himself for a particular profession as the assumption had been that he would step into his father's shoes in due time. Now with the business badly overextended, there would be little for him to inherit.

It was also no secret that Logan Gwaltney considered Cissy his. That alone was enough to bring out the competitiveness that always simmered just below his surface. He had met other girls, dallied with a couple, and bedded those of lower station that he considered worthy only of a convenient romp in the sheets. Other than physical release, they could offer him nothing. Yes, Cissy would suit him fine. Just because he married, it would not mean that he would have to substantially alter his life, merely redefine the parameters of his daily existence in mundane ways. With his eyes slit in concentration, he watched her tugging furiously at the weeds. Their roots were leaving the life-sustaining hug of the sod in big clumps, along with more than a few unfortunate flowers.

"Cissy, stop wrecking your flower bed for a moment. I want to ask you an important question. Please?"

"Just because my hands are busy, it doesn't mean my ears are deaf."

"Of course not, my dear. But if I'm going to propose to my girl, I do want her full attention when I do so."

Caught off guard, Cissy could only stammer, "What, what did you say?"

She stared at him in surprise, her pique momentarily forgotten in the shock of his words. Nate grinned, and dropping to one knee, took her hand in his.

"My dearest, lovely Cissy, do me the honor of consenting to be my bride."

"Your *bride*?" she could only repeat the word numbly. In the back of her brain, the realization that he made no claim of love began to germinate. Cissy ignored it in the momentary realization of her daydream. "Yes. Oh, Yes, Nate! But you must of course ask my father before we are officially engaged."

"I will, now that I have your permission. I thought perhaps I would stop by his office in town after I leave you."

"Wonderful! Oh, I am so happy. I must tell Miss Evangeline," Cissy's beam slowly faded when she thought of how much Evangeline had always liked Logan. Perhaps, she would wait and let her father tell her.

"Let's marry soon so you will be my wife when I march off to war. I want someone waiting for me and writing me letters and praying for my safe return." Nate laughed, "And of course, celebrating my brave deeds."

"I'm sure you'll be very brave, but I really don't want to think about you going off to fight," Cissy said. She was so immersed in thoughts of her wedding gown and the festivities that she barely noticed Nate's departure.

No more than an hour after he left her, Nate was sitting in Graham's office.

Graham looked at him across the paper littered expanse of his large mahogany desk. Picking up a stack of papers, he quietly shifted them to the left side. Still he did not respond to Nate's request for his blessing. Through narrowed eyes he watched the young man shift and squirm in his chair. Graham chuckled at how much he enjoyed the discomfort he was causing.

Finally he began, "Mr. Pearson, I can certainly understand why you or any other young man might want to marry my daughter. She's beautiful and charming. And of course, she comes with the added attraction of being...do forgive the conceit...a very wealthy man's only heir. I..."

"Excuse me, please, but I am unaware of her financial particulars and indeed of your own," Nate stammered nervously.

"Of course you are. How unkind of me not to note that

you're new to the local community and therefore not as privy to us all here as others might be." Graham smiled but his eyes were cold. He continued, "Nevertheless, I might add that despite my daughters many charms, she is a very head-strong and opinionated young woman and one I've thoroughly enjoyed spoiling. She will lead any man who thinks to control her a merry chase."

"I am not unaware of her many attributes, sir, and feel that we will suit very well."

"You feel you will suit? It seems to me there is some lack of ardor in your courtship of my daughter, young man."

"Not at all, sir. I am most eager that we marry."

"I don't recall challenging your *interest*. As for my blessing, I must decline for the moment. You have only known one another a very short time. A hasty marriage in the face of your imminent departure for the battlefield is ill advised. If you have enough love and commitment between you, time will not be your enemy. Furthermore, the information that has circulated regarding your circumstances in your home community would cause any father to be cautious."

"Mr. LaRoque, any man that has spread malicious lies about me and my standing in Kinston I challenge to meet me on the field of honor. I will not stand for the impugning of my good name and that of my family." Nate could only bluster. He did not know what information might have reached Graham LaRoque's ears. Whatever it was, and despite LaRoque's opposition to a hasty wedding, he intended to push Cissy into one as quickly as possible. That would also silence the insistent letters from his father that he return to Kinston and make an honest woman of the girl he had bedded and impregnated. All she could bring him was her body and a brat he didn't want. Unlike Cissy, she had no fortune to offer and no prospects of one. Yes, he would have Cissy, and soon.

"The local officials aren't too fond of dueling. I suggest you save your gunpowder for the Yankees." Graham stood signaling an end to the meeting. His voice stern, he added, "I will speak to my daughter tonight. I suggest you not return to my home until I invite you to do so."

Biting back anger and forcing his voice to pleasant modulation, Nate said, "Of course, Mr. LaRoque. I shall await the invitation with great eagerness. Until then, I bid you good day."

"Mr. Pearson." Graham nodded his head in dismissal.

Graham paced his office in agitation for over an hour. In exasperation, he told his office staff to carry on without him and left for the day. He needed Evangeline's calming influence and wise council. Cissy was going to be furious with him. Regardless of her anger, he had to stop this foolishness before it was too late.

He did not leave Evangeline's until after dinner. He wanted to stay with her, hold her in his arms, and claim both her heart and her body as his. The need in him was so great, that he thought of visiting his widowed mistress, longing for the momentary comfort her body could provide. He rejected the thought immediately. He wanted no substitute.

Graham squared his shoulders as he walked from the woods between his home and Evangeline's and into his yard. Cissy could tell from the look on his face that Nate had spoken to him and he was not happy. She felt her heart sink as she watched her father slowly climb the veranda steps. He did not see her sitting in the wicker chair by the large fern jardinière.

When he reached the top step, she stood and called to him, "Papa, I'm here. I've been waiting for you."

"I thought you might be. Let's sit out here a minute. I think we need to have a little talk."

Cissy resumed her seat and waited for her father to begin. For long minutes they sat in silence, neither willing to be the first to broach the subject that loomed between them.

Chapter 6

"You don't understand, Nate. I am all the family my father has had for a very long time. I can't just elope with you. It would break his heart into smithereens. All he has done is ask us to wait until we know one another better. I'm sorry the meeting did not go well between you." Cissy could tell by his face that her words were not enough to quell his anger. Biting her lip, she continued, "Besides, what if something were to happen to you in the war. I would be a widow. I don't want to be a widow. It isn't that I don't love you. I do. I'm just asking you to wait. Papa says if you really love me and I really love you, that a few months won't matter. You said yourself that the war will be over soon. So why not wait until then?"

"Would you send me into war with a broken heart? You know I want to marry you. If you are uninterested, if you don't love me enough to marry me now, then say so."

"That's not fair. You know I do."

"You have to decide, Cissy. Marry me before I go to war, or we will never marry." His voice was cold and he kept his eyes studiously focused on the bole of a large oak that stood on the verge of her yard, refusing to look into her face.

"Give me a couple of days to think about it, at least."

"Very well, two days. Since I am forbidden to be here, I will leave now. It's ridiculous that I cannot even come to the house, but must stand here in the woods like some low-life. However, since that is the only option, meet me here in two days, same time."

He mounted his horse, snatching angrily on the reins to wheel the huge gelding around in the small clearing. Softly Cissy implored, "Don't you want to kiss me goodbye?"

He did not look down. Digging in his spurs he galloped off, leaving her standing in a swirl of dust. She shrugged, thinking he might not have heard her. Coughing, she watched until he was out of sight. The tears in her eyes were not from the dust. With a heavy heart, Cissy cut through the woods to Evangeline's house. Although she suspected the woman was as opposed to the wedding as Graham, she was the nearest thing Cissy had to a mother. And a mother to talk to her and understand her pain was something she very much needed.

Cissy stopped on the edge of Evangeline's yard and peered through the dappled screen of leaves. Tied to the hitching post and shifting from side to side in patient equine boredom, stood Logan's horse. He visited Evangeline often now that his mother had died. Mrs. Gwaltney had fallen ill of pneumonia the previous winter and slipped quietly away. His father had buried his grief in brandy. As an only child Logan was left to shift for himself and in his loneliness for a home life, he had turned to Evangeline. While Cissy was glad that Logan had found a second mother in the woman they both adored, she was in no mood to visit with Evangeline if it were to include an accusatory and angry Logan. Turning she slipped back through the trees and into her own yard.

She tossed and heaved in the bed that night like some chained creature struggling to be free of the entwining sheets. When the weak light of morning sent a watery shaft of light through her window, she gave up the effort to sleep and left the rumpled bed. Despite her father's mandate, she had decided that she would marry Nathaniel Pearson. Of course she loved Nate she reassured herself, so why not marry. Although he had never phrased it in baldly direct terms, she knew he must love her as well to want to marry her. Thus decided, Cissy determined not to wait for Nate surreptitious visit of the next day.

Her brow furrowed in concentration, she tried to picture her father's face when he realized she was gone. Surely, he would come around she reassured herself. Best not to think on that, she decided, or she would never have the courage to run away.

When her father left for the office she would finagle some way to ride into town with him. It was not his custom to question her. With no mother to arrange the purchase of medication or other feminine supplies and apparel, her father had made it a point to never inquire too closely into his daughter's shopping needs. Cissy dressed with care in one of her most flattering day dresses, soft lime batiste with royal blue trim, pulled on walking boots and grabbed a matching straw bonnet. When her father descended the stairs to the dining room, she was already at the table.

"Goodness me, I didn't expect to see you up and about so early, missy."

"I hope you don't mind, Papa, but I need to do some shopping today. I thought perhaps I could ride in with you and we could have dinner later at the Gaston House Hotel. We haven't done that in ages. I could have Toby drive me home afterwards and then come back for you later if you need to stay in town this afternoon." Cissy held her breath as she looked expectantly at her father.

"I have a long day today, sweetheart. I have two ships arriving, providing they are on schedule. It is important that I meet them and review the manifest as we are awaiting a shipment of armaments from England. They are critical to the Confederacy. I must be there to ascertain they have arrived. If not, it's critical that my captains depart immediately with new orders. For that matter, it's vital that they depart immediately with orders for the additional items that we must have if we plan to sustain a conflict for any length of time." Graham expelled a long breath, "Of course, you may ride in with me. I will try to meet you for dinner at the hotel but I can't promise. Come to the office around noon and we'll see. If the ships have just arrived, it will be impossible to get away even for a quick bite. Otherwise, after we have eaten, I'll have Toby drive you home."

Cissy did not stop to consider where she would find Nate, but since he had said he was not an early riser, she assumed he would still be at home with the Taylor's at that hour of the day. She also did not dwell on the impropriety of calling on him. Such brazen and unmaidenly comportment would shock his aunt and uncle, but then, she giggled, an elopement would be even more shocking. She twitched with impatience. Soon Nate would know that she would marry him. When her father's carriage stopped at the office, she sprang down without waiting for her father's assistance and was ready to scurry away.

"Wait, Cissy. It's still early. Come in with me for a moment. I would like to show you something that came in last week. I thought perhaps Miss Evangeline might like it for her birthday. It's a lovely piece and I'm quite taken with it, but of course, I will defer to your judgment in such matters."

Cissy started to protest. But if she did so, perhaps she would arouse her father's suspicion. Besides, she wanted to see the gift he had selected. For a moment she was sad. Depending on when she and Nate left, she might miss Evangeline's surprise birthday party. Guilt welled up when she thought of leaving her father to cope with the party arrangements without her help. Cissy squared her shoulders and put the fear that she was being rash in a back corner of her mind. Perhaps if she ignored the feeling, it would go away. She had time to do this for her father. Besides, it was early for the shops. Only a few merchants had begun sweeping in front of their stores and opening shutters. What could a few moments more matter, she mused? "Of course, Papa. You have wonderful taste, so if you like it, I'm sure I will as well. What is it?"

"You'll see. Not to be impatient, missy."

Cissy walked into his office and sat in the chair that stood by the window. It had been her favorite spot since she was a little girl. Looking through the wavy glass of the window she could watch the workers as they scurried about their morning tasks on the Union Point dock, named for the junction of the Neuse and Trent Rivers. A couple of local fishermen, a tall thin son and his round short father, were sorting their nets. Feeling her gaze, they lifted their faces and waved at the window, smiling at the lovely girl they had watched grow into adulthood.

Her father glanced out the window and saluted the two men. "Looks like Jim and Charlie are planning on going out this morning. Doesn't look much like fishing weather though. I wouldn't be surprised it we have a storm. It's just too hot and muggy not to."

"Oh, dear, I hope it doesn't rain until afternoon."

"Nothing we can do about the weather one way or another...not even pretty girls that don't want to get rained on," Graham remarked with a chuckle. "Let me get that safe open and I'll show you the gift I chose."

Cissy gasped when he held up the ivory and lace fan. Delicate and airy, it unfurled like a flower spreading its petals to the sun. "Oh, Papa, it's exquisite, an absolute work of art. I love it. I know Miss Evangeline will, too. It's just so perfect."

"I wish it were more. I want to give her so much more, but propriety doesn't allow and she would never accept." For a moment his face was shadowed by sadness.

Knowing where his thoughts had gone, Cissy wrapped her arms around him and hugged him close. "I know and so does she. She loves you as much as you love her. It's just terrible that you cannot be with one another."

"Years ago I was rash and foolish, missy. Don't be as stupid as I was. There is much truth in the old adage: 'marry in haste, repent at leisure.' The only thing that I don't regret from my marriage to your mother is that she gave me you."

His words hammered her heart. For a moment, Nate's face flashed before hers and she doubted her planned course of action. But then, she told herself, Nate wasn't shallow, shrewish and unfaithful like her mother. Her own marriage would be wonderful. Nate was handsome, charming, and such a good dancer; and of course, he must love her to want to marry her. Yes, her marriage would be wonderful. "I'm going to go now, Papa. I'll come back around noon and maybe we can have dinner." Her conscience gave a momentary prickle at the lies, "Even if the ships come in today, you still need to eat something."

Graham rose from the safe where he had carefully tucked the fan. "I'll see you then. Now be careful out there on the street. There are a lot of rude men in town practicing at being soldiers. A pretty girl like you is bound to attract attention."

"You know I'll be careful, so don't worry." Cissy kissed his cheek and was gone.

Rushing down South Front Street, she hurriedly turned the corner onto Craven Street. Just down on the right loomed the Taylor's home, quiet and still shuttered on the lower level. Cissy hurriedly pushed open the gate and stepped onto the brick walkway. Catching a quick breath for courage she prepared to advance on the house. The sound of sibilant murmuring arrested her journey. Turning in the direction of the whispers, Cissy crept toward the concealing screen of shrubbery. Stopping in the embrace of the dark green branches, Cissy listened. Although the idea of eavesdropping was momentarily troublesome, recognition of Nate's voice made her draw even deeper into the bush until she could see beyond into the inner garden.

Hidden from the house by a latticed gazebo, Nate stood with his arms around a very young and obviously pregnant girl.

With a pang of jealousy she noted that the girl was very pretty even in her shabby attire. As Cissy watched, he pulled the girl closer and kissed her with a passion that Cissy had only previously imagined. She watched in amazement as Nate gripped the girl's bottom and pulled her hard against him as he allowed the kiss to move from her mouth to the tips of her breasts. The tears on the girl's face told Cissy that the two had been having a heartfelt discussion before the fervid embrace. For a moment she wondered what it might have been and then shrugging her shoulders in resignation and loss, she silently withdrew from the concealing hedge and left the Taylor's yard. Dejected and heartbroken, her dreams of marrying Nate forever gone, Cissy wondered down Craven Street. She did not stop until she reached New Street. Fat drops of rain dimpled the dust at her feet with the promise of a coming deluge. Cissy turned right and trudged down to the waterfront street that would take her back to her father's office.

Her tears merged with the heavy rain that now pounded on her bent head. Her clothes were drenched, her hair a bedraggled and sodden mass that clung in wet tendrils to her face and neck. Tired in heart, mind, and body, she was miserable through and through. She wanted only the comfort of her room, a dry nightgown, and the soft embrace of her bed where she could at last cry in peace. She could only pray that providence would deliver her from the necessity of facing her father in her current state. The gods were kind.

She was so happy to see Toby waiting at the curb with the carriage that she could gladly have hugged him. "I'm real sorry, Miss Cissy, but your father say for me to take you on home. His boats done come in and he got to see to business. He say he see you tonight for supper." Toby paused, then continued. "I suspect you going to be glad to get home and into some dry clothes."

"That I will." Cissy breathed a silent prayer of gratitude.

She felt as though the clop-clop of the horse's hooves were the sounds of her heart beating a heavy rhythm, reassurance that she would live even if it were broken. The ride home seemed to last forever and she was grateful that a frustrated Toby at last gave up the effort at conversation. She wanted to run away inside herself, shut away from everyone, until she could find a way to deal with Nate's betrayal of her love. Until she could heal herself, she had no energy to spare for relating to others. Even the weather seemed to be in mourning. The heavy rain had tapered off into a steady drizzle, the leaden skies promising it would not end soon.

Cissy stayed in her room the remainder of the day, drapes drawn and face averted from the door. At suppertime when Tizzia tiptoed into the room to check on her, Cissy had pretended sleep. She could not face her father with her face swollen from weeping. She could not make small talk. She could not pretend that all in her world was normal. When she failed to appear at breakfast the following morning, an alarmed Tizzia knocked on her door and then boldly entered.

With determined good cheer, her longtime maid and friend, threw back the drapes and exclaimed, "It's a plumb beautiful day out there, Missy. You need to get on up now. Bessie went and made you pancakes and some of that good country sausage you like. You need to eat something. You didn't eat nothing last night. Your Papa is purely worried there is something mighty wrong with you. I had to shoo him out of the house this morning before he would even go to work. Now, why don't you hop on up and put on something pretty. I'll fix that hair of yours and you'll look just like an angel. Miss Evangeline is coming over to dinner, so your Papa'll be back here by noontime. Ain't no need to go all mopey and worry everybody."

"I'm not hungry," Cissy mumbled from under the protection of her lace-trimmed sheet. "Please, just go."

"Nah, I can't go doing that. Now you tell Tizzia what's got you so worked up you can't even eat. You hear, now? Whatever it is, we'll fix it."

Cissy sat up in bed and glared at her maid, "I don't know how you propose to fix the mess I'm in."

"What you mean?" Tizzia asked in alarm. "You ain't done nothing stupid like have you, something that gets girls in trouble?"

"I've been stupid all right. I promised to marry a no-good philanderer who has just broken my heart," she declared defiantly.

"Promising ain't doing. Ain't no man that messes around with other women is worth worrying about. You just be glad you found out before you married that skunk. The ones I feel sorry for are those that don't find out nothing until it's too late. Yessum, you're mighty lucky. You thank the Lord Almighty, you done found out before you tied the knot."

Her face woebegone, she looked into Tizzia deep dark eyes and asked, "Why? Why did he want to marry me when he's kissing and fondling on someone else?"

"I ain't even going to ask you how you know. I'll just say again: it's good riddance. I guess you're talking about that Nate feller that's been sniffing around here. I knew he was bad news the minute I laid eyes on him. No doubt he liked your papa's money real well and it ain't no lie that you're the prettiest girl in the whole town. Yeah, he ain't the only one that would jump at a chance to marry you. You just be careful next time that whoever it is *really loves you* and not your daddy's money. You make sure of it before you go falling too hard for his sweet talking ways."

"Phooey on men! There won't be a next time. I'm through with the lot of them."

"I don't 'spect you going to like this much, but I need to say something about this whole mess. Thing to me is: you just got took in by the wrappings. Here he is a nice looking, nice talking, real smooth acting man. Ain't nothing wrong with any of that. Trouble is you didn't wait to find out if there was anything nice under the skin. You got yourself a girl's crush. That ain't the same as a woman's love. A grown-up woman knows a man has to have something good inside, something she can depend on. Give yourself time to grow up a little more, then you'll see this Nate thing won't nothing. Right now it hurts your pride and that is a thing a person hates, young or old. But wounded pride ain't going to kill you."

Cissy threw back the covers and marched over to the armoire. "I want to look pretty. I don't want anyone to know about this, so don't you dare tell. Not Papa or Miss Evangeline. And for sure, not Logan."

"Yessum. My lips is sealed on this one, for certain. Let me help you now. Your papa and Miss Evangeline be here soon. You don't want to look like you been knocked down. You stick your nose up high and act like you got no troubles, no heartache. Word'll get around. Cook that Nate's ole goose when he find out you don't care nothing about him."

"Good!" Cissy announced grimly.

With her head high, Cissy was waiting serenely on the piazza when Evangeline walked over for dinner. Her father was not yet home, so Evangeline seated herself in a wicker chair close to the one Cissy had claimed.

"You look lovely today, darling. I confess I was a bit worried about you when Graham told me that he has forbidden you to marry Nathaniel Pearson until after the war. I know that must hurt, but in time I think you will see the wisdom of waiting." Evangeline reached over and squeezed Cissy's hand in sympathy.

With firm resolution, Cissy gave a small brittle laugh before replying, "Oh good heavens, that was just a silly, childish crush. I'm quite over all that. Nate is pleasant enough, I suppose, but I really don't know anything about him. I am quite relieved, actually, that Papa stopped me from doing something stupid. Once I thought about it, I decided I don't especially care for him very much at all. I certainly don't want to be engaged to him, or anyone else for that matter."

Surprised, Evangeline sat back in her chair and leveled her eyes on Cissy. She had known her too long and too well not to sense pain behind the dismissive words. The girl had been much too infatuated for the feelings to vanish overnight. Something had caused the sudden disclaimer of interest. Deciding not to push the issue, she merely responded, "That's that, then."

Graham rode up at that moment and swung easily down from the saddle, "My two favorite ladies waiting for me. I'm a lucky man." He flipped the reins around the rung at the hitching post and stepped onto the piazza.

"I'm glad to see you feeling better, Cissy. When you didn't come to dinner, or to breakfast, I began to worry. I considered bringing the doctor back with me. I'm happy to see that wasn't necessary."

"I'm fine, Papa. Just a headache, but it's gone now." Cissy stood and kissed him on the cheek. "Let's have dinner. I don't know about you and Miss Evangeline, but I'm starved."

Ignorant of the discussion between the two women, Graham was careful to avoid mention of anything to do with Cissy's suitor. Evangeline was a ready ally in keeping the conversational waters unruffled, thus the meal progressed smoothly. When the apple pie had been served and appreciatively devoured, Cissy excused herself and retired to her room. As soon as the dining room door closed behind her, Graham reached for Evangeline's hand and pressed a tender kiss into her palm that sent a hot pang of longing through them both.

"I don't know what happened but she seems to be her usual

self again. Did she say anything to you before I arrived?"

"Only that she is relieved not to be engaged to Nate. It seems she has had some kind of epiphany in regards to that young man. I think we can both breathe a sigh of relief on that score. I do confess a certain curiosity as to what brought about such a sudden change though."

"I can't imagine. She went into town with me yesterday morning. Toby brought her home early as I was too occupied with the ships that came in yesterday to dine with her in town. When I arrived home she had already retired to bed. Toby said she seemed rather subdued on the ride home, but didn't think much was wrong with her other than being drenched by the downpour while she was walking back to my offices. I feared she might have caught a chill, but that doesn't seem to be the case. I do think she seems rather remote though." Graham smiled at the woman he loved, "Tell me if you think I'm being just a foolish doting father?"

Evangeline melted into his eyes, longing to tell him how much she loved him. Scolding herself to respond to his question and not her own needs, she replied, "I don't know what happened in town, but I suspect something occurred that reflected poorly on Nate. She's pretending a brave nonchalance, but there is something underneath that careful front I can't put my finger on. I think she may have suffered her first heartbreak. We all know Nate isn't worthy of her. I suspect something happened to convince her of it as well. Whatever it is, her pride is stilling her tongue."

"She's a proud one, my Cissy, and a tough little thing. If she's been wounded, she'll find a way to pick herself up and go on. She had to grow a thick hide to survive her mother. I tried to give her enough love to make up for it, but knowing her mother did not love her has left her with an empty place inside. I don't know what she would have done had it not be for you stepping in and mothering her."

Evangeline recognized the truth in his assessment but resisted the urge to comment. Since she had admitted her love for Graham, she had avoided discussing his wife with either him or Cissy. Somehow it did not seem quite so sinful to her to long for another woman's husband if she could pretend the woman did not exist. Cissy and Graham had filled the empty place in her own heart. Still, there were times in the night when she reached for the other side of the bed and was surprised to find it empty. Then she would remember that her husband was dead and the man she had grown to love could never answer the physical longings that gripped her. When she found herself wishing for Monique to disappear forever from their lives, she would say a quick prayer of contrition for the direction that her thoughts flew without volition. She told herself daily that the love they gave her was enough. But, she wanted more, much more. And she knew Graham did as well. She wondered who answered his physical needs and cursed herself that her own standards held her to such stern and rigid resolve that some other woman enjoyed the intimate caresses she pined for.

The beautiful fan and the party in her honor only added to the flame of her love. For Graham and Evangeline, lost in the joy of the moment, Cissy's half-hearted participation could not dim the joy of the evening.

Chapter 7

Comte Rene de Guibert turned from the tall French doors that overlooked the plaza. His face was like a granite mask, as hard and cold as stone, imperious and hostile. He did not like the man that stood before him, never had. He was a wastrel and a scoundrel, the subject of many rumors, the principal of many duels, and the man on whom his daughter had wasted herself. He glared at his willful daughter's lover and for a moment almost delighted in the news he would deliver. Making a barely perceptible shrug, he dug into his waistcoat and produced the telegram that had arrived the previous afternoon. Without comment he handed it to Marcel who had demanded an audience.

Marcel had arrived the previous day to find the house shuttered and the servants unwilling to admit him. Unsettled by the refusal of entry into the house where he had long been a familiar, Marcel had no choice but to leave. He had stewed all night, anxious to meet with her parents and discover if there was any validity to the rumors that had begun to circulate in the drawing rooms and private clubs of Paris.

Marcel felt his hand begin to tremble as he read the tersely worded telegram informing the Guibert family that Monique LaRoque, nee Guibert, had been lost at sea. The ship bearing her to New Berne had steamed into a storm and sunk, taking all aboard into the cold and watery embrace of an Atlantic grave. His dreams of a fortune had sunk along with the ship. Unless he thought of something soon, he would be as dead as his late lover. He recognized that he felt neither grief, nor any remorse for the lack of it. His only emotion was fear for his own hide. Forcing himself to observe the social necessities, he shook his head sadly as he returned the telegram to Monique's father.

"My condolences, sir. Her loss is a tragic and heartfelt one for us all."

Rene took the proffered telegram, nodded his head in acknowledgement of Marcel's expression of sympathy and without further ado left the room. Shortly on his heels a butler arrived to show Marcel out. Her father's coldly formal behavior spoke volumes about any future welcome he could expect in this house where he had spent so many illicit hours in the arms of his lover. Either her parents were not as oblivious as she had thought, or their cynical acceptance of the arrangement was now concluded by her death, along with any welcome he might expect in future.

He stood in the street and pondered where to go and what to do. He had limited funds and no friends to turn to for more. He had tapped into their generosity too often and repaid too rarely. The usurious gangsters who currently owned him body and soul were focused only on recovery of what he owned, not incurring yet more debt. His only option appeared to be a hasty departure. To stay in Paris was for the moment an unhealthy option. Damn Monique for an inconvenient and ill-timed death, he swore. He would need time to cultivate another needy and wealthy woman, and time was a luxury he lacked. Not only that, but he found Parisian drawing room increasingly chilly, his presence barely tolerated due only to the illustrious caché of his family's name in the past. But, just as the family fortune had been frittered away, the honor attached to his name had slowly dissolved as well. He knew his foibles well enough to acknowledge that his own activities were responsible for the final loss of what little money and respect his family still retained. Thus he realized he would have to seek his fortunes in distant fields. Paris with all of her dissolute pleasures he must abandon.

Marcel threw what he could carry into two valises. Taking a last glance around his quarters to assure that nothing of value remained, he caught the glint of sunlight on the small, framed portrait that Monique had insisted he have. She had been only seventeen when she sat for it. Seventeen? Suddenly he knew where he was going. She was gone, but her daughter was not. Perhaps he was a trifle old for her tender years, but he was vain enough to easily accept that his looks were still exceptional and youthful. He possessed the added weapons of charm, guile, and a thorough cynicism. And in New Berne he would have no unfortunate rumors to combat.

Taking passage at Le Havre, he sailed for Nassau. He arrived a much less confident man than when he had left France. Constant mal de mer had left him wan and weak. Cursing the sea and the necessity of voyaging thusly, he staggered from the wharf onto land, grateful that he had survived. More than once he had entertained frequent doubts that fate might deem otherwise. Marcel used the next week gainfully, gambling in the dens of vice that robbed naive sailors of their hard won wages. He felt no compunction at pocketing his winnings from these lowly men he secretly scorned. The fact that he employed a marked deck to achieve his current riches bothered his conscience not at all.

At the end of the week he procured passage on The Cecily, a heavily laden freighter bound for New Berne. The irony of the ship's ownership brought a sardonic smile to his features. If things went according to plan, he would one day own the ship on which he sailed thanks to his intended seduction and marriage to the owner's daughter. It seemed fortuitous that the ship that carried him north bore the name of his intended bride. He laughed aloud as he stood at the deck watching Nassau fade into the early morning mist. If the daughter were as comely and as passionate as her mother, she would be a welcome substitute. She was not only far younger and in the freshness of her beauty, but innocent and thus malleable. Even the prospect of the coming days, that would find him once more at sea, could not dim the elation he felt building within his chest. Yes, this new world would make him a wealthy man as it had so many others. And unlike those who came years before him, his work would not be hard physical toil in the face of wilderness. He would ply his skills in the drawing rooms and taverns of New Berne.

It was a gray day when Marcel steamed up the Neuse River into New Berne's port. Compared to the skyline of Paris with its grand palaces, elegant residences and gracefully ornate bridges, New Berne was unimpressive. Despite being one of the largest towns in North Carolina and frequently referred to as the *Athens of the South,* its modest clapboard homes and red brick buildings elicited only contempt from the Frenchman. He shuddered delicately as they bumped into the wharf and rudely dressed men hastened to tie off the ropes of the ship.

Graham watched the mooring from his window. The cargo shipped from London via Le Havre, to Nassau and then on to New Berne was one that not only he, but also the local militia, awaited with eagerness. Unless things had gone sadly amiss, the cargo hold was full of badly needed rifles, bayonets, and ammunition. In his mind he was already reviewing the contents of the hold and the agents that would need notifying of the arrival of the ordered goods.

Graham glanced at the passengers as they disembark. A tall elegant man strolled arrogantly among them, his nose lifted in disdain. For a moment he seemed vaguely familiar, but before Graham could ponder further, he saw the captain making his way to the office of LaRoque Shipping. Leaving the window, he walked out of his office and met the captain in the outer reception area.

"Captain Jonas, do come in. I trust your voyage was an uneventful one."

The captain nodded his head and followed Graham into his

office where he wearily seated himself without waiting for an invitation. Graham noted the man's grim face and wondered what the problem might be. Jonas had never been the merry sort, but he was normally happy to reach homeport.

"I must say, Captain, you seem remarkably subdued for a man just returning home from weeks at sea. Did you have problems filling the munitions orders?"

"No, no. That's all as specified, I'm happy to say." Jonas rubbed his bristled chin and then stood. The bulbous nose and red cheeks that announced his fondness of drink seemed to visibly grow more florid. "I'm mighty sorry Mr. LaRoque, but I've got some bad news. I truly hate to be the one to bring it to you."

Graham waited with alarm, wondering what the captain had encountered on the voyage to have him so upset. Finally tired of the harrumphing captain, he asked, "Just spit it out. What is it you need to tell me?"

"It saddens me to...." Again he harrumphed before continuing, "I extend my condolences, sir. I was informed in Le Havre that the ship bearing your wife capsized in a storm at sea. All aboard are presumed to have perished, I fear."

"You're sure of this? My wife was aboard the lost ship?"

"Aye. That I am." The captain studied the toes of his shoes before looking up to meet Graham's eyes. "Ain't no doubt."

Perplexed, Graham did not realize that he had asked aloud, "But why? I wrote her and expressly told her to stay there until this war here is resolved. Why would she come now after staying away so many years?"

"That I couldn't say, sir." Bob Jonas reached into his pocket and extracted a folded paper. He handed it to Graham. "This is the passenger list of the Mermaid. The owner of her company asked me to give it to you."

Graham quietly read the document. "Obviously, for whatever reason, Monique ignored my request and booked passage.

It was a terrible decision with the direst of consequences for her, sad to say."

"Aye, that it was, Mr. LaRoque. Again, I would like to say how sorry I am for your loss."

"Thank you, Captain."

Graham quietly closed the door behind Jonas and sat in the chair behind his desk. Absentmindedly he picked up a letter opener and toyed with it. He waited for some grief for the woman he had once wanted, loved, wedded and bedded to assail him. The only thing he felt was a small remorse that their marriage had existed in name only for so many years. How long had it been since he could see her face in his mind's eye? How long had it been since he thought of her during the day or in the lonely hours of night? How long since he had stopped caring? How much of the blame for their failed marriage was his when he had not demanded she return with him those many years ago? Had he not turned a blind eye to her dalliances in Paris, would she have stayed on? Was he secretly so glad to be free of her that he encouraged her infidelity by his complicit silence?

He thought of their daughter and wondered how to tell her that her mother was dead. Even though Cissy professed no love or desire to see her mother, surely the reality of the woman's death must cause some belated sense of loss. Then, he thought of Evangeline. He scolded himself to squelch the joy that blossomed in his breast when he considered the impact of his unexpected freedom. Despite all odds to the contrary, he could at last ask the woman he had loved for so long to marry him.

He was so lost in thought that he did not see the elegant man standing outside his window gazing fixedly at the sign proclaiming LaRoque Shipping Company. He did not see the calculating stare that shifted from the sign to pierce the dusty glass, there to latch onto his vague image. Graham disappeared from the stranger's line of sight as he moved to the hat rack to collect his hat and jacket. He must go at once to his daughter. And then he would tell Evangeline. After a memorial service and a suitable period of mourning, he intended to make her his wife.

When Graham walked into his home, he found Cissy sitting quietly by the window in the solarium where a potted palm cast striated shadows over her bowed head, an opened book lay unread under her hands. She was so lost in thought when he entered that she did not hear him, did not look up. He studied her still form and felt the misery radiating from her, wondering at its source, not realizing how badly Nathaniel had bruised her heart. Seeing her melancholia, he hesitated, unsure how to tell her of her mother's tragic death at sea.

As if sensing his eyes on her, Cissy looked up into the troubled face of her father, "Hello, Papa. You're home early. Is something the matter?"

Graham walked over and seated himself on the wicker settee and draped his arm over her shoulder as though to protect her from the words he must say. "Cissy, I have some sad news. Despite my request to your mother that she not come, she apparently decided to book passage anyway..."

"Oh, fiddle-faddle. I don't want her here." Cissy interrupted. "Why would she come? She doesn't like it here."

"Cissy, you need to hear the rest of what I have to tell you. Your mother will not be coming after all. You see, her ship sank at sea and all aboard were lost. Your mother is gone, darling. I'm sorry. Despite the years she has been away, she was still your mother and my wife."

Cissy went as still as stone, her face as unreadable as a marble statue. For long minutes she said nothing. "I'm sorry, Papa. I know I sound nasty and unloving, but it is hard to mourn a mother who turned her back on me from the time I was an infant. I have already mourned. I mourned for years that my own mother could not love me when I so wanted her to. I mourned for years that there was something wrong with me that she could not love her little girl like other mothers do. When she wrote you and never me, it hurt. I gave her up so long ago, that now the idea of her death seems as remote as some story in a romance. I don't know how I am supposed to feel pain for her now when so long ago I stopped letting her hurt me."

"Cissy, in many ways you are still that hurt little girl. But, at the moment this isn't about you. We must both pray for her soul. Instead of anger and resentment of all that was not, we need to remember that a part of our family is gone. Monique in her own way was a lost soul, a victim of her own frustrations and needs. Let us feel pity that her life was lost in this way. Let us grieve for her in a way that is charitable and kind."

"Of course, you're right, Papa. I know you've been lonely and hurt, too. At some point, you must have loved her. You married her, lived with her, and made her a mother. There must have been some good times with her." Cissy looked into her father's eyes. "Oh, Papa, it makes me sad that I have no good memories of my own of her."

"You were young when she left, darling, too young to have many memories whether good or otherwise. In her own way, I am sure she must have loved you. What mother does not love her child?"

When she did not respond, Graham patted her shoulder and continued, "Tomorrow I will check with Father Paul to arrange a memorial service for your mother. We must also write her parents. They are old and she was all they had. We must remember that. They will truly mourn her loss." Graham made up his mind to send them enough money that their later years would be comfortable. Perhaps, when he asked Evangeline to be his bride without the customary year of mourning, it would ease his conscience that he had done the decent thing by Monique's parents.

While Graham made plans for the memorial, Monique's

former lover pursued his own devious direction. Once he was established at the Gordon House Hotel, he began to explore New Berne and meet people. He was anxious to charm and entice into confidences those that he encountered on his rounds. When he professed a profound sympathy for the plight of the southern states, he won instant rapport with most of those he met. One in particular seemed to be particularly venal, of a kindred mindset, as it were.

Marcel studied the man over a hand of cards. He had carefully dealt the deck and was confident that the man opposite him would lose the sizeable pot that Marcel had subtly coerced him into building. Pearson was proud, too proud, and that worked to the Frenchman's advantage.

Nate Pearson's eye twitched and his hand trembled slightly as he pushed the last of his money onto the table and called the bet. With three aces and a pair of threes, he was certain of victory and yet the Frenchman seemed to have uncanny luck. Slowly Nate watched as Marcel quietly laid the remaining ace of hearts on the table. One by one the other cards followed: the king of hearts, queen of hearts, and the jack of hearts. Nate was holding his breath praying that the remaining card was not the ten. Marcel slapped the last card onto the table and held his hand over it for a moment before he slowly slid it away. Nate's triple and pair was no match for the royal flush that now lay face up on the table.

As Marcel raked his winnings into a neat pile, the others at the table let out a collective sigh. None had believed that the wily Frenchman would beat Nate's hand. A couple of the men shifted restlessly in their chairs and fingered their drinks. The bastard had uncanny luck as far as they were concerned. Maybe too much luck.

Finally the oldest, George Smithe, a merchant with a propensity to drink too much and gamble too often, stood and nodded to the group. He remarked with a frown, "It's a damned good thing you're engaged to that LaRoque girl, Nate. Looks to me like you're going to be short on cash after tonight. Her daddy's money is going to be mighty welcome I suspect."

Nate rose from the table as he debated his response. With drunken nonchalance he slurred, "Oh, I think I can manage without Mr. LaRoque's wallet or his daughter. I find myself reconsidering my previous offer of matrimony in favor of a more tractable wife and father-in-law."

Several eyebrows rose at the rudeness of the remark, especially considering his previous braggadocio at his engagement to the girl. Smithe shrugged, "Well then, I guess it's a good thing you're headed for Cape Hatteras. Trash talk about LaRoque in this town won't win you any friends. I'm sure Gwaltney will be relieved, though, to have you out of the running. He set his cap for Cissy LaRoque from the time he was a boy."

His pride pricked, Nate responded with asperity, "If she had wanted Logan Gwaltney, she would have never considered me as a serious suitor and I can assure you she did. That is until her father stepped in."

"I thought you said you're the one to call it off, not Graham LaRoque or Cissy?" Jeff Burns had never cared for the brash newcomer and could not resist the chance to needle him.

Marcel's interruption was as smooth and oily as a keg of imported eels. "Let me buy you a drink, Mr. Pearson. It's the least I can do. That was a fine game you played. Had I not been lucky enough to draw that queen of hearts in the final draw, the game would have been yours."

Happy for the change of subject, Nate accepted the invitation. Soon Marcel had extracted all of the information he could glean about the ill-fated courtship between Nate and Cissy and had determined that the other young man posed no serious challenge. Indeed, as best Marcel could ascertain, the biggest obstacle would be her father. Time was increasingly critical to his purpose with the pending nuptials between Graham LaRoque and his widowed neighbor, Evangeline Forrest. The woman was still of an age to produce children and conceivably a male heir for the LaRoque fortune. Before that could happen, Marcel had to be safely wed to Cissy. Then he would assure there would be nothing to stand in his way of controlling the estate after the untimely death of her father. Unless he planned to arrange for the demise of the Forrest woman as well, it had to be done soon.

Nathaniel Pearson, frustrated and humiliated when Cissy failed to meet him by the large oak on the appointed day, was glad to be leaving New Berne. The excitement of war and the opportunity to leave the area for fresher fields afar had become more than appealing to him. The only regret that he harbored when he left for Fort Clark on Cape Hatteras three days later was leaving Logan Gwaltney behind. It was galling enough to have been jilted. It would be even more so were he to be bested by the likes of Gwaltney. Unlike Nate, who had managed to get himself attached to a regiment headed for the outer banks, Logan had joined the North Carolina seventeenth regiment, recently reorganized into the twenty-sixth, and would remain in New Berne for the foreseeable future.

Unaware that an even more dangerous suitor than Nate waited in the wings, Logan once again found himself making several visits a week to either the LaRoque or Forrest residences. Despondent and withdrawn, Cissy was lukewarm in her acceptance of his renewed courtship. Logan was unsure if her mood was the result of Nate's departure or the loss of her mother. Fearing that it might be the former, he redoubled his efforts to be amusing and was awarded with an occasional smile that never quite reached Cissy's eyes.

Logan soon had more to occupy him that courtship. After the battle of Bull Run in July, the Federals busied themselves blockading the vital ports of the south under General Winfield

Scott's Anaconda Plan, designed to squeeze the rebels from every direction and cut off needed access to supplies. With the armies readying for winter quarters, the effort to subdue the rebelling states would be waged primarily at sea. Logan, at the suggestion of Cissy's father, was assigned to monitor ship movement along the inland shores near New Berne. An occasional foray to the Outer Banks and lookout duty at Cape Hatteras light kept him away for several days at the time. He made it a point to visit with Cissy before and after such excursions. With Graham as a liaison and mentor, he had a secondary motive for calling at the LaRoque's.

Unbeknownst to Cissy, with the governor's collusion, Graham had begun raiding Union ships off the dangerous coast of North Carolina. From Cape Hatteras, the bluer waters of the northward moving Gulf Stream could be seen with the naked eye. Ships traveling north to the ports in New York and New England availed themselves of the stream's speed in order to reduce the time needed for northbound vessels. From his vantage point in the lighthouse, Logan could signal Graham's ships tucked out of sight behind the dunes when Union vessels were off shore. The ploy had been honed to a fine point during the days the pirate Blackbeard roamed these shores in the previous century. From their berth behind the sheltering dunes, Graham's recently armed ships could dash out and seize an unsuspecting Union ship before it could man adequate defense. Although the piracy was sanctioned by the state, it was a dangerous venture for the ship's crew if captured by the Union. The risk was deemed worthwhile due to the potential materiel and goods that could be seized for Confederate use.

Because Logan was seldom in New Berne for more than a necessary trip for supplies and Graham was busy managing his ships and keeping them from Union hands, neither was aware of Marcel's campaign to glean all that he could about LaRoque and his daughter. Although his questions had caused some idle concern in the minds of some of New Berne's citizens, none had been alarmed sufficiently to inform Graham about the curious Frenchman. Most, knowing of LaRoque's own French ancestry put it down to mere curiosity about a fellow Frenchman.

Even had Graham known that someone was inquiring about Cissy and him, he had no energy for gossip. He was too worried about keeping the shipping lanes open to the ports of Europe to which the South must turn for the many things it did not make and could not make on its own.

Sitting in Evangeline's parlor, he mused on his daughter. "Cissy worries me. I can't quite put my finger on it, but she seems a little remote and distracted. Logan has noticed it, too."

Evangeline was careful in her response, "Nathaniel Pearson was hurtful. She is young and will heal, but I suspect she'll never be so naive and trusting again."

"I've watched Logan patiently wooing her. I suspect it costs the lad to rein in his feelings while she remains so cool and aloof. The more I watch Logan evolving into a self-controlled, responsible, and trustworthy man, the more I like him." At times, Logan seemed like the son he had always wanted, but after Cissy, Monique had been adamant there would be no more children. He smiled then. Perhaps, his child rearing years might not be ended after all.

Leaning forward he gathered Evangeline into his arms, "Are you determined to delay this wedding. I'm getting mighty impatient."

"So am I. It isn't much longer, darling."

"Another day is too long as far as I'm concerned."

They kissed goodnight at the door, and he walked into the dark of the woods. The glow of candlelight in the windows of his house steered him through the deep shadows. He felt restless. Sleep would be elusive tonight. His mind was preoccupied with his coming wedding. He chaffed at the forced delay, but knew that Evangeline was right when she balked at his unseemly haste. After years of waiting, a few months more could hardly matter.

Graham shifted his study chair to take advantage of the light breeze flowing from the river. The night was hot and humid. He decided to wait for a cooler hour before seeking his bed. To pass the time he picked up the newspaper from his desk. He had been so busy during the day he had not noticed the headline that now demanded his stunned attention. His fears were confirmed. The Union would ignore the North Carolina coast no longer.

The New Berne Progress devoted most of the front page to the August 28th and 29th battles for possession of Cape Hatteras. Poorly defended by a small group of green 7th North Carolina Volunteers commanded by Colonel William Martin and under concentrated fire from seven Union gunboats, first Fort Hatteras and then Fort Clark fell. With only three Union soldiers wounded, the Federals proclaimed a needed victory to assuage the morale rattling loss at Bull Run. Conversely, with several Rebel deaths, a number wounded, and nearly seven hundred captured, it was a serious blow to southern confidence.

With Oregon and Ocracoke inlets poorly defended, Graham knew their days were numbered as outlets to the sea from North Carolina's sound ports. That would leave only Beaufort inlet protected by Fort Macon. If the old Harlowe-Clubfoot canal had been restored and enlarged as he had urged, he could use the Beaufort inlet but it had long since lapsed into disrepair. As it was, Hatteras and Ocracoke inlets were the closest to New Berne, and thus he had most depended on them for outlet to the sea. The sound ports of Washington, Plymouth, Elizabeth City and Edenton were dependent on the same routes. In the upper reaches of the sound, through the Albemarle-Chesapeake and the Great Dismal Swamp canals, small ships in the sound could access such northern ports as Richmond and the ports along the Chesapeake.

Thinking hard Graham envisioned the military strategy that lay ahead for the eastern part of the state. With an island like Roanoke as a potential base for operations, the Union could control the large inland sounds and their inlets and would have a backdoor route into the large port at Norfolk as well as a base for assault on Richmond. If the north could capture vital shipping lines via water as well as those by rail, it could quickly starve the South into capitulation. A base in the eastern part of the state would allow for assaults on the vital Wilmington Weldon railroad that hauled supplies from the port in Wilmington to Richmond and Lee's army in Virginia. Should Wilmington fall, the south would be in deadly peril.

Even so, Wilmington was now the safer option for his ships, as Wilmington lay some twenty miles inland on the eastern shore of the Cape Fear River. There any approaching enemy would have to run a gauntlet of fire from fortifications along both banks to reach the port. With two inlets, Old and New Inlet, ships had a choice of egresses to the sea further frustrating attempts at blockade. He resolved that the coming morning would find him on a ship bound for Wilmington where he would secure sufficient berthage for all but a couple of small ships in his remaining New Berne based fleet. He was so busy making plans to protect his shipping interests that he almost failed to read the remainder of the article. With a deeply inhaled breath of frustration, he continued. When he reached the bottom of the article, he read among the names of those killed in action Nathaniel Pearson of the Lenoir County Braves.

When Cissy appeared for breakfast in the morning, he took her hand and apologized. "Sweetheart, I am going to ask you to go to Evangeline and stay with her for a few days. I must go to Wilmington immediately and arrange for my ships. I have yesterday's paper in my study. You may read it to inform yourself of the necessity for my trip. When you are finished with it, please give it to Evangeline with my apology for not seeing her before I leave."

Cissy studied him with alarm, "You look tired, Papa. I don't think you slept well last night."

She rose and hugged him around the shoulders. Leaning over to kiss the top of his head, she assured, "Of course, I'll go to Evangeline. I'll leave as soon as I can tuck a few things into my valise."

Graham softly added, "Cissy, there is one more thing I must tell you. Nathaniel Pearson died in battle at Cape Hatteras. I know you once considered him a dear friend, therefore I am sorry for your loss."

Chapter 8

Cissy sat in the shadows on the far side of the Stanlys' elegant ballroom. The tall palm beside her, almost the color of the satin gown she wore, added further protective coloration. Had the ball been for any other reason, she would not have come. She was in no mood for partying. However, when Mrs. Stanly insisted on hosting an engagement party for Graham and Evangeline shortly after his two-month stay in Wilmington, she had been left with no choice but to attend. She watched her father smiling joyfully at Evangeline and felt great happiness for them both. Even so, she could not quite squelch the momentary twinge of jealousy that nudged at her as she watched happy couples swirling about the floor propelled by an energetic orchestra. She was so preoccupied with her thoughts that she did not see Logan approach.

"Cissy, I've been looking everywhere for you. Come on now and give me a dance. You don't want to worry your father and Miss Evangeline by pouting in the corner. You know I didn't mean to upset you earlier when I teased you about them beating us to the engagement party. Forgive me and let's dance," Logan cajoled.

Cissy studied him for a long moment. In truth she did not want to upset her father and Evangeline on their special evening and if she stayed hidden for the night it would. A fleeting frown creased her brow as she stared into Logan's earnest eyes. Would he never understand that she was uninterested in marrying him or anyone else? Grudgingly she responded, "All right, I'll dance. But, don't you dare pester me anymore about marriage. I'm just not interested."

"My very dear, Miss LaRoque, I would not dream of causing you further distress. Now, seeing as how you are in a bit of a pet, pray do stay off my toes."

Cissy sputtered with indignation, "*Me stay off your toes*, you oaf. You know very well that you are the one that's always stomping on *mine*. I swear, I take my life in my hands when I dance with you."

Logan laughed with high humor, "Then let's risk it. I like that song they're playing, 'Lorena.' When I march off to war, I'm going to be singing it, but I'll change the lyrics to 'Cecily' for the one I leave behind me."

"Don't even mention war tonight. I don't want to think about something so depressing." Cissy firmly pushed the memory of dancing with Nate to the back of her mind.

"Ah, so the thought of me going into battle depresses you?"

"I warned you, if you talk about war anymore you'd better find someone else to dance with because I won't."

"There are some mighty pretty girls here tonight. You'd better not toss me over too easily."

Logan continued to tease as they danced, eliciting little in the way of response. Determined to lift her mood, he refused to be put off. Over her shoulder he could see a tall, elegant man watching them closely. He had not seen him in town before. He assumed it must be some friend of the Stanly family, so he was not surprised when he spotted their cousin Polly Burton at the stranger's side, her arm looped casually through his. Logan chuckled to himself. Despite Polly's earlier infatuation with him, she seemed to have abandoned him to Cissy in order to pursue the new man in town.

Tired from dancing, Logan and Cissy made their way to the dining room where a heavily laden table beckoned them. They took their plates onto the veranda and ate quietly. The silence was broken by voices around the corner from them. Cissy recognized the sibilant hiss of Sally Jane Mayfield and the low tones of Polly Burton. Listening despite herself, she heard spiteful Sally Jane's caustic comment.

"Honestly, wouldn't you think Cissy would be ashamed to show her face after Nathaniel Pearson jilted her? I heard him say she was not as ladylike as she wants everyone to believe."

A third voice, that Cissy recognized as Elizabeth Berkeley, known as Lizzy, cattily interposed, "Of course, Nathaniel did have a bit of a reputation. Perhaps, that's what she was attracted to. And, furthermore, I don't understand how you can watch while she takes Logan away from you. I know the two of you were getting along really well until she took him back. Of course, she'll drop him again as soon as she can steal another girl's beau."

"Do stop, Sally Jane, and you too, Lizzy. You don't know what you're talking about," Polly scolded. "Forgive me for speaking ill of the dead, but Cissy was always too good for the likes of that disreputable rake, Nathaniel Pearson. As for Cissy taking Logan from me, it's really more me trying to take him from her after Nate came along. Everyone knows Logan's been sweet on her forever.

She sighed, "Besides, I think I could be smitten by that suave Frenchman, Marcel Lambert. He's a marquis. Isn't that just the most exciting thing? He's such a divine dancer and so handsome. I wonder if he is so very old. Even so, I could just swoon from looking at him. I do so hope he asks me to dance again."

"Well, mark my words, the minute Miss Cissy LaRoque learns you're interested, she'll be after Mr. Lambert in a flash and poor Logan won't stand a chance. And, you won't either."

Lizzy leaned in, "I wonder if she *is* fast with men. She certainly seems to have no trouble attracting them."

"She's very beautiful. I think you're both being unfair."

"Pooh, you'll see. She wants everyone's beau. Besides, even if she isn't fast, if her father wasn't so rich, I'll bet she wouldn't have all these men chasing after her."

"Really! I can't believe you can say such things. Lizzie, you're still angry because Joey Reynolds told you she's pretty. You're jealous that he might like her better than you."

"I never! You know Joey has all but asked me to marry him."

Her nose quivering like a hound after a new scent, Sally Jane cooed, "Oh, how exciting. You must tell me."

Logan felt the waves of anger radiating from Cissy and could not blame her for feeling angry. Taking her by the hand, he pulled her to her feet. "Come on. Don't pay any attention to Sally Jane or Lizzy. They're just jealous, spiteful, troublemakers and always have been."

"Do people really think I'm only worthwhile because my father has money?"

"Cissy, if your father were a pauper you would still be attractive to men and a worthy person in your own right. You're fun, intelligent, witty, beautiful, and independent. And, oh, I don't know...just plain wonderful. It doesn't matter to me who your father is or isn't. You know how I feel about you and I always have, even before I knew anything about what money and position really mean."

Cissy smiled into Logan's eyes, "I know. You've always been my good friend."

"Daggummit, Cissy. I am more than a *friend* and you well know it."

"For goodness sake, don't get in a huff. I can't stand anymore aggravation tonight." Cissy squared her shoulders, "If I wasn't depressed enough before, I surely am now."

"Don't let them see they upset you. It will only encourage Sally Jane and Lizzy to be more obnoxious next time."

"You are so right. I won't give them the satisfaction." Cissy lifted her chin defiantly and turned to Logan. "I think we should dance again."

Outwardly Cissy appeared to be enjoying herself. She was not. She was badly shaken. Was it only Sally Jane and Lizzie that would say such vicious things about her? As the evening drew to a welcome close, Cissy could not help but notice the dashing Frenchman had pursued every unattached female there except for her. Her vanity was piqued by the omission. She wondered if it were because Lizzy or Sally Jane had whispered unkind things to him about her.

Ensconced in the carriage beside her ecstatic father and equally ebullient future stepmother, she struggled to project a lighthearted mood. "Well, Miss Evangeline, it won't be long now before we'll all be going to the same house when the evening is done. I think I'm going to look forward to that."

Graham gave Evangeline's shoulder a teasing squeeze, "Cissy, my love, you are not the only one anticipating that event I assure you. I still can't believe she agreed to move in with the two of us headstrong LaRoques."

"Now you decide to tell me your faults!" Evangeline pulled a face that was lost in the shadows of the night, "In that case, I wonder if it would be a perfect scandal if we just went on living separately after we marry? That way if y'all get too stubborn and obstreperous, I don't have to deal with you."

Graham pulled her close and whispered in her ear, "Don't even think about living in another house, much less any bed but the one I'm in."

Later, pacing restlessly in her room, Cissy smiled at their joy in one another and the coming wedding. As for her, she wanted a chance to prove her worth and that did not include marriage. It wounded her to think that people might think so little of her that she was seen as merely the pampered daughter and only child of a wealthy man. Did they really think she was nothing more than a shallow flirt, and an immoral one at that? She had suffered rejection by her mother. With Nate she had experienced the pain of an unfaithful and manipulative suitor.

Even the reassurance of Evangeline---her surrogate mother, her father's love, and Logan's steady support were not enough to take away an unsettling sense of insecurity.

Somehow she was determined to find a way to show them all that she was not some idle and insignificant ornament. For a wild moment she thought of cutting her hair, dressing in her father's cast-offs, and joining the rebel troops. But a glance in the tall peer glass in the corner of her room disabused her of that notion. Even with chopped hair and men's clothing, her figure could not be disguised. Having no concept of what it entailed, she gave fleeting consideration to the idea of watching ships like Logan and reporting on them to her father. She had to reject that notion, as Graham LaRoque would never permit her the freedom to roam the countryside.

It was a determined and more mature young woman that rose from her bed the following day. Because of Monique her childhood had been frequently painful. As a consequence both Graham and Evangeline had conspired to compensate, failing to realize that it was an unrealistic ideal world they created for her, one that found her indulged with luxuries and humored at every turn. Their loving acts and good intentions had not given her the armor to deal with the adult world in which she had emerged like some beautiful, fragile butterfly. Accepting that her future happiness and self-worth were hers alone to earn, she resolved to approach her life freed of the blinders of the past. The wings of the butterfly must become those of an eagle if she wished to soar.

Graham looked over the rim of his coffee cup as Cissy entered the dining room. He sensed some change in her from the way she carried herself, her firm stride, and the determined tilt of her chin. "You look chipper this morning, sweetheart. I trust you slept well?"

"I feel wonderful." Cissy gave him a dazzling smile as she seated herself across from him. "Papa, I've decided since you don't have a son that it's time you taught me something about the business. That way if you get sick or have to be away, I will at least have some idea of what to do until you can take over again. With a war underway and your shipping so critical, surely that is a good thing?"

"But, Cissy, I have an excellent office staff. You don't need to worry your pretty head about that." When Graham saw the crestfallen look that swept across her face and the sudden sadness that filled her eyes, he was stricken that he had not appreciated the depth and sincerity of her offer. "Perhaps, I answered too hastily. I don't have time today, but if you would like you may come to the office with me tomorrow and I can show you some things that you can do to help."

"Thank you, Papa. That's wonderful. I promise I won't get in the way and I will really work hard. I so want to do something productive, something that matters, that's important."

Once again happiness lit her eyes. He beamed at her eagerness and resolved to find little inconsequential things to occupy her so she would feel that she was making some contribution. Graham chuckled to himself, confident that she would soon bore of the office and be back to shopping for pretty bonnets and a round of afternoon teas. He wondered what he could find for her to do. With his shipping business transferred to Wilmington and only a couple of small ships retained for his use to commute back and forth, the office was much reduced in activity. Small ships that were unsuited for ocean going he had donated to the Confederacy to ply the inland waters. His ships and others, either donated to or purchased by the state, were soon called the "Mosquito Fleet," named for their ability to annoy the Federals with their darting maneuverability in the sounds of North Carolina. Were it not for Cissy and Evangeline's protests at abandoning their homes and moving to Wilmington, he would be in Wilmington already where he could more closely monitor his concerns. As it were, he had to depend on telegraph and ship communication between the two ports.

A few days after the ball, Graham picked up the daily paper and carried it back to his office where Cissy was sitting at a desk sorting through invoices for filing. He waved the paper at her and pointed at the headline. "My ladies need to reconsider the move to Wilmington. This coast is going to be a Yankee magnet. It says right here that the Federals under General Thomas Sherman have seized Port Royal and now control all of the sea islands off the coast of South Carolina and Georgia. They won't forget us either. They already maintain control of Cape Hatteras and have blocked Hatteras inlet so they have an established base here for launching an invasion. New Berne and the port cities around Pamlico and Albemarle Sound are targets they cannot ignore for long. I do not want you and Evangeline here if that should happen."

"Papa, I don't *want* to be here *if* they decide to attack us, neither does Miss Evangeline. We have the ship. If it looks as though the Yankees are coming, we can put our things on board and go to Wilmington. In the meantime, do we really want to leave our house and Miss Evangeline's for squatters to occupy?"

"We can leave some of the servants to care for them. That's not an issue."

"Then you had better talk to the servants. I know for a fact that Tizzia, Bessie, Toby and Leroy all plan to skeedaddle if we do. We *freed* them. We can't make them stay. I know they want to go with us if we leave. Besides if it isn't safe for us, do we want to expose them to danger after all they have done to take care of us?"

"Ah, Cissy. You make good points. Still, it makes me very uneasy to sit here like ducks in a pond waiting to get shot."

"Don't worry so, Papa. We'll be fine."

"I hope you're right. I do so hope you're right."

Both turned at the knock on the office door followed by the immediate entry of a tall an elegantly groomed man who hesitantly stroked his mustache as he awaited an invitation to enter.

"Yes, may we help you, sir?" Graham studied the stranger as he had previously when encountering him, and again noted a vague feeling of familiarity. Still he could not place where he might have met him previous to his arrival in New Berne. Perhaps, he thought, on board ship while traveling on business. So intent was he on his own musings, Graham did not notice the sudden flush that infused Cissy's face with color, nor the quick clasping of her hands, which she hastened to hide in the folds of her skirt.

"Please, forgive the intrusion, Mr. LaRoque, Mademoiselle." Marcel noted the speculation in Graham's eyes and was glad that he had had the foresight to grow the mustache and closely trimmed beard. "With the news of recent reverses in the fortunes of this new Confederate government, I grow alarmed that I might be caught here with no way to return home. I am not prepared to leave immediately, however I would like some reassurances that if I delay I will still be able to make my escape should it become necessary. Since you have ships plying the waters between here and foreign ports, I thought perhaps you could provide some insight."

"Please, be seated and allow me to introduce my daughter, Cecily LaRoque."

"It is my deep honor and pleasure to make your acquaintance, Miss LaRoque." Marcel bowed low over her hand. "I must say that I noted your beauty on previous occasions but was not fortunate enough to receive an introduction. I am Marcel Lambert, the Marquis de Rochefort."

"Mr. Lambert," Cissy said as she nodded her head in acknowledgement.

"Mr. Lambert, I would like to assure you that at no point will you need to worry about transportation, but I cannot. The port here and the others on the Pamlico and Albemarle are in some peril with the fall of Hatteras Island to the Union. With winter coming and what is still a relatively weak navy, I do not foresee any imminent threat. However, they will use this time to build their strength. With the coming of spring, all bets are off. The sounds are too strategic for the Union to ignore. I fear the Confederacy has yet to share my evaluation. If you have some concern for your welfare, you might remove yourself to Wilmington which is much more defensible. That, of course, is assuming your business does not require residency here."

"Ah, the prospects seem gloomy indeed. Unfortunately, I have not concluded my affairs here."

"Forgive the intrusion into your privacy, but might I ask the nature of your business in New Berne? This is a small town and some of the locals have speculated as to what might have brought you to our fair city."

For the next hour Marcel gave an extravagant vision of all he planned in the way of business ventures, the depth of his financing, and the breadth of his experience, as well as an inventory of highly successful past ventures. He was amazed at his own creative capacity for invention and warmed to the task as he went along.

When Graham returned to his office after escorting Marcel Lambert out, Cissy exclaimed, "My goodness, Papa, he is certainly an impressive gentleman."

Graham snorted. "Cissy, when you are as old as I you will learn that folks that blow their own horns as hard as that are generally full of nothing but hot air."

"Surely you don't think he's lying, do you?"

"Time will tell, time will tell." Graham shook his head, "Let's go home. I think we have done enough here for today."

Marcel was pleased. Not only had he now achieved the prerequisite formal introduction to Cecily LaRoque; but also he had noted the admiration in her eyes, both for his facile tongue and his appearance. Next he needed only to arrange an accidental meeting. The fact that she seemed to be working in her father's office made the opportunities to do so easier. He continued his winning streak at cards giving him the necessary funding to maintain the appearance of a gentleman of consequence, and he listened carefully to those with whom he played, gleaning useful tidbits of information as time passed. It was only a week before the opportunity presented itself to take his overarching ambitions to the next level.

As if by accident, he met Cissy as she emerged from the newspaper office where she had gone to place her father's advertisement for seamen for his blockade-runners. With so many men enlisted in the service of the Confederacy, staffing his ships at optimum levels was becoming harder just when the need for them had increased exponentially.

"Miss LaRoque, what a pleasure to see such a lovely face on this fine morning." Marcel took her hand in greeting, and bending low, kissed the air just above her flesh. As he did so, he could feel the slight tremor in her fingers. Hiding his satisfaction at her reaction to his touch, he smiled brightly. "I was just on my way to the Gaston House Hotel for a cup of tea. I would be honored to offer you refreshment as well."

Remembering Lizzy and Sally Jane's words, she bit her lip to stop a ready acceptance of the invitation. "Thank you, but I regret I must decline. I fear I have another engagement at the moment. Perhaps another time."

"But, of course." He nodded his head as she slipped past him. She did not see the sudden impatient fury that lit his eyes, nor the malicious stare that followed her. She did not hear him swear under his breath.

Cissy spent the rest of the afternoon working in her father's office, grateful that she was doing something beyond passing time in idle pursuit. However, she knew that the filing and other menial tasks assigned to her were simply her father's way of keeping her occupied and feeling needed. His clerks were far more familiar with office routine and function, and despite their patient assistance, she knew she was more in the way than not. Even with that knowledge, it was at least a beginning.

So intent was she on her thoughts that she did not hear the jingle of the bell just over the office door. It was not until she felt the presence of someone just over her shoulder that she turned in greeting. "Oh, Logan, I didn't hear you come in. I guess you are here to see Papa about what's happening along the coast or something?"

"No, Cissy. I came to fetch you. I have a buggy and it's a beautiful afternoon, so would you permit me to drive you home? Your father will be closing for the day in less than an hour, so come on and let's go."

Cissy hesitated. It was a gloriously beautiful day and fresh with the first hint of winter's coming chill. She knew her father would not object if she left early to ride with Logan, however she said, "I'll ask Papa. If he doesn't mind, I'll go with you."

Cissy walked into her father's office and received his distracted permission to ride home with Logan. She did not take time to inquire into the worried expression on her father's face. Soon she was climbing onto the black leather seat of the two-seater buggy that Logan drove.

Reaching into the boot behind the seat, Logan extracted the last autumn roses he had gathered that morning from his late mother's garden. "These are for you. With cold weather coming, I suspect there won't be any more."

"How beautiful they are. Thank you so much for picking them for me."

They rode along Pollock Street turning left at the end onto the river road that would take them to her home. When they were in the residential area where the homes were tucked behind hedges to gain privacy from the road, Logan took her hand in his. "Cissy, I leave tomorrow to go to Fort Mangum in Raleigh for training. After that, I don't know where I will be."

"Oh no, Logan. Don't go. Papa needs you to keep an eye on ships for him. Isn't that enough contribution to the Confederate cause? Do you really have to run off and get shot at, too?"

"Cissy, you can't mean that? I thought you supported the cause?"

"Of course, I do. It's just that what will we do here if all of the men leave? Who will protect us then? Papa is gone so much now with all these trips to Wilmington. I confess Miss Evangeline and I are really nervous at being left with only the servants to protect us. Except for old Toby and Leroy, the rest are women."

"If there were any danger here, the army would come to protect the town. New Berne is too important to just let them sashay in and take it from us."

"We're more worried about the Buffaloes and runaway darkys than about the Yankees." Neither Cissy or Evangeline shared Graham's pessimism for New Berne's chances of eluding Union notice.

"There haven't been any problems from either group around here, as far as I know. Do you think your father would leave you if he thought you would be in danger? You know better."

"I know, but I still feel uneasy when he's away. Knowing you are nearby makes us feel safer."

Logan pulled on the reins bringing the horse to a stop, turning to her he exclaimed, "Ah Cissy, I hope safety isn't all that I can give to you. I came today to ask for your hand in marriage. Your father has given me his blessing already. I love you, always have and always will. Tell me you'll marry me so I leave knowing you will be waiting for me when the war is done."

"Logan, please don't ask me that. I do care for you; I'm just not ready to be anyone's wife. I want to feel like I'm a person in my own right and not just an appendage of some man. I need to do *something* that makes me feel worthwhile."

"You're still down about that gossipy, spiteful Sally Jane and Lizzy. I'd like to wring their meddling necks." Logan chewed his lip a moment thinking on how to proceed. "Cissy, men go out into the world to make a living for their wives and children. We go to war to protect you. That's a man's role. That's the way it is and always has been. Women get married and make a home."

"Fiddlesticks! Women are just as smart as men and can do things, too."

Logan struggled to keep his patience, "Yes, they are. I'm not saying they aren't. I'm saying you are all I need and want. You don't need to change. I love you the way you are now."

"But, I don't love me just now. I feel as though I have to fill me up before there will be any of me to spill over on anyone else." Cissy kissed him on the cheek. "Don't be mad at me. Try to understand. I promise I'll write while you're gone. Just please be careful."

Despondency stilled Logan's tongue for the remainder of the ride to her house. With gentle hands he helped her descend and escorted her to the door. When he pulled Cissy into an embrace at her door, she allowed him to kiss her. He held her with a fiercely restrained passion, a frustrated hunger, and an overwhelming sadness that he must leave her, not knowing if she would ever be his. Neither of them could foresee what the future would bring, what war would mean for them and their fellow southerners. Logan breathed a prayer that someday, if he were lucky enough to survive, he would win her for a wife and that nebulous tomorrow would be theirs.

Chapter 9

Sitting at the dinner table with the two women that meant more to him than any others, Graham could not help his heart swelling with joy despite the many worries that filled his day. Sipping on his red wine, he smiled with pleasure.

"Papa, I was talking to Mr. Pennington in town the other day and he was telling me about that French speaking girl, Sarah Gilbert, that lived with him for a couple of years. He says she married Mr. Slater after the war broke out. You remember him of course, he had the dancing academy where I had dance lessons?"

"Oh, yes, Rowan Slater wasn't it?"

"That's right. At any rate they left town and the academy is empty. Mr. Pennington thinks we need a new dance school. He advertised in his paper but no one is interested, apparently in light of what's going on with this awful war. He asked if I might be interested in opening one since I told him I wanted something to do. What do you think of that idea, Papa?"

Graham glanced with surprise at Evangeline who shrugged her own ignorance of Cissy's new scheme. "Darling, it is imperative we think about moving to Wilmington. That being the case, I don't think the timing is right. If you are still interested, after the war, we'll talk about it. I know I don't have much for you to do at the office with almost everything transferred to Wilmington, but you could help Evangeline sort through things. I'm sure she would like to bring some of her own pieces over here. Perhaps, the two of you could look through your mother's things and decide what you might wish to keep, or what you could donate to those who have need of it. We must sort through things, especially if we are to move."

"Are we to move everything then, Graham?"

"Unfortunately, no, my dear. I think only the most valuable and necessary pieces."

Cissy felt her spirits sink. She so badly wanted a project beyond the walls of her home, but no matter what she tried there always seemed to be some obstacle. Hiding her disappointment, she nodded her head, "Miss Evangeline, I'm happy to help anyway I can."

Her voice soft, Evangeline asked, "Would you like to call me Mother, darling? I feel as though I have been a mother to you since you were a little girl. Now that your father and I are married, it seems appropriate."

On the first day of 1862, Graham had married the woman that had stolen his heart long years before. They had sailed to Wilmington for a working honeymoon leaving the logistics of combining households for later. Evangeline had assured him that she understood the importance of his business affairs to the war and she did not mind the dual purpose of the trip. Although he had hurried through the day in order to be with her at night, he still had left much undone and she knew that he must return shortly.

"Graham, darling? Graham?"

Startled from his thoughts, Graham looked up in confusion, "I'm so sorry. Forgive me the inattention, my love. I fear I didn't hear you."

Evangeline reached over and patted his hand, "I asked if you had thought any further about having a ball to celebrate our marriage. Since the wedding itself was such a discreet affair, I thought perhaps we should have a party to include our friends. With so much sadness and fear, I think people need a few moments of joy."

"I am far too preoccupation with the state of affairs between here and Richmond pertinent to our waterways to have thought of a party. If you and Cissy wish to plan one, of course, please do. However, I fear we'll have to work the date around another trip to Wilmington." He gripped her hand and looked into the eyes of the woman he could now call wife, "Please forgive this bridegroom of yours. You deserve far better from me."

"I'm very satisfied with my bridegroom, so don't apologize for doing the things you must."

Cissy slipped quietly from the table, unnoticed by them, as she walked onto the veranda and stood under the cold light of a winter moon. Looking up into the haloed brightness of the early January night, she thought of Nate, now dead, and Logan who was camped somewhere trying to stay warm in the midst of winter sheltered only by a flimsy tent. Unconscious of the movement, she tugged her shawl more firmly around her shoulders and shivered. She had missed Nate at first after he had jilted her, but no longer. Now she could regret his death as anyone would the needless loss of such a young life. At last she had admitted to herself that it was more wounded pride that had tugged at her, not some lasting emotional attachment to him. As for Logan, it surprised her that in the still of the night before sleep swept her into oblivion, it was his face that swam before her vision, smiling his love in silent pleading. She did miss him far more than she thought she might. That seemed normal she decided; after all, he was her oldest and best friend. She still could not see him as a suitor.

It was an uneasy household that retired to their beds that night. All were conscious of the heavy burden that living in the midst of the early days of war brought. Hope for a brighter tomorrow mingled with concern for what the ultimate cost that uncertain tomorrow might bring. Intending to bring the South to its knees, even as they slept, Winfield Scott's great Anaconda was stirring, ready for a crushing constriction via the waterways of the Confederacy. Graham alone understood just how personal that plan could become to the lives of the three that rested under his cypress-shingled roof.

For Logan there was no roof and no bed. He rolled over for what seemed like the millionth time, trying to find a comfortable position on the hard sandy soil that held his meager bedroll. He was grateful that the cold windy weather kept the pestiferous sand fleas at bay. Still sleep would not come. Weary of the struggle, he arose from his pallet and walked to the top of the dune that gave him a sweeping view of both sound and sea. Were Union forces to come it would be here. It was his responsibility to see them and quickly get word to his fellow Rebels and then to Graham LaRoque. Logan felt the weight of responsibility and the loneliness of his windswept outpost. He longed for the comfort of home and the face of the woman he loved. He could only hope that she missed him a little, thought of him some, and perhaps felt the stirrings of love. He hoped, but in downcast moments reason told him otherwise. He watched as the first warm glow of sunrise lit the eastern horizon and painted the tips of rolling waves a golden hue.

Graham was awake at sunrise as well. He must get to Wilmington and his ships. Momentary annoyance at the obstinate objection of his wife and daughter to a move there arose in his breast. He could not stop the great breath of exasperation that escaped his lips.

"Graham, are you awake so soon?"

"I'm sorry my dear. I did not mean to disturb your sleep."

"It's fine. I'm ready to get up anyway."

Graham rolled over and tucked her in his arms, his chin resting on the top of her head. "I wish you girls would come with me to Wilmington. I don't feel right about leaving you here and I can't stay. I don't think it's safe here anymore. The North is not going to leave us alone much longer, darling."

"But, Graham, they've done nothing since they took Hatteras last August. I gather they have only the smallest force there.

Surely, if we were important, they would have more soldiers there and would have tried to capture more of the sounds last summer."

"They didn't have the fleet to be overly ambitious then. Now they've had months to get ready. Don't think they twiddled their thumbs with idleness. With Hatteras in Union hands, Wilmington is safer than the cities on the sounds. New Berne is going to be in for a taste of war once they determine to take the sounds. Strategically they must and they will. It makes me much too anxious each time I leave you two here, especially now that there is only the one small ship left behind."

"We can always take the train should the need arise. I promise if we think we are in danger we'll leave immediately and come to you. I really would like the time to go through the things in my house and see what I might like to incorporate here. Cissy and I also must decide which pieces should go with us. Give me a bit more time and then we'll all move to Wilmington."

"If the Federals come, your furniture will have little meaning in the face of the threat to your lives, and it could well be too risky to take the train even if civilians are allowed to use it. At that point, the army will need it to get soldiers here to stop the invasion."

"Please, don't make me feel so guilty and stubborn, darling. I don't want you to leave for Wilmington angry with me." Rolling over she pressed her lips to his.

Forgetting his concern, he stroked her sleek derriere and began to make love to her. His need for this woman he had loved so long overwhelmed him with an insatiable intensity. As his hands and kisses brought her to arousal, Evangeline's passion answered his and they were soon lost in ecstasy.

Evangeline and Cissy stood in the driveway as Toby drove away with Graham, taking him to the ship that would carry him to Wilmington. Both women stood with tears spilling from their eyes. Both women were aware of a nudge of guilt that they remained despite his vehement objections. Yet neither was willing to leave their homes: Cissy the one she had known forever and Evangeline, both the one she claimed now, and the one she had left.

"I suppose we should walk on over to my house and see what more we would like to bring over here."

Cissy glanced at the lowering clouds. "I think we had better bundle up. It looks like we're in for rain."

"As cold as it is, it could well be sleet or snow. I confess I fear for your father when he sails in such threatening weather."

"Papa knows the sea," Cissy hesitated before adding, "Mama."

Evangeline gave her a warm hug, "Thank you, Cissy. Now, let's get our cloaks and get busy. When Toby gets back with the buggy he's going to come help us load things up."

Evangeline's servant Beulah and the two women worked the rest of the day and the next as well. At the end of the second day, they walked once more through the house where Evangeline had spent her first marriage and then the long years of widowhood. Stripped of her paintings, the finer pieces of furniture, and the ornaments that she treasured, it had a forlorn and lonely look. Absentmindedly Evangeline rubbed her forehead leaving behind a smudge from the dust that clung to her hands.

Beulah scolded, "Now, Miss "Evangeline you done got yourself plum dirty. I do declare if I didn't tell y'all I could handle this."

"I know you did, Beulah. There was so much I didn't know where to tell you to start. It's something I had to sort through myself. I couldn't have done it without you two though." Evangeline patted the shoulder of the woman who had cared for her for more than twenty years. "Are you sure you're going to be okay living in this house alone? I hate to leave you, but I don't want to leave it empty. I feel better about it knowing you are here to take care of things for me. I had planned to send Tizzia over so you would not be alone, but she found herself a husband and moved to James City with the other free Negroes and runaways."

"If I needs you, all I got to do is walk through them there woods and get you."

Evangeline's sucked in her lower lip and gave a small shrug, before sweeping Beulah into her arms. Both women's eyes were shiny with unshed tears when they parted.

Having sent Toby on with the final load, Evangeline and Cissy walked home through the brown winter woods as little pellets of ice began a pinging dance on the tree branches and the magnolia leaves that surrounded them. Sensing her stepmother's mood was as bleak as the weather, Cissy commented, "With your things moved in, our house will feel more like home to you soon. We'll set up a studio for us to paint in and those paintings of yours will really brighten things up. I love the secretaire you gave me. It's going to be perfect in my room. And just wait until Papa sinks into that big leather chair you have for his office. We'll have to pry him out."

"Ah, Cissy, I know. It's just my old house looks so sad. I feel a little sentimental about leaving it this way. I suppose I should sell it but with the war on, there isn't much market. Anyway, I have a new home now and I love both it and my new family. You mustn't think I'm not happy. I am. You and your father have given me a new life and so much love."

"You've given us more. I never realized before how empty our house felt until you came. We tried to pretend the two of us were enough, but it wasn't true. Papa has wanted you since I was a little girl and I wanted you to be the mother I never had. If it had not been for you 'adopting' Logan and me, I don't know what we would have done for a mother."

"Have you heard from Logan? I don't recall seeing a letter lately."

Cissy mouth twisted into a wry smile, "I haven't. I guess I finally ran him off."

Evangeline laughed and shook her head. "Not a chance. That boy has been in love with you since you were seven. It'll take a heap of doing to get rid of him. I'm sure, as soon as he is able, he'll get word to us he's safe. I confess I worry that Graham has him creeping around out there watching for Yankees. Since they occupied Hatteras your father has been looking over his shoulder at every shadow. He's certain they will try to take New Berne. I keep telling him that our boys are going to keep them so busy in Virginia that they'll have no time for us, but he doesn't believe me."

"Logan agrees with Papa. But I don't care. I still don't want to go to Wilmington. Surely the Yankees won't bother with us for long. Our boys will lick them good before they have a chance to do much more than raise a little dust."

They quickened their steps as the sleet began a steady drumbeat. Both were shivering with cold as they stood in the back hall shaking ice from their cloaks and hair. The fire in the dining room and the warm bowl of soup resting on the table alongside a loaf of Bessie's freshly baked bread was a welcome sight.

As they seated themselves, Bessie entered the dining room carrying a bottle of red wine. "Y'all needs something to warm you up on a night like this one. I'm scared we in for a big ole ice storm. That sleet coming down to beat the band. That sky so gray out there this won't be letting up no time soon."

Turning to leave the room, Bessie suddenly remembered the letter in her pocket. "This come for you yesterday, Miss Cissy. I forgot to give it to you last night when y'all come in."

"Thank you, Bessie." Cissy immediately recognized Logan's writing on the envelope. "Speak of the devil: Logan has finally written."

"I hardly think of Logan as the devil and neither do you. Do open it and see what he has to say."

Cissy pushed her soup to one side and slid her knife under the edge of the envelope never noticing that the knife still had butter clinging to its blade. Quickly she scanned the letter and then began reading to Evangeline. The letter was not long, merely a short description of the monotony of his days and the misery of the weather. "Oh, listen, he says that he hailed Papa's boat on the way to Wilmington and had a short visit with him."

"I do so hope your father is in Wilmington by now and sitting by a warm fire. I would hate to think of him still on the boat in this nasty weather." Evangeline smiled and teasingly inquired, "Does Logan say anything about how much he's missing you?"

Cissy shrugged her shoulders and didn't respond to the question. "Let's finish our soup before it's cold. Would you pass me another slice of the bread please?"

Evangeline passed her the requested bread and resumed eating her own soup. She suspected by the blush that colored Cissy's cheek that Logan had indeed included a personal message for her. She was careful not to push too hard and scare Cissy away. She and Graham both hoped that Cissy would accept Logan's courtship. They had talked about it and decided that the best thing they could do was to keep quiet and allow the two young people to resolve the issue of their own accord. Despite protestations to the contrary, it was obvious that Cissy had missed and worried about Logan.

That night, February 7, while Evangeline and Cissy lay snug in their feather beds listening to the sleet pelting the tin of the roof, Graham was still on board ship. Low tide and adverse wind had delayed them slipping through the shallow waters north of the inlet at Beaufort. Across from the port, the rampart-topped brick walled Fort Macon was held by Confederate troops. Although he did not know it, the muted rumble that came to him over the water was not thunder, but the booming of distant cannon. Roanoke Island was under attack by a huge flotilla of Union boats under the command of Louis Goldsborough. The attacking ships also carried a large body of soldiers under General Ambrose Burnside. Had he comprehended the Anaconda had come to life, he would have sailed back for his wife and daughter and they all would be safely on route to Wilmington. Restless, he stood in the icy storm close against the wall of the upper cabin and looked out at the gray heaving sea. Graham tugged his hat lower on his head as he braced himself against the wind. As he stood there, the clouds began to separate into ragged tatters. In the dark gaps he could see the promise of stars and clear skies for the morning. Glad for the coming change of weather, he bid the Captain goodnight and sought the warmth of his bunk.

As Graham slid into the arms of lethe, Logan was making his way back to New Berne with all haste. He suspected the time of waiting was finished. The Union had arrived in mass on the Carolina shore determined to close off the ports that lay on the sounds and the inlets that gave access to those ports. Judging from the size of the fleet that passed his hiding place, Logan surmised that it would be only a matter of time before Roanoke Island lay in Federal hands. He cursed silently and steadily as he rode hunched over his horse to keep the sleet from sliding down his neck and chilling his already frigid body. If only Graham had delayed his journey by a day he could have warned him to take the women with him. As it was, Logan could only hurry to New Berne with his message for the troops there and send a telegram to warn Graham of the impending danger. It should be waiting when he reached port in Wilmington. Logan worried for Cissy and Evangeline, wishing they had heeded Graham's urgings. Although the Yankees were not yet on the way to New Berne, surely it could not be long now.

Chapter 10

Dawn was but an hour away when Logan walked into General Lawrence Branch's headquarters in New Berne. The hastily aroused and disgruntled general was pulling on his dressing gown when he walked into his office. Logan did his best to snap to attention before he gave the general the unwelcome but anticipated news.

"Damnation," General Branch swore. "The four thousand poorly armed boys I have are going to be no match for a force like that. I have told Richmond until I am blue in the face that I need at least sixty-one hundred. Hell, half the ones I have are ailing with first one thing and then another."

Wheeling around, he ordered his still groggy aide, "Get some boys out there digging to extend our lines as soon as it's light. I want a defense running from the brickyard down to that little creek that intersects with the railroad. Tell them to run down the creek a ways and extend the line into the swamp so my flank will be protected."

Turning back to Logan he pointed, "You look half dead, son. Get yourself some rest and then report back to me. I'm going to need every man I can get."

"Yes, sir. I'll do that." Logan saluted and left the still swearing general.

Once the telegram agent had been aroused and a message dispatched to Graham LaRoque, Logan began the ride to Cissy. Dawn was pinking the eastern sky when he rode into her yard. Seeing the house still dark, he rode to the back and entered the kitchen. He was weary, sleepy, cold and wet to the bone.

Quickly he stirred the embers in the fireplace and added fresh wood, shivering as he worked.

The fire took hold and began to burn smartly as Logan struggled from his wet coat. Hanging it by the fire to dry, he next bent to his shoes, tugging at the wet leather laces. A still yawning Bessie walked into the kitchen just as he pulled off his socks and draped them over his boots on the hearth. Logan coughed deeply. A shiver started in his spine and rattled his teeth into a chatter as the chill air of the kitchen hit his wet feet.

Taking in the miserable looking man, she shook her head in dismay. "Lord, have mercy, if you ain't a sight for sore eyes. Get out of the rest of them clothes before you catch your death. I'll get some of Mr. LaRoque's things for you to wear until we can get yours dry. Soon as I do that, I aim to fix you some breakfast."

"I'd be mighty grateful, Bessie. I'm about hungry enough to eat those empty iron pots."

"You poor lamb. Now go on and get out of them clothes. Don't worry about me none, I seen naked boys before."

"Yes, ma'am." Logan blushed as he began unbuttoning his shirt. He didn't mind taking the shirt off, but the thought of removing his pants and drawers was another matter. He was sitting in the chair by the fire when Bessie returned with dry clothing.

Bessie dropped the bundle she carried on the kitchen table. Arms akimbo, she barked, "You planning to sit there and freeze to death in them wet britches. I told you to take them wet clothes off. Now get on it, boy. Wrap this blanket around youself, if it bothers you to peel them off in front of me. Act like I ain't never seen no white boy naked before."

Bessie grinned to herself as she turned her back on the embarrassed man and began slicing pieces of country ham to put in the black iron skillet that sat by the fire. "I done put that coffee pot by the fire there last night so it would be ready to go.

When you get a minute stick it on the fire for me. Some coffee will take the chill out of them bones of yours."

Thankfully he and Graham were much the same height so the clothes he pulled on were a reasonable fit. As soon as he draped his clothes to dry, Logan shrugged the blanket about his shoulders and put the coffee on the fire as directed. He felt faint with hunger as the first aromatic curls of smoke arose from the sizzling ham fat. Biscuits oozing with butter were a specialty of Bessie's and he happily noted they were on the menu. Regardless, he intended to enjoy to the last morsel his first home cooked food in weeks.

After putting a pan of biscuits into the brick oven still warm from the banked fire, Bessie wiped flour from her hands and gave a couple of stirs to the grits that were bubbling away in an iron pot. "Going to have this ready in just a few more minutes. You look like you could eat a pile of breakfast this morning. Skinny as you is, I suspect you ain't been getting much in the way of vittles. Don't they fed you soldier boys?"

"I've been sort of stationed off to myself, Bessie. About all I've had to eat is hardtack for the last few days and not much of that. I can't ever remember being so hungry. Times were I thought my stomach had caved in and the sides had glued together so it wouldn't ever be able to hold food again. The way it's growling right now, I sure do hope that's not the case."

"I doubt your insides is going to reject ole Bessie's cooking. No sirree. You going to be eatin' a mess of breakfast this morning. If you up to it, you can help me carry this into the dining room. Lordy, Miss Evangeline and Miss Cissy going to be plumb surprised to see you. They for shore is." Bessie pronounced with emphasis.

Sneaking a biscuit before picking up the dishes, Logan took the tray bearing the ham, grits, biscuits, syrup and jelly, and walked into the dining room chewing the last savory bite. As he unloaded the dishes onto the table, the door into the hall opened and Evangeline walked in. Blinking her eyes rapidly, she stared at him in shocked silence.

"I'm not a ghost, Miss Evangeline. It's really me. I'm intending to have some breakfast with you ladies, if you'll have me?"

Recovering rapidly from her surprise, Evangeline pulled him into a warm embrace. "You're always welcome here, Logan. It is so good to see you. I confess after Graham told me what you are doing, I have worried for your safety."

"Except for being a mite lonesome, it's not such bad duty. Most days are pretty pleasant except for when the weather is cold and miserable like it has been lately. I do wish that this war would end fast so I could stay at home and eat decent food and sleep in a clean warm bed."

"Please, God. The sooner this world returns to normal, the better I will like it. I stay upset listening to people talk about battles and the threat of Yankees coming here."

"It's not just a threat anymore."

"What does that mean, Logan?" Logan had not heard Cissy walk into the room.

Turning he looked into her emerald eyes, sparkling with the vitality of youth and a happy spirit. He wanted to hold her and cover her face with kisses but hesitated to press her to respond to the yearning need to express his love. Instead he restrained his impulse and replied, "I fear the Yankees are finally set on invading us. They have landed on Roanoke Island with huge navy and land forces. There is no way our boys can hold them off...too few of us and not enough weapons."

Evangeline gasped, "Oh, dear God! Does that mean they are coming here? Graham is going to be so upset."

Both women waited for his response. He pondered how to convince them to leave without creating undue fright. "Ladies, there is no way we are going to avoid a confrontation. New Berne is as valuable a port for them as it is for us. In fact, it looks as though they appreciate our importance more than the folks in Richmond do. As you know, the railroad from the port here leads to Goldsborough. From there it intersects with the Wilmington-Weldon line that leads to Richmond. That's just one of the factors that makes us a sitting duck. The Yankees'll come all right. I'm aiming to get you to Mr. LaRoque in Wilmington before they do."

"Oh, dear. Let's not talk about that for the moment. Sit down, Logan, Cissy. Let's eat Bessie's breakfast before it's cold." Evangeline felt a determined resolve forming in her mind. She would get Cissy to safety but she would remain to protect the two houses. She could not fathom that their former countrymen would sink so low as to threaten homes and harm women were they to seize the town.

Cissy broke the uncomfortable silence that followed Evangeline's remark by asking, "While you eat, tell us about what you've been up to, Logan. Judging from that plate of breakfast you've piled up, the army's been starving you to death."

Stifling a cough, Logan chortled, "I do look like a pure hog taking so much food. I apologize, ladies."

"For goodness sake, you know we don't care how much you eat. Heavens, you can eat that and that much more, if you're still hungry," Evangeline assured.

"Thank you, ma'am."

"So, Logan, tell us what you've been doing and what's happening. We have been so anxious since Papa left. The only news we get is the little bit that gets into the paper and most of that is over-blown conjecture."

Logan talked of his days by the sea, watching, always watching for the first sight of an invading force. When he had seen the first dot on the gray tossing sea, he had rubbed his eyes in surprise that anyone would dare such weather. As he watched more dots began to emerge on the distant horizon. He felt a deep sinking in his gut and stood slowly to stare in awe at the coming storm...not of nature but of man. Shaking himself from the mesmerizing sight of so many ships bearing down on the thin barrier islands that formed North Carolina's fragile outer banks, Logan hastened to gather his things and load them on his small sloop. If he could keep from capsizing he would be fortunate. Regardless of the danger, he had to reach camp where he could procure a horse and then race for New Berne to spread the alarm. He thought for a moment about trying to reach Roanoke Island ahead of the invasion to warn them of their eminent danger, but then surely they would be watching, too.

At last he fell silent, his plate empty and his mind too weary to continue.

"Logan, come upstairs. Bessie has prepared a bed for you. It looks as though you are half asleep in your chair."

"Thank you, ma'am. I'm purely tuckered out." He rose to follow Evangeline, smiling an apology at Cissy as he left. He wanted to say something, but a fit of coughing left him gasping.

Cissy called after him, "Sleep well. We'll visit some more when you wake up."

Logan slept the rest of the day. He slept all that night. He slept the next morning. When he did not appear for the midday meal, Cissy waited no longer. Going to his door she knocked. Hearing no answer she knocked again, harder. Still the silence beyond the door held. Daring to enter the room where a man lay sleeping, understanding that it was not the proper thing to do, and yet not caring, Cissy opened the door. Logan slowly turned to her, struggling to rise from his pillow. He opened his mouth to speak but only a raspy creak emerged before violent coughing racked him. His eyes glittered, dark and burning with fever. Without waiting, Cissy spun on her heel and raced for Evangeline who was working intermittently in the studio, not from inspiration Cissy thought, but rather desperation to escape the moment when they must leave.

Running into the room, she cried, "Come quickly, please. It's Logan. I think he's very sick."

Evangeline raced behind Cissy as they ran into the hall and up the stairs to the room where Logan lay. Even before they entered the room, they could hear his labored breathing. Evangeline rushed to his bed. He was on his side, facing the window, no longer conscious. Holding her hand against his burning forehead, she glanced back at Cissy who remained frozen at the door. "Get Bessie, darling, and send Toby for the doctor. Tell him to hurry."

Cissy began, "Is he...?"

"Go! And hurry, Cissy."

Tripping in her haste, she righted herself and plunged down the stairs where she dashed into the kitchen. She alarmed Bessie by blurting, "Go upstairs. Logan's sick. Very sick, I think. Where's Toby?"

"He's in the barn feeding the horses." Bessie didn't wait for another question. She was running for the stairs as fast as her legs would move her. Cissy headed for the barn just as rapidly.

Cissy and Evangeline sat in the parlor by the window. The late afternoon sun picked out a lacy pattern on the floor as it streamed through the windows. The doctor had been with Logan for over an hour, and still they waited. Although both women were busy knitting much needed socks to send to New Berne boys serving in the army, neither was making much headway. Constant dropped stitches had them both tearing out almost as much as they were knitting.

"Oh, botheration!" Cissy exclaimed as she started pulling out her last row of stitches. "I simply cannot concentrate on this."

Throwing the unfinished sock into her basket, she arose from her deeply tufted chair and began pacing the room. Evangeline shrugged her shoulders and pitched her own sock into the basket. Leaning back on the sofa, she rubbed her forehead and heaved a sigh. "I'm no better. I do wish the doctor would come down and tell us how Logan is doing. The longer we wait hearing nothing, the more anxious I become. Considering the conditions these poor boys have to endure in all kinds of weather, it's a wonder any of them survive."

Cissy halted in mid stride. "Surely you don't think he will die?"

Evangeline lower her lids to conceal the terror in her eyes, "Of course, not darling. That remark was purely rhetorical. Logan is a strong healthy young man. He's going to be fine."

The clock in the hall chimed the hour. Both listened to the peeling of five dolorous chimes. Bessie crept into the room and at Evangeline's nod of permission, silently took a seat by the door. Each woman sat consoled by the presence of the others as they prayed for the man they had known since he was a ragtag boy.

Lost in their individual worries, they did not hear Doctor Leonidas Brown as he wearily descended the stairs and entered the parlor. "Harrumph." He cleared his throat before continuing, "Excuse me ladies; I need a word with you before I leave."

All three heads swiveled toward the doctor. Evangeline rose to her feet and pointed to a chair. "You're weary, sir. Please be seated and rest yourself."

"No, no. I must be going. Your young man is very ill, pneumonia. I have managed to get his fever down a bit and he's resting. However, he is a long way from being out of the woods. I left some elixir by the bed. When he wakes, give him a tablespoon full, but no more than that every four hours. He needs a mustard plaster on his chest to try to break up some of the congestion in his lungs. Someone will need to sit with him for the next day or so. Whenever he awakens, make sure he drinks water. A good bracing chicken broth will help if you can get him to take it. If his fever goes back up or he seems comatose or unresponsive, you send for me no matter the hour. Regardless, I'll be back in the morning. I suggest you take shifts sitting with him for the next day or so. Whatever you do, if that fever goes up, get him cooled off as fast as you can. Open the windows, sponge him with water, whatever. God in heaven, what I would pay for some snow right now. If that fever goes higher, it would help bring it down."

"Thank you, Doctor. I'll prepare a mustard plaster right away. Bessie, would you make some broth, please. Cissy, go up and sit with Logan until we can prepare the things we will need. If you need us, just call and we'll come."

Cissy climbed the stairs with trepidation. She had never known illness in others, had never been responsible for another's welfare. Other than wiping his forehead with cool cloths she had no idea what to do or how to do it. Bracing herself outside his door, she walked in and sat in the chair that the doctor had left by Logan's bedside. Fidgeting with uncertainty, she looked about the room, looked at anything to avoid looking at her childhood friend. Nagging at the back of her mind was the fear that he might die. Running out of options of where to look, Cissy at last turned her eyes on Logan. She was shocked by his pallor, but more shocked by the fact that she had never really looked at him as a man. Her memory was more of them as children. She wondered when she had lost sight of Logan's transition into manhood. She studied his regular features and was surprised to see that he was handsome. Ha, she thought, no wonder the girls are after him. Tentatively she reached out her hand and drew back the sheet that covered his chest, exposing his body to the waist. Furtively she glanced at the door, amazed at her own daring and curiosity about a man she had know since childhood. With pursed lips, she studied the heavily muscled upper torso, evidence of a man who used his body for something other than scholarly pursuits. Reaching out once more, she touched the top of the cover daring herself to expose more of Logan's body. Logan groaned and stirred. Terrified by her own temerity, she hastily pulled the sheet back to his throat.

"Logan, are you awake?"

Her answer was another groan. "I have to give you some medicine. Please, don't go back to sleep until I can give it to you."

Cissy fumbled with the spoon on the table by the elixir, dropping it to the floor in her anxiety. Scooping it up she put it back on the table as she struggled to un-stopper the bottle of medicine. That done she picked up the spoon and filled it. "Open your mouth, Logan."

Logan remained inert. Cissy lifted his head with her free hand and pushed the spoon between his slightly parted lips. Slowly the liquid trickled in. Sputtering with the effort to swallow, Logan struggled to push her hand away. His voice was a weak rasp when he complained, "Daggummit, Cissy, are you trying to choke me to death?"

"I'm sorry. The doctor said to give you medicine."

Cissy could just discern the mumbled words, "Just want to sleep. Don't want that foul stuff."

"I'm sorry. It's doctor's orders." He didn't hear. He was already lost in sleep, soft snoring escaping through clogged nostrils.

Cissy patted the covers back in place and stood. His body was burning with heat. She raised the window, struggling against the reluctant sash. The cold air that swept into the room left her shivering. She moved as close to the small fire in the hearth as she dared and huddled by its meager warmth. Logan continued to snore, interrupted by intermittent coughs. Cissy listened to the ticking of the mantle clock and prayed that Bessie or Evangeline would arrive to relieve her. She wanted to help and her inability to do so made her furious, both with herself and with his illness. She was also frightened. What if he should die? The idea of death in one so young and healthy looking was unsettling, terrifying even. She wondered if her teeth chattered from fear or the icy wind sweeping in through the window.

She could not wipe the anxiety from her eyes. Evangeline saw it when she entered the room...saw those eyes reaching for her, for assurance, for comfort, for denial. "He's going to be fine, Cissy. He's a sick man now but sleep and care will help that strong body of his overcome this. I've made a mustard plaster for his chest and Bessie is coming with some broth. Did he awaken yet?"

"He did. Twenty minutes ago. I gave him medicine like the doctor said."

"Good. Now go on and get some rest and try not to fret. I'll sit with him now."

"Can I do something to help?"

"Not at the moment. I'll send for you later to spell me."

Cissy left the room. The upstairs hall felt cavernous and empty. Logan's stentorian breathing seemed to echo down its length. Although the day was bitterly cold, Cissy felt she could not stand the house a moment more. Grabbing her hooded cloak from the armoire in her room, she snuggled it close about her body and left. Walking down the carriageway towards the road, she noted the wetly dripping Spanish moss as it swayed slowly in the slight breeze from the river. The freezing rain had stopped, leaving the day damp and raw. When she reached the road she turned left towards town, not with the intention of walking so far, but desiring only to escape the confines and worries of the house. Her deep concern for Logan made her ask whether she had grown to love him, or if it were the simple worry one would feel for any friend of long standing. She was so engrossed in thought that the sound of the carriage wheels did not register. It was only the cessation of the noise of the wheels and clopping hooves that brought her back to the present. Glancing over her shoulder, she thought the man in the carriage looked vaguely familiar, but she did not look long enough for him to register in her mind. It was not until he spoke that she recognized him as the Frenchman she had rebuffed that day in town.

"Oh, good day to you, sir. I do apologize, but I seem to have forgotten your name." Cissy did not want company, wished only that he would slap the reins and drive on. It was apparent the man had no intention of leaving as he draped the reins carefully and swung down beside her.

"Allow me to renew our acquaintance, Miss LaRoque. I am Marcel Lambert, the Marquise de Rochefort. We've met on a number of occasions, yet far fewer than I would have preferred. You have chosen quite a dismal day for a walk. Might I offer you a ride home?"

"I don't mind the weather. I needed some fresh air and exercise." She turned to walk away but was detained by a firm hand on her elbow.

"Then you must consider my companionship. It is unseemly for a young lady to walk unescorted on a public road."

"Don't presume to school me in decorum, sir."

"Not at all, Miss LaRoque. I am only concerned for the safety of such a pretty young maiden as you. You must permit me to walk with you for a bit. As a gentleman, I could not forgive myself were I to abandon you." Marcel forced a genial smile, squelching his impatience to conquer the impertinent little bitch. Soon she would grovel for him, beg him for his favors. The thought made his face grow warmer and his smile wider.

A part of Cissy was flattered by the suave and handsome Frenchman's attention, but some niggling doubt about him gnawed at her. What made her withdraw from him, she could not have said. But, there was something that did not feel right about Marcel Lambert. Some unformed question niggled at her mind, one that she had not asked and he had not answered.

He chatted on unaware of her inner turmoil. "Miss LaRoque, do permit me to call you Cecily."

"Cissy, please."

"Cissy, I find your beauty irresistible. I was quite despairing of meeting a lady of such bounteous charms when I first arrived on these shores. Now that I have, I do hope that you will permit me the pleasure of calling on you?"

"I'm not sure that I will be here. It's seems that we will be evacuating in the face of an invasion by enemy forces."

"A much over-vaunted concern, I suspect. No doubt your parents err on the side of caution. Have you determined when you will depart?"

"I'm uncertain. Our friend Logan is ill with pneumonia and staying with us. I'm sure we will not leave while he is unwell. Hopefully he will recover soon. When he does, Papa will insist we come to Wilmington with him."

"Ah, yes. I did hear that your father is away at the moment." Marcel squeezed her elbow slightly, "You failed to answer my question, Cissy. Will you allow me to call on you?"

"Oh, that." Cissy hesitated, groping for a way to decline without appearing rude. "I'm not sure that is advisable at the moment. You would not wish to visit when everything is in such turmoil."

"Ah, but I do. I find you even more beautiful than your mother." He wanted to kick himself the moment the words slipped out.

"What did you say?" Cissy gaped at him in confusion before demanding, "Did you know my mother?"

"No, no. I have only heard rumors to that effect and all assure me that you are even more lovely."

"I see."

He could tell by the expression on her face, the way she pulled her shawl more firmly about her, that she suspected his reply. "Ah, I cannot remember, but perhaps I met her in Paris at some function. I believe she resided there for a period prior to her untimely and most unfortunate demise."

"Yes, she did." Cissy felt a sudden chill. She did not want to think of her mother and she was tired of the confident and aggressive man. "You must excuse me, sir. It is past time I returned home."

"I insist you allow me to drive you in the carriage. You are must be tired and cold. It would be inconsiderate of me not to do so."

Cissy started to object but recognized the determined resolve in the man's face. It would save time to just let him drive her, rather than arguing about it. Her voice flat and remote, she conceded, "Very well."

Marcel helped her into the carriage and carefully draped the blanket across her knees before driving her home. After a hastily mumbled thank you, she wasted no time in disappearing behind the front door, closing it firmly in his face. He was furious that once again she had rejected his attentions. Feeling stupid for even mentioning that he might have known Monique, he drove back to his hotel alternately cursing both her and himself. His trip had been all but wasted. With her father away, he had intended to begin a whirlwind campaign to win her affections. He walked into the hotel mulling over options for how best to do that.

Chapter 11

Graham stood at the window overlooking the Cape Fear River. Colonel John Hedrick, newly assigned to strengthen fortifications at Fort Fisher, was standing at his side. They watched as Graham's latest ship to safely return from England maneuvered into port.

"I hope the Parrot guns I ordered are on that ship," the colonel remarked. "I've toiled with all my might and just about killed my men trying to get the earthen batteries built but they are still disconnected. It's discouraging to say the least. Unless my guns are on that ship I don't suppose it will matter, though."

"Richmond needs to wake up. Wilmington is vital if the Confederacy is to survive. I think Norfolk will go anytime now. That will leave this as the next closest large port."

"You're ruling out Beaufort and the sound ports then?"

"Once we lost Hatteras Island last August, it has become only a matter of time. Not much has happened to strengthen our defenses, train and arm troops, or organize for a naval attack. Richmond is focused on two things: Washington and Richmond. As far as they are concerned, it's to hell with the rest."

Both men turned as Graham's clerk came into the office, "Excuse me, sir. This telegram just came for you."

"Thank you, Zeke." Graham opened the telegram and began to read, "Roanoke Island lost. Imminent attack expected other ports."

"You look like you've seen a ghost. Is something wrong?"

Hedrick asked.

"Speak of the devil: we've lost Roanoke Island. Now the Union has a base for off-loading land forces as well as for controlling the sounds." Graham's mouth went grim. "I'm a damned fool for listening to my womenfolk. I knew it. Damnation, I knew it."

"Sir?"

"I tried to get my wife and daughter to come with me. I let them get around me despite my better judgment. New Berne could be under attack any day. I've got to get them out of there. I left a ship, but there is no way they would be safe to attempt water passage with the sound full of a Union fleet looking for trouble. I'd better get a telegram to them. Thankfully, we can always take the train to Goldsborough and from there to here."

"I agree. The water is no place for them now. However, you might try to get that last ship sneaked out of there if you have a man brave enough to risk it. We're going to need all of the ships we can get. No telling how much of the Mosquito Fleet we'll lose in this fiasco."

"Zeke," Graham called, "I need you to send a couple of telegrams for me as fast as your legs can carry them." Graham scribbled a hasty and emphatic message to Evangeline. They must leave. All arguments to the contrary were now moot. And he would try to save the remaining ship, if his men could move her south. He and Hedrick stood in mutual shock as they contemplated the import of this new attack.

Graham looked at the doorway to see Zeke standing there, "What is it? I thought you would be running to the telegraph office by now."

"You just received another telegram, sir. Maybe I should wait until you've read it, too."

"No matter what it says, I want those telegrams sent now. Now!"

Zeke left the office at a run.

Glancing at Hedrick and taking a deep breath as though to steel himself, he slid his finger under the flap of the envelope as cautiously as a man opening a sack of rattlers. He read silently, his mouth tightening into a grim line. Without comment he handed the paper to Hedrick.

The colonel took it and unconsciously began to read the tersely worded telegram aloud: "Elizabeth City lost. Mosquito Fleet destroyed except for CSS Beaufort and CSS Raleigh. Cobbs Point Battery and all forts on Croatan Sound lost. Fall of Edenton, Albemarle Sound forts imminent. New Berne in potential peril."

"Holy Christ, all hell's breaking out! Excuse me, Graham. I'm going to haul fanny back to Fort Fisher and get those batteries built if I have to confiscate every slave in Brunswick County. If those guns are on that ship of yours, hire someone to get them to me. I'll see you're paid if I have to do it myself."

Graham waved his hand dismissively, "Don't worry about it. We'll work something out."

After Hedrick left, he sat at his desk holding his head in his hands. He was torn. He needed to be in Wilmington, but his wife and daughter were in peril. His clerks would have to handle things until he could get to New Berne, collect them and return. With the rapid fall of the sound ports, New Berne's time was running out faster than water in a sieve. Standing he began to put vital documents into his safe, collecting files that could wait until his return, and stuffing the most urgent into a box on his desk. Striding to his door, he threw it open and bellowed, "Marsh, I need you to get the manifest from that captain and see what's on the ship that just came in. If it's Hedrick's guns, hire someone to get them to him fast. And you, Robert, take these files here and deal with them as best you can. If you run into a hitch, telegraph me in New Berne. Tell Zeke I'm headed home to get my family. I need him to manage shipping for the next few days. Same goes for all of you, any problems you can't handle either sit on them if you can, or if it's urgent, telegraph me. Hopefully, I'll only be gone a few days."

Marcel felt the need for haste as much as Graham, but for different reasons. Wooing Cissy was proving more than a minor challenge. He had arrived at the house in early afternoon on the pretext of checking to see if there might be something he could do to assist them in the absence of her father. Part of his agenda was a fierce desire to thwart any inroads the patient might be making on Cissy's sympathies.

Resettling himself on the sofa after he had risen at Evangeline's departure to check on Logan, Marcel turned to Cissy who was openly fidgeting. It was obvious that she would have preferred to be the one leaving the room. Coaching himself to remain collected, he modulated his voice to dulcet tones, "So, Cissy, with Mr. Gwaltney in residence, am I to assume that he has some special status in this household? A fiancé perhaps?"

"For Heaven's sake, why would you assume any such thing? Logan Gwaltney is like a son to Evangeline since his own mother died. He's here because when he arrived it was obvious he was too sick to go any further."

"I take it then you and the esteemed Mr. Gwaltney are not engaged to be wed?"

"Let me put your mind at rest on one score. I am not interested in marrying him or anyone else. Why on earth would I do that, especially now with a war on? First off, I don't intend to marry some man just to say I'm not a spinster. I'm young enough I don't need to rush into marriage. Secondly, I don't intend to marry someone whose idea of marriage is keeping me imprisoned here having children while he's out spending my father's money. Thirdly, if I never marry, it's none of anyone's business but my own. If that sounds rude, I do apologize, however I quite mean it."

Marcel narrowed his eyes not realizing how sinister he

looked when he replied, "Perhaps, you need a man to persuade you of the pleasures of romantic love."

"Well, don't presume to volunteer."

Marcel would have enjoyed slapping her and taking her precious virginity on the spot. Her spirited defiance aroused his lust. Unfortunately, he had no choice but to cloak his real intentions. "Bravo, my dear, how refreshing it is to met such an unorthodox young woman."

"You must excuse me, Marcel. I seem to have developed a terrible headache. Allow me to show you to the door." She did not wait for his reply, just walked to the door and held it open for his exit.

"Good afternoon, Cissy. It was my pleasure to visit with you again." Marcel bowed low over her hand and then walked to his horse and untied him from the hitching post. Once mounted, he gritted his teeth and savagely jerked on the reins of the horse. Digging sharp spurs into the animal's side he raced down the lane to the road.

'That bitch, that bitch' became a litany that played over and over in his mind. He was going to enjoy bringing her to her knees. Her mother had been too easy. This bitch was one he intended to conquer. In the beginning his goal had been to get her father's money; now it was a sexual vendetta, too. It riled his ego that any woman would so summarily reject him. It riled him even more that it was one so young. In his experience she should have been far more malleable and much more susceptible to his practiced charm. Her reticence on that score forced him to consider a more radical approach to get her to the altar and her father's money in his own hands. LaRoque's wife was an added complication. He had to act before she could become pregnant with another potential heir.

He was so lost in his schemes that he did not even notice the telegraph rider galloping towards him. It was only when he drew abreast and halted his horse that Marcel looked up.

"Pardon me, Mister, I'm looking for the LaRoque house. You any idee where it is?"

Ignoring the question, Marcel remarked, "You seem to be in quite a rush to get there. Is there some urgency?" Marcel studied the man. Noting his uniform, he surmised he was with the local army troops. Judging from the fuzz on the boy's cheeks, he was a green and naive recruit.

"Damned tootin' there be a rush. I got a telegram here for Miz LaRoque from her husband. I was told to git it to her fast as this hoss could trot. You know where thar house is at?"

"Allow me to save you some bother. I'm a friend of the LaRoque's, and as it happens, I'm on my way there now. Permit me to deliver it for you. That way, you can get on back to town and get ready for the enemy invasion. I hear you boys are busy digging embankments around town."

"I just don't know about that. My sergeant didn't say nothing about handing it off to someone else."

"My good man, I'm sure he would agree that you are far more needed there than here, especially when a friend of the LaRoque's is willing to help you out."

"Well, I don't reckin' it matters none." The boy handed the telegram over. ""Thanks, mister. I 'preciate it."

"Not at all." Marcel pulled his horse into the shrubs at the side of the road and waited as the boy turned around and headed back the way he had come. When he was out of sight, he wasted no time in ripping open the telegram. Providence was about to deliver Graham into his hands. With the information contained in the telegram, he knew which train Graham would be on. He had only to make sure when it arrived and when Graham started for home. He would see to it the man never reach his destination. With that obstacle removed, he would deal with the reluctant daughter.

Unaware of Graham's telegram and planned arrival, Cissy and Evangeline occupied themselves with a household routine that revolved around Logan. Despite their diligent care, he remained gravely ill. The months of exposure and poor diet had weakened his system and left him susceptible to the infection that racked his body. Weak and feverish, he slept more often than not. Whenever he awoke, one of the two women would be instantly by his side with warm broth and water. It took persistent persuasion to coerce him into taking the broth they spooned into him. Exhausted from the effort, he would fall back into fitful slumber alternating between racking chills and raging fever. The doctor visited frequently and judging more from what he did not say than from what he said, it was obvious that he was worried Logan was not yet on the mend.

Cissy found herself sitting more and more by Logan's side. Sometimes she read aloud to him, but more often than not she just sat watching his labored breathing. Despite continuing to reject the idea of marriage to him or anyone for the foreseeable future, she began to realize that her former fondness for Logan had changed. She no longer looked at him and saw a brother figure. He was a man and an attractive one, one that she felt herself responding to even as she squelched the impulse to begin a romantic relationship based on that newly realized attraction.

Cissy dropped the book she was holding into her lap and allowed her eyes to close. She was tired. Still disturbed by the Frenchman, she had slept in fitful snatches the night before. Again she could not define what it was about him that made her hackles rise. He was without fail polite, charming, well groomed, and as handsome as any man she had ever seen. Still something rang false. Something about the man continued to needled at her like some vague shadow image from the past. A sudden spasm of coughing from the bed jerked her attention back to the moment. Reaching for the mixture of honey and whiskey on the small round table by the bed, Cissy lifted it to Logan's lips when the paroxysm passed.

He lifted his eyes to her in silent gratitude and offered her a gentle smile.

"Your fever seems to be subsiding. Hopefully you will be on the mend soon. It's just awful to watch you sick and not be able to do more to help you."

"Ah, beautiful angel, just opening my eyes to see you here is a wonder in itself. I ask nothing more from you," he proclaimed with a croak. "Except perhaps, you might ask Toby to come help me. All of that liquid y'all keep filling me with demands release."

Cissy blushed. "Of course, I'll have him come up right away."

Logan tried to laugh at her embarrassment, but only succeeded in stimulating another coughing fit.

"Rest quietly. Toby should be here in a moment. If I cannot find him, I could have Bessie come up. Would that be acceptable for you?"

He managed to wheeze, "That's fine."

Cissy scurried from the room, intent on finding Toby.

When she descended the stairs she could see Evangeline standing at the front door. She could not see who stood on the other side of the cracked door, but it was obvious from her stepmother's determined hold on the door that she was not going to allow the caller to enter. Cissy stopped at the bottom of the stairs and waited until Evangeline closed the door.

"Who was the unwelcome guest?"

Startled, Evangeline turned around, "Cissy, I didn't hear you come down." Nodding her head in the direction of the door, she commented, "Your new suitor is a difficult man to turn away. I must say, I don't know when I have ever been quite so rude. I would not even let him in."

"Marcel? That man just cannot take 'no' for an answer. I have told him I am not interested and still he comes. I am so glad you did not allow him in."

"From what you told me after yesterday's encounter, I thought as much."

"Have you seen Toby? Logan needs some assistance and would like his help."

"I think he's in the kitchen with Bessie drinking the last of our coffee unless your father manages to get some more to us. I'll tell him to go up."

"Thank you. If you don't mind, I'll slip out the back way and get some fresh air. I've been sitting so long, I could use a good stretch."

"Make sure Marcel is gone first."

"Don't worry I will."

Marcel had indeed left. He had galloped down the road towards New Berne and stopped in a section of woods where no houses lined the road. Now he lay hidden in the woods to watch as his hired henchman shot Graham dead. He considered doing it himself but was afraid that he might miss. This had to be done and done right: quick, clean and fatal. The thug he had hired was noted for his ability with a gun. Now it was but a matter of time. Marcel shook as he waited, partly from the chill of the wind blowing from the water, but more so from a sudden case of nerves. His time was running out along with his funds. Glancing once more at his watch, he noted the hand slowly crawling towards four o'clock. The train should have arrived by now and with no one to meet him, Graham would have hired a horse from the livery stable and been on his way. He turned in the saddle to see if he could spot the hired gun, Zeb Lamb. The woods were quiet except for the chirring of squirrels and the squawking of a couple of jays engaged in contesting their turf. The low undergrowth and thickly needled long-leaf pines effectively camouflaged anyone who might lie in wait. Again he stared at his watch wondering what was keeping the man. He noted the sun sinking into the treetops. It would be dark soon; too dark for what needed doing.

Zeb, from his perch on the limb of a true that had enough leaves to hide him yet still provide a clear view of the road, exhaled in disgust. He damned well wanted that promised money, but he couldn't stay in the tree forever. With night fast closing in, the temperature had fallen to bone-numbing cold. His fingers were stiff from gripping the rifle and he was shivering. "Aw, hell," he exclaimed softly.

Tired of waiting, he dropped to the ground and gathered the reins of his horse. He'd do the job another day. The damned Frenchie wasn't the one freezing his ass off, he thought, not knowing that Marcel was nearby and as cold and miserable as he.

Watching him ride off down the road, Marcel's face was a mask of cold fury. The fates seemed to be conspiring to frustrate him at every turn. His rage engulfed him as he watched Graham LaRoque calmly trotting past the very spot where Zeb had laid in wait. Damned the man, he swore. Had that idiot Zeb waited a few minutes more, it would all have been over. For a moment, he debated doing the job himself but he could not risk missing his shot and being caught, or worse yet, shot by his alerted victim who wore a side arm slung low on his leg. Marcel mounted his horse when Graham was far enough away not to see him and returned to town. He was so angry with Zeb he could have killed him. Unfortunately he still needed him. He would have to find him and quickly arrange for another try. When LaRoque was dead, he would take pleasure in finding a way to finish off Zeb Lamb, a detail that would need cleaning up. He couldn't risk the man talking.

Happy to be home and oblivious to the danger he had just avoided, Graham spurred his horse as he galloped into the lane leading to the house. In his haste, he did not see Cissy before he was upon her. The horse reared in fright throwing Graham into a tumble at her feet.

Cissy screamed in shock, "Papa! Papa!"

Barely conscious, her voice came to him as though a long tunnel. He could only groan in agony as he writhed at her feet. Despairing of capturing the spooked horse to ride to the house, Cissy had no choice but to leave her father where he lay and run for help. She had taken only a few steps, when she whirled back and knelt by her father.

"Papa, if you can hear me, please don't move. I'll be back with help as fast as I can."

When she reached the house she dashed into the front hall to find Evangeline just descending. Too winded to speak, she could only stand there gasping in fright.

"Dear Lord, Cissy. What on earth is the matter? You look like you've seen a ghost."

"Papa..." she wheezed.

"Cissy, calm down and tell me what's wrong. What about your father?"

Cissy panted, "He's hurt. He fell off the horse coming into the lane and he's not talking. Please, get Toby to get the wagon so we can bring him to the house."

"Graham's home? You find Toby, Cissy, and tell him what needs to be done." Evangeline snatched her shawl from the rack by the door and ran. Her heart was pounding in terror. *Dear God, she prayed, don't take Graham from me, too.*

Marcel rode into New Berne not knowing that Cissy might well have unwittingly solved all his problems. When he reached Pollock Street, he turned towards the Gaston House Hotel where he left his horse tied to the hitching post. He tossed Kersey, the slave boy, a nickel to return the hired horse to the stable. He's was too tired and out of sorts to deal with it himself. After a warming toddy and a hot supper, he walked to the tavern by the river where Zeb hung out. Entering the overheated tavern, he noted a table of soldiers playing poker. His eyes narrowed in greed as the pile of money in the center of the table continued to grow. He badly needed a win. The last few days had not gone well. The men that frequented the public room at the Gaston House had begun to suspect his skill at cards was due more to artifice than acumen. For the last week, he had been unsuccessful in wining the sums he had come to depend on as they now avoided playing with him. These green soldiers looked like easy marks and the pot on the table called to him.

He spotted Zeb at a table near the fireplace and mouthed "Later," as he jerked his head towards the door. Zeb looked down and slowly lifted his head in acknowledgement.

Walking over to the soldiers, Marcel asked, "You boys mind if I join you? I'm not much good with American style cards but I sure do enjoy playing."

A tall rangy soldier pushed a chair with his foot and invited, "Come on. Take a seat. Your money is good enough for us."

Chapter 12

Evangeline swept the sugar bowl and creamer from the long pine kitchen table. They fell in shards around her feet. With her focus on the unconscious man that the others held, she was oblivious to the sound of their breaking, to the crunch under her feet, as she hastened to help them lower him to the waiting surface.

"Fetch Dr. Brown, Toby. Do hurry. I know his leg is broken but I don't know what else might be wrong." Evangeline bit her lip to hold back the tears.

"Don't you worry none, Miss Evangeline. He's tough. I'm sure the doctor will get him fixed up in no time. I'll fetch him as fast as that horse'll carry me. I sure do wonder why he didn't tell us he was a coming home. It sure don't seem like him, now do it?"

Evangeline didn't answer the man. She wanted to scream at him to stop yammering and just go. Again she bit her lips. Reading her expression, Toby nodded once and scurried from the kitchen.

Cissy tore her gaze from her father's face and looked into Evangeline's worried eyes in a silent demand for reassurance that her stepmother did not feel.

Yet, Evangeline struggled to master her emotions and answer calmly. "He's going to be fine, Cissy. We just have to pray. And we must hope the doctor arrives quickly. Perhaps you would bring a blanket from our room. I don't want him to become chilled."

When Cissy left the kitchen, Evangeline turned to Bessie,

"Please, put some hot water on. Maybe you should poke up the fire, too. We need to keep him warm. Also, are there clean linens we could tear into bandages? I don't know what the doctor is going to need, but I do want to be ready."

While Bessie hastened to do her bidding, Evangeline pulled a chair to the table and sat by Graham's side. Lifting his hand, she murmured, "Please, wake up, darling. Talk to me. Tell me why you have returned from Wilmington. We had no idea you were on the way or we would have met you at the station. Oh, do wake up. Please be all right. I love you so much. I've missed you terribly. I don't know why you returned so soon, but it doesn't matter. I'm just glad you're here. Logan's here, too. He's been sick with pneumonia and we thought we would lose him, but he seems to be a little stronger today. I..."

Her voice trailed away to nothing. He couldn't answer her. He couldn't hear her. Her eyes were shining with unshed tears when Cissy returned with the blanket. Taking it from the shaking girl, Evangeline cautiously tucked it around Graham. When she reached to tuck it around the broken leg, he moaned. Startled, she jumped back. "Oh, my God. If I hurt you, I am so sorry. Oh, Graham, I'm sorry."

"You didn't mean to, Mama. Please don't be upset with yourself. We must stay strong for papa. I do hope the doctor is not out on a call when Toby gets to town. Is there anything we can do for him until the doctor arrives? He must be in awful pain from his leg and who knows what all."

Helpless at her lack of medical knowledge, Evangeline wrung her hands with frustration. "I wish I knew something to do, but I don't. I wish he could wake up and tell us where he hurts."

With nothing else to do, Cissy sat on the other side of the table and softly caressed her father's arm. Choking back a sob, she cried out, "It's my fault. If I hadn't frightened his horse he would not have been thrown."

"Hush now, Cissy. This is not your fault. How were you to

know that he would turn into the lane just as you reached the road? It's that fool horse's fault if anything. It certainly is not yours. Your father would never want you to take on that burden of guilt."

Cissy lifted haunted eyes to Evangeline but made no comment.

Evangeline knew she remained unconvinced. Hoping to distract her, she pleaded, "Cissy, darling, would you go check on Logan? With all that has happened I completely forgot about him. Perhaps you could take up a bowl of stew for his dinner. I'm sure he's hungry by now. There really isn't much we can do here anyway until the doctor arrives."

Cissy nodded once, before moving to the pot of stew and ladling out a bowl of it. She then poured a glass of cold milk and added that and some cornbread to the tray that held the steaming bowl.

Evangeline moved to her side and kissed her gently on the check, "If your father wakes up, I'll call you. I know you're as worried as I am. Thank you for seeing to Logan for me."

Cissy merely nodded in mute agreement as she left the room with Logan's tray.

Logan was sitting against the head of the bed when she entered. The smile that lit his face was as bright as firelight when he saw her. As he studied her face the smile faded into just an ember of remaining warmth. "Is something wrong? You look as though you've seen one of Bessie's 'haints.' Don't tell me I look that bad just when I think that I'm at last on the mend?"

"It's not you. It's Papa. I think I may have killed him." Tears began to seep from her eyes and roll down her cheeks where they hung heavily until they dropped onto her dress making dark spots of wetness.

"Good Lord, Cissy! You would never do that. Now tell me what in the world is going on?"

When she had finished telling him of the day's events, Logan wordlessly beckoned her to him. Cissy moved to sit beside him on the bed. He pulled her into the protective circle of his arms and held her there as his mouth moved in sibilant words of comfort against her hair. Slowly she felt her body relax into the comforting embrace as his whispered assurances dried her tears.

"There now, it's going to be all right, Cissy. Your father is one of the strongest men I know. He's not going to die and leave you and his new wife. He's a fighter and he'll fight to be here for you, especially now when he knows how threatened we all are in the midst of this war. You need to trust in that and stop blaming yourself for an accident that no one could have foreseen. I may not be capable of running any races yet, but in a day or two I should be up and about and able to help you with your father. I don't want you and Miss Evangeline worrying about me. Mr. LaRoque is going to need all the help you can provide for a while. I'll fend for myself with a bit of help from Bessie and Toby." Logan kissed the top of her head before she sat up and leaned away.

"Thank you, Logan." Cissy smiled and shyly reached out to caress his cheek, "You are a dear, you know?"

"I know. But, I'm glad you're beginning to come around to the idea." Logan could not help the smile that lit his face like sun breaking from behind dark clouds.

Startled by the sound of rapidly approaching hoof beats, Cissy rushed to the window and parted the curtains to peer into the gloom of the yard. "I think it's the doctor. I have to go."

Logan urged, "Go on. When you know something, come back and tell me what he says."

Cissy called over her shoulder as she ran from the room, "I'll do it."

Evangeline knelt by the bed where Graham lay oblivious to the world. Her brain felt as though voracious demons had taken possession, determined to consume her every thought and give her no rest, no comfort, and no hope. She tried to form a prayer but it died on her lips. Tears poured down her cheeks and the doctor's words hammered against her heart: *'If he survives, he could be a total invalid, paralyzed, unresponsive, dependent as a baby for his every need. You need to prepare yourself. Perhaps, it would be better if you pray for God to take him. There is nothing more I can do for him.'*

Some voice kept trying to get her attention, to break through the stranglehold of her thoughts. She stirred herself enough to ask, "What? What did you say?"

Cissy again shook Evangeline's shoulder. She found herself parroting Logan's words to her. "I said the doctor is just a self-educated quack. He's useless for something like this. Don't listen to him. My Papa is going to get better. I don't know how, but he is. He has to. We need him and he knows it and he knows how much we love him. You just trust my Papa. He's going to beat this."

Evangeline turned her head and looked into Cissy's eyes. "I can't stand it. I just can't bear the thought of losing him."

"You're not going to." Cissy whispered, *"Stop it! Do you want him to hear that? I know you don't. He needs to believe he is going to make it. We need to believe he's going to make it."* Choking on the words, she added, "Besides, he did help Logan even if he isn't the best doctor in the world."

"This is about the brain. No one knows much about that, unfortunately."

"No, but we do know about Papa. He's a fighter and he'll do it. We just have to help him and believe as hard as we can."

Evangeline shook her head, "You don't know what it's like to lose everyone you love. I do. It nearly killed me before. I can't do it again."

Fierce with her stubborn insistence, Cissy grabbed Evangeline by the shoulders, "Stop it. You must not say these things."

The two women looked into one another's eyes for a long moment. Then, Evangeline sighed, "You're right of course. Forgive me."

"There's nothing to forgive. We're both terrified, but we're going to do whatever it takes. Logan says he will help, too, just as soon as he's a little stronger."

Evangeline lifted her eyes to the ceiling, "Lord, what a time for the Yankees to be threatening us: both Graham and Logan sick in bed, and here we are just two lone women. I do hope the Yankees don't find out who your father is and about his shipping business. But, I don't know how they can help but do it."

"What danger are Papa and Logan to anyone when they're both sick in bed and incapable of threatening those mean old Yankees, anyway?"

"I don't know. I suppose I'm just fretting about the Yankees to take my mind off my more immediate worries."

"Did the doctor say if there is anything we can do to help Papa?"

"Nothing. We have to wait for him to awaken on his own. The doctor said he would be back in the morning."

"I know you want to stay with Papa. I'll go see if Logan needs anything before bedtime. May I get you something?"

"No, Cissy. I'll be fine. I think I'll just sit in the rocker by the fire so I'm near if Graham wakes up. You go on to bed. If I need you, I'll come for you."

Evangeline moved stiffly in the chair. At some point she had nodded off, but now with the fire dying in the grate the room was becoming cold and uncomfortable. Leaning over, she added more wood to the fire and used the bellows to bring it to a warming flame. Once more she looked longingly at her husband and willed him to return to consciousness. Yet, still he lay inert and senseless to the world. Weary with worry and yet unwilling to retire to bed, she sat on as the bleak dawn of a gray day began to lighten the eastern sky.

Cissy found her sitting in the chair staring into the fire when she entered the room shortly after awakening. "Mama, you must be exhausted. You go on to bed now. Sleep in my room if you want and I'll stay with Papa until you're rested. It will do no good for you to get sick from not taking care of yourself."

"Did you rest, darling?"

"Not much," Cissy confessed. "But more than you."

"Have you checked on Logan this morning?"

"He's fine, sitting up in bed and begging for breakfast. Bessie is on the way with his tray now. Why don't you go eat something and go to bed for a while. The doctor won't be here before ten or eleven, so you might as well try to sleep a little. I'll call you if Papa wakes up."

"Did you have breakfast already, Cissy?"

"Bessie's bringing me a tray here. I told her I was going to stay with Papa while you take a little nap. Now, go on, please."

Cissy resumed Evangeline's vigil in the rocker by the fire. She snuggled her shawl around her shoulders and stared into the flickering flame. From time to time her reverie was interrupted by the dropping of a piece of blackened wood onto the bed of embers, or a sudden sizzle when fire ate into the resin of the fat lightwood used to keep the oak logs burning at a steady pace. She was so lost in the hypnotic dance of combustion, that at first she did not hear the low moan from her father's bed. Shaking her head to clear her thoughts, she listened. Her father was moving fitfully, his pain obvious from the crease across his brow.

Moving to his side, she placed a cool palm on his forehead and stroked it. "Papa, can you hear me?"

Her only response was a low moan. Whether it indicated awareness of her presence or was a mere expression of suffering, Cissy did not know. "I'm going to call Evangeline, Papa. I'll be right back."

He lay still again with nothing to guide her as to whether or not he heard.

"Oh, do wake up," she cried as she turned to leave the room.

When Cissy returned with Evangeline, Graham was stirring restlessly. His eyes opened briefly only to close again. A low moan issued from between his dry lips, spurring the two women to his side.

Evangeline bent low and kissed his brow. "Graham, can you hear me, darling?"

Graham's eyes fluttered open in an unfocused stare. Again he groaned. His lips moved slowly and he rasped, "Hurts."

"I know, darling. I'm so sorry. The doctor is on the way. He left me some medicine that will help the pain. Do you think you can take it?"

Graham struggled to focus on Evangeline's face. He wanted to smile his reassurance that he would be all right, but he did not know if he had done so or not. He supposed he had not, as her expression had not change from that same anxious look of inquiry. He managed to croak, "Water."

"Of course. I'll add some laudanum. That should give you some ease." Evangeline turned to Cissy after she had stirred the opiate into the glass of water, "Help me hold him up, please, so we can get this into his mouth."

Cissy eased her arm under her father's shoulders and began to lift, "I'm sorry if I hurt you, Papa."

His only response was a blink of acknowledgement before he tiredly closed his eyes. His head was pounding and his leg throbbing. He could not decide which was worse and it hurt to even try. Gnawing at the back of his mind was the vague notion that there was some danger he needed to warn them of, however the thought refused to form. As the laudanum eased the pain that racked him, he slipped back into sleep.

Cissy met Evangeline's eyes, "It's a good sign he woke up, right?"

"I think so. We will let the doctor know when he comes. Perhaps, he can tell us more."

During the coming days, Graham's sleep was haunted by vague memories of something left undone, and his waking moments were so clouded with laudanum to control the pain that he lacked the ability to voice the worries that racked his sleep. Evangeline and Cissy watched over him as he tossed restlessly and plucked in frustration at the covers they struggled to keep tucked around him. They sensed that he was troubled by something more than his injuries and could only surmise that it had some connection with his unexpected return home. Fortunately for the women, Logan was now recovered to the point that he could move about the house for ever longer periods and even talk of his return to the front. He relieved them once a day to sit with Graham while they attended to their personal needs. He sensed their relief that they could devote their time solely to Graham rather than divide it between the two men.

Logan sat in the rocker by the bed, whistling a tuneless song as Graham slept. He seethed in quiet fury as he recalled the earlier visitor at the front door. With both women attending the patient, Logan had answered the door to find the Frenchman he detested standing there in obsequious sympathy. He snorted to himself when he remembered the Frenchman's fury when he had been firmly turned away. Logan had no tolerance for his protests that he had come merely to express his heartfelt concern to the charming Mrs. LaRoque and her lovely stepdaughter at the injury suffered by Mr. LaRoque. Despite Marcel's best efforts to elicit some information about LaRoque's condition, Logan had revealed nothing. Something about the Frenchie made his hackles rise and it wasn't just jealousy of the man's obvious interest in Cissy. At the thought of Cissy, Logan smiled, pleased that he had caught her sending more than one considering glance his way. It had taken all of his willpower not to push her for more.

Lost in his musings, he did not at first feel Graham's eyes on him. At last sensing that he was being watched, Logan looked at Graham and noted the first lucid stare that he had seen since beginning his daily vigil. "Mr. LaRoque, it's good to see you awake. May I get something for you: water, laudanum, something to eat?"

Graham shook his head slightly to keep it from pounding, "No. Laudanum makes me confused. Just some water, please."

Logan assisted Graham in sitting up against the headboard and then held the glass of water to his lips. Graham drank greedily and then exhaled, "Good. So thirsty."

"Are you in pain, sir?"

"Hurt like hell. Have to endure it. Can't stay doped up. Need to remember..." Graham's eyes looked a challenge of inquiry.

"I don't know, sir. What is it you need to remember? Is it why you came home? Is it about the fall of Roanoke? I got sick after that and don't know much about what has happened since then, other than what I saw in the newspaper Toby brought yesterday. Elizabeth City is gone. The mosquito fleet is done for. They've blocked the Albemarle and Chesapeake Canal. The paper says the Union will probably move on New Berne any day now."

"Have to get Evangeline and Cissy away. Wilmington..." Graham closed his eyes, exhausted by the effort to think.

"So, you came home so you could take them away before the Yankees get here?"

There was no answer. Graham again was lost to the world.

Logan waited for the women to relieve him at his bedside station. Then he walked to his room and gathered his things. It was imperative that he report for duty and learn as much as he could of any imminent peril to the inhabitants of this house that had become so much a home to him. Perhaps he could arrange for train transportation to Wilmington for the three of them as soon as Graham was well enough to travel. And, if Graham did not heal... Logan left the thought unfinished, refusing to recognize the possibility. Regardless, he felt conflicted by an obligation to not only help the three of them, but to return to his regiment as soon as possible. The odds were going to be overwhelmingly in the Union's favor: more men, better weapons and equipment. Every man capable of resistance needed to be in the trenches when the Yankees invaded. Logan would be in there fighting for his home, for those he loved, and for the dream of a tomorrow with the woman he loved.

Despite Evangeline and Cissy's pleas that he stay on until fully healed, he persisted in his determination to report for duty. They watched as he rode down the lane and waved when he turned to salute them before he rode from sight. They were not the only ones waiting for his departure.

Marcel smirked from his post in the verge of the woods as Logan cantered past. He had kept watch for the last couple of days hoping for just such an eventuality. With Logan gone and Graham gravely ill, he could put his contingency plan into effect. The rumor in New Berne had Graham all but dead.

The doctor, puffed with importance, had spilled the information over a game of cards shortly after the accident. He had assured all at the table, "The man can't recover from a head injury of this type. If he does, he'll never again be functional. Better if he dies now."

Marcel had garnered the information along with much of the braggart's purse. With Graham neatly out of the way without even having to pay his henchman for the job, Marcel gloated at how well his plan was coming together. He worried a little about the newspaper articles warning of the eminent danger of an invasion and puzzled how that might affect his own hide, not to mention the financial prospects of the LaRoque empire.

Even if the Yankees took over, there should be sufficient resources to provide him with a secure future. The primary concern was to waste no time securing Cissy as his wife. Then he had merely to seize control of the LaRoque fortune and liquidate as rapidly as possible before fleeing to safer climes. Evangeline would be dealt with as needed. As for Cissy, she might prove entertaining to keep around as long as she learned to bend her will to his own. If not, she was expendable as well.

While Logan cantered into town to report to the headquarters of General Branch, Marcel rode up to the LaRoque residence and presented himself at the front door. He could only smile at his good fortune when Cissy herself answered the door.

"Hello, Cissy. Forgive the intrusion, but I have been most concerned about your father and the terrible unhappiness his accident has caused for you all. I wish to extend to you my every assistance should you need it in the face of the peril we may find ourselves in at any moment." Not pausing to give her the opportunity to dismiss him, Marcel continued, "I fear the papers are full of dire warnings about the danger for us here. Many of the citizens have already fled. I have managed to procure three passes on the train to Wilmington which I am pleased to offer you."

Despite her first inclination to close the door to the man, Cissy found herself unexpectedly touched by the magnanimity of his offer. "That is very kind of you and the offer is much appreciated, however, my father is still too ill to move."

"Has he not regained consciousness, then?"

Cissy's face lit with happiness, "Yes, he did wake up for a minute. It gives us such hope that he will recover soon."

Marcel forced a brilliant smile that never reached his eyes, "That's wonderful news. Do let your father and step-mother know that I have arranged passage for you should they so desire."

Chapter 13

March in the Carolinas brought the rebirth of rampant springtime. By the 13th of the month, camellias, daffodils and fragrant jasmine added a note of color to the landscape. Already tiny buds on the trees were unfurling in a pale green haze. As the days grew longer, her father had begun improving. With worry for him lessening each day, she found herself growing restless and bored. With Logan gone, the house seemed strangely empty. She dared not question why his absence seemed to matter so much. It was far easier to go on thinking of him as her childhood playmate and friend.

Listless with boredom, she walked over to her bedroom window and drew the lace under-drape to one side. The trees surrounding the house were dark silhouettes against the gray rainy chill of early day. Even the birds seemed to be moping as no cheerful songs from avian throats enlivened the heaviness of the morning. As though her thoughts had summoned him, she saw Logan emerging like some apparition from the thick fog that had blanketed the area for the past two days.

Cissy dashed down the stairs and hurled herself out the front door. Judging by the urgent lashing he was giving his horse, something was badly wrong. She had never seen Logan mistreat an animal, but it was obvious that he had pushed this one to the point of heaving exhaustion. Studying his face as he reined to a stop, she read there a strange mingling of excitement, tension, concern and dire haste.

"It's too late to leave, Cissy," he panted. The railroad is no longer running and the sound is too dangerous to venture escape by boat. The Union forces have landed at Slocum Creek and are headed this way. I just came to warn you. We have to pray the shelling doesn't reach this far and you'll be safe. Find what food and valuables you have and stash them where they will be secure, then stay inside. I hope to God we can stop them, but it doesn't look damned likely." He grinned ruefully, "Forgive the curse, but I'm a bit overwrought. I can't stay. I wish I could. I'm without leave as it is. If I don't get back to duty before I'm missed, they'll have me up for court marshal."

"Surely we can take Papa's boat and leave?"

"No, it's too late I tell you. I'm sorry. I tried to get you on the last train to Kinston, but they were permitting no more civilians to board. They are planning to tear up the rail bed to keep the Yankees from using it if we lose. You could take a wagon, make a pallet in the bed, provided it's safe to move your father and try to get out into the countryside. However, the rain has made the roads a mess, and with so many evacuating I don't know where you will find to stay that isn't already filled. Most of the townsfolk left days ago."

Cissy bit her lip with worry then shook her head. "No. I don't think we could move him far in a wagon. The roads are too rough and his condition is still too precarious to risk that. That's why I thought a boat..."

"You can't. You'd be running into the whole damned Union fleet before you know it. They'd blow you out of the water for target practice. They've already sunk about every boat in the sound." Logan slid from the saddle and pulled her into his arms, "I'm so sorry. Know that I love you and I'll come back to see you as soon as I can. There's just no telling when that will be."

Cissy nodded her head once in understanding before she found herself pulled closer to his hard body. She felt and smelled his dusty, sweat-stiffened uniform as he held her. Bending his head to her upturned face, he kissed her with all of the love and longing in his heart. Something inside her breast began to stir beneath the hungry passion of his lips. Without volition, her lips parted beneath the onslaught of his kiss. Thrilled and terrified by her response, she pulled back and whispered, "Be safe, Logan. Come back as soon as you can."

"You be safe, too. As soon as this fight is over, come hell or high water, I'll come back if I can." He left unsaid the truth that was reflected in both their eyes: he could be killed, wounded or taken prisoner. No one could foresee what the coming hours would bring.

Cissy touched his cheek in a soft caress. "Please, be careful."

"Don't worry. I've got too much to live for to let a damned Yankee finish me off. I told you: I'm going to marry you and grow old loving you. We're going to have a passel of children, you and I. You may not know it yet, but I do. So mark my words, Cissy darling, I'll be back."

Cissy just shook her head, "You are just too much, Logan. Now, drat it, take care of yourself and get back to duty before they hang you. I'll tell Evangeline and we'll figure out what to do. I'll get word to you somehow if we decide to leave."

Logan climbed back into his saddle and blew her a kiss, "You've not seen the last of me. I'm coming back for you, girl, and that's a promise."

With a sharp tug on the bridle, he wheeled his horse around and galloped down the lane at the same pell-mell pace that he had arrived. Cissy shivered in apprehension at what his news could mean to them all. Sucking in a deep breath, she squared her shoulders and walked through the door into her home. Somehow she must find the courage and strength to help her stepmother in the days ahead. Cissy climbed the stairs with quiet determination allowing resolve and energy to flow into her trembling limbs. She paused outside her parents' bedroom door and then lifted her hand and knocked.

"Yes?"

"It's me, Mama. I wonder if you could come out for a moment? There's something I want to tell you."

Evangeline opened the door and then closed it softly behind her back. "Your father is sleeping. What is it? You look as though you've seen a ghost."

"Logan was just here. He says people in New Berne have fled. The Yankees are going to be attacking any minute. He says it's too late for us to leave by boat or by train, and Papa's not strong enough for a wagon or carriage."

"Oh, my God, Cissy. Is he sure?"

Cissy nodded her head. "He's sure. He said to hide our valuables and enough food to get us by for a while in case the enemy comes here. He says we could be shelled if the guns aim this way. I think we'd better move Papa downstairs to the back of the house. It should be safer for him in his study than up here."

"Get Toby to help me." Evangeline glanced at the closed door, "Your poor father is going to be so worried for us. I blame myself for getting us into this mess."

"Don't. I didn't want to leave either. I'll have Bessie start gathering what food we might need and have her hide it in the cellar. I'll get the silver and my jewelry, what money Papa has in the office, and anything you want hidden, and figure out where to put it. I think maybe under the house. I can dig a hole there up next to a chimney foundation."

"Your father's things are in the top drawer of the dresser. I'll get them for you. I'll be right back."

Evangeline disappeared behind the door, leaving Cissy fidgeting in the hallway until her stepmother could return.

They worked for the remainder of the day securing as much as they could and making Graham comfortable in his study. Night found them exhausted but too nervous for sleep. The thick fog of the following morning blanketed the landscape in eerie grayness. At dawn Cissy was standing sleepily in the hall foyer when Evangeline hurried down the stairs and thrust a package into her hands. A sudden rumbling noise that reminded her of rolling thunder broke the quiet of the morning.

"This is the last of it, my late husband's family jewelry. Bessie unpacked it for me from the trunk in the attic. Hurry and hide it. No telling how long we have. I fear that's cannon fire we're hearing."

Cissy and Evangeline both turned in alarm at the sound of rapid hoof beats drumming their way toward the house. They watched as Marcel jerked his horse to a halt at the bottom of the porch steps and launched himself from the saddle. Neither of them moved as the immaculately groomed man leaped up the steps two at the time and arrived panting at their open door.

Leaning over the upper banister, Evangeline cried, "What on earth is the matter?"

"I managed to obtain two railroad passes, madam. You ladies must leave at once," he gasped.

"That's impossible. I don't know what kind of game you are playing but we have it on excellent authority, sir, no longer are civilians permitted aboard the train."

"Your pardon, madam. I assure you I can arrange passage for you and Miss Cissy."

"I will not leave my husband, sir."

"And I'm not leaving my father. Logan assured us there is no escape now, except by wagon, and Papa is not strong enough for that. We're staying. Please excuse us. We have no time for social amenities at the moment." Cissy, took Evangeline's hand, "Come, Mama. We have too much to do to waste our time in futile conversation."

Furious in his frustration, Marcel bowed. Struggling to keep his face bland as he stood erect, he apologized, "Forgive me, ladies. I meant only to help. I see you are occupied and I must now see to my own safety."

A sudden barrage of thundering cannon gave credence to

his words as he fought to gain control of his terrified horse. With the beast momentarily subdued, he swung into the saddle. The women had already turned away as he galloped down the lane.

"Come, Cissy, we must convince your father we are fine. He is beside himself with worry and furious at his helplessness."

Before Cissy could reply, they were again halted by the sound of hoof beats approaching the house. This time she turned to see the doctor barreling his way toward them. "Go to Papa. I'll see what the doctor wants."

"Thank you, darling. Bring him in if it's about Graham. Perhaps he wants to check on him before the battle makes travel impossible."

Cissy nodded and ran down the steps to wait for the doctor. As he drew closer she could see a film of sweat painting a glistening sheen on the doctor's balding pate. Reining in his horse he rummaged in his saddlebag to find a cardboard rectangle. "Here, Miss Cissy. Y'all use this quarantine sign. Put it on your door. If the Yankees think there is a smallpox infection in the house, I think they will leave you be. You cannot let them get your father. With his shipping interests in Wilmington, he'd be a prize catch. If they come you tell them it is just you and some sick womenfolk. Soon as things quiet down, I'll be back to check on you. Now get on inside. It's going to be mighty dangerous around here for a few hours."

"Thank you, sir. Please, take care of yourself."

"Do my best, child. Do my best." He wheeled his horse around and was gone before she could say goodbye.

From his vantage point in the edge of the woods, Marcel had watched the doctor come and go. He debated about abducting Cissy then and there, but a loud barrage of cannon fire cut short his ambitions in favor of hasty retreat to a safer locale. He would return unless he could find another heiress with fewer obstacles to the fortune.

Only a few miles away, gray clad soldiers faced their first battle. Struggling to wheel one of the two recently arrived 24-pounders into position, Logan had no time for thoughts of anything but maintaining the rebel position in the brickyard of the local kiln. Surrounded by fellow soldiers of Branch's 7th, 27th, 35th, and 37th regiments, Logan took comfort in the nearness of so many of his friends and neighbors. His efforts to get the gun into position were interrupted by a fierce attack from the 21st Massachusetts at 7:30 in the rainy cold of morning. Firing his rifle as he rolled behind the useless 24 pounder, Logan watched as the enemy surged towards them. When the enemy pulled back, it appeared the rebels would seize the victory, however his relief was quickly replaced by cold fear for his life as they charged again with increased numbers and vigor. The screams of the dying and wounded joined the panicked cries of unseasoned, terrified boys who were getting their first taste of the brutal reality of war. Soon Logan and his fellow soldiers of the 7th regiment were swept up in the tide of men who had begun to flee towards the bridge over the Trent River leading into New Berne.

Logan raced over the bridge bent low to escape the bullets that zinged past his head. Soldiers were still pouring toward the fragile route to relative safety when it was set aflame to prevent the Yankees using it to follow them across the river. His heart sank as he turned to watch as the unfortunate ones who had not escaped in time surrendered to the blue horde. Soon flames from the burning railroad bridge added to the smoke that swirled above his head. After just six hours of battle, the town was lost.

Commander Rowan of the Union forces wasted no time in ordering his fleet to begin shelling New Berne. Terrified women and children ran shrieking through the streets seeking non-existent safety. Howling dogs and screaming horses were joined by the alarmed clucking of chickens as they fluttered around backyards as eager as humans to escape the din of bursting shells, falling metal splinters, and the crackling of burning buildings. Leaving New Berne to the invading forces, Branch ordered his men to retreat to Kinston, beginning a disorganized and pell-mell rout on the more than thirty miles of muddy and rutted road. Logan slipped quietly from the ranks of his comrades to again make his way to Cissy before resuming the clandestine monitoring of enemy movements.

Galloping down the streets of the panic stricken town, Logan grimaced at the acrid smell of the smoke that swirled around him. It would be a lucky thing if the town did not burn to the ground. It was fortunate that days of rain and fog had left the timbered buildings, trees, and bushes well soaked. Fortunate, too, that the roads were nearly impassable for heavy Yankee guns, giving the rapidly moving rebel infantry time to beat a miserable path away from the site of their ignominious defeat. Thinking of the recent battle, Logan was amazed the poorly trained and armed soldiers had held out as long as they had.

"Dammit, you stupid excuse for a horse!" Logan swore under his breath as he narrowly escaped being unsaddled when his horse reared at the sound of a shell landing somewhere in the mud of the street behind him where it buried itself harmlessly. "Like lightning, it ain't the ones you hear land you worry about, you sorry excuse of a nag."

Shaking his head and keeping a firmer hold on the reins, he doggedly braved the rain of hot metal fragments as he gained the edge of town and the road to Cissy's house. On leaving the town, the shelling was soon behind him. Although it still made the horse skittish, life was no longer in peril and the animal quickened his pace, as eager as Logan to escape the noisy bombardment. Logan fretted. He had only moments to spare before he would be forced to flee. Somehow he must formulate a new plan for getting information to General Branch, find a new base camp, and measure the parameters of survival in a

Union occupied territory. As a spy, one slip, one error could easily cost him an unpleasant dangle from the business end of a rope. He rued the day he had agreed to become a gatherer of information rather than a regular infantryman. The companionship of boys he had grown up with, learned to spit tobacco with, chased girls with, was far preferable to a lonely campfire in the woods. The only bright spot was the freedom that it gave to move about the countryside independent of the army. And that freedom meant that he could keep his eye out for the safety of Cissy and her family and the occasional visit.

Cissy was standing at the end of the lane when he turned in. "Whoa," Logan pulled the horse's reins. "What are you doing out here, darling. There's no telling when those blue bellies are going to be swarming all over this place. A lone girl and one as pretty as you is not something I want to think about meeting up with that bunch. You need to stay with your folks in the house. I just pray to God they will leave y'all alone. But I don't count on it. They're going to need housing for that hoard and New Berne's not that large a town. They'll be coming here for sure and I want you safely inside when they do."

"They're not going to mess with us. The doctor gave us a quarantine sign saying there's smallpox in the house. Not even the all-mighty Yankees have bullets that'll kill that. Nope. They won't be bothering us." Cissy tossed her head in dismissal of the idea.

"Not if they get to the house. But out here you're not in the house. You just can't be out here alone anymore, Cissy. And for sure not now!" Worry for her made him angry and he didn't want to leave her that way. Struggling to soften his voice, he added, "I couldn't stand it if anything happened to you."

"I know I have to be careful. It's just it's been so awful shut up in the house and listening to all the racket of battle and not knowing what is happening. I figure, since you are worried about the Yankees coming here, we lost the battle?"

"That we did. Our army is headed for Kinston as fast as the muddy road will let them. Unfortunately a bunch of our men got killed or captured, God rest their souls. New Berne is being shelled and some of it is burning. I just hope the Yankees think enough of the town as a base that they put the fires out before the whole town goes."

"Oh, no," Cissy cried. She stood with her eyes closed and head bowed trying to come to grips with the new reality of her world before asking, "So what are you going to do? Are you going to Kinston, too?"

Logan shook his head. "General Branch wants me to continue providing information to him. He needs to know what the Yankees are doing and where they plan to head next. Any advance indication gives our army time to prepare."

"You are only just now arisen from sickbed. It's going to be no good for you to lay out in the rain and cold. Couldn't you be with the army somewhere, let someone else do the spying?"

"Our army isn't going to be residing in a fine hotel, Cissy. Most of them are lucky to have a tent and a tin pan for cooking. As a lone man, I can find corn sheds and haylofts and I have a good tent. I'll be fine." Giving lie to his words, a sudden burst of coughing left him gasping for air.

"You surely don't sound it. Come on to the house. With that quarantine sign on the door you can maybe sleep warm in a bed tonight at least. The rain and foggy cold aren't good for you so soon after being sick in bed."

"I'd like nothing better, but I can't risk it." Logan's face went grim, "The sign may help you avoid occupation or outright eviction, but with the Yankees in need of lodging, they're going to be looking for houses to live in. Yours and Miss Evangeline's are two of the nicest and roomiest houses on this road and you're close enough to town for it to be convenient. If they ask who's sick, don't just say one person.

Add some others. As for Evangeline's house, Bertha will just have to do the best she can to take care of it. The Yankees will take it over unless I miss my guess. That means they're going to be right on your doorstep. And there's no telling how long they'll be here either. Don't take any chances, Cissy. A bunch of men in an army don't always behave like gentlemen. I fear for you, for all of you left to face them."

"We'll manage somehow as long as we can get food and keep that quarantine sign up."

"That will last for a few weeks, no more. Then what?"

"We'll have to come up with something else somehow."

"Do you remember the hollow tree down in the woods were we buried that pet raccoon of yours?"

Curious as to why he would mention that at this of all times, Cissy replied, "I haven't thought about it in years, but of course, I do."

"If you need to get a message to me, wrap it in something waterproof and put it inside the hollow. I'll check periodically and leave a note for you, too, from time to time. I don't dare come to the house until things quiet down or they move on. You'd be in serious trouble if you were caught harboring me."

"If you need us and we can help, you come anyway. Those damned Yankees can't run my life for me."

"They are going to make changes in the way we run our lives, I promise you." Logan pulled her into his arms, "Take care, my Cissy. I must leave now. I wish I could take you somewhere safe from harm, filled with happiness and good, but it's no longer possible. We must just find a way to survive the coming trial. I love you."

Cissy gave him her lips. As he hungrily took the kiss that she gave and then demanded more, she realized the possibility that she loved him, too. Before she could find the courage to tell him, he had stepped away from her and mounted his horse. She lifted her hand in silent farewell as he melted into the woods leading away from New Berne. She could only pray that he would be safe, that they all would.

Pulling her shawl over her head to protect her hair from the drizzle that had once again begun to fall, she hurried into the house. They all must be alerted what the lost battle would mean for them. And someone would need to tell Bertha what Logan had warned to expect.

Chapter 14

General Foster wasted no time in putting out the fires that threatened the town. If it were to be his base he needed those buildings for housing and offices for his army. The homes of hastily departed citizens were soon occupied and those of the stubborn or hapless few that remained were soon playing host to as many soldiers as could be accommodated. But there were too many soldiers and too few buildings to stop there. It wasn't long before Foster's soldiers were bedding in homes along the perimeter of the town. Evangeline's, occupied by only her faithful retainer, was a prime residence and did not escape notice.

Cissy was sitting at the breakfast room table picking with little interest at her food. She was frustrated and worried. It had been a week and she had heard nothing of Logan. Her father still seemed dazed and helpless much of the time. Evangeline was so concerned she rarely left his bedside. They had heard nothing more of what was happening in town since Logan's quick visit on the day of the battle. Bessie and Toby spent their time preparing the garden for spring planting and collecting what food they could glean from outlying farms and stashing it in unlikely places as a hedge until harvest season.

Cissy had been left to her own devices. She was not only worried; she was bored. Taking a deep breath, she resumed counting the roses in the wallpaper. Tired of that, she arose and walked to the window. Not even the sight of a fresh spring morning cheered her. Once again she wished that she had some useful occupation. She was tired of being an ornament, tired of nothing of moment that she herself had created or contributed. With the occupation, even social visits and parties had ceased. Other than occasionally reading to her father, there was nothing for her to do. The quarantine sign on the door served to exacerbate her isolation. She could not even go into town or nearby neighbors' houses to assist with rolling bandages, picking lint, and the myriad of other tasks that occupied the feminine gender intent on its own patriotic contribution to the southern struggle. For one wild moment she considered chopping off her hair and joining the army as a man, but she knew herself too well to think that she could or even wanted to pull a stunt like that. The idea of sleeping on the ground, wearing lice infested clothing, eating soldiers' rations, being shot at, and marching endless weary miles held no attraction for her.

Unexpected pounding at the rear entry was a welcome distraction. No matter who or what it was, anything was better than sitting in helpless worry and frustration. Cissy dropped the sheer under-drape and hurried to the door.

"Beulah!" Cissy exclaimed. "You look like you've seen a ghost."

"Ain't no ghosts. It's them Yankees. They done and come to Miss Evangeline's house and just moved theyselves right on in. That didn't pay me no never mind at all. Just told me if I wanted to stay I could keep hot food on the table at mealtimes and keep the house clean. I told them blue-bellies I been keeping that house clean for more'n fifteen years and they ain't about to stop me now. But Lordy, they shore do make me nervous. You got to call Miss Evangeline down here so I can tell her what's going on over yonder."

"Oh, my! I'm surprised they haven't been over here, too," Cissy exclaimed.

"They ain't been over here 'cause I done tole them about how y'all got the smallpox. Bessie explained to me about that sign the doctor give you to put on the door. So I said the whole passel of you is pretty near sick in bed with it. They don't want nothing to do with no smallpox, I can tell you. No sirree. I don't think they going to be messing with y'all no time soon."

"There is some ersatz coffee in the kitchen. Why don't you go have a cup with Bessie while I ask Mama to come down."

"I do that, Miss Cissy. Don't be long now. Ain't no telling what they do to your step-mama's house iffn I ain't there to watch it."

Cissy barely listened to the conversation between Beulah and Evangeline. She was too busy formulating a plan of action, a way to make a difference and to have a purpose in the new arena in which she found herself. Logan had unwittingly given her the venue. Now all she needed to do was to find a way to make the information she gave him something more vital than the current state of her health and disposition. With Yankees next door in a house she knew as well as her own, she had access to information that Logan and those he served might well be able to use. She smiled with pleasure at the possibility that she could be of use to her friends and homeland.

Evangeline glanced at her and asked in puzzlement, "What on earth are you grinning about, Cissy? Didn't you just hear Beulah say we have Yankees next door in my house? For heavens sake, they could decide to move in on us at any minute. I must say I find nothing pleasant about the whole situation. I certainly don't see anything to be smiling about."

"It isn't that I'm happy about it, Mama. Please don't misunderstand. It is serious indeed, especially if they decide to come here. I'm as worried for Papa as you are," Cissy hastened to reassure. "But you know the saying is to *'keep your friends near and your enemies closer.'* Perhaps, we can learn things that will help us protect ourselves, and others from whatever they're up to."

"Don't go getting dangerous ideas, darling. I know you are

frustrated and bored, but this is not a game we are playing. It is deadly serious for us all."

"That it is and we have dead neighbors and friends to prove it and others still in harm's way. But, if we should learn something that might help, I intend to get a message to Logan to let him know."

"I think you should forget about it. If Beulah hears something that is important to us, she will tell us."

Beulah gave Cissy a conspiratorial grin. "That's right! We gonna be spies on them Yankee boys. I gonna learn all I can and I'll tell you so you can tell Mister Logan. Yep, we gonna teach them not to go messin' with us southern folk."

Evangeline put her hands on her hips in exasperation, "Don't either of you get any glorified ideas. These men are not playing games. We *do not* want to call any unpleasant attention to ourselves. Just think of what they might do to Graham. They could even turn us out of our home if they realize there's no smallpox here. For goodness sake, just don't do anything to upset them or make them suspicious of us. I beg you both."

Beulah harrumphed, "Now, don't you go frettin'. *I ain't gonna be stupid*."

"Oh, do be careful, Beulah. You don't have to stay over there. Come back here and stay with us. Bessie could use some help with Graham still not well."

"If I thought I was needed here worser than looking out for your house, I'd come a runnin' but I know you just sayin' that. Besides that house over there has been my home for as long a time as it was yours. I don't intend to see no trespassin' Yankees messin' it up. "

"Just *be careful*, Beulah. The house is not worth having you hurt, or worse." Evangeline hugged the old woman before she left to slip quietly across the yard and into the woods. She breathed deeply before turning to Cissy.

"There is nothing we can do, darling, other than staying out of their sight and praying they leave us alone. Please keep that in mind. Until your father is well enough to return to Wilmington, we must keep the Yankees away from here at all cost."

"I understand your concern. I heard it the first time and I hear it now. Please don't worry. I don't intend to do anything to ever jeopardize my father. Surely you know that?"

"Of course, Cissy. I know you would never intentionally do something like that. I'm just asking you not to act rashly out of some misguided notion of heroism."

"Don't worry, Mama. Like Beulah, I'm not stupid."

Evangeline did not push her further and for that Cissy was grateful. After going in to greet her father for the day and spend a few moments reading to him in late afternoon, Cissy ambled out into the yard. Evangeline watched her from the upstairs window, fearful that Cissy would slip from the yard and go to her former home. When the girl settled onto a wicker lawn chair and laid her head back as though to doze, Evangeline's bosom heaved in relief.

In the house through the woods, Beulah stood in the kitchen mumbling as dark descended on the land. "They think they so smart, damn them Yankee hides. Just cause I'm over sixty don't make me some dumb ole black woman. They done and sent me off cause they don't want me hearing them making them plans against us folks. I know what they up to, yessir, I does."

She did not hear the door open softly and jumped with surprise when she felt a hand on her shoulder. Almost fearing a ghost or some other such unwelcome caller, Beulah forced herself to turn her head, "For the love of God, child. You just about scared the breath outta me. What in tarnation you doing sneaking up on me like that?"

"I just can't stand doing nothing. I thought I would come over and see if you had learned anything from those soldiers in the house."

"They done and run me out here to the kitchen minute some colonel feller named somethin' or other rode up on his big ole horse. They real scared I hear somethin' they talkin' about. Uhuh, I know what they up to."

"Well, I just think I'll find out."

"You best stop and think about that now, Miss Cissy. You can't go causin' no messes for Miss Evangeline and your papa. It's one thing for me to go sneakin' around, it be another for you to." Cissy had left the kitchen before the words left Beulah's mouth. Beulah hissed into the empty doorway, "You get yourself back here, you hear me now. Don't you go messing around with them Yankees. Lord have mercy, what is that child goin' to get into now?"

Ignoring the hissed command, Cissy scurried around the house. The lamplight streaming from the dining room window cast shadows across the lawn. Hugging the dark forms of azalea bushes that skirted the house like ruffles on a petticoat, Cissy edged ever closer to the window. Not nearly tall enough to see through the window, Cissy tried jumping to see if she could gain a momentary glimpse of those cloistered within. That proved to be a futile and tiresome endeavor that left her feeling decidedly stupid.

Staring at the wall that loomed before her, she decided that her only choice lay in climbing the trellis that was attached to the wall and covered with climbing roses. The idea of tangling with all of those thorns was even more daunting a prospect than attempting to climb such a makeshift ladder in hoops and voluminous skirts. For one wild moment she contemplated shedding her dress, hoops, and petticoats, and climbing in her chemise. Years of training in the tenets of maiden modesty brought shudders at the prospect of being outdoors clad in underclothing suitable for nothing beyond the private confines of her own boudoir. She stared at the trellis in mute determination. Narrowing her eyes in concentration, she studied the pattern of the climbing rose to determine a path of ascent that would bring the least contact with the thorny branches that twined through the lattice. Satisfied that she had sufficiently mapped her journey, Cissy hiked her skirts and put her right foot on the lattice. Reaching as high as she could, she tested her weight on the flimsy slat and noted with relief that it seemed solid enough to hold her. With great caution, she eased up another step and then another.

Just as she gained the height of the windowsill and was within view and sound of the men huddled in discussion around a map spread on the dining room table, Cissy heard the first creak of the lattice slat that held her. With great caution, she eased her weight onto the next highest slat and renewed her grip. Now her line of vision was much improved giving her clear view of blue uniformed soldiers as they bent over the large map that covered much of the surface of the mahogany table. Straining to hear their voices, Cissy leaned closer to the window. A pesky spider web caught just in the edge of her hair breaking her concentration on the voices within.

Reaching up to brush it from her hair, Cissy could feel her tenuous hold on the trellis slipping. The old wood beneath her began to break away as she scrabbled for better purchase. She tried to stifle an involuntary scream, but an inadvertent squeak and the thrashing of her feet were enough to alert the blue clad men huddled around the dining room table within. Before she could reach the ground, she could feel rude hands grasping for her. Infuriated by their too familiar purchase on her body, she twisted and kicked as they clawed at her. At last, one bold fellow dodged a fierce blow, managing to seize her despite ferocious resistance to his intentions. Hauling her into his arms, he disentangled her from the trellis all the while working to elude the blows that continued to hammer him from her balled fists.

His companion laughed at his contortions. "What the hell

have you tangled with, a mountain lion?"

"She's a cat alright, a damned hellcat." He gasped as she managed to free one hand and rake her nails across his cheek. "Scratches like one, too."

Between the two of them, they succeeded in hauling her into the house. The men that had been seated at the table discussing battle maneuvers stood as the trio entered. Setting Cissy on her feet, the two soldiers hastily stepped out of range.

She looked at the hard faces of the men in the room and felt a cold panic beginning to rise within. Cissy wanted to run, but she was trapped in that circle of blue. She refused to allow fear to conquer her. Aware that if she did not want them to learn what she was up to, she had better figure out a way to brazen it through, Cissy glared at the two men who had captured her. "How dare you presume to manhandle me this way."

The officer who had been detailing his plans while she eavesdropped, pointed at her and sternly demanded, "Miss, would you kindly explain what you are doing here?"

"Would you care to introduce yourself, sir?" she responded with saucy impudence, green eyes snapping defiance.

The man looked at her with annoyance mingled with resigned exhaustion, "My name is Colonel Ryan Madison. And yours?"

"Cecily LaRoque, *Miss LaRoque* if you please."

"You may call me *Colonel Madison,* Miss LaRoque." Cissy caught the faint gleam of admiration in his eyes as he studied her before continuing, "Now with the formalities out of the way, I want to know what you were doing spying on us. I would hope that you've considered the penalty for spying is death by hanging?"

Cissy leaned forward, arms akimbo, and declared, "I was doing nothing of the sort. How dare you even imply such a thing? I was merely looking to see who has the audacity to just usurp this house and make themselves at home."

With an insouciant wave of his hand that encompassed the house, Madison stated flatly, "You might have presented yourself at the door and informed us of your intentions. It seems to me that if your mission was one of mere curiosity as to the occupants here and the safety of the premises that would have been a more appropriate and maidenly way to accommodate your interest. As it is, you apparently felt that you would learn more clinging to that trellis out there and overhearing our conversation."

"I didn't hear what you were discussing and I wouldn't understand such military matters if I did."

"If you didn't hear, how could you know the *matters* were *military*?" Thinking hard, Madison narrowed his eyes, reminded of an early conversation with the muttering black woman that grudgingly served them. "LaRoque. Isn't that the name of the folks next door who are under quarantine for smallpox?"

Thinking rapidly, she replied, "It is, indeed. They're cousins of mine and I was just checking on this house for them since they cannot do it themselves."

"You don't live with them then?"

"Ah, no. I live closer to town."

"Are your parents in the habit of allowing you to roam the countryside at night, unsupervised, in the face of an occupying army with men eager for the company of a pert young miss such as yourself?"

"Unfortunately, I am not always obedient, sir."

"So it would seem." Madison clamped down on a chuckle that threatened to escape. "It's full night out. I would be remiss as a gentleman to allow you to leave unescorted. Permit me to accompany you safely home. Since I was just preparing to return to town, your house will not be out of the way."

Cissy struggled to keep her face from showing her dismay. Ducking her head she feigned a cough to buy time to think.

There was no way she could allow him to escort her to some non-existent home closer to town and she could not tell him that the quarantined house next door was her residence.

"A glass of water, perhaps?" Madison offered tentatively.

Clearing her throat, she declared, "Oh, no thank you. I'm fine now. And please don't concern yourself about me. Beulah is accustomed to walking me home and will be doing so tonight. My mother has asked to see her, you see."

"How convenient for you. Then I will bid you a goodnight, Miss LaRoque. It has been interesting to have you *drop in* on us this evening, however I suggest that in future your visits be made in the traditional manner." This time Madison bowed to hide his own features. He could not help being a bit smitten with the beautiful and dynamic young woman. He worried that her audacity would bring her to ruin. He also rued that his status as an officer in the enemy army kept him from pursuing a closer acquaintance. Lonely and with no woman of his own to write pensive letters of longing, he asked himself why not seek her company in the days to come? Reconsidering the option, he blurted, "Perhaps, if you will give me the location of your home, I might call on you in future to assure myself of your continued welfare?"

He held his breath as he waited for her reply, reading a kaleidoscope of emotions flickering across her features: confusion, pleased vanity, and fear.

"Thank you for your interest and concern however, I am most regretful, Colonel Madison. My parents would never condone a social visit from one of the enemy. I bid you a good evening."

"That is my unfortunate loss, but I understand the difficulties." He was surprised at his level of disappointment. Colonel Madison bowed his head in dismissal. "My pleasure, ma'am."

Cissy hastened from the dining room, her steps quickening

as she gained the rear of the hall and the egress to the kitchen precincts. She could only pray that Beulah had not yet retired for the night. Bursting from the back door, she squeaked when she was suddenly grasped and pull close against another body.

"For Heaven's sake, Beulah. You nearly scared the life out of me!"

"What done happened in there with them Yankees, missy? I been worried near to death about you."

"I heard enough to know they don't intend to just sit around here enjoying the scenery. They're planning to grab Beaufort and Fort Macon. I need to warn Logan what they're up to just as fast as I can."

"You need to get on home now and worry about that problem tomorrow. Your folks is going to be real worried about you if you don't show up for supper. You gonna have to run if you plannin' to get there 'fore they start lookin' for you."

"Beulah, I need you to walk with me a ways down the road until that Yankee colonel rides on back. He's probably going to be looking for us on the road. We don't have to go far. If Mama or Papa ask where I am, I'll make up something."

"You done and landed yourself in one fine kettle of fish, missy. Them Yankees gonna be suspicioning you now. Yessir. We gotta be more careful around here."

"I think I just learned a lesson on that," Cissy snorted. "I'm going to have to think twice and act once in future, and that's for sure."

"I don't think nothin' about having' to go traipse down the road in the dark. No sir. I ain't goin' to be doing this no more. You just goin' to have to figure out another way to git yourself out of your messes without sticking me in the middle of it." Beulah grumbled and muttered as they walked down the road in the direction of town. "My feets is hurtin' somethin' bad, standin' on 'em all day like I does takin' care of that house and workin' for them Yankee soldiers. Now I got to walk down this here road like I'm going somewhere. All I want to do is set down in my chair and eat my own supper."

Cissy wisely refrained from reminding the woman of her earlier interest in spying on the Yankees, and offered nothing more than a consoling, "I know, Beulah."

They were both glad when the Yankee colonel saluted them as he rode by. As soon as he rounded the bend and was lost from sight, they turned back toward home.

The night sounds were the same as always, adding normalcy to the soft footfalls of the two women, yet Cissy realized, as did Beulah, that the world they had known would never return. They were walking into the night but also into a new tomorrow that would bring new fears, new uncertainties, and new challenges. For a moment Cissy considered the yesterday that she had lost and wondered how much of it would survive this war and who among them would not. A brief image of Logan smiling at her with love warming his eyes flitted across her mind. She wished that she could have been more giving of her heart to this long time friend of hers. Would she ever be ready to give more of herself to him, or did long familiarity as a friend and almost brother, render that a sterile romantic notion on his part? Unconsciously shrugging her shoulders in dismissal of such thoughts, she turned her mind to the knowledge she had garnered. She must arise early and find the hollow tree where she could leave a message for Logan. Perhaps, forewarning would help their beleaguered, outnumbered, ragtag, and makeshift forces. Perhaps, in some small way she could help to avoid even one death of someone she knew. Perhaps, this war would give her a purpose, a sense of contribution, and worthiness based on something she had accomplished on her own initiative. She lifted her chin in determination. Somehow she would make a difference. Maybe it would be a small one, but still a difference.

Chapter 15

Cissy lay still for a moment luxuriating in the softness of her bed. The morning was cool and judging from the gray light sifting through the window it was still early. Shuffling noises and sibilant whispers in the hall outside her door induced her to leave the warm comfort of her bed and tie her wrapper around her, curiosity trumping any thought of lingering longer.

When she opened her door she first saw a nervous Evangeline standing with her hand pressed to her mouth. Then looking a few paces in front of her, doing his best to maintain a wobbly balance, stood her father. With a look of grim determination on his face he slowly walked forward, tottering and pausing with each step as he balanced on his crutch.

"Graham, for goodness sake, if you're determined to go downstairs at least let me hold on to one side of you." Evangeline's voice caught on a sob of frustration. Seeing Cissy, she turned to her pleading, "Please make your father see reason. He is still too weak to try to navigate the stairs, and his leg is not yet fully healed."

"You stay out of it, Cissy," Graham barked over his shoulder. "I'm tired of that damned bed and I'm going downstairs and having my breakfast at the table. I keep lying up like some invalid old lady I never will get well. I'm tired of being coddled, tired of being read to like some simple minded idiot, and I'm damned tired of being cooped up."

Cissy glanced at her stepmother and shook her head in sympathy before whispering. "I'm sure he wouldn't refuse to escort you down. So just go take hold of his arm. Don't ask."

Raising her voice, she addressed her father, "Well, remind me to let you do the reading in future. My voice is about worn out. And since you seem determined to break your neck, far be it from me to stop you."

Graham muttered 'women' under his breath, before grabbing the banister and contemplating the descent. It did look damned daunting, especially with only one leg to bear his full weight. Grudgingly he accepted Evangeline's arm while refusing to acknowledge his secret gratitude for the stability it offered. Frustrated with himself and his predicament he nonetheless felt like a heel for being so irascible with the two women he loved more than anything else on earth.

Although he knew that New Berne had fallen, the quarantine sign on the door prevented much in the way of news reaching them. Graham fretted about the prospects of getting the women to safety with escape by boat too risky, the railroad cut between New Berne and the Confederate controlled area to the west of the town, and Yankee troops in residence and patrolling the surrounding countryside. A buggy or wagon that perforce must stay on the roads was also a risk when there was no way of knowing whom one might meet. Runaway slaves now called Contrabands, outlaws, and bushwhackers added to the perils they would face traveling. Alone, a horse could carry him to Kinston where he could catch the train to Goldsboro and from there to Wilmington. It was imperative he return there and resume managing his ships. With the Yankees in control of the sounds, Wilmington was critical to the South's effort to ship goods abroad in return for the goods and materiel vital to the new nation. Heavily dependant on imports from both the North and Europe prior to hostilities, the non-manufacturing South could not survive without those brave ships willing to dare capture and cannon in order to get through.

He flexed his jaw with frustration as he stumbled into his

seat in the dining room. He had to heal, and quickly. Wanting to reassure Evangeline, he erased the scowl from his face and struggled to smile. "Forgive me, dear heart. I fear I am something of a bear today. This accident was at the worst possible time and my recovery is agonizingly slow. I don't mean to take my frustrations out on you."

Looking into his eyes, Evangeline lifted his hand and kissed it. "I'm happy to be your wife even when you're a bear. I know you're annoyed and bored by the inactivity when there is so much you need to do. You don't need to apologize."

"Where's Cissy? I thought she was right behind us."

"I suspect she wanted to give us time together and give herself the chance to dress before coming down. She's not upset with you either. So don't worry about that."

"I shouldn't have growled at her earlier. I just want to apologize."

When they finished their breakfast, Evangeline helped Graham to the back parlor where he could sit by the window and watch the water through the trees. Spring flowers and new green leaves added color to the scene. They could hear birds and chattering squirrels as they flitted about building nests in the branches. He had always enjoyed nature, especially in springtime.

"I wish I could sit on the porch, but with our new neighbors in your house over there, I suppose it would not be so smart."

"We will have to figure something out soon. That quarantine sign won't last forever."

"I wonder why Cissy is so slow to come down. I thought she would have joined us in the dining room long before we finished breakfast."

"Don't worry, Graham. Cissy is fine and she's not sulking because you snapped at her. If I see her, I'll tell her you want her to come here."

"Does that mean you're leaving me to putter about the house?"

"I can delay those chores if you would like me to keep you company. My knitting is here so I can finish that pair of socks while we talk."

If they had known why Cissy had not yet appeared downstairs they would not be enjoying their chatter and contemplation of the pleasures of early spring in eastern North Carolina. As for Cissy, she was annoyed. The first obstacle to challenge her progress was a sentry on the edge of the woods. She forced herself to wait until he moved further away allowing her to slip past unobtrusively. Next was a thicket of brambles that tore at her skirt and petticoats, ripping off a section of lace. She bent to retrieve it, managing to ensnare her hair in the vicious thorns and thoroughly scratch herself getting extricated. Then, mosquitoes hungry for a taste of her blood, buzzed around her head, their hum serving only to increase her ire. As if that were not enough, she twisted her ankle stepping around a root and was forced to hobble onward, each step bringing a twinge of pain. Cissy hissed a few choice words that her family would have been scandalized she even knew. With face flushed and temper hot, she finally reached the tree where Logan had instructed her to leave any messages. Extracting the oilcloth wrapped missive from her pocket, she quickly slipped it into the protected hollow. Now if only Logan would come for it in time perhaps her aggravations would be worth it. As she trudged homeward the idea of spying had lost some of its appeal. Scolding herself, she thought instead of the sacrifice that so many were making and tried to be content with her small contribution to the southern effort.

So concentrated was she on clawing through the brambled undergrowth without inflicting further damage to her clothes and person that she did not hear the horseman that met her just as she emerged from the woods.

"Miss LaRoque, you do seem to have a penchant for getting yourself into fixes. You look as though you've tangled with a bear and come out the loser." Ryan laughed at the flush of wounded pride that colored her face.

"The last thing I need this morning is some sarcastic remark from you, Colonel Madison."

"So tell me, is this the typical route for your morning constitutional?"

"No." Cissy refused to elaborate and stood waiting for him to ride on. She could not help noting his handsome features and sky blue eyes. He sat erect in the saddle, his uniform molding a well-shaped and very masculine figure. Blushing at her dishabille, Cissy dropped her gaze to her feet and waited for him to leave.

Refusing to be put off by her rudeness, he swing down from the saddle and offered his arm. "Permit me to escort you, Miss LaRoque. The least I can do is offer protection should you meet up with any more bears."

"I do not need protection, sir."

"I beg to differ, Miss. Now, where is it we are off to?" Ryan struggled not to laugh at the glint that sparked in her eye at his words.

"*We* are not off to *anywhere*, Colonel." Cissy put her hands on her hips and glared at him.

Ryan grinned at her and remarked, "My, my. We certainly are testy this morning."

"Colonel Madison, my disposition this morning or any other is no concern of yours. Now, please excuse me and be on your way."

"My dear, Miss LaRoque, I fear I have provoked you with my courteous request for the honor of seeing you safely home." Ryan bowed to hide the laughter he felt bubbling up inside.

"Ah ha, you're not totally insensitive."

"More like wounded to the core by your rejection of my chivalry."

"I'm sure you'll survive. Now please be so kind as to go on

your way and leave me to mine."

"Good day to you, fair lady. I look forward to seeing you again, albeit I might prefer a far friendlier frame of mind."

Cissy snapped her head in a brief bob, "That you should not anticipate, sir."

Clapping his hands to his heart theatrically, Ryan announced, "How could I not when mortal man cannot resist one of such charming demeanor?"

Cissy snapped her head up and stalked off. 'Damned his Yankee,' hide she thought. Despite herself she liked him. But he represented danger for her and her family, her town, her friends...and his knowing look was too unsettling.

Watching her stomp away, Ryan acknowledged his attraction to her, but he did not trust her. She was up to something. He could see the guilt on her and it worried him. He must have her watched but he fervently prayed that she would do nothing that might bring her to harm. He recognized the desire he felt for her, but it was not his habit to debauch an innocent, and surely this belle of the south was one. In the past his amorous adventures had been confined to the willing arms of hungry widows, eager for his embrace and free of the constraints of virginal expectations of future marital bliss. Having seen little happiness in his own parents' union he had no desire to tread the path to a permanent relationship with any woman. Use them to allay his need for female comfort he would and did, but beyond that he had hitherto been immune. Perhaps, were circumstances different, he might have pursued this girl on the cusp of womanhood in a more traditional manner. The exigencies of the moment precluded any such impulse. Turning in the saddle, he glanced back just as she turned around to look over her shoulder at him. He was too far distant to read the expression on her face, but his vanity was pleased that she had looked for him. He did not want to consider the possibility that her glance back might have been for determining her safety from his scrutiny. Shaking his head in acknowledgement of the futility for any potential amour, he turned resolutely around and galloped off.

Hearing the increased pace of his departure, Cissy exhaled in relief and hastened home. Her hope of sneaking up to her room and repairing the damage she had suffered to her appearance was a vain one. Both Evangeline and Graham were standing in the hall when she entered. Both sets of eyes registered shock.

Her father demanded in amazement, "Dear Lord, Cissy, what on earth have you been up to? You look like you tangled with a bear and lost."

Cissy chuckled to herself. That made twice she'd been accused of being mauled by a bear. "Sorry, Papa. I went for a walk and got caught in some briars. Y'all excuse me, please. I need to clean myself up."

Graham and Evangeline looked after her in amazement as she climbed the stairs to her room. "I never saw my daughter quite that disheveled. Not even when she was a child. I wonder if she is up to something. It's just not like her."

A shiver of fear ran icy fingers up Evangeline's spine. She cast a fervent prayer heavenward that Cissy was not sneaking around trying to spy on the Yankees. Struggling to keep her voice normal, she responded, "I think she's just bored, darling. She's young and the isolation is getting to her. With no one visiting she's left to her own devices. I will caution her to be careful. With Yankees in my house next door, we must all be cautious."

"Dammit," Graham growled. "Just as soon as I can get on a horse, we need to get out of here any way we can."

"But, Graham..."

"No! The two of you refused to leave before but now you have no choice. I must go and I will not leave you behind."

Evangeline judged the adamant expression on his face as

evidence that silence was her best course. But, she was still determined to stay and protect their servants and homes if she could. At least she could celebrate his renewed vigor and the beginning of a return to health. While he was home she would enjoy his company. Giving him a coquettish look, she implored, "Graham, I'm rather bored myself. Why don't we retire upstairs for a little nap prior to lunch? I would delight in lying next to you."

"Ah, somehow I don't think we'll nap. However, if you'll help me up those stairs I believe I know how to resolve some of our boredom."

"I do hope so. I do so hope so."

Graham swatted her bottom and whispered in her ear, "Hussy. Lead the way. I have plans for you."

Evangeline purred, "I have some of my own."

Cissy had no way of knowing that Logan was at that moment in South Mills preparing the defenses for the canal locks there through which the Confederates hoped to transfer ironclads from the boat works in Norfolk into the Albemarle in an effort to expel the Union. On the morning of April 19, Union Brigadier General Jesse L. Reno reached Elizabeth city and marched his troops north towards South Mills. Meeting daunting Confederate opposition he withdrew and returned to Elizabeth City and from there to New Berne.

Logan had no time to celebrate. Leaping to his horse, he tore through swampy terrain in hopes of evading enemy outposts in order to reach the surrounds of New Berne. He could not rest until he ascertained whether or not Cissy and her family were safe. First he found the hollow tree and was pleased to find the oilcloth bound packet telling him that the LaRoques were safe despite Yankee occupation of Evangeline's former home. He read the news of the intended attack on Beaufort and Fort Macon with interest. Unfortunately the news left him no time for a social call on his ladylove. Getting the message to the

Confederate commanders took preeminence over personal considerations. Nonetheless, Logan tore the lower unused paper from Cissy's note and hastily scribbled a message to her assuring her of his gratitude for the information and his continued health. Thoughtfully he added an additional note before wheeling his horse eastward towards Beaufort.

Cissy awoke at dawn the following morning to a torrential downpour. Periodic flashes of lightning followed by booming claps of thunder convinced her to pull the cover around her ears and snuggle back into the downy bedding. She had hoped to visit the hollow tree to see whether or not Logan had picked up her message, but the storm spelled doom for that plan. She admitted to herself that clawing her way through the undergrowth back and forth to the tree was not an appealing aspect of the job she had set for herself. Realizing how minor her own inconvenience were in the face of what so many men were now coping with daily while living in crude tents exposed to the weather, facing hostile bullets, and the ravages of diseases that swept through the camps, she chided herself for her squeamishness. Her discomforts were minor compared to that and hopefully her contributions would somehow matter. At least she was doing something. At least she was no longer an indulged and useless ornament. Beyond the physical discomfort, was a vague fear that she might be caught by the enemy and face retaliation not only against herself but also against her family. Then too, she did not want to worry her father and stepmother by the sudden and uncharacteristic change in her daily routine. Perhaps it was a good thing that the storm forced her into a normal pattern for the day after the unexplainable condition they had found her in the day before.

Cissy need not have worried that Graham and Evangeline would be monitoring her activities. They too were snug in bed enjoying the renewal of the physical aspect of their marriage, which had per force been put on hold during Graham's absence and then by his injuries. With his returning health came a surge of passion for the woman he loved.

Marcel was in bed, too. He lay in the arms of a willing whore while he watched the rain run down the windowpane beside the bed. Even the dirt on the window could not hide the foulness of the weather or the dingy sheets and room. He looked at the woman beside him and sat up in disgust. Obviously the previous evenings consumption of whiskey had dulled his aesthetic sensibilities. In the gray light of morning he was appalled that he had sunk to using cheap slatterns after enjoying the favors of bored French aristocratic women and high-class courtesans. But, then, such as they were not in abundance in the port of Wilmington. Easing from the bed, he reached for his clothes hoping he was dressed and away before she awakened. Fastidiously he tied his cravat and slipped into his coat. Holding his shoes he tiptoed to the door. The creak when it opened was like a gunshot in the morning stillness.

"Where you off to, ducky?" The blowsy woman pulled the sheet away and sat up, casting her eyes on the chair by the bed that served as a table. Furious, she screeched, "Where the hell is me money, you son of a bitch Frenchy. Ain't so high toned that you wouldn't try to cheat me out of what you promised, is you?"

Cursing under his breath, he turned, "My pardon. It must have slipped my mind due to the earliness of the hour."

He walked back to the bed and put a dollar in her hand, noting broken dirty nails and what looked suspiciously like a syphilitic scab on her face. Disgusted with himself, he beat a hasty retreat. The scab did not worry him. He had long been afflicted by the French pox. However he did regret the loss of money for such a sorry excuse of a trollop. He had precious little to lose after this last spree of cards and drinking. He was fed up with Wilmington on every level. At just under ten thousand citizens it was the largest town in North Carolina, but it was still a provincial one. Despite not being up to his urbane standards, it was still time to leave before the law caught up to him for card-sharking and other shady dealings. Even if the law did not come after him, the tempers of those he had conned and cheated could not be trusted.

When he reached his hotel he wasted no time stuffing his clothes into a valise. The only issue as he saw it was where to go next. He still wanted the LaRoque fortune, but was the timing right? When he snapped the latch on his luggage, he stood still for long moments debating the choices open to him. Suddenly he knew what he must do.

Marcel walked into the LaRoque shipping company office and pretending an intimacy with Graham LaRoque, asked if he might be permitted an audience.

Zeke arose from his desk pulling his cuffs down as he did so. He was sufficiently discomforted by the haughty elegance of the Frenchman to pat his wayward hair with absentminded futility. "Beg pardon, sir. I can't oblige at the moment. Mr. LaRoque ain't returned yet from New Berne. I confess to being mighty concerned for his welfare."

In stilted arrogance, he replied, "I see. By happenstance I plan to travel in that direction. Should our paths cross, I'll relay your concern."

"We'd be some kind of obliged to you if you'd do that, sir."

"That's no problem. Good day to you."

Marcel left the office. In the street with his back to the door, he beamed. New Berne. There was still a fortune waiting there, particularly if Graham LaRoque were dead or dying. This time he would not fail in his objective. He could not afford the luxury of time and he was sick of this country. The pleasures of Paris sang a siren song in his blood, stealing his sleep, haunting his days. Nothing here enticed him into a desire to linger longer than necessary. The war made it insufferable. But, even without the war, he would have hated it. Its provincialism, piety, and paucity of the pleasures he valued held no appeal. He wanted to go home, but to go home meant money. He had none. He had to win a fortune, win enough to pay his debts in France and give him the future he wanted for himself. Cecilia LaRoque was still the best avenue to achieving his goals. Shifting his valise to his left hand, Marcel dug in his pocket for the money to buy a train ticket to Kinston. He was whistling when he walked up to the ticket agent's window and bought a ticket. He was smiling while he waited to board the train. Now that he had a goal and renewed determination, his future seemed brighter. This time he was going to win. Every fiber of his gambling instincts urged him forward. He welcomed Lady Luck as his traveling companion.

Chapter 16

Graham was adamant. He was leaving and his women would go, too. Their arguments and tears fell on deaf ears. He'd left them before. This time he would not. Go they must.

The day prior to their departure, the weather had improved enough to allow Cissy to make a trip to the hollow tree to see if Logan had retrieved her message. It was likely to be the last opportunity for her to do something for the cause. She had wanted to go back to Evangeline's house and spy on the officers there, but prudence cautioned her as to the folly of that. Now was not the time to call attention to her family, particularly the presence of her father. Dressed in her oldest dress and without the voluminous petticoats that so hampered her previous excursion into the woods, she slipped from the sleeping household and into the shadowy embrace of the still dark forest. With the sun only just creeping above the horizon, going was slow, as she could not see well enough to avoid any but the most obvious of impediments. None of the discomfort mattered once she reached the designated tree and extracted the carefully wrapped packet Logan had left for her.

She skimmed quickly over the contents to assure herself of his safety before sitting on a tuft of grass and savoring the words he had written. She smiled with pleasure when he remarked how proud he was of her for obtaining valuable intelligence. She held the letter to her breast, eyes sparkling, and thought of other adventures that might bring foreknowledge of future Federal movements. Remembering she would be gone and her career as a spy at an end, she dropped the letter into her lap.

It was so very provoking, especially in light of the information Logan provided. Emeline Pigott, had become a ready agent for the Confederacy. She would serve as a conduit for information when the need for urgent relay obviated leaving it in the tree, not knowing if Logan would be able to reach it in a timely way. Just when she had the opportunity to be a cog in a vital network to thwart enemy ambitions, she was being snatched away to Wilmington. For one rebellious moment she thought of defying her father and remaining. But that was not an option and she knew it. She could not stay alone and her father and Evangeline would never leave her behind. Even Evangeline had been persuaded to see the necessity for leaving the occupied town.

Cissy reread his letter once more and then carefully wrapped the note she had written telling him that she would be in Wilmington with her family and could no longer help unless he could find something for her to do in Wilmington. She had thought long and hard about how to end her note. Logan always included a remark about his feelings for her and longings for a future together. She had thought more and more about that future and the idea of marriage, and marriage to him in particular, no longer seemed so unacceptable. With that in mind, she had signed her note for the first time with "love and prayers for your continued safety and return to me. Yours faithfully, Cissy." While not as an effusive a declaration as those he had written, it was a big step for her and one that made her decidedly uneasy.

"Oh, well," she said aloud. "It's done now."

No Colonel Madison was waiting for her when she emerged from the woods this time. For a moment she was almost disappointed. Despite a growing awareness of Logan, she could not help the thrill of excitement that Ryan Madison inspired in her. He was a man to turn any girl's head. She dared not let him turn hers. With that thought cleared away, she slipped into the house and up to her room where she neatened herself and prepared for a day of packing.

The things they would be able to take were limited with only a pack mule for food, necessary clothing, and valuables. Evangeline was determined to protect as much of what was left as she could by bundling it securely to hide the contents, tying with strong knotted ropes, and then having Toby haul it all to the barn where he would stuff it under the hay. Both Bessie and Toby were grumbling good-naturedly at the heavy packages they were hauling. Neither servant was thrilled that they would stay behind to tend the house. It would be lonely for them, and the unknown frightening to contemplate. But, like Beulah, this was their home, too, and they wanted to do what they could to preserve it.

Cissy could see Evangeline's pain at leaving behind almost everything they owned with the likelihood that the house would be occupied and ransacked by enemy troops not long after their departure. It hurt to part with things that she, too, had treasured since childhood. Perhaps they would mean nothing to another, but they were special to her. The shell she had found on the beach during a childhood excursion, the first painting that she had done under Evangeline's tutelage, a card from her father celebrating her sixteenth birthday, and an image of her with her mother taken during that fateful trip to France when she had last seen her. Taken when she stilled longed for her mother to love her. In the picture, her mother was holding her by the shoulders and smiling. Cissy had kept it as a reminder of that moment of maternal warmth, so rare to her childhood. Looking at it now brought the sting of regret for all that could have been, never was, and could never be.

She went to bed exhausted but resigned to leaving for Wilmington come morning. Sometime in the night she awakened and was sick in the chamber pot beside her bed. By dawn, Cissy was ill. Feverish and miserable, she was still abed when Evangeline came to her room to see why she had not appeared for breakfast. Her eyes were bright with fever and her face flushed when she looked up at her stepmother's anxious face. She turned her head away and coughed.

"What's wrong, Cissy?" Evangeline pressed her cool hand against Cissy forehead and winced. "Dear heaven, you're burning up. There is no way you can go to Wilmington today. You stay here and I'll get some herbal tea to help with your fever. Are you nauseous, too?"

Cissy merely nodded her head and closed her eyes, too tired and sick to do more. One part of her brain registered that she was not going to be leaving for Wilmington after all. But sick in bed, there was nothing more she could do anyway to help Logan and the confederacy.

Evangeline left Cissy and descended to the dining room where Graham was finishing his breakfast. "Where's Cissy," he demanded. "She knows we're must leave as quickly as possible. Of all the mornings to lollygag about."

"That's not the case at all, darling. I fear Cissy and I won't be traveling with you today. She's burning up with fever. There is no way she can be exposed to the elements, nor sit in a saddle for thirty miles as sick as she is. And of course I can't leave her."

"Damnation!" Graham began in exasperation before catching himself. "Ah, forgive me. Of course we can't go. I would never dream of exposing her to the rigors of traveling when she's unwell. What seems to be the problem?"

"I think she's caught the grippe that's been going around. Perhaps we should have Toby fetch the doctor for her."

"That's wise. The sooner she recovers the quicker we can be on our way. Not that I put all that much stock in his medicines, but still it's something." Graham walked to the window and peered through the drapery, his frustration evident in his rigid posture. "You go, Graham. Go today. There is absolutely no need for you to stay. As soon as Cissy is well, we'll have Toby escort us as far as the train depot in Kinston and we'll come to you."

Graham's face went gray with agonized indecision. "I don't want to leave you again. I'll be sick with worry if I go without you."

"She's young and strong. I'm sure in a week or so we can follow you. You can do nothing here that I can't do for her. And everyday you stay here I fear for your safety if you're discovered." Evangeline walked close and pressed her hands to the sides of his face. "You dear old thing, do you think we're so helpless? We'll be fine. Now go tell Cissy goodbye and be on your way."

"I know you're right. It just kills me to think of leaving with Toby the only man in the house to protect you."

"I know how to shoot and so does Cissy. We have the pistols you gave us. We'll keep them near while we're here and when we travel we'll carry them in our pockets. We'll be fine, Graham. Now go up and tell her goodbye while I help Toby unload our things. You'll travel faster and safer without us anyway. As soon as Toby is finished, I'll tell him to fetch the doctor."

He nodded his head in reluctant assent. Evangeline hastened out the door and was calling to Toby long before he reached the top of the stairs. He winced with pain when he reached the landing. He was still having trouble with his leg, but he could afford to wait no longer. He for sure would not be doing any running if the Yankees were to chase him. Until his leg grew stronger he wouldn't be doing any running for any reason.

For the next three days Cissy lay in bed too listless and feverish to do little more than note Evangeline's quiet ministrations. When the fever finally broke, she was left with a hacking cough that made sleeping a hit or miss possibility. It was another three days before she began to feel that she was at last on the mend. She vaguely remembered her father coming to tell her goodbye and that they would be joining him as soon as she recovered. Cissy lay in her bed on the sixth day conflicted as to what to do. She did not want to go to Wilmington. She wanted to stay and help Logan with information that she could glean, but Evangeline would never permit it. Young ladies without the benefit of matrimony were never left un-chaperoned. Virginity was a fragile and highly prized commodity in the market for a husband. Girls who flouted that rule found themselves ostracized by both family and society. For that reason, families protected young women with a plethora of rules, obligations and strictures. Cissy was no exception.

When she arose from sickbed, she felt a guilty flash of relief when Evangeline next fell ill. She had a few days to continue her spying before Evangeline recovered and they would have to leave. After making her stepmother comfortable and giving her a dose of the medicine the doctor had left, Cissy scurried from the house and was soon standing at the kitchen door of Evangeline's former home softly calling for Beulah.

"Mercy, child. Come in here and visit with me. I ain't had a chance to do nothin' but work for a week now. I could sure stand a little rest and some talkin.' How you all be doin' over yonder?"

Cissy explained breathlessly, "Papa's gone back to Wilmington and we were supposed to go too but I caught the grippe and now Miss Evangeline has it. This is the first chance I've had to get out."

"You just set here and I'll get you a cup of that good Yankee coffee. They won't be missin' it none." Beulah went to the cupboard and removed a cup, which she filled and sat on the table. "There's sugar and milk right there. You fix it up like you want now."

"Thanks, Beulah. It's been weeks since we had any real coffee or sugar. I'd love some." After taking an appreciative sip of the soothing liquid, Cissy asked, "You heard any talk from those Yankees that our boys might like to know about?"

"That I did. I heard 'em say theys goin' to attack some place called South Mills where the Dismal Swamp canal is. They say it'll put the stopper in that ole piece of ditch so the Rebels can't use it no more."

Eager to know all the woman might know, Cissy leaned forward, "Did they say when?"

"Can't rightly say, but it sure sounded like it be soon like."

"Well, just knowing where they are planning to attack should be of some use even without knowing exactly when. I'll get a note to Logan letting him know."

"You heard from that boy?"

"I had a note from him just before I got sick saying he's doing fine."

"Anything I can do to help out with Miss Evangeline? They's a Yankee doctor stayin' in the house. Maybe I can get some medicine from him."

"Doctor Brown left something for me and there's enough for her, too, at least for the moment. As long as he has medicine I'd rather get it from him than some Yankee."

"Well, Yankee or not I'm goin' to fix you a package of coffee and sugar to take on home with you. I know it's hard to get in town right now. I hear them Yankees talkin' about how they plan to starve us out since everything has to be brought in on them boats like Mr. Graham's. Yessir, they figurin' on blowin'em plumb outta the water. It's pure miserable times. That it is."

"I'd better get on home and see if Miss Evangeline needs something. I'll let you know before we leave. Bessie told me to say that she and Toby will help you if you need anything while we're gone." Cissy hugged her goodbye, "Thank you for the coffee, Beulah. This is a welcome gift even if it is Yankee coffee."

When Cissy returned home she found Evangeline sleeping. Using the opportunity she penned a quick note, slipped off her petticoats and was soon making her way through the woods to the hollow tree. She had decided to make two notes: one for the tree in case Logan should come by in the next day or so and the other she would take to Emeline Pigott. There was no letter from Logan in the tree so she could only worry about his whereabouts and well being.

She had no opportunity that day to deliver the other note. It was too late in the day to go to the Pigott woman whose house was across town and would require a horse to get to. And she needed to tend Evangeline who was hot with fever and had begun the hacking cough that still plagued Cissy when she became too warm or over-exercised.

By the time she had helped Evangeline to a bit of broth that quickly came back up...some medicine that lost no time following the route of the broth...and into a clean gown, it was almost noon. She had to leave immediately if she wanted to deliver the message to her contact before the intelligence was too old to be of any avail. With Bessie alerted to assist Evangeline if she should need help, Cissy had Toby saddle her horse and she was soon on her way. It was the first time she had left the premises to go to town since before the occupation.

When she reached East Front Street she began to see the aftermath of the shelling the city had endured during those hours of attack. And everywhere, like a swarm of ants on a hill, blue clad soldiers scurried back and forth on errands she dared not imagine. The activity intensified when she turned onto New Street. At the intersection of Broad, she stopped in amazement. The John Stanly Wright house sat hunched under the weight of a proudly waving Union flag. One of the men standing on the porch in a group of officers turned her way when she rode near. Cissy recognized Colonel Madison and lost no time ducking her head. She did not want him to recognize her. Nor did she have time to waste avoiding his questions and charm.

"Miss LaRoque," he hailed as he descended to the street.

Drat, she cursed under her breath. Pasting on a slight smile, she responded, "Good afternoon, sir. You must excuse me. I'm most pressed for time."

He watched her snap her reins and gallop off leaving him in a cloud of dust. With a wry shake of his head, he turned back to the porch to face a teasing by his fellow officers who had witnessed the rebuff.

"That little rebel gal doesn't seem to take to you. And here we were thinking your handsome mug had swept them all off their feet. Maybe the rest of us stand a chance after all."

"Ain't that the little spitfire our men pulled out of the trellis a while back?"

"Lord, she sure is a pretty thing. I wouldn't mind pulling her out of my trellis?"

"Hadn't heard that one. Come on Madison, we want to hear this story."

He looked from one to another of them and shrugged his shoulders, "Just a young lady I ran into the other day."

"I could have sworn she was the one you caught spying on us."

"Nope, can't say as she is." Ryan wondered why he was protecting her. He wondered more so if she needed it. And he wondered where she was off to alone, unprotected, and in a decided hurry. "You'll have to excuse me gentlemen, Major General Burnsides is waiting."

Brigadier General Jesse Reno turned back to the group. Like several others he had watched the lovely young woman gallop off. "Right, Colonel Madison. We'd best get on with it. Perhaps another time you'll tell me about the 'trellis spy?'

"Not much to tell, really," Ryan assured as they walked back into headquarters. With Reno scheduled to leave for South Mills any day, he hoped the man would forget to ask again. If the story gained too much interest and circulation, Burnsides might well order Cissy LaRoque apprehended for questioning. He hated to think of her confined in the Jones house that now served as a jail for Confederate sympathizers.

The next several hours swept her from his mind as he listened to Reno and Burnsides discussing the campaign against South Mills. With news that the South was building ironclads in the ship works in Norfolk, Burnsides was eager for action. If they could seize control of the Dismal Swamp locks at South Mills, they would have closed an important Rebel avenue for bringing ships from Norfolk into the Albemarle Sound. Burnsides gave the expedition to Reno, assigning him command of the troops of the 21st Massachusetts and those of the 51st Pennsylvania. As a Colonel of the New York 3rd Calvary, it was a relief when Ryan heard he would not be involved. A lawyer by training and from a Baltimore family of Southern sympathizers, he knew he wasn't as gung-ho as many of his fellows. He was not a coward. In fact he was braver than many. His curse lay in the ambivalence caused by dissecting both sides of the argument with intellectual dispassion.

Cissy had reached her destination and now could only curse her stupid blunders. The woman's words lashed her as she stood with her head down to hide the tears that had welled into her eyes.

"You silly, foolish girl. Look at you. Fancy clothes, a thoroughbred horse, and the stamp of wealth all over you. How long do you think you would last if one of these runaway slaves or good-for-nothing white robbers got hold of you. They'd kill you and not look back for that horse of yours, not to mention what they would do to that curvy little body. Not only that, you come trotting up here to a simple farmhouse like you're making a social call. Since when did you come calling on me? What would you offer as an excuse for coming here? You know nothing of me, or I of you and yours. I can't afford any attention called to me. I'm too close to the enemy camp for comfort as it is. What I am doing is vital for getting information about enemy troops, what their strength is in arms and numbers, and what they're up to. I know Logan Gwaltney meant well when he sent you to me, but I doubt he knew how you would go about it." Emeline paused for breath before continuing, "You come here again, you'd better be a lot more low key than this and with a lot more needed information. I have already sent on word that the Union is going after South Mills. You have wasted your time and put me in jeopardy for nothing."

Cissy lifted her head defiantly, "Yes, I've been stupid and I probably will be again, but I'm learning and I'm trying. I will remember what you've said and I'll use it. However, to say that my information is worthless is unfair. How was I to know whether or not you already knew?"

"You're right and I'm sorry I scolded you for trying. You have to understand this is a serious business. This country has never hung a woman, but in wartime, who knows what could happen if a woman makes the enemy mad enough. I don't want to be the first one that goes to the gallows and neither do you."

"I'll be more careful next time. I promise."

"That's fine. Now run on home before it's dark. And for the love of God, be careful. You got a gun on you?"

"Yes ma'am. I have a pistol my papa gave me and I know how to use it if I have to."

"Good. Well, run along. If you learn anything vital, you can bring it to me. We never know when it might help." Emeline relented enough to smile and pat the girl's shoulder, "Keep safe, you hear?"

Cissy started her trip home far more somber than she had begun it. The woman's words rang true and that truth hurt in its starkness. Every moving shadow in the woods caused her to startle. The horse sensed her unease and snorted and skittered. Jerking herself back to attention, she patted the horse and soothed him with soft words. He soon calmed and she rode through the back streets of New Berne skirting past the academy building and the First Presbyterian Church. Even though she still saw soldiers, there were far fewer than on the other side of town. Her sigh of relief was cut short when she turned onto East Front Street. Moaning at her ill-timed arrival to the road home, she reined in her horse beside the man that was waiting for her.

"Miss LaRoque, fancy meeting you here."

Chapter 17

Marcel rolled over on the dingy bunk and cursed loudly when his arm refused to move with him. The firm clasp of the iron manacle on his wrist reminded him where he was and why. The memory brought a new spate of curses to join the ones that were already ringing in the air.

"Shut up in there, you damned Frenchie. I've had enough of your lying, cheating mouth."

Marcel shut up. The sheriff was furious with him and more than ready to do more than deliver another hefty blow to a body that still ached from the beating of the night before. How was he to have known that the last man he cheated at the poker table was the sheriff? How could he have foreseen that the sheriff would be in the station when he went to buy the ticket for Kinston? He'd turned his head quickly and walked the other way after recognizing the man he had played cards with. His was the money Marcel had used to pay for the prostitute. But, he had looked a second too long. As he waited by the tracks, a heavy hand had landed on his shoulder and spun him around, followed by a vicious jab to his belly. Marcel collapsed like a folding fan. His first memory afterwards was awakening in the miserable cell.

The sheriff was not a forgiving sort. He left him there without water or food until seven that night. And the food he brought, Marcel would not have eaten had he not been so hungry.

When the sheriff saw Marcel's look of disdain when he removed the cloth over the chipped plate, he snorted in derision, "Ain't up to your expectations, huh? Well, get used to it. Besides, if I can manage it, you won't be swallowing for long anyway. Be kind of hard to swallow when your damned neck is stretched by a rope."

"I have done nothing to warrant hanging. Besides, this is just a misunderstanding. *Alors,* if you feel I wronged you at cards, I'm happy to make restitution."

"And just how were you figuring on doing that? I already took what was in your wallet and you're still twenty bucks short."

"Release me and I'll get you the rest. I swear it."

"You conniving son of a bitch, you think it's going to be that easy?" With that, the sheriff spun on his heel and walked out.

Merde, Marcel cursed. He did not need this shit.

He could not know that as he lay in his narrow, lumpy bunk, Graham was tossing miserably on his own bed in the luxurious townhouse he had rented for him and his family. Not knowing when nor how they would manage the trip, not knowing if Cissy had recovered left Graham in no mood for sleep. Instead he fretted at his helplessness. The nagging pain in his leg was minor compared to the fear that permeated his heart. Punching his pillow in a futile quest for sleep, he rolled onto his back and watched the ripples on the ceiling, reflections of moonlight on the water behind the house that sat high on the bluff above the water of the Cape Fear. The river was as restless as his slumber.

Graham had arrived late in the day and walked without delay to his office. There he was greeted with surprise by the staff he had left in charge. Too many days with no supervision for important decisions had taken a toll on their nerves. Their relief was palpable when they saw him in the doorway.

"Praise the Lord, I am mighty glad to see you back. It's been a hectic time for sure with all the stuff going on with the Yankees up in the Albemarle."

"Heard they took New Berne."

"How did you get out?"

"What happened to your leg to make you limp like that?"

"You get your family out?"

Graham looked from one to the other. "I don't know who to answer first. Yes, the Yanks have New Berne, and as far as that goes, any damned thing else they've a mind to take. Our boys are out numbered, ill trained, and mostly with no proper weapons to fight them. They took New Berne in a few hours despite some hot fighting from our forces. If we don't hold on to Wilmington, this State is a goner."

"So, what happened with you and your family, sir?"

"Zeke, I had to get out before I put us all in danger. The Yankees have taken my wife's former home next door. With them on the doorstep, it was only a matter of time before they cottoned on to who I am and made me prisoner. My wife and daughter were all set to come with me but Cissy fell sick with the grippe and I had to leave them behind. It is my fervent prayer that they'll be here in a few days more."

Marsh glanced pointedly at Graham's game leg, "And that leg of yours?"

"Fell off my damned horse and broke it; had a concussion. Otherwise we would all have been here before the Union occupied New Berne. My leg's on the mend, just not back to full steam yet."

Graham paused, "Now, let's talk about what's been happening here. I want to know what ships are in port, which ones are expected, and what's scheduled to leave. I need to see the cargo manifests. Anything else I need to know, let's hear it."

Zeke replied, "Last of our ships, the Craven and the Carteret, made it out of Beaufort just in time. I seem to recall the papers said they started bombarding the fort on March 23. Last I heard Fort Macon was still under siege. But, at least we have the last two ships out of harm's way for the moment. Craven is here in Wilmington, the other down in Charleston. Having two more ought to help with blockade running."

"Unfortunately, we have no way to refit them for blockade running unless we can get them to Nassau. A better steam boiler would add some real speed. Both ships are fast hulled and very maneuverable," Graham mused aloud. "What about the last one I ordered from England, the Clyde Steamer? Is it here yet?"

"No, sir. Should be here any day though."

"Did you get Tom Burroughs to pilot it?"

"We did and the English runner, Jonathan Steele, has agreed to skipper." He knew Graham would be thrilled at that as Steele was the best runner around.

"Good. Now let's look at those manifests." Graham nodded to Marsh, "Did those guns arrive that Colonel Hedrick ordered?"

"He still don't have those Parrot guns he ordered and he's about fit to be tied."

"Can't say as I blame him. Richmond needs to get its head out of the sand and realize our ports have got to stay open or we can just go ahead and quit right now. Any one with half a brain can see that if the Yankees wanted to they could take North Carolina today. Most of our troops are in Virginia and the few left don't have the firepower to kill much more than some squirrels for supper." Graham's voice rose in anger as he continued, "What the Confederate hierarchy can't seem to see is that if they lose North Carolina, the route to supply Richmond and the army in Virginia will be in Union hands and Virginia will be cut off from the rest of the Confederacy. Once that happens, maybe they'll stop worrying about something besides fortifying Richmond. I blame that damned fool Huger in Richmond and Judah Benjamin for this mess. General Huger is scared silly the Yankees are going to sail over from Hampton Roads and shoot at him while he sits in Norfolk surrounded by 15,000 idle troops. And Secretary of War Benjamin can't seem to look past Richmond. In the meantime their actions are going to make those ends certainties. Both their heads should roll for this debacle. Losing North Carolina's sounds and the ports north of here was an unnecessary tragedy."

Graham lay in bed reviewing what he had learned that day from his men and how to utilize the resources he had to best advantage in the ever-shifting landscape of war. Graham smiled into the night when he recalled the profits he had made in Cuban coffee, molasses, sugar and fruits, all seized from Union merchant ships running off the perilous North Carolina coast. Privateering activities, sanctioned by first Ellis and then Governor Clark at Ellis's death, had proved a boon to his business and to the South. Yet with the fall of Roanoke Island the previous summer he could no longer operate from Hatteras Inlet. The other inlets he had depended on were closed as well. Only the two inlets into the Cape Fear remained. He mentally tallied his ships and their locations and plotted shipping strategies in light of the changed dynamics of the occupied waterways and increased Union threat. He did not need Governor Clark's recent letter to remind him how badly needed Cuban goods and those from Europe off-loaded in Havana and Nassau had become.

Punching his pillow yet again, he rolled onto his side and gazed out the window to the far bank of the river where tall marsh grass waved in the early dawn mist. Perhaps, he would have a telegram today from the station in Kinston telling him that his women were on the way. Cissy was young and strong. Surely her recovery would be rapid.

Hers had been, but Evangeline was miserably sick, weak from nausea, and ever aware of the fragility of the joyful burden that nestled in her womb. Having miscarried numerous times before giving birth to her late daughter, she was determined that this child of Graham's would be born healthy and full term. This would be her gift of thanks to the man who had brought love back into her life, who had given her a reason to live, a home, and a happiness that she had never hoped to know again. Lying in her bed, she curled around herself and clasped her hands over the still small mound of her belly. She would protect this unborn child with every fiber of strength she possessed and against all odds. A soft smile lit her pallid face and she prayed that this would be the son that Graham had longed for.

After a time, she struggled to half sit in her bed. Hours had passed since she had seen Cissy. The absence of one who had been so attentive to her needs was worrisome. She knew her stepdaughter was restless, her life on hold due to the war, and bored from weeks of isolation. Where could she be, Evangeline mused?

At that very moment, Cissy was beyond vexed. Of all of the people to run into, Colonel Madison was the last she wished to see. He now lived in Evangeline's house next door. She had lied as to her own domicile. He suspected her of being up to something of a clandestine nature. She surmised that meeting her so frequently was less than accidental. All in all, his continual presence was a threat and an interference with her agenda.

"Ah, excuse me, Miss LaRoque, perhaps you didn't hear me? I said fancy meeting you here."

"Fancy has nothing to do with it, sir. I find myself wondering if these meetings are less than happenstance. I most assuredly am not seeking your company."

"Ah, you wound my heart, not to mention my male vanity. I was unaware that women find me so repulsive as to scorn my company out of hand. Surely I deserve the opportunity to convince you of my stellar qualities." Ryan laughed inwardly at her discomfort.

"I suspect what you are in possession of is some considerable degree of conceit, sir. I have not sought, nor have I any desire to discover your qualities, sterling or otherwise."

Ryan laughed at her stilted reply before remarking, "That was *stellar* qualities, I believe."

"Oh, mercy," Cissy exclaimed in exasperation. "You're wasting my time. I must get home before my family begins to worry."

"My very thought. And since the day is growing late, I fear for your safety; so, I insist on accompanying you. There is not telling what kind of nefarious Yankee you might meet up with."

"Quite so." Cissy remarked with some asperity. Once again she was forced to try to outwit the man so he would not realize the actual location of her home. With her father safe in Wilmington the discovery would not carry the same hazards, yet she did not want the colonel to gain any additional information that might imperil future clandestine activities.

As they rode side by side down the river road, Cissy stewed over the dilemma of whether to admit her home and thus her father's identity or to brazen it out. In the end, it was an unnecessary worry.

A sudden gallop of hooves to their rear alerted them to another horse in hot pursuit. The man whipping the horse onward yelled, "Colonel! Colonel Madison. Hold up, sir. I got a message for you."

The jocularity faded from Ryan's face as he nodded dismissively to Cissy and wheeled his horse to meet the captain that raced towards him. He called over his shoulder, "Forgive me Miss LaRoque, duty trumps pleasure."

Not bothering to answer, Cissy spurred her horse to reckless speed and raced homeward, determined that Madison would not catch her should the man not long detain him.

"Damn, that little she-cat can sure sit a horse. Look at her go. You'd think the devil himself were after her." The captain studied Cissy's retreating back in amusement. "She sure does seem to keep turning up."

"Captain, what is the urgency?" Ryan demanded in vexation as he too watched her hasty decampment. The captain had not understated her horsemanship. She was little short of amazing on horseback.

"General wants you back at headquarters, Colonel Madison, sir. Says it's mighty important, sir."

Ryan glanced back at Cissy's rapidly vanishing figure for a lingering moment before replying, "Thank you, Captain. Any idea what's up?"

"Sir, you know the General ain't going to make no confidant out of me."

When Cissy finished with assisting her stepmother to bed, she wearily crawled between her own comforting sheets. Her mind and body were tired enough that she was soon lost in sleep, oblivious to the intrigues swirling in the air of eastern North Carolina.

As she slept, General Ambrose Burnsides paced the gas-lit parlor in high dungeon. "Damnation, between Reno and that rash upstart Colonel Hawkins, we've managed to lose the South Mills engagement. Those damned Culpepper Locks are still in Confederate hands. If the sons of bitches manage to squeeze some ironclads through there we can just pack up and leave town."

"With all due respect sir, I hear that Colonel August Wright and his Georgia boys were formidable adversaries for our forces." Ryan paused, "So, what's next?"

"We have no choice but to ignore the Dismal Swamp situation for now and press on at Fort Macon. I'm placing you on temporary assignment with General John Parke at Carolina City. We need to get that railroad bridge over the Newport River up and running again to support the General. I want to put a stopper in the line of supplies running between Morehead and Beaufort and Colonel White's forces holed up in Fort Macon. You are to act as liaison between my headquarters and

General Parke's until we can get the bridge reopened and the telegraph lines and railroad repaired.

At the same moment in Confederate headquarters in Kinston Logan listened to General Branch as the man stared intently into his eyes. "You understand the importance of this message you need to carry. It must remain confidential. Memorize it and then destroy it. From now on you will act as courier between my headquarters and those of Colonel Moses White at Fort Macon."

"He's under siege with less than 450 men, I believe?"

"Correct. His job is to hold that fort. We lose that and we lose the port at Beaufort, which will serve to make the Yankee position even more entrenched. I confess it looks like a hopeless task considering the opposition's strength in men, munitions, and battleships." Branch took a deep breath, "You have someone you can liaison with to cover your spy network while you're up in that neck of the woods?"

"I have a couple of women in mind. I'm not sure which one is best. One is older and more experienced, but she's under strong suspicion. The other, my fiancée, lives next door to a bunch of Union officers but she's green at this type of thing."

"Is she pretty?"

"Most beautiful woman you'll ever lay eyes on." Logan glowed with pride as he said it.

Branch chuckled, "Never saw a man that's a man who couldn't have his head turned by a beautiful woman. Question is: is she smart enough to fool a bunch of Yankees?"

Logan thought for a long moment while Branch fidgeted at his desk, "She's smart, sir, but, I wouldn't want to put her in harm's way any more than she already is, if it's anything too risky."

"Hmm. We've got to move our intelligence pick-up point a little further out of Union occupied territory. We need someone that can ride ten miles or so out of town, leave intelligence at a safe drop off point, and then get back into New Berne. Could this gal of yours pass for a man?"

"Up close, not in a million years. Maybe from a distance if she wore men's clothes and a hat." Logan paused, "She's a terror on horseback. It's like she and the horse become one. Never saw any woman that could ride like that."

"I think she sounds like the one to use. Let me get things in motion on this and I'll get back to you with the details. I assume you have a system for contacting her?"

"Yes, sir." Logan left the general's office wondering what he had just gotten Cissy into and what hazards the future might bring her.

In a matter of hours, Logan used the obscurity of a fog-shrouded pre-dawn morning to creep silently up to the rear door of Cissy's house. A few careful twists with a wire opened the rusty lock of the door that had never been locked prior to war and occupation. With his shoes out of sight in the hedge by the door, he crept on stocking feet up the stairs and to the closed door of Cissy's bedroom, a sanctuary of maidenhood who's boundaries he had never crossed. To do so ran counter to every propriety of his time, and he well knew it. Softly he turned the knob and stood just inside the door, now closed behind his back. For a long moment he studied her still sleeping form, imprinting it on his mind. Not knowing when he might again be with her. Not knowing if perhaps he were looking on her for the last time. With her unaware of his presence he could stare to his heart's content, let his eyes caress the lines of her body and the face that was as beautiful as an angel's in her repose.

As if sensing the nearness of another person, Cissy stirred in her sleep. Breaking his trance, Logan hurried to her side. Leaning close, he put his finger against her lips as he bent to whisper in her ear. "Wake up, Cissy. I have to talk to you and I don't have much time."

Cissy sat up in alarm, "What on earth do you think you're

doing in my bedroom? What's wrong? Is it Papa?"

"Shh. Don't wake up the household. Your father is fine as far as I know. That's not why I'm here."

"What is it?"

"Cissy, I have to go away and we need your help. The general thinks that you're our best bet to courier messages from here to our drop off point about ten miles out of town."

"Me? Ten miles? How am I supposed to do that?" Cissy was suddenly wide-awake and more than a little alarmed. "Goodness, you're serious aren't you?"

"I'm afraid so. Mrs. Pigott is under suspicion. It's too risky to use her for vital messages until things cool off a little over there. It's dangerous and I hate asking you. But, you can ride like a demon and you're a safe courier. You are still safe aren't you?"

Cissy pulled her upper lip in as she thought. The idea appealed to her desire to be involved in an important way. She debated telling him about the Yankee colonel that kept dogging her. Shaking her head, her decision made, she took his hand. "I'm fine, no problem. Now tell me what you need."

Logan simply stared at her. He heard her say something but the blood roaring in his ears drowned all but the need for her from his mind. "I love you. I want you so much. I want to hold you and stay with you and make love to you. Goddammit. I hate this war."

"I hate it, too, Logan. But it's a reality we can't change." Cissy looked into his eyes and the cold fact of the words she had uttered melted under the heat she saw there. She could not stop the words that burst from her lips. "Logan, I think I love you, too. I don't know how to feel. You were my friend for so long that it takes some getting use to you as a man, as someone I love that way. I...."

Whatever she had planned to say was stopped by lips that claimed hers, demanding an answering passion. Logan wrapped possessive arms around her pulling her against his throbbing heart. Lifting his lips from hers, he whispered, "Oh, God, forget it, Cissy. I couldn't live if something were to happen to you. It's too dangerous."

White heat filled her belly igniting a passion that squashed all but the need to feel his lips on hers, his hard body against her soft one. Wordlessly she pulled him down to her and fitted her lips to his. Lost in the kiss she could not have said when her gown had slipped from her shoulders leaving her breasts bare and aching with the need to be kissed.

Logan could not resist touching her, caressing her, even while his head was warning him to stop. Her soft moan ripped through his body eliciting a fiery heat in his groin. For a moment longer he gloried in her nearness, the feel of her and then with a strength he did not know he possessed, he pulled away.

"I want you beyond need. I love you beyond all limits of feeling, but I cannot do this. How could I leave you if I made you mine in this the most elemental way that a man can claim a woman, not knowing if you carried my child, and whether or not I will ever return from war. Just know that I will love you until the last tomorrow and then beyond."

Cissy gently withdrew from his arms and pulled her gown up to cover her nakedness. Placing her hands on each side of his face, she whispered, "I know. Just be safe Logan. Come back to me when this war is over. Come back and love me."

"Ah, sweetheart, that is my dream, my hope, and my only salvation."

Cissy drew a deep breath to calm the strange turmoil that still rage in her body, "So, tell me exactly what it is that your general wants me to do."

Fifteen minutes later, Logan left her room with the same stealth with which he had entered. Cursing the need to go, cursing the need to expose her to danger, he crept into the early light of morning. The gray fog, coating the tender green leaves of spring with droplets of moisture, suited his mood, and mimicked the tears that swam in his eyes. As he did each time he left her, he cast a silent prayer to heaven that God would see them both safely through the coming months.

Chapter 18

Graham studied the terse message, unaware that it was through Cissy's daring that it had been smuggled along with others from enemy territory to the drop off point near Tuscarora from whence it had been passed to the telegraph office in Kinston. He bit his lip in grim concentration, unsure what to do in light of the unexpected news it held. Dropping it onto his desk, he walked to the window where he stood staring at the crowded harbor that lay sparkling in the late afternoon sun. None of the scene framed by the dusty wood registered beyond his retina. A part of him wanted to sing for joy. The other part was numbingly terrified. His longing and worry for his wife and daughter hurt so much that he felt as though a knife were twisting in his gut. Counter to the pain ran a thread of unalloyed excitement and joy that his wife carried his child, perhaps even the son he had so longed for despite his love for his daughter. Even were the unborn child another girl, he rejoiced at the gift of life in a period of so much death. He rejoiced in the child that he had created through love of his new wife...a wife that had brought him happiness and peace. He could not help but question what this might mean for his family's safety when they still were firmly ensconced in enemy territory and he was bound to Wilmington. If only he could get a message through to them, perhaps even get them out of New Berne before Evangeline's pregnancy advanced to the stage of sequestration. Graham pounded his fist against the windowsill.

"Damn this misbegotten war. Will it never end and when it does, what will be left for us here?"

Zeke stuck his head around the door, "You say something, sir?"

Graham waved his hand dismissively, never turning from the window. He had to find a way to get his family out and he had to do it soon.

A few blocks away, from the window of his small cell Marcel glared at the same harbor that Graham's office window overlooked. He did not pay any more notice to the scene than Graham did. He wanted to reach Graham's family, too, and his reasons were far more nefarious. Unfortunately for him, he was unable even to cross the street much less several counties. The hostility of the sheriff had abated none at all. His prospects for release were as likely as a host of sexy naked angels singing him to sleep at night. When that imaged crossed his mind he snorted in vexation and sexual frustration. It had been days since his less than satisfactory transaction with the whore and his strong libido left him longing for a woman.

The image of Cissy LaRoque filled his mind. He would have the bitch, one way or another, and he would make her beg for more just as her whore of a mother had done. His need to conquer the arrogant girl was at least as strong as his determination to dominate her. What surprised him was that his sexual goal was nearly stronger than his quest for the LaRoque fortune. He must compromise, seduce, and if need be, abduct her. He would force her into marriage since a willing agreement seemed unlikely. The idea of forced intercourse was becoming more erotic to him than that of a complacent and accommodating woman. And he had to take her soon while she was still the only heir to the LaRoque financial empire. If he had known that Evangeline carried Graham LaRoque's child he would have been even more frantic. He had to find a way out of jail and get to New Berne before something spoiled his plans. He pounded the windowsill at this new impediment to his scheme. Cursing furiously he slashed his hand across the small table scattering the tin plate and cup left from his noon meal.

"Shut the hell up, you piss-pot," the sheriff yelled out. "You wreck that cell, I'll just add that to what you already owe me."

"Sorry, Sheriff. I tripped over the table." There was no response and he had expected none. The sheriff was a taciturn man at best.

Once more Marcel tugged at the iron bars of the window as he had done repeatedly since his incarceration. One seemed looser than the others but without tools he had no way to gouge the mortar that held it in place. Mere shaking was accomplishing nothing except perhaps as an outlet for some of his frustration.

In the weeks to come both Marcel and Graham were destined to stand at their respective windows as each repeatedly pounding his fist in frustration at the thwarting of a somewhat mutual desire: Marcel to reach Graham's daughter and Graham's desire to reach both his daughter and wife. Neither was happening. And for Graham, the inability to get to them was compounded by no further word from New Berne as to their welfare.

In the fourth week of his incarceration, Marcel woke to a gray morning without the energy to move from his lumpy cot. Although the weather was warm he shivered. His brain felt foggy and his body hot. His gut rumbled. By late afternoon his fever had risen and the cramping in his belly had intensified. When the sheriff brought his meager supper, he wearily raised his head and mumbled. "So cold. Please, a blanket."

The sheriff wasted no time backing out of the cell, knocking against the noisome chamber pot as he did so. It teetered back and forth as he watched in terror that it would tip and spill its vile contents. The last thing he wanted was to deal with a sick prisoner who could sicken him and anyone else around. He stood at the door of his office and cursed, "Dammit to hell."

Like the rest of Wilmington, he was terrified. A blockade-runner was reputed to have brought the dreaded Yellow Fever into port and it was raging through the town, killing more than a few.

Miles away, Cissy carried the basin of vomit from Evangeline's room struggling to quell the gag reflux the odor inspired in her own body. She was as frustrated as her father or Marcel. For Cissy the inability to get word to Graham was not for lack of desire. Much of her time was spent helping her stepmother. Evangeline was struggling with her pregnancy and often unable to rise from a sheet-twisted bed. Cissy could only look on with helpless anxiety and fret as to how best to extricate them from New Berne. The need to be gone became more critical with each passing day. She remembered her father's urgings to leave and regretted her obstinate refusal to see the wisdom of his words. If only they had known then about Evangeline's pregnancy...

With a death-lock on the South resulting from both the Union blockade and occupancy, food was becoming scare for the local citizenry. The LaRoque family was no exception. With daily depletion of the stores in the pantry and smokehouse, Cissy's anxiety grew. It was too soon for the garden to be of much help and the recent weather was not conducive to the effort to grow a sustaining quantity of vegetables. With coffee and other even more basic food stuffs either unattainable or too costly to buy, the LaRoque family, like all of the other locals, found themselves looking at a looming day of want and hunger.

Even the simple things like buttons, needles, and hairpins had become a luxury and women were scrupulously careful not to lose them. There would be no replacements. With the demands of soldiers at war, medicine was difficult to obtain and doctors had followed the army doing what they could to save shattered bodies leaving treatment of the citizenry to granny women and old home brewed remedies. Drapery and carpets, sheets and rags, extra pots and household implements had long since gone to the war effort. Carpets and drapery went for coats and bedrolls. Sheets and rags were torn into bandages. Metal items were melted for bullets. More and more southerners felt as though their very bones were being picked. When Cissy's gowns began to engulf her thinning figure, she thought it was no longer a mere colorful expression but was fast becoming fact.

The lack of things heretofore taken for granted was not her chief worry. How to escape to Wilmington was. The awareness of suspicion growing around her person kept her closer to home than she would have liked. Not only was the possibility of any spying and transporting of messages curtailed, but she dared not go beyond her property for fear of being harassed by the Union soldiers that seemed to be a constant presence at the end of their lane. The question of Ryan Madison's involvement in the surveillance was soon laid to rest.

Shortly after noon, with Evangeline sleeping peacefully, Cissy had slipped her horse through the woods in a route parallel to the lane in order to reach the river road where she hoped to ride north and then west to reach the drop off point. She carried two messages: one for Logan saying she had been unable to get any information for the moment due to constant monitoring of her comings and goings, and one message for her father explaining that Evangeline was still too unwell to travel. As she emerged from the sheltering trees a soldier was instantly at her side, his hand on her horse's bridle to restrain any further progress.

"Miss LaRoque, just where are you off to, ma'am?"

"Do not presume an acquaintance, mister. We have no introduction," Cissy snapped. "Besides, since when is it any of your business where I go?"

"Since I was told to see to it you don't go riding off somewhere that Colonel Madison wouldn't be too happy about."

"I fail to see how, when, and where I go can be of any

significance to your all-powerful Yankee officers. Isn't it enough that you have taken over our town, about starved us to death, and killed our men-folk? Do you have to make war on helpless women, too?"

"I purely regret all that, miss. I'm just following orders."

"You might tell your officers that my stepmother is with child and not doing well at all. I am simply trying to find our doctor for help. That is if you haven't either killed him or run him off? Now you just let go of my horse and allow me to get on with it."

"I'm mighty sorry about that, ma'am. I'll tell Colonel Ryan. We have a doctor right next door we can send over now that we know where you live. You won't be needing to ride any further."

Perplexed as to an answer and furious that they had discovered her true residence, Cissy stood glaring for long silent minutes before admitting, "She could use one even if he is a damned Yankee."

"Yes, Ma'am. I'll see to it, ma'am. Now you best be riding on back home. Don't trouble yourself to go through the woods again. I'm sure the lane is an easier route. By the way, Miss LaRoque," he paused, grinning as he added, "Those pants look mighty good on you, if I do say so myself. I nearly took you for a man, I did."

Cissy bit back the sharp retort and calmly replied, "It seems it is the safer way for ladies to travel with so many unprincipled soldiers occupying our roads. I assure you it is not my preferred attire."

"Real fetching, ma'am, whatever the reason." The soldier winked impishly, "If I thought I could get all the ladies to travel around in pants, I'd be inclined to be one of those rogues myself."

Cissy snorted for answer and tugged the horse's bridle to set him on the path home, her unanticipated escort trotting behind.

Inwardly she seethed.

Blithely ignoring her mood, the young soldier whistled in happy appreciation to be with a beautiful young woman on a spring day so balmy and soft it made his heart ache with yearning. Corporal Barney Reed was lonesome for the company of someone to talk to about something other than war and soldiering. He was lonely for a woman. He longed for a soft tender caress from a caring feminine hand. He thought he would have willingly died at that very moment for just a soft kiss, even a gentle peck on his newly whiskered cheek. Nudging his horse he moved up so that he was riding beside Cissy.

"Forgive me for saying so, ma'am, but you are about the prettiest girl I think I ever did see. I am real sorry you see me as the enemy because I would never do anything to harm you or any other woman. It's a shame things have to be this way right now. I sure never counted on being no soldier. My pa was figuring on me helping him in his store. Instead I got myself drafted and ended up here. It's a long ways from Vermont. I hate it that folks around here won't even speak to us. They'd bout as soon spit on us as give us a howdy-do."

Cissy did not respond, but he watched as some of the stiffness went out of her body. Encouraged he continued, "It's a real pretty town. I guess if I can't be home this is a good place to be. It sure beats some of the other duties I could have pulled. Not nearly as dangerous as being on the march and fighting all the time. I don't care one bit for this soldiering business."

"Then why don't you just go on back home?" There was no apology in her tone for the coldness of the inquiry.

"That would get me hung for desertion. I can't see much sense in trying that."

"I suppose not," Cissy commented. "What's your name, soldier? Since you know mine it is only fair I know who you are."

"Corporal Reed, Ma'am. Barney Reed. My friends all call me Barn. I'd be pleased were you to consider me a friend."

Cissy turned, almost blinding him with as sunny a smile as had ever been cast his way. Much to his sorrow they had reached her home and he had no excuse for lingering, as he would have liked. "I'll see to it your step-mama gets a doctor over here today. He is a real good one. I'm sure he'll have her better in no time."

"Thank you, Barn." Once again he basked in the warmth of her smile.

For a moment Cissy despised herself for the duplicity of her actions. She could not have said at what point her mother's words to her as a young child had appeared unbidden in her mind. As clearly as though it had just happened, Cissy heard them ringing in her ear. She remembered the very evening her mother had caught her listening behind the parlor door.

Monique wanted a necklace that she had admired at the jewelers. Graham had resisted her request that he buy it. The argument had raged across the supper table for over an hour before it had died with the interruption of a request from Toby for Graham to check on the new horse who seemed to have some kind of colic. When Graham returned from the stable, Monique had called him into the parlor. In his absence she had donned a lacy dressing gown in a soft pink shade that enhanced both her complexion and her curves. Handing him a glass of port, she had smiled up at him, softly brushing his arm with her breast as she did so. Cissy had not been able to hear all of their words but knew from the low sounds they made that they were kissing. She had recoiled behind the door when her father left the room whistling as he walked up the stairs, loosening his cravat as he ascended. Monique snuffed the candle and prepared to follow.

Catching sight of her daughter as she left the parlor, she laughed scornfully, "Men are easy to manage. Be sweet. Make them think they are wonderful and that you are dying for their caresses. We may be the weaker sex, but we have the strongest weapons. Smart women learn to use them."

"I don't see any weapons, Maman."

"You are such a stupid little girl. I'm not talking about guns and knives," she hissed. Monique smirked at her daughter before turning to the stairs. Cissy watched in puzzlement as her mother glided up the stairs after her father. The following evening Monique flaunted her new necklace at the supper table.

The memory had lain dormant in Cissy's mind until the soldier had ridden up beside her and begun to talk. With that long ago conversation nudging her and with an adult's comprehension, she knew what she must do to gain both information and some freedom. The soldiers were lonely: far from home, family and girlfriends, and hungry for a smile, a little flirtation, and some joy amidst the dull and thankless job of occupying New Berne. It would cost her little in the way of effort to pretend interest and encourage men like Barney to pay her some attention. In return she might be able to glean surreptitious knowledge from them that she could pass on. And, if she could allay the suspicions that had arisen in the Yankee camp, perhaps she could garner a bit more freedom to move about without being followed or turned back.

Cissy walked into the house with a spring in her step that immediately reached a thudding halt when the aroma of frying fat back assailed her nostrils. She groaned at the thought of another meal of meat that she had previous scorned. With the current shortage of food she had no choice but to eat it or go hungry. No doubt the accompaniment would be cornpone and black-eyed peas. She was sick of them, too. The unvaried fare was proving even worse for Evangeline. More often than not, her meal came up with far greater rapidity than it had gone down. Cissy looked on with helpless concern, unable to provide more appetizing fare, unable to take the gaunt, hollow-eyed look from her stepmother's thinning face.

When she walked into the sunroom, Evangeline looked up from the chaise longue where she spent most of her days. "Mama, I asked a soldier next door if they would send their doctor over to see you. He's supposed to be very good. Hopefully he can help you feel better."

"Oh, my. I had hoped our regular doctor could come out."

"It's difficult for us all to get around just now, besides, half the time he's pretty useless anyway. We might as well let the Yankees be good for something besides nuisance value. If their doctor can help, we should give it a try. At least they still have medicine that we can't get." Cissy did not want to worry her further by announcing how tightly she was being watched. It would only further add to the woman's troubles, for not only was the pregnancy a difficult one, but she constantly fretted about getting to Graham.

Evangeline blamed herself for the fact that they were isolated in enemy occupied territory. She had not foreseen their current predicament or her pregnancy. Had she left as her husband asked, they would be with him now. If they did not find a way to leave soon, it would be too late in her pregnancy to risk the rigors of getting to Kinston to catch the train for the long ride to Wilmington. As it was, she questioned whether or not she had the stamina to even attempt to leave.

"God bless, Bessie. I know she is doing the best she can but I cannot abide the smell of that pork another minute. Would you mind terribly opening the window and closing the door? Maybe that will get the odor out."

"I'm sick of it, too. Unfortunately most of our preserved food has been used up, the smoke house is about bare, and there's not a lot to be had in town even if I could get there. Both armies have scraped the countryside clean from what I hear. Toby has tried to scrounge up some game and Beulah sent over the last of the food in the pantry at your house. She says the

Yankees have so much they don't bother with the things she had on hand. She has to account for every bit of what she cooks for them for fear some of us Rebels might eat a bite of it."

"I'm sorry, darling. I don't mean to complain and I know that you are all doing the best you can. Hopefully, when we get to Wilmington, your father's ships will keep us supplied with things that are healthier for us and this baby I so desperately want."

"Your baby is going to be fine. We'll leave for Wilmington as soon as you are strong enough to make the trip." Cissy gave an encouraging pat to Evangeline's hand, "We are all going to be fine, so don't worry, Mama. Just try to get well."

"Do you think Toby could go fishing? Or maybe find some fresh greens in the woods... I'm so hungry for something different. Maybe, I could keep something else down. As it is, I can't get strong because everything we have is making me nauseous."

"I'll ask him. If he doesn't want to, I'll try myself. Logan taught me to fish years ago when we used to play by the river. I never did catch anything, but I wasn't trying to then either."

Any response Evangeline might have made was halted by a light knock on the doorjamb. "Miss Evangeline, there's a Yankee soldier here says his name is Dr. Daniel W. Hand and he's been sent over here to tend to you." Bessie stood firmly in the doorway of the sunroom, her bulk blocking the women from seeing the man behind her. Casting a suspicious glance over her shoulder she continued, "You wantin' to see this here doctor, ma'am?"

"Thank you, Bessie. Please allow Dr. Hand to enter."

Cissy patted Evangeline's shoulder reassuringly as she stood to leave. "I'll go downstairs now and leave you with the doctor."

She was sitting in the parlor pretending to read, when Dr. Hand descended the stairs and walked up to her. He did not ask permission to sit, just sank wearily into a cushioned chair near hers. Cissy raised her eyes to his in silent inquiry.

He shook his head and closed his eyes briefly, "I'm sorry, Miss LaRoque. I'm no female doctor but it seems to me your stepmother is a trifle old to be carrying a baby. She is weak and ill nourished. The best I can do is have Beulah bring over some chicken soup and crackers. Maybe she can keep that down. Mrs. LaRoque tells me that the food available here is unpalatable at best and makes her ill. What I can send may not do any better. I'll send over some ginger root and chamomile for tea to help with nausea. She's also very weak. I have heard of a granny woman remedy for strengthening the ill using a brandy mixture with egg yolk, powdered sugar and a bit of cinnamon."

"We have no chickens left since both armies long since made use of them. There's no brandy in the house, nor cinnamon, and all sugar has long since been used, powdered or otherwise." Cissy stated grimly.

"I'll have Beulah make up some brandy tonic and send it over with the chicken and rice soup. Give Mrs. LaRoque a little to see if she can keep it down. If so, two or three tablespoons a couple of time a day will help build her up." He paused, "I'll see if I can find you a few chickens and a rooster. I don't think our larder will miss a little sugar and some of the other staples you are short on. There's a bottle of brandy, or maybe two, that I suspect are going to go missing."

"We are grateful. However, if it will create difficulties for you, we of course will understand your predicament."

"Not to worry. Being the staff doctor gives me a little leeway." He rose from the chair and bowed, "You must excuse me, Miss LaRoque. Should you need anything more, don't hesitate to call on me. I confess it feels good to deal with the more normal side of human ailments after a spate of wounds and the maladies of war."

Cissy walked him to the door and smiled into his eyes with genuine warmth for his kindness. "Please, feel free to call again, Dr. Hand. You are more than welcome here anytime you need a little freedom from army life."

In the following days while Evangeline was resting, Cissy made it a point to talk with the sentry at least once daily to glean what information she could. Twice he had let slip details that she knew Logan could use. With his growing trust of her, Reed had not questioned her when she remarked about the need to take her horse out for some exercise. Despite orders to the contrary, he had let her go, gazing after her retreating back with longing.

Chapter 19

Like a torrential rain that gathers into rivulets, then runs into brooks, then into a river...all those atoms of water bound for one destination...so were the gathering forces that would determine the course of the LaRoque's lives and fortunes.

Impatient with the lack of news from his wife and daughter, Graham booked a ticket on the train to Kinston. From there he planned a circuitous route to his family, one intended to avoid his capture by the occupying forces. This time he meant to deliver his wife to safety if he had to carry her in his arms every step of the way back to the train depot in Kinston. Cissy he trusted to be able to ride or walk according to the dictates of the moment. A sudden problem with the delayed arrival of an important shipment of armaments for the increasingly stressed armies of the South postponed his departure. He was determined that it would be only a matter of days before he was on his way north. In the interim he could only pray that Logan was still conducting clandestine operations in the area and keeping a wary eye out for any threat to his family.

As Graham gazed unseeingly at the harbor awaiting the blockade-runner that should have arrived three days past, Logan was stretching his hand into the black dankness of the hollow tree praying for a message from Cissy. As on the previous four visits, his grouping fingers found nothing but decayed wood and disturbed beetles. Aware of the risk of venturing to her home, Logan shrugged his shoulders in acceptance of the possibility of a hangman's noose.

His position was tenuous at best as he operated as a spy loosely connected to General Branch's command despite the recent transfer of Branch and his troops to Virginia where he had valiantly led in the Seven Days Battle...part of the Peninsular Campaign, losing over a third of his men in the process. Logan had wanted to go fight alongside his friends and neighbors, but Branch had left him behind to garner intelligence from a regional network of spies. It was a mixed blessing for Logan. He wanted to be near Cissy. He had to know the woman he loved was safe. He had to know she did not face starvation as so many he encountered every day. He himself had notched his belt into the last hole and even that had grown loose.

The South was being brought to its knees by an empty stomach. With men gone to war, those left behind could no longer grow enough to feed themselves nor satisfy the deprivations of the armies, both friend and foe. The first round of mules and horses had long since been confiscated to carry officers or pull carts, wagons, and caissons. As they died in battle, even the old nags had been taken off to do duty until they too would fall to the fire of bullets or cannon, fatigue or starvation. Fields lay choked with weeds, un-tilled, un-planted...not that seeds were that available, had the labor been. Using what few seeds remained from the previous season's crop, families struggled to plant small gardens and jealously watched every green sprout with zealous concentration. Those tiny bits of vegetation meant the difference between survival or the gnawing pangs of hunger. Wives wrote their husbands begging them to come home and some did that spring, taking 'informal leave' to help get crops into the ground so their families could feed themselves in their absence. Generals shook their heads in frustration at the depletion of their ranks. They looked the other way knowing that their men's obligation to family carried a command and nobility that charity demanded they accept.

As Logan climbed onto his skinny mount, his mouth salivated at the idea of one of Bessie's ham biscuits even as his brain accepted the futility of the anticipation. Carefully he guided his horse through the trees and brambles, stopping often to listen. The carefree singing of birds and the quiet whisper of the wind in the trees assured him that he was safe thus far. Nearing the edge of New Berne, he grew ever more cautious. Skirting to the left of town, he rode north until he reached the river. From there he began a cautious approach on foot. The last two miles were a tough slog, the trek exacerbated by marsh, swamp, and tangled vines and brambles. Even as Logan cursed at the briars that tore his skin, the roots that tripped him, and the mosquitoes that swarmed him in a buzzing haze, he was grateful for the cover the dense undergrowth afforded. Sweat beaded his forehead and ran into his eyes making them sting. He paused to wipe them with a soiled handkerchief that had been weeks without benefit of a washing. Leaning against a tree to catch a moment's rest, Logan startled at the crackling of a nearby branch. Dropping to the ground he shimmied under a bush and waited with bated breath.

He was so near he could smell the dirty uniform of the Yankee soldier that appeared to be patrolling the perimeter of woods around the LaRoque's home. He could only hope that the soldier's nose was not as sensitive as his own for he feared his odor was no better. Logan snorted soundlessly when the soldier paused to urinate, grateful that he had aimed the stream in another direction. He would have hated to appear on Cissy's doorstep reeking of urine as well as unwashed clothes. His business finished, the soldier continued lurking about the boundary of the yard. Logan gritted his teeth with vexation at the slow progress the soldier made as he circled the property. At last the man moved to the far side of the house. Logan muttered a quick prayer followed by a curse before running like one possessed towards the safety of the kitchen door.

Marcel was running, too. Running for his very life. He had overpowered the simpleminded jailer's assistant when the boy served his evening meal. A horse standing by a hitching post in the alley down the street gave him the escape method he needed for fast decampment from the environs of Wilmington. He dared not stop at the local station and purchase a ticket for fear the sheriff would pick up his trail. Then it crossed his mind that he had not a penny in his pocket for food, ticket, or anything else. He would have preferred the comfort of a train ride, however, that was no longer an option. He was a wanted man and a horse thief. He left behind a sheriff who wanted nothing more than to arrange for him to dangle from a gibbet. He was still weak from fever and unfamiliar with the eastern North Carolina countryside, but somehow he would find his way to New Berne and that LaRoque bitch he intended to conquer.

He had lost too much time already. This time he did not intend to fail. But first he needed money and food. A game of cards was out of the question, as he had no funds with which to gamble. He had only his wits, the clothes on his back, and the stolen horse on which he rode. Staying on the edge of the road where he could quickly dart into the trees along the wayside should someone approach, Marcel made his way out of Wilmington and onto the road toward the small hamlet of Colliers. There he hoped to find food and money. He had no choice but to steal if charity was not forth coming.

Night fell before he gained the outskirts of the village. He made his way to an abandoned shed, the farmhouse nearby nothing but a hollow shell of rotted timbers crowned by jagged halo of twisted tin roofing that had collapsed inward. The rusted metal glimmered faintly in the dying light as he crawled into the dryness of the shed and leaned with disgust against the wall, his horse occupying the rest of the narrow space. He had debated leaving the horse outside but he dared not risk it being found or running off.

His stomach growled with hunger and a cramping residual discomfort brought fear his bowls would once again run like water leaving him even weaker and more fevered. The idea of dying in this God-forsaken backwater, soiled by his own feces, brought a fresh spate of cursing to his lips. He slept fitfully, grateful when the first rays of light sifted through the cracks in the crude wall.

Walking his horse out of the shed, he struggled to gain purchase on the saddle and heave himself up. His horse looked over his shoulder in silent accusation at the man who sat on his back. Almost begrudging his awareness of another creature's discomfort, Marcel realized the horse was thirsty and hungry, too. A small creek not far from the shed provided a solution for their thirst. As he rested for another assault on the saddle, the horse took the opportunity to graze on nearby grass. Sparse as it was, it was a feast for the starving beast. Marcel idly watched him snatching at the thin grass, slobbering as he masticated.

After perhaps a half hour, the Frenchman rose with great weariness and hauled himself into the saddle. It was mid-morning when he spied the ramshackle farmhouse and rode into the dirt yard. A gaunt woman stood by the clothesline, a wet dress clutched in her hands. She stared at him with hollow eyes, too tired to care who he might be or what he wanted. The thin wailing of a child broke the stillness between them.

"Beg pardon, madam. I am hungry and unfortunately without funds to pay you. I would be most grateful for any charity you could offer in the way of food." Marcel started to swing his leg over the saddle but was stopped short by her abrupt command to stop.

"You just set right there, mister. Ain't no cause for you to be gettin' down in this here yard. I ain't got nothin' for you here. Now just ride on."

"Regrettably, I cannot do that. Again, I ask you for food."

"My, ain't you a high fallutin' dandy for all you're poor." She snorted, "I'm poor, too. I need what little I got for me and my young'un. Now git."

Marcel studied her for a moment and then slid from the saddle. Striding past her he entered the house and walked over to the table where the remainder of her breakfast of cold beans and cornpone sat congealing in grease. Ignoring the naked child who sat on the bare plank floor in a puddle of urine, Marcel ate without looking up. The woman sidled into the house as he stood chewing on the cornpone. She held an old pistol in wobbly, chapped hands.

Squaring her shoulders and raising the pistol shoulder high, she barked, "I done told you to git. I don't want to have to shoot you but I will if I have to. Now you leave us be, hear?"

Moving quickly despite his ravaged state, Marcel wrest the gun from her grasp. Sticking the weapon in his belt with one hand, with the other he backhanded the woman viciously across the jaw, watching with satisfaction as she crumpled to the floor. The child stopped mid-sniffle and gaped open-mouthed at this stranger and his mother's still form. Shoving the child out of his way with a booted foot, Marcel quickly scoured the kitchen for food. He snatched a threadbare pillowcase from the narrow bed in the corner and stuffed left-over cornbread and a slab of fried fatback into the bag. Looking around the room, he noted a cracked teapot on the mantle. Instinct told him to look inside. Greedy fingers closed around a few Confederate notes and a gold piece. He wasted no time stuffing them in his pocket. Casting a final look around the dingy room, he left just as the woman began to make whimpering sounds. He noted that he had not killed her, even though it mattered little to him one way or the other. It did not bother him that she and her child were one of thousands in the forgotten byways of the rural south that were faced with starvation and deprivation, poverty and hopelessness, ever at the mercy of the marauding armies and renegades, ever fearful of surviving, and almost despairing of doing so.

Marcel rode from the dingy shack gloating. He had a loaded pistol, a gold piece and food. Another such visit or two and he would find himself with enough money for a good game of poker, a bath, and then a new suit of badly needed clothes. His proclivity for elegant clothing, and a fastidious nature, demanded a mien appropriate to one of his high aristocratic breeding. It never dawned on him that the honorable men that were his forebears would have been disgusted could they have lived to see such a pompous, cruel, callous, and degenerate wastrel besmirching their proud name. He trotted past Collier calling no more attention to himself than the bark from some hound in a dirt yard too lazy to do more than idly scratch an errant flea or two. He rode through Richland and found nothing to delay him. No restaurant, hotel, or tavern beckoned.

About five miles beyond the village, he decided to explore a lane that led down a winding path through fields that lay fallow on either side. Just around a wooded bend he saw a curl of smoke rising from the chimney of a modestly large house. Marcel swung down from the saddle and walked the horse into a stand of trees where he tied him to the branch of a small dogwood tree. From there he cautiously approached on foot, staying well within the obscuring shadows of the trees. There was no sign of activity in the neatly swept yard, not even the ubiquitous hound. Hunkering down, he waited for some sign of activity. The only change was the sudden lighting of a lamp in the darkening windows of the house. Creeping forward, he cautiously approached, the only untoward noise the sudden clucking of a chicken scratching near the side of the porch.

Sidling up to a window, he peered through. The only inhabitant appeared to be an elderly woman who had just settled down at the table to eat her evening meal. He watched as she bent her head in thanksgiving, her lips moving as she prayed. Emboldened by her solitude, Marcel quickly stepped onto the porch and knocked.

Long minutes later, the woman called tremulously through the stout planks of the door, "Who is it?"

"Forgive the intrusion, madam. I find myself on the road without hope of a place to spend the night, or of a meal to sustain me. Would you be so kind as to accommodate my modest needs for the night? A bite of food and a pallet in your barn would suffice."

"You're welcome to bed down in the barn. As for the food, I have precious little, but I will put something on a plate and set it down on the porch."

"I'm in your debt, madam."

Several minutes passed before she again called through the door. "You step on back in the yard yonder and I'll slide this plate out onto the porch. When you're through eating, put it back by the door and go on to the barn and settle down. Light comes, you best be gone from here."

"Indeed I will. You are most kind." Marcel did as instructed. When he stepped back onto the porch to fetch the plate, it was a pleasant surprise to find a piece of chicken, a biscuit, and some green beans on a china plate. Standing by the side of the plate was a glass of milk. He would have preferred a good French wine but that would have signaled his arrival in an unexpected heaven that he had no reason to anticipate. Taking his meal to the side of the porch, he settled himself on the edge letting his feet dangle. He was surprised at the toothsome quality of the simple supper. When he had finished he carried the utensils to the door and set them down, calling a thank you to the woman.

There was no reply. Shrugging his shoulders he left the porch to fetch his horse. Finding a water trough by the barn, he let the horse drink his fill. In the dim twilight, he could just make out a mound of reasonably fresh hay inside the barn. Marcel unsaddled the horse and used the saddle blanket to make a crude bed in the edge of the hay. Long before the first stars twinkled beyond the barn door, he was fast asleep. His only companions in slumber were his weary horse, a cow who took no notice of either of them, and a tabby cat that rubbed against the sleeping man's shin before stalking away in disdain.

As the first rays of dawn stole on furtive footsteps through the weathered door, gray from years of mornings...years of sun, and rain...Marcel shifted on the straw. The slight stirring of dust made him sneeze. He sat up in blinking awareness of the new day and new opportunities. He wasted no time saddling the horse and leading him back to the edge of the swept dirt yard. From the vantage point of the same dogwood tree that had earlier held the reins, he studied the house once more. It was still quiet and dark, the old woman still sleeping he hoped. Once more he crept to the house. Silently he slipped his boots from his feet. With great caution he raised the window. It was easy to haul himself through and slide unheard onto the smoothly waxed floor. He stilled his body and took shallow breaths to better detect any movement from the nearby bedroom. When the only sound to break the stillness of the early morning was the cheerful chirping of the birds, Marcel stood.

Getting his bearings in the strange room, he looked around for anything that might be useful to him. Despite the neat and prosperous appearance, nothing caught his eye. Turning to the larder, he surveyed the contents and surmised that he would not starve on the next leg of the journey. The old woman had food and enough to spare. A pity, he thought, that there was no obvious money.

"*Sacre bleu,*" he muttered. "She doesn't live this way on nothing."

Walking to the silent darkness of the bedroom door, he

entered. "Hey, old woman. Wake up."

The still form in the bed stirred feebly. "What. What do you want? Who are you?"

"Who I am doesn't matter. I need money and it appears you have some. Give it to me and I'll be on my way."

The old woman sat up, the sheet clutched to her thin breasts, "I have no money for the likes of you. I remember now. I let you stay here last night, and out of Christian charity, fed you. And this is the way you repay my kindness? You barge into my house uninvited, invade my bedroom, and then demand my money. If my sons were here, you'd be a dead man by now."

"Your damned sons aren't here, old woman. I am. Now where is the money? Give it to me and I'll be on my way."

"I told you I have no money," her voice pitched higher on a note of desperation.

Ignoring her, Marcel walked over to the chest and began tossing the contents onto the floor. Finding nothing, he proceeded to up-end her trunk, watching with disgust as the old woman's worthless mementos spilled onto the woven rag carpet. Furious that she would defy him, he turned to the bed. He barked, "Get up, you damned bitch."

She stared at him in terror, too frightened to move.

"I said get the hell up."

Impatient with her feeble struggles to rise, he grabbed her by the arm and yanked her from the bed. He was surprised by the lightness of the woman as she drooped against him. "Where is your money? Tell me and I'll leave you in peace."

Terrified, she could only stutter incomprehensibly.

Marcel was furious and impatient. If she had money he would find it, with her help or without. A vicious punch to the woman's head knocked her senseless to the floor. She jerked spasmodically as a rattle of air left her lungs, and then lay still. Without bothering to check, he knew she was dead.

He searched for an hour and was ready to give up when the

rug on which he was standing seemed to have some flex in the boards underneath. Snatching the rug back, he bent down and felt with his fingers. As he pried, a board began to move. Pulling it up, he reached into a cavity in the floor and withdrew a woman's purse. The clinking of coins was as sweet to him as any music he had ever heard. Inside he was pleased to find over fifty dollars in gold pieces. His immediate financial worries were finished. Pocketing the coins, he hastened to the larder and grabbed the few items of food that he could carry with him. If he needed more before reaching New Berne, he would stop and buy something with his new wealth.

The little agrarian village of Ordinary seemed to deserve its name as best Marcel could tell on his canter through. Although the food in the saddlebag was not the preference of his French palate it was sufficient to keep hunger at bay. That being the case, he saw no need to waste time in the unappealing little hamlet. He would have preferred arriving in New Berne with decent clothes, but time was critical and the likelihood of finding suitable attire in Ordinary was remote. He camped that night not far from the town of Trenton. He thought of riding into the small town nestled on the banks of the Trent River, but it was a detour and he was in no mood to add to the length and discomforts of his trip. The sooner he reached some greater semblance of civilization the happier he would be. As he tossed on his crude bed on the grass, he pondered how best to escape with his intended bride. Again the thought of money and the need for more occupied his mind. Even if he succeeded in marrying her, how was he to obtain her father's fortune? And how was he to carry out his plans in the interim.

His horse cast him a baleful glance the next morning. He was apparently as sick of his new master as his master was of the necessity for the stolen horse. With no oats, meager grass, and only occasional stops for water and rest, the horse had been ill used. That was of no moment to Marcel. For him the horse was good for one thing: transportation to New Berne. Once there the animal could die in his tracks for all he cared. Digging vicious heels into the horse's sides, he forced him into a reluctant canter on the final stretch of his journey. So far, Marcel considered it uneventful. He had not been recognized or questioned as to his identity and purpose during any of the long miles. With his destination a mere few hours away, he grew ever more confidant. He devised an agenda as he rode. Marcel smiled with pleasure at the first item, a bath in the Gaston House Hotel followed by a shopping expedition in the local haberdashers. Then back to the tavern at the hotel where he intended to find a few soldiers eager to lose their government pay. Once he had the funds he considered necessary for the completion of the initial stage of his plans, he would seize Cecily LaRoque. Again a smile creased his face as he contemplated taming his little tigress. Soon she would purr for him just like her mother.

Chapter 20

With the practiced insouciance of a true dandy, Marcel delicately flicked a speck of lint from the sleeve of his new jacket. He was annoyed at the news he'd just learned over a game of cards, although he dared not show it in public. Even the pot of money he raked into his saddlebag could not relieve the fiery anger that seared like a hot iron. Mastering the rage that threatened to overwhelm him, he forced himself to smile as he rose from the table.

"Please excuse me, sirs. I fear the day had been a long one and I must retire. Perhaps, tomorrow we can play again so you gentlemen have the opportunity to recover your losses."

The men stared at his retreating back. None of the looks were friendly. He was too formal, too suave, too European, and just a little too confident for their tastes. Had they realized how thoroughly they had been bilked, his life would have been worth little. Hardened in battle and bored at being stationed in this remote southern town far from the action of Virginia's battlefields, they would have welcomed a foe to thrash, even if it were a lowly card-cheat. As it was they saw only an arrogant, conceited foreign popping-jay who played a lucky game of cards.

Marcel ignored their palpable animosity as he strode to the door. He needed the coolness of the evening air to quiet his nerves. Outside only one thought consumed his mind: the bitch's stepmother was pregnant. The good doctor he had just made considerably poorer had chatted idly about the woman he had recently treated and her comely stepdaughter. Now he had to not only marry Cissy, but must eliminate both her father and the stepmother. Always Marcel had known that delay meant complications. Once again the adage had proven true. Added complications meant added risks. That he did not like. Could he have been in the LaRoque's kitchen at that moment he would have been livid.

Logan sat at the table holding Cissy's hand. While the meal he had just finished was filling, the cornbread and fatback could not compete with the biscuits and ham he had longed for. That no longer mattered. He was with the woman he loved and all he wanted to do was to make time stand still.

"Will you marry me then, Cissy? You say you love me and God only knows I have loved you forever. Must we wait?"

Cissy raised trouble eyes to his. He held his breath not knowing if he wanted her answer or feared it. He was no fool. He understood and accepted the obstacles that lay ahead. In the middle of war with both of them spying on the enemy, their prospects for survival were increasingly dim.

"This is no time for us to talk of this. We don't either one know if we will even be alive tomorrow. You have risked your life to come here and you are going to risk it again leaving. I have to get Evangeline to Wilmington if I can. With a baby on the way and her health precarious, I dread even thinking about it. I can only think how desperate I would be if I were in her situation. If I were carrying your child and you were far away, if I had no way of knowing if you were even alive, if you would be there to care for us, if there would be enough food to feed a child..." Cissy swallowed hard and continued, "It's too much to think about, Logan. It's just too much."

Logan watched the tears well into her eyes and spill onto her cheeks. Leaning forward he licked each salty tear with his tongue, whispering soft words of solace. "It's okay, darling. I know. I do know. I just want so much for life to be normal. I'm so tired of living in the woods like some kind of animal: hunted, lonely, cold and hungry. This is no life for either of us. I understand that this isn't easy for you either. I wish I could make magic and suddenly everything would be right again."

Cissy gave a rueful smile. "I wish you could make magic, too. Unfortunately, you can't. When the war is over, promise me you'll come back and ask me again?"

"God willing, Cissy. God willing." With great reluctance Logan reached for his hat. "I have to leave. I wish I could stay but I can't. It's too dangerous for both of us."

"I know. Before Evangeline and I go, I'll still try to find out what I can about the enemy and leave it in the drop off. At least, until I figure out someway for us to leave, I can be useful."

Logan shook his head, "No! Don't even try. Don't you see it's too dangerous now with them watching you? You are under too much suspicion. I have others that I can turn to for information. You've done enough. The important thing now is to try to get you both to Wilmington. I've not heard anything from your father, but I am sure he must be trying, too. Has he sent you any message?"

"Nothing; and I don't know if mine got through telling him about the situation here. Right now, Evangeline is too ill to move so there isn't much we can do. As soon as she's better I'll try to get passes through the Union lines so we can leave. I've made friends with some of the Union officers so maybe they will help me. Flirting with them is how I have been getting information for you. The sentry has been pretty lax about letting me slip past."

Jealous anger threatened his emotional control. Fighting it, Logan snorted, "And that is supposed to comfort me? It's hard enough to leave you here surrounded by damned Yankees. The last thing I want to imagine is you flirting with the enemy, information or not. Just quit it, please. Stay away from them. And run, Cissy, run away from here the first chance you get. It's no good you two staying here. The minute Miss Evangeline can travel you get that pass. Wilmington is much better for you than here."

Chagrined by his righteous concern, Cissy nodded. "I know. She does seem to be improving with the medicine that Yankee doctor gave her. Hopefully in a day or two we can leave. I can try to slip a message to you to let you know we have gone."

"No need, I can find out through other and safer methods. You don't need to risk it. Just get to Wilmington as quickly as you can. Promise me." He did not want to even think about the possibility that they would be unable to book passage on the train. That, however, was increasingly the case as the army needed every inch of capacity for carrying troops and supplies.

"Of course I promise."

"Now, kiss me good bye, Cissy darling, before I begin playing hide and seek with your Yankee watchdogs."

Cissy stepped into his embrace and turned her lips to his, startled by the whirlwind of emotions and need that engulfed her. Just when she thought the kiss would end, they both lost themselves in sensation once again. Her knees weakened and she clung to him shaken by the indefinable need that consumed her. She had heard that passion between a man and a woman could be a powerful thing. The relationship between her father and stepmother had hinted at that. But never had she felt such a sexual awakening and demand for fulfillment.

"Ah, Cissy, I could stay here forever kissing you. I love you. Be safe, my darling girl."

"I love you, too. And you be safe. You are in far more danger than I am." Reaching up she caressed his cheek as he stepped from her arms.

"I'll see you in Wilmington." Logan smiled in farewell before slipping into the shadows of the porch. There he lay silently waiting for the watchman to make his pass around the perimeter of the yard.

Cissy watched as he raced from one concealing shadow to

another before being swallowed by the enveloping darkness of the forest. The hands that she had clutched in nervous tension relaxed. She did not have the luxury to linger longer. It was past time to give her stepmother her medicine and a bite of supper.

She beamed as Evangeline finished the last of her meal. By the flickering light of the candelabra, she could see that the woman already looked stronger. "It's so good to see you feeling better again. Hopefully you won't be sick anymore and we can go to papa."

"My sweet girl, let's pack tomorrow. I think with your help, I can do it. We've been here far too long already and I confess I miss your father terribly."

"I miss him, too. But are you sure you're ready for that kind of journey. You realize we will have to ride by horseback from here to the depot in Kinston. That's over thirty miles."

"Heavens, Cissy, I grew up on a horse. We can take our time if I need to rest, but I don't want to have to spend the night somewhere. I do know some people in Dover if we must stop for the night. I'm sure they will take us in if need be. Somehow I'll manage. And I really do feel much better. I think that Yankee medicine is helping after all." Evangeline reached over and patted Cissy's hand. "Stop fretting. I'm going to be fine. Now, see if you can arrange passes for us to get through the Union lines and we'll leave. Perhaps that colonel next door would help."

"Are you very sure you're strong enough? Papa would never forgiven me if I endangered you in anyway."

"By the time you get those passes, I'll be fit as a fiddle. You stop worrying about me, dear."

The following morning after a vastly improved Evangeline joined her for breakfast, Cissy walked across the lawn and followed the well-worn path she had used since childhood through the woods to her stepmother's former home. The soldier that was patrolling the yard glanced her way as she crossed into the woods, but seeing the direction, had not followed her. As she emerged from the woods on the far side, another sentry walked over to her.

"Excuse me, miss. May I ask why you're here?" He doffed his hat and grinned at the pretty woman, hoping that she would smile in return, unlike the other local women who merely sneered at him when he tried to be friendly.

Cissy did not disappoint. "Good morning. I would like to speak to Colonel Madison if he's still here?"

"He is, but he won't be for long. Come with me and I'll take you to the house."

"Thank you very much, but I see that won't be necessary."

The soldier turned to look where she indicated with a nod of her head. He remarked, "Best hurry on over before they bring his horse around."

"I will. Thank you." Again she flashed him a beaming smile. The warmth of it lingered in the air as she walked hurriedly down the path to the front piazza where Ryan Madison stood waiting.

Ryan watched her as she came up the walkway, happy to see a beautiful woman and looking forward to her wit. She never failed to amuse him. He chuckled to himself when she gave him the benefit of a huge smile, wondering what it was she wanted from him, for surely she wanted something. She had not been quite so friendly on previous encounters.

Forcing a stern tone to his voice, he demanded, "Well, Miss LaRoque, what brings you over this beautiful morning? You're not out information gathering are you?"

Ignoring the comment, she responded, "It is lovely, isn't it? But, then we are blessed with an excellent climate here, I think. Except, of course, in the middle of summer when it is so very warm unless there is some wind." Cissy continued to chatter, nervous about the possibility that he might refuse to help. He said nothing.

An impatient glance from him toward the stable, caused her to blurt out, "I suppose I have interrupted you on some mission or other, and I do apologize. However, I wanted to thank you and the doctor for the medicines for my stepmother. She is much improved."

Ryan glanced over his shoulder as the orderly brought him his horse. Turning back to her, he smiled. "Normally nothing would please me more than to enjoy your company and your unanticipated appreciation of my Yankee self, however, General Foster has requested my urgent presence this morning. His order takes precedence over my pleasure at your unexpected company. I'm going to have to ask you to excuse me." Ryan was amused by the stricken look that flickered across her face. He doubted that it was his charm that made her want more of his time, as she had previously seemed impervious to that. Taking the horse's reins he swung into the saddle with practiced eased.

Cissy grabbed the horse's bit. "Wait. Please, I need to ask you something."

She looked up into his eyes as he waited for her to continue. "You realize the situation we are in here. I need to get my stepmother to Wilmington so we can join my father. She doesn't want to be in New Berne when the baby comes. Could you get us a pass to get through your lines?"

Ryan hesitated in his reply as he enjoyed the sudden spark of sexual awareness that blazed between them. Seeing that she was rattled by his smoldering regard, Ryan broke eye contact as he assured her, "Of course. While I will miss your reluctant company, it is much for the best that you go to your father where he can curtail your curiosity about our Yankee doings. I fear, that were you to stay here, I would be visiting you in the Pollock Street jail at some point. The sentry says you have been a good girl lately, but we can't count on that lasting, now can we?"

He could not resist teasing. Even so, his worry was a genuine one. Calling his orderly over, Ryan said, "Sgt. Porter, would you take Miss LaRoque inside and arrange for her to get a pass. When she is ready to go, send Corporal Reed with her until she and her stepmother are safely through our picket lines."

Turning back to Cissy, he smiled, "I must say I will miss you. But, it's wise for you ladies to go. Don't worry about your home. I will see to it that it comes to no harm."

"Thank you so much, Colonel." Tears of relief welled into her eyes.

"Good bye, Miss Cissy. Good luck and safe journey. Perhaps we will meet under more pleasant circumstances someday."

Ryan rode away thinking that New Berne had just become a little less pleasant with the loss of his lovely protagonist. He would miss seeing her no matter how sporadic it had been.

Cissy lingered on the path watching him ride down the lane before turning to follow the sentry into the house to receive the promised pass. She liked Colonel Madison and despite her deepening regard for Logan, she felt an undeniable attraction for the man. His looks were nothing to discount, but it was more than that. She appreciated his humor and wit, his confident masculine demeanor. And while disconcerting, his frank sensuality enticed her.

In the dining room where she had first met Madison, several officers were chatting with excitement. Left alone to await someone to help her, she could not resist drawing near to listen. The information she learned was urgent. One last time she must slip past the sentry to get it to the hollow tree in hopes that Logan would check once more for a message from her.

The pox-marked officer that helped her chatted interminably, determined to enjoy the pleasure of looking at her and being with her as long as possible. She was irritated at the delay and eager to deliver this new information that could prove vital to the South. It galled her to have to flirt and indulge in meaningless repartee with the man. Twice she had nearly opened her mouth to hurry him up before prudence took over and cautioned her not to antagonize him. Had he not been called elsewhere, Cissy had no idea how long he might have detained her. The summons spurred him to action. When he handed her the pass, she stuttered a hasty 'thank you' before scurrying from the room.

Cissy forced herself to walk when what she really wanted to do was run hell for leather. She forced herself to smile at the waiting sentry and warn him that her horse was restless from being stabled. Prettily she wheedled him into allowing her the freedom to leave the premises in order to exercise her horse. Cissy yelled to Toby to saddle the mare as her heels hammered a rapid staccato on the stairs. Wasting no time, she was soon attired for riding and as the weather warned of autumn, she wheeled back long enough to grab a short jacket. The hasty kiss and implausible explanation she tossed to Evangeline took mere seconds.

Not long after Cissy rode away. Trouble rode in. Marcel paused in the path leading to the LaRoque home, gloating that in a mere matter of time he would own the house and all that entailed. Clucking his horse forward, he rode to the hitching rail and alit onto the brick surround of the piazza. He checked himself in the reflective panels of the windows on either side of the door. His suit was perfect. He looked much younger and far more prosperous than he ever had thanks to that old lady's money. Satisfied with his reflection, he lifted the heavy brass knocker. Thus he set into motion the culmination of all of his scheming.

Feeling the best she'd felt in weeks, Evangeline was the one to answer the door. Astonishment that he had evaded the sentry and walked to the front door was plain on her face. She had no way of knowing that Corporal Reed was one of the men at the card table the previous evening and thus knew Lambert.

"Mr. Lambert. Good day to you. What brings you into our midst once again?"

Bowing formally, Marcel declared, "I have come at the behest of your husband. He is most concerned for his family's safety and since I, as a Frenchman and a non-combatant, can travel more freely than he, he asked me to fetch you back to Wilmington for him."

Confused that Graham would have asked this reprobate to accompany them south to safety, Evangeline hesitated to reply. Nor did she invite him in.

Locked in her calm gaze, Marcel fidgeted. Hastily he explained that leaving immediately was the only option open to them. Glancing pointedly at the rounding mound of her abdomen, he repeated the need for departure. Evangeline listened in silence giving no clue to her thoughts. Trying a different tack, he inquired if Cissy were at home. Evangeline just continued her mute stare.

He asked himself what was the problem with the stupid bitch. Surely she didn't want to stay in an occupied town when she had been offered a chance to rejoin her husband and deliver her baby at a safe distance from enemy lines. He wanted to reach out his hands, wrap them around her throat, and strangle her for being so unresponsive. Shoving his hands in his pockets to prevent such volatile action, he took a deep breath and cautioned himself to stay calm.

Despite the curb on his temper, he felt his face turn red with frustrated anger. Marcel took a deep breath. If necessary he could simply kill her on the spot and then deal with the others. The appearance of the sentry on the far side of the lawn scotched that plan. He could not afford to do anything until he had them on the road from New Berne and well beyond prying eyes. Once on his way to Kinston, he would see to the woman.

There were many dark roads and murky swamps on the thirty-mile journey. Disposing of her would be no problem. Then he would see to the bitch of a stepdaughter.

"Beg pardon, madam. It seems I have called at an inopportune moment." Marcel bowed and left.

Evangeline stood at the door watching him ride down the path. She didn't know why, but she had shivered the minute she laid eyes on him and comprehended in some intuitive way that he was a villain. She was glad Cissy had not been at home. The offer of a safe passage to New Berne under his aegis might have appealed to Cissy considering the girl's current state of boredom and frustration. Evangeline wanted to go as well, but the man's offer was unsettling for reasons she could only intuit but not name. It seemed incomprehensible that the Graham she knew would have entrusted them to the likes of Marcel.

Chapter 21

He was grateful for the good fortune that led to the unexpected encounter.

"I don't believe you! My father would never have sent you to escort us to Wilmington. What on Earth makes you think you can get away with telling me that? Why? Why would you even want to in the middle of a war? Why not just go back to France?" Cissy glared at Marcel. "Now get out of the way, I have some business to attend to."

Marcel studied the young woman with cold dispassion. If he could not con her into willingly going with him, coercion was his only alternative. "Unfortunately, my dear, my business takes priority over yours. Now hand me the reins of your horse and come along like a good girl."

"You go to Hades! I told you I am not going anywhere with you." Cissy snatched the reins hard to the right to wheel her horse away from him, digging in her heels as she did so. She was determined to get the information she carried to the drop off point. The mare leapt forward leaving Marcel gaping after her.

He damned her under his breath as he spurred his own horse to the chase. The little mare was no match for the new horse he had purchased. In a matter of moments he drew abreast of her and snatched the reins from Cissy's hands, leveling his pistol on her at the same time. Giving a diabolical cock to his right eyebrow, he snarled, "I have no desire to harm you, so don't force me."

Not bothering with a reply, Cissy frantically plotted her

escape. If he took her back to the house, the guard would come to her rescue. She had only to cry out. Why had he really come for her and her stepmother? No matter which direction her thoughts turned during the ride through the woods in the direction she had just come, nothing made sense.

When he jerked her horse to a stop a half-mile from her home and ordered her down, Cissy refused. Wasting no time on argument, Marcel reached up and yanked her from the mare. Despite her scream of protest, he hauled her to a small tree and securely lashed her hands around it. He warned her to keep her mouth shut if she knew what was good for her. When she promptly screamed, Marcel tied a gag around her mouth leaving her struggling in mute protest as he rode away.

She had never been more frightened in her entire life. Not knowing if he meant to leave her there for animals to ravage, not knowing his intentions at all, Cissy strained against the rope to free herself. When her wrists were raw with abrasions and she had managed to only pull the knot tighter, she sank to her knees with frustration. The beauty of the day was lost on her as golden leaves drifted about her head and squirrels scurried about hoarding for winter. Exhausted from her efforts to free herself, she sank further against the ground, glad to find it dry and padded with wind-dropped foliage. Perhaps she dozed, she could not have said, but when conscious thought returned day was fading, and her hope of rescue along with it. Over and over, she tried to determine his motives for abducting her. And, where and what was he up to now? And, always nagging at her mind was the need to get that vital message to Logan. The Confederates must be prepared for what the Yankees had planned. Perhaps, she alone held the key to averting an attack. Thinking that, she jerked once more against the restraining ropes only to be rewarded with pain and a slow trickle of blood at her wrists.

Again Marcel had smoothly talked his way past the naive

Barney and knocked on the door of Cissy's home. Against her better judgment, Evangeline had opened it to him only to find a pistol shoved into her stomach with a curt order to start packing. Now she was scurrying to cram the few items he allowed for her and Cissy into one small valise. At her every hesitation, he waved the pistol to hasten her on. With her heart pounding a steady staccato and her hands shaking, it was no easy matter to pack the essentials.

Taking a deep breath, Evangeline cautioned herself to stay calm for her own sake, as well as, that of her baby and her stepdaughter. Fearing an interruption by Toby or Bessie that could put their lives in danger, she dared to confront him, "Mr. Lambert, I don't know your motivation for this outrageous behavior, however, I must warn you that their are others on the premises. My servants could interrupt at any moment, and there are also the soldiers that are guarding the house for you to worry about. Why don't you simply leave here and let's forget this unpleasantness? I will not file charges against you. I promise. Furthermore, you can see I am in no condition for arduous travel. I beg you, show some compassion for our welfare."

He did not trouble himself with a reply, just nodded his head at the valise and pointed the gun at the door as a directive to exit. Taking her arm in a vise-like grip that made her wince with pain, Marcel jerked her out the bedroom door and down the steps.

"Say one word of warning, madam, and you are a dead woman," he growled in her ear.

Evangeline nodded her head in agreement and kept her eyes down as he smoothly talked their way past the guard. Of all the times for the guard to allow unquestioned egress, she grumbled to herself, he would choose this one. Even Toby, at her command to quickly saddle her horse, did not question why she would be leaving with Marcel Lambert.

Toby had not challenged the request because he had glimpsed the outline of the gun pressed into her side despite the Frenchman's effort to hide it beneath his coat. It would do no good to get them both shot. When he had tightened the girth of the saddle, Marcel ordered Toby to help the woman up. He caught Evangeline's eye as he obeyed the terse command, waggling an eyebrow and shifting his gaze in Marcel's direction as he did so. He hoped she would get the message that he understood she was being forced to leave. She knew him well enough to comprehend that he would get help as soon as they were out of sight.

And he would have, except for the unexpected blow to the back of his head that sent him crashing unconscious to the stable floor. Evangeline gasped in shocked disbelief at the violence inflicted on the man and could only pray he was not dead. Even more terrified by Marcel than she had been before, she griped the pommel of her saddle with knuckles whitened from the pressure of her grasp. She prayed that Bessie or Cissy would find Toby and help him, and then get help for her. Once again, she wondered what was keeping Cissy.

Cissy was at that moment sitting on the ground with her limbs asleep from her cramped position. She shifted as best she could to ease the aches and wondered for the millionth time how long it would be, or even if, Marcel would return for her. Despite the lengthening shadows that advertised the coming of dusk, her thirst, her hunger, and her utter misery, she decided she preferred to face the perils of the night rather than to deal with what could only be his evil intentions.

The noise of someone approaching gave her sudden hope that rescue was at hand. When Marcel rode into the clearing leading Evangeline's horse, her heart sank with dread. Evangeline was still far too frail for such rough treatment and the truth of it showed in every line of her body and the stiff concentration in her face. It was obvious that it took every ounce of her strength just to sit in the saddle without toppling over.

"Oh, Cissy, what has he done to you. You poor darling." Evangeline forgot her own fears and weariness at the sight of her beloved stepdaughter who struggled to stand by sliding up the rough bark of the tree to which she was securely tied. The frantic look in Cissy's eyes mirrored her own despair.

Turning in the saddle, she appealed to Marcel, "Oh, please, undo her. We are no danger to you. We have no weapons and we wouldn't know how to use them if we did. Won't you please untie her?"

Marcel didn't know what to do. He was in the middle of the woods, miles from habitation, food, and water. He had considered none of that in his hasty abduction of the two women: one pregnant and obviously unfit for travel, and the other young and rashly impetuous. While he felt little concern for Evangeline's welfare, he had to keep Cissy in his control until he could bind her and the LaRoque fortune through matrimony. For the time being, the older woman was a useful tool in controlling Cissy. When that ceased to be the case, she was expendable. Future plans did nothing to ameliorate the discomfort of the moment. With nightfall, the shortsightedness of his preparation was readily apparent. He could not seek shelter from a nearby homestead with two abducted women, and he had not brought the supplies necessary for roughing it in the woods. With only saddle blankets to protect them from the ground, the night chill seeped readily into his bones increasing his irritation and the misery of cold and hunger.

Cissy and Evangeline were cold and hungry, too, and added to that was the terror of a man capable of unknown violence and evil. When he finally settled into sleep, the two women nested close to one another for shared body warmth.

Softly, not even sure that Cissy was awake, Evangeline began to whisper to her. "If I don't make it through this, I want you to know how much you have meant to me, you and your father both. When I met you that summer day when you were just a little girl, I was empty of life. I felt like a shell on the beach abandoned by the living thing that it had once held and just existing at the mercy of the elements that buffeted me. Little by little, from that day on I began to come alive. And then, I fell in love with your father. The happiest day of my life was when he told me that he loved me, too. You made me a part of your family and gave me back my life. Your love filled me with joy and renewal. Now I'm carrying this baby and I so want it to live. I pray to survive this for my child's sake, but if I don't, you must remember that I am so grateful for these years together and you must tell your father for me that my love for him is for eternity."

Holding back a sob, Cissy murmured, "Please, don't talk that way, Mama. We're going to make it. I am and you will, too. Toby will send someone to help us."

"Toby was struck down. We can't know if he is even alive."

"Bessie will know something is wrong when we weren't there for dinner. She will tell the Yankee soldiers. They'll find us." She could not bear to hear Evangeline talk of death. The pain of that possibility on top of the pervasive terror of what they might face at Marcel's hands, was too much. She squeezed her eyes shut as though she could squeeze from her mind the idea that Evangeline losing her life might come to fruition. When Evangeline did not immediately answer, Cissy hoped that she had fallen asleep. She did not want to talk of these things.

After several minutes, her stepmother took a deep breath before continuing, "I hope you are right. But if not, you are young and strong. You must get through this. If you can escape this evil man, do it and don't worry about me. I don't have the strength to keep up and I would only hold you back. I have no proof, but I believe it's you he's really after. I think I'm just a nuisance. He'll use me to try to control you because he knows I am too weak to be a danger. Be brave, darling. Get away somehow."

Evangeline drew Cissy into her arms. "Promise me."

"I can't just leave you."

"Yes, you can and you must if the opportunity arises. Now, promise me. You run, Cissy. You run as hard as you can."

Reluctantly Cissy nodded her head. "I promise, but I will find help. You are going to make it, too. *You must promise me that.*"

"I will try my very best, darling. I promise." Evangeline put all of the fervor she could muster into the pledge, but she doubted her body was equal to the challenge demanded by her heart and the stubborn insistence of her stepdaughter.

Grateful for the layers of clothing and shared body warmth that provided meager solace, and ignoring the discomfort of bound limbs, they finally drifted into fitful sleep.

The thin light of dawn sifted through brown-tagged branches as birds began to sing in the day. Cissy was the first to stir. For a brief moment she was confused. Then her eyes snapped open as she remembered where she was and why she could not stretch her aching limbs. She glanced over at her stepmother. The woman's feet protruded from the coarse saddle blanket leaving them exposed. Cissy gasped when she spied Evangeline's badly swollen ankles. The rope had cut viciously into the tender flesh. Forgetting her own prickling limbs and the ropes that held her bound, she struggled with stiff fingers to try to loosen the ropes around Evangeline so that blood could begin to flow again. Hampered as she was, the effort was futile. The white heat of anger and hatred that swept through her was like nothing she had ever experienced when she saw the damage this man's cruelty had caused the only real mother she had ever known. It gave her the courage to fight whatever the man had planned for them. And not only would she fight, she was going to win.

"Wake up, you fool. Dammit, come help me!"

Marcel sat up, taking a moment to orient to what had awakened him. "What in deuces do you want? It's barely day and I'm tired."

Reckless with fury, she cried, "I don't give a damn what you are. You come here and untie these ropes around Evangeline's ankles. You've nearly cut off the circulation, you stupid man."

Too tired and miserable to resist the peremptory order, he surprised himself by complying.

"Now, undo mine. Perhaps, it surpasses your understanding, but I have need of a moment of privacy."

Again, he untied the ropes he had so carefully knotted the evening before. His temper began to rise as he noted that she had just called him stupid. "Don't go far and don't think you can get away, you bitch. I'll kill her if you try."

"You've just about done that already. She's unconscious and for all I know she's already dying. She's been seriously ill and has no strength for the rigors that you have put her through." Holding Evangeline's hand in hers as she said this, she felt a subtle squeeze. She immediately understood her stepmother's intention. She wanted her to get away and go for help. Yet, how could she leave Evangeline behind? Picking up her saddle blanket she carefully tucked it around her stepmother. Then she stood and looked into Marcel Lambert's hard eyes. The realization that she wanted to kill him shook her with its intensity.

His voice cut like a knife through the fog of angry resolve, "You stay near, you hear? Even better, perhaps, I should come with you while you do your business then I won't have to worry about what you're up to. I've got no problems with that. In fact, I might enjoy it."

She ignored his nasty laugh and suggestive remark. Her biggest priority was the need to allay any suspicion. Perhaps, she could get to the horses and get away before he realized what she was doing. Although she did not want to leave Evangeline she knew she had no choice. The woman could not take another night like the one past, nor could she survive a hard day in the saddle, continued exposure to the elements, and little food and water.

"Just how am I supposed to get away? I don't even know where we are, nor do I know how to saddle a horse. And I for sure can't mount one barebacked," Cissy lied. "I have no desire to be lost in this swamp and I expect you to get us out of here. Now, kindly allow me to relieve myself."

Suspicious, but aware of his own full bladder, he accepted her words. "Do it. And if you know what's healthy, don't waste time getting back here."

Cissy suspected Evangeline was faking unconsciousness as a way of protecting herself. If Marcel thought she would die, perhaps he would just ride away and leave her there. Cissy prayed that was the case, because she was leaving if she could. She had lied when she had said she didn't know their whereabouts. She had used this path on previous occasions when she delivered notes to the drop off point. She was acquainted with people on a small farm not far from the clearing. If she could get to the Davenports, she could get help for Evangeline and then she would deliver her message for Logan.

The minute she was far enough through the bushes and bramble to not be seen, she gathered her skirts and raced to her mare. Quickly she untied her reins and those of the other horses, before leaping onto her horse's unsaddled back. For once, she was thankful for all of those daredevil years and the tomboyish skills she had developed as a consequence. She slapped the flanks of the other horses at the same moment she put heels to her own. The first few feet were slow, but once she gained the path, she raced away, Marcel's shouted command to halt ringing in her ears. Even the ping of a bullet ricocheting off a nearby oak did nothing to halt her escape. It did bring a lump into her throat, however, as she considered the danger to which she had abandoned Evangeline. She could only trust that the woman would find some way to convince him that she was too far gone to bother with. The second bullet was closer and for a moment Cissy thought of turning back. Gritting her teeth, her shoulders blades anticipating a bullet at any moment, she hunched flat against her horse. Gripping her mane in desperate fingers, she urged the sturdy little mare to greater speed.

Cursing at the top of his lungs, Marcel whirled on the woman who lay unmoving on the ground, curled into a fetal position. Striding to her side, he viciously dug the toe of his boot into her ribs. Evangeline did not move. Only a faint groan escaped her lips. Marcel stood back studying her. She looked like hell. He kicked her harder and again was rewarded with only a soft groan. There seemed no point in killing her; she was too far-gone to be worth the waste of another bullet, especially when he had only three bullets left in the pistol he had taken from the young mother on the farm near Colliers. Once again he cursed himself for the lack of foresight. He should have bought more ammunition in New Berne. Instead he had thought only of a bath, good food, and new clothes. That had been nice but it did nothing to prepare him for his current course of action. Cursing steadily, he left the woman and stalked after his horse.

Evangeline lay unmoving. It had taken every ounce of willpower to emit only a small groan and remain limp and at his mercy. She had wanted to shriek in terror and agony, in fear for herself and her unborn child. But, the man had to believe that she was unconscious, had to think that she was dying. For all she knew, she might well be. The only glimpse of mercy she had to grasp onto was the fact that her baby seemed unharmed. As if in answer to her silent prayer, she felt the fetus stir and kick against the palm of her right hand that she had cupped protectively around the extended mound of her abdomen. She breathed a silent prayer of thanksgiving and then waited. She dared not move as long as there was some danger that he might return for her. She didn't know if she could move anyway. Every breath was a labor and she idly wondered if perhaps he had broken a rib. As she lay there, to help ignore the pain, she lovingly recalled the days of her marriage. Graham's face floated into her vision just as she lapsed into unconsciousness.

Leaves fell from the trees, dappling her still form with the bright colors of autumn. Birds called to one another as they flitted from branch to branch. A squirrel scamper close and then darted away to add another acorn to his winter stash. The sun rose higher in the sky, sending arrows of golden light to dance on her still body. The world around her continued in its timeless path and still she did not move. The child, nestled in Evangeline's womb, protested the position of her body, and kicked against her side urging her to move. But, she did not.

Chapter 22

Graham urged his horse forward. The animal was as exhausted as he was. Even the day had expended itself and was slowly fading into night. The trip to Kinston had been a nightmare of happenstance. In one station he was allowed to proceed, and in another tossed from the train to make space for troops and thus forced to waste precious hours waiting for the next opportunity. It had taken far longer than he could have imagined, but at last he was within an hour of his home. He found himself longing for the comfort of his wife's embrace, his daughter's face, and the prospect of the first hot meal in days. Despising himself for asking the old rented nag to hasten her step, Graham nonetheless dug in his spurs. They could both rest soon.

Shrugging his coat a bit tighter as he hunched down into its warmth, Graham turned from the ruined rail bed that he had followed since Dover. It was time to seek the protection of the wooded paths that would eventually lead him to his home. The going was slower but he had no choice if he wanted to elude the Yankee pickets. After the arduous trek he had endured to attain this proximity to home, he had no intention of imperiling the opportunity of getting his wife and daughter to safety by stumbling into the hands of Federal troops. He would be home by nightfall if luck held.

Some sixth sense and then the faint smell of pipe tobacco brought his progress to an abrupt halt in the thick brush bordering his land. Proceeding cautiously on foot, Graham dropped to the ground when he saw the figure of a Union soldier standing on the edge of his lawn. What the deuces was the man doing patrolling LaRoque property? Cursing under his breath at yet another impediment to his goal, Graham lay on his belly waiting for the man to move on.

After what had felt like hours, but was in reality mere minutes, the soldier ambled past Graham's hiding place and strolled towards the wooded path to Evangeline's former home. Graham wasted no time. Tugging the old nag along, he edged into the dark interior of his stable only to halt in terror when he heard an unexpected groan. Walking forward cautiously, he nearly tripped on Toby's supine form. "Good God, man. What has happened to you?"

The only response was a groan and a feeble stirring. At least Toby was not dead. Graham dashed for the lantern that always hung just inside the barn door He grabbed the flint from where it dangled from a nearby nail. Once the wick flared with flame, he quickly shuttered its sudden glow so that only a thin ray of illumination pierced the darkness. With the lantern shedding dim light on the straw littered barn floor, he looked back to where Toby lay. His forehead was spattered with a rust-like crust of dried blood, but other than that he appeared unharmed. He didn't want to drag the man to the house and feared that he could not lift him on his own. Graham reluctantly left him, and wasting no time, was soon in the safe harbor of the kitchen. There he found Bessie hunched over the table in tears. In front of her were untouched dishes she had managed to prepare from their own meager supply and the supplemental food the Yankee doctor had provided.

"Bessie, what on earth is the matter?"

"Lord have mercy, you are the answer to my prayers. The good Lord done and brought you home in the nick of time," Bessie cried. I don't know what to do, Mr. Graham. I can't find neither Miss Cissy nor Miss Evangeline. They didn't come down for supper so I went looking for 'em. It looks to me like they done and left. Things are all scattered around in their rooms and it just don't feel right. It ain't like Miss Evangeline to be messy. I'm just plumb scared something bad's happening. They wouldn't leave without telling me about it unless somebody done stole 'em away. I been so worried. I called out the door for Toby and he ain't answering neither. I don't know if the Yankees got 'em all or what."

"What do you mean? They aren't here? I can't image why they would leave alone. And Toby's not with them. I just found him in the barn. He's been hurt. Do you think you could help me carry him in here so we can see what's wrong?"

"It's the devil's work for sure." Bessie shook her head as she arose from the table. "Course I can help you. Let's git him in here and then we'll figure out what done happened to the misses."

By the time they got him to the kitchen, Toby seemed to be coming around. Seating him in the chair that Bessie had vacated earlier, Bessie hurried for water to wash his wounds while Graham examined the sizeable lump on his head. When they had him cleaned, Graham gently shook the man, "Toby, can you talk? Tell me what's happening, if you can."

Toby seemed to arouse himself with great effort and lifting his hand to his head, he gingerly explored the tender bump. His head dropped to his lap and he looked up in some confusion. Muttering, he remarked, "I must be dead. Can't be Mr. Graham here. He's down in Wilmington."

"No, Toby. I'm here. I came to get y'all and take you to Wilmington with me. Now tell me what's going on, if you can?"

"Danged it I know. Miss Evangeline come out to the barn with that Frenchie guy and told me to saddle up her hoss. I saw he was up to no good. Looked to me like he was holding a gun on her. I tried to let her know I would get help without rousing suspicion, but before I knew what was a happening he done and knocked me out."

"Where was Cissy?"

"I saddled up her horse a good bit before all this happened. She said something about getting some important message to Logan. I ain't seen her since."

Graham was thunderstruck. His daughter was galloping around the countryside unescorted and his wife was in the company of the nefarious Frenchman. He had heard numerous rumors concerning Marcel Lambert since their initial meeting in New Berne and none of them were flattering. He also seemed to have a vague memory of the name having some connection to his late wife's circle of acquaintances in Paris. Why he would have forced Evangeline to escape with him was beyond Graham's comprehension.

"Toby, do you know where Cissy planned on meeting Logan to get this message to him?"

Toby shook his head.

"Bessie?"

"She been going to somewhere down near Tuscarora. I spect I ain't supposed to know, but I heard Miss Cissy talking with Mr. Logan about it and her spying on them Yankees next door."

Graham's mouth dropped in disbelief. How could his daughter have allowed herself to become embroiled in such dangerous activities? Remembering her frustration with her lack of some useful purpose, he suddenly had the answer. He was proud and furious at the same time. He could only pray that Logan would protect her. Now, he must find some way of discovering what Marcel Lambert meant by abducting his wife and where he had taken her. Bessie ruined any hope that Cissy might be a separate issue when she explained that clothes and personal items for both of them had been taken.

At that moment, Evangeline was daring to move. The cold from the ground was seeping into her bones from lying so long in a stupor. She had regained consciousness minutes before, but was afraid to signal the fact in case Marcel was nearby. Waiting patiently for any noise that might betray his presence, she finally determined that he had not returned. Fear seized her at the thought that he must have caught Cissy. That being the likelihood, the only hope of salvation had now been thrust into her own feeble hands. Gathering some inner residue of strength, Evangeline brought herself onto all fours and then slowly stood. Listening with her breath in her throat, she waited. The only sound to break the silence of the early evening was the snort of a horse. Her heart soared. Now, if only she could saddle the animal and mount up, she could go for help. That is if she could stay conscious. Fighting back the darkness that threatened to reclaim her, Evangeline stumbled in the direction of the sound.

Heaving a sigh of relief, she leaned into the side of her horse. The animal heat radiating from him gave warmth to her cold and trembling body. "Hold on old fella. I'm going to get a saddle on you somehow and then find a log or stump so I can mount."

After what seemed like an eternity of struggle, she had managed to do both. That done, she sat on the horse's back in total quandary. How was she to find help in the middle of a swamp and in the dead of night? Glancing up at the sky as if seeking Divine guidance, her gaze fastened on the Night Star. Ever since her childhood she had found comfort in its steady presence. As long as the stars kept their places in the heavens, there was order in a chaotic world. Since the swamp seemed to run in an east-west direction, she decided trusting the stars to help her find the way was her best option. She could only pray that it would lead her to help for herself and Cissy before her meager strength was expended.

Weary past exhaustion and struggling to stay conscious, Evangeline jerked to attention when the alarmed barking of dogs broke the chill silence of the night. Raising her head, she could see in the distance the outline of a farmhouse and outbuildings. Spurring her tired horse forward, she cautiously advanced. Evangeline fervently hoped that the sleeping owners of the farm would awaken and call off the dogs before they could spook her horse. The thought of being thrown and what it could do to her unborn child made her quake in terror. Relief came in the form of the gleam of sudden lantern light and a sharp command for the dogs to hush.

"Hello," She called. "Help. Please, help me."

The farmer ran into the yard in his long underwear. A gun in his left hand was aimed in her general direction. "Ride up close so's I can see you, missy. You out here alone?"

"I'm alone and I desperately need help. I have no weapons and I mean you no harm." Evangeline rode into the light and waited.

"Good God Almighty, woman. What you doing out here in the middle of the night in your condition?" He walked up to her and hauled her from the saddle where she sank weakly against him, her legs incapable of support. The man yelled, "Ma, git Jonathan and git out here. I need some help. We got us a sick woman on our hands."

Soon hands were lifting her and carrying her inside. They gathered around her, a perfect halo of faces all peering intently at their unexpected visitor. The husband and wife were joined by a stair-step of sons that she judged to range in age from three to maybe fourteen.

"Ma'am, I'm Loretta Jones. This here is my man, Caleb, and my sons Jonathan, Benjamin, Shadrack, Joshua and baby Micah. We aim to help you best we can. I spect the first thing you need is something warm to eat. You just set right here by the fire whilst I get you something."

The woman was all efficiency, "Pa, how about gittin that coffee pot going for me? Benjamin you go git me some more firewood and some kindling. Joshua bring me another blanket and wrap it around her quick like."

It felt so good to be warmed by the fire. The bowl of left over soup was as good as the most elegant meal she had ever eaten. They were a kind family and their concern for her was apparent. When she had eaten the last bite of soup and drunk a tall glass of clear spring water, she smiled her gratitude and began her story. They listened intently, their eyes never leaving her. When she had finished, tears were running unchecked down every cheek but Caleb's stubbled ones, and even his eyes had a suspicious sheen. Wiping her tears away with her hand, she concluded, "Now you have it. For the life of me, I don't know what that evil man was planning, but if he has caught my daughter, I fear for her."

Caleb patted her hand, "We're going to git her back. Jonathan, ride into Dover and git the sheriff and have him bring some men. I'll ride around the local farms and see who I can find to help us. Most menfolk are off fightin' but there's a few of us left, plus some too old to go to war, but they ain't so old but what they can't help search. Now we're going to help you to bed. I suspect some rest would be real welcome. Don't worry none. If your young'un can be found, we aim to do it."

Evangeline snuggled into the feather bed and was soon deep in sleep.

At that moment, Bessie stood in the parlor of Evangeline's old home staring at the blue clad men that surrounded her. Beulah stood off to the side wringing her hands in her apron, her face a network of deeply etched worry lines. Carefully Bessie relayed the story as Graham had coached her, leaving out any mention of him. As one of the foremost blockade-runners out of Wilmington, they would love to take him into custody. Considering each word before she uttered it made the telling slow and at times circuitous. At Graham's direction, she allowed them to think that Cissy had been at the house when Evangeline was taken. Since Bessie had told him someone had packed a few essentials for them both, Graham assumed, in all probability, they were together.

Colonel Ryan Madison studied the woman. He knew she was holding something back, but he could not doubt the basic truth of what the distraught woman was saying. Nothing else mattered at the moment. Dr. Hand caught his eye, mirroring the concern that he himself felt.

Ryan was honest enough with himself to acknowledge that for him, it was more than worry for the welfare of the women. He felt a towering rage that the innocent girl might be sullied. He admired Cissy, not just for her extraordinary beauty, but also for her spirit. He enjoyed her intelligence and that indefinable sparkle that made her exciting. Her nascent sensuality made him long to teach her the pleasures of loving. Yet, he had denied himself any overt action in that direction, accepting that she was too young for him, too recently an adolescent. The thought of some rakehell harming her, robbing her of her purity and zest, was enough to enrage him to the point of murder. Maybe, he admitted, in some dark corner of his mind he was a little jealous that some other man would seize the prize that he had thought of on many sleepless nights when the need for a woman plagued him.

Turning to his aide, he thundered, "Tell that nitwit Barney to see which direction the tracks go and then get his ass saddled up. And round up some men. Take three or four from our Third New York Calvary. And you, Sergeant Wright, isn't it?"

"Yes sir, Ben Wright. Tenth Connecticut."

"Do you have someone you can spare?"

"I can come, sir. Friend of mine, Pvt. Elias Peck, is a good man. I'll get him.

"Can you ride well enough to keep up with the calvary?"

"We may be city boys from Greenwich but we can ride. Get us some horses and lead the way."

"Somebody get these men some horses and pack up. We

leave in twenty minutes. We'll search as far as we can without running into Rebel territory. Let's hope to God we can catch up to those women before they come to any real harm."

The doctor spoke up, "I'm coming, too. Mrs. LaRoque is in no condition for rough treatment. If we find them before some ill befalls them, she's going to need my help."

Bessie and Beulah linked arms as they watched the men hurry from the room, taking comfort from one another. When the soldiers were out of earshot, Beulah remarked, "Mr. Graham be fit to be tied iffn he knew what become of his wife and child. Lord, that poor man. It'd kill him was something bad to happen to them."

"He knows. He over at the house now. He come to get us and take us to Wilmington just a little spell ago and found old Toby laid out in the barn. Look like that varmint whacked him on the head. Mr. Graham say he's goin' to go lookin' for 'em, too. We just gotta hope the Yankees don't find him ramblin' around out yonder. They sure would like to git they hands on that man and stop his boats from runnin' past that blockade."

"Lord Jesus, what a heap of mess we is in."

"Ain't it so. I done and prayed and prayed. I couldn't stand nothin' to happen to them."

After exchanging final commiserations with Beulah, Bessie walked home to see if there was anything more she could do for Toby. She walked into the kitchen to find Toby still at the table.

Graham was there too and had just finished stuffing food into his saddlebag. He wasted no time in telling the two servants goodbye before leaving to begin his search. He had noted horse tracks leading west when he arrived. He could only surmise that Evangeline and the Frenchman were heading after Cissy, or were with her. Either way, his instincts told him to head in the direction of Dover. By midnight he was too exhausted to continue, the night too dark, and his horse ready to collapse. He made camp in the swamp, determined that at first light he would be on his way.

At daybreak the sound of men talking low and the clopping of horses awakened him to a rosy dawn. Hastily he packed his things, fed the horse a handful of oats and let him drink from the swamp water, brown from the tannin of decayed leaves. Swinging into the saddle, he followed in the direction of the men he had heard. Some ten minutes of riding brought him near enough to call out.

"Ho there. Could you wait up a minute?"

The group of mostly old men and adolescent boys turned to stare at the stranger as he approached. It was obvious they were impatient to be off and Graham was delaying them.

"Howdy, men. I wonder if you might have seen a man with a pregnant woman and maybe a young one, as well. My wife and possibly my daughter were kidnapped. If any of you could help me search, I'd be very grateful."

"Tarnation man, I suspect its your wife I got at my house. The missus is tending to her." Caleb Jones introduced himself and then the others before relating Evangeline's story to Graham. As Graham listened, he knew beyond a doubt that Cissy had been Lambert's goal from the beginning. He didn't know if Lambert wanted her for her body or the fortune that she would share with her unborn brother or sister. Whatever it was that the man wanted with Cissy, Graham was determined to find his daughter and crush the Frenchman like the vermin he was.

Chapter 23

Logan decided he was getting damned tired of hunching down in bush and briar, in cold and rain, in heat and mosquitoes. He was weary of being constantly wary, fearful of being caught and facing the hanging meted out to spies. Once again, he was hiding. Despite the chill of the early November day, sweat was poring off him. He could smell its rancor, the sign of nervous fear, the adrenalin rush that nailed him to the spot, breath bated, afraid to even blink. He cursed steadily to himself as he buried deeper into the pine straw and drifted leaves. The bluecoats must not capture him now. The newly procured message in his pocket added urgency. He must avoid any impediment to delivering the news it contained. The Union was planning an incursion into eastern North Carolina while Lee's forces were occupied in Virginia. Foster was to march west through Kinston and destroy the Wilmington-Weldon railroad bridge five miles distant from Goldsborough. The railroad, and thus the bridge, formed the vital aorta between the port in Wilmington and the Confederate capital of Richmond to which it carried the food, the war supplies, and all other goods necessary to both the civilian and military populations. Were it to fall, the capital and Lee's army would be isolated from the remainder of the south and the days of the Confederacy limited. He had to deliver the message.

Straining his ears to hear above the sound of the Yankee squad as they unsaddled to give their horses a rest, only the name Cissy LaRoque penetrated his brain. Logan dared to edge closer to see what they were saying about her. His worry that she would be caught and punished was even greater than the terror he felt when he thought of being captured himself. The message he carried was vital, but not even the Confederacy was enough to replace Cissy as the primary focus of his very being. He had to help her if she was in danger.

"Dammit, how much further can we penetrate into Confederate held territory before we run into a hornet's nest of problems?" The voice was querulous.

"Are you complaining, Corporal Reed? If you had watched the LaRoque's the way I instructed, this whole exercise would not be necessary. I don't want to hear anymore griping out of you. Is that understood?"

Judging by the man's reaction, Logan suspected Reed had not intended for the officer to hear his remark. His posture and voice were hang-dog when he replied, "Yes, sir. I apologize, Colonel Madison, but I'm feeling mighty skittish about now. We ain't that far from Kinston. From what I hear, they got a sizeable army holed up there."

"I'm well aware of that, Corporal. If you are too frightened to continue with us, feel free to turn back, however I promise you it will not be overlooked."

"No, sir. I ain't turning back. I'm just saying...."

"You're not saying anything that the rest of us don't know." Logan listened as the Union officer continued in a hard and determined voice, "I intend to go on for at least another mile or so before turning back. The LaRoque women are in danger. If the black servant is to be trusted in what she says, one has to believe that to be the case. If we still have found no trace of them by shortly after sunup, we will have to turn back. There aren't enough of us to hold off many of the enemy if we should run into them. As it is, I feel a responsibility to help the LaRoques if we can." Madison looked pointedly at Corporal Reed as he added, "I remind you, had it not been for negligence on our part in guarding the premises the Frenchman could not have slipped in and seized them."

"But, Colonel Madison, ain't that Cissy suspected of being some kind of spy?"

"Corporal, you say one more word and I'm going to tie you to a tree and leave you for those Rebels you're so worried about." Madison cursed, "Mount up. No point in wasting any more time debating."

The cold of the early morning was nothing compared to the sudden chill that descended on Logan's heart. All he could think of was what he had just heard. It was bad enough that they suspected Cissy of spying. It was worse that the contemptible Marcel Lambert was likely the one who had taken her and Evangeline. Logan had no choice. The message would have to wait. He had to do what he could to find them and free them. And he would relish the chance to provide a long overdue killing for Lambert.

When the jingle of harnesses and the clopping of hooves had faded away, Logan stumbled to his feet. He was cramped from huddling in rigid fear of detection. Brushing the leaves from his clothes, he pulled his hat low on his head, stamped his feet to renew circulation, and walked back to where he had tethered his horse. With the coming of light, it would be easier making his way. But, where was he to begin? He had no clue where Lambert might be taking the women, nor why.

Logan knew the woods. He knew where the bogs were, where the clearings that had existed since Indian times lay, and he had a good idea of the likeliest paths to take in order to avoid the main roads. That helped him. This not being the terrain of either the Yankee soldiers or the Frenchman, he could only pray that such arcane knowledge would serve him in his quest. Now if only the difficult topography would confound the others and force them to the main routes, he could discount two problems. He would be able to more easily elude the Yankees and the routes that Lambert might take were greatly reduced. He decided his best option lay in paralleling Trent Road in the hope of finding Lambert. If the man was using the easiest route to reach Kinston and the depot was his destination, it was the logical choice. That was a great assumption he realized, but time was precious and he could not search everywhere.

Midmorning he stopped his horse within sight of Trent Road, and swung down from the saddle. He needed a break. Digging in his knapsack, he found a piece of hardtack that he struggle to chew and swallow. He figured sawdust would be just about as palatable. He had just re-corked his canteen when he heard a woman scream, followed immediately by strenuous cursing in English and then French.

No longer caring if the Yankees were near or not, Logan leaped into his saddle and furiously slashed his horse as he headed in the direction of that voice in distress. It had to be them.

After Cissy had dropped off her message, she had turned back toward New Berne along the path that she had used on so many previous trips to deliver messages. Since she had seen nothing of Lambert since she had escaped, she assumed that he had lost her trail. That was her first mistake.

The adrenalin coursing through her veins was putting pressure on her bladder. She had fought the urge as long as she could before stopping. The second was stopping to relieve herself and leaving the horse only loosely tethered. He had moved off several yards while left unattended, forcing Cissy to waste valuable time chasing him until she could catch him again. A torn edging of lace from her petticoat clung unnoticed on a small thorn, where it waved like a flag announcing her direction.

The third mistake was a single-minded focus on returning to New Berne. So concentrated was she on her goal that she forgot to listen for a pursuing horse. It was not until the thundering hooves were upon her that she was alert enough to spur her horse to greater speed. It was too late. Once again her mare was no match for the Frenchman's horse. Marcel reached over and hauled her from the mare onto his own horse.

"You little bitch, I think it is time I tamed you once and for all," he snarled. "Your whore of a mother was a lively bedmate. I intend to find out what kind of woman you are."

"You try and I'll kill you, so help me God." It would be days before the meaning of his remark about Monique would penetrate her brain.

"Don't over-estimate yourself and don't under-estimate me," he responded coldly. "I find myself weary of the aggravation you have put me to. Cause me anymore, and you will regret it."

"I'll die before I stop fighting you."

"That can be arranged in due time." There was no mirth in his laugh.

Struggling to escape, Cissy managed to rake his face with her nails leaving a path of lines that welled with a thin seep of blood. Immediately he jerked the horse to a halt and dragged her from the saddle where he dumped her unceremoniously on the ground. For a moment she was winded from the impact of the fall. Catching her breath she began to rise, but he climbed on top of her pressing her back onto the earth. As he struggled to shove her skirts and petticoats away, panic filled her. The scream that tore from her throat was ignored. A savage rip took care of the impediment of clothing. Marcel began to unbutton his own britches. Heaving and twisting under him, she fought with all of her strength. Fumble as he might, his one free hand was insufficient for undoing the buttons.

"I warned you," were the last words she heard before a stinging slap sent her spiraling into darkness. Marcel stood to unfasten the buttons. He no longer felt the same need to rush. He would wait until she started coming to and then she would learn what it meant to defy him.

He did not have to watch her for long. She began to stir and he was ready for her when she opened her eyes. "I would have preferred a more pleasant introduction for our first bedding, however, since you seem so intent on being uncooperative, you leave me no choice."

Cissy watched him lower himself onto her body, stunned and more frightened than ever before in her life. Screaming in terror, she jerked her knees up to protect that most private part of her. She succeeded in a manner that her innocence had not prepared her for. Marcel writhed in agony. Gasping in pain as he clutched his groin, he snarled, "You'll pay for that."

A cold, steely voice replied for her, "Not her. You. Stand up and drop that gun." Glancing at Cissy he softly asked, "Cissy, could you walk over there to the woods and straighten yourself?"

Rising on shaky legs, Cissy clutched her clothing against her body, her eyes never leaving Logan's face. He motioned his head for her to go, the pistol that was leveled on the Frenchman steady and sure in his hand. He did not want her to witness him shooting Marcel to death. Cissy stumbled as she began to walk away causing Logan enough of a momentary distraction for Marcel to pull his own gun from his pocket and fire.

Again Cissy screamed. The sound was lost in the sharp retort of Logan's pistol as he put a bullet through the Frenchman's heart. Only then did he stagger and fall to his knees. He was hit. He didn't know how badly until he could remove his shirt and search the wound. Instantly Cissy was by his side. Kneeling she wrapped her arms around him and lowered him to the ground. For a moment the sweetness of having her near distracted him from the impact of the searing pain that had begun to throb in his side. When she leaned against him, he yelped in agony.

"I'm so sorry. I didn't mean to hurt you. What can I do to help?"

"Help me get my shirt loose so we can see how bad I'm hit." Logan grunted as she tugged the shirt from his trousers.

With gentle fingers and bated breath, Cissy explored his wound. "I don't think it is serious even though I know it must hurt terribly. It looks as though it just grazed your flesh here just at the ribs. The bullet didn't go in."

"Good. However, it feels as though it may have cracked a rib. It hurts like a son of a bi... Never mind. Do you have something that you can use to bandage me up so we can get going? I don't want to stay here."

"Give me your knife, Logan. I can cut some strips from my petticoat to use for bandages. It's pretty much ruined anyway."

"I'd like to kill him twice for what he did to you. I'm sorry you had to see this though. Shooting and killing are no sights for a woman. It's hard enough on us men."

"Logan Gwaltney, I am purely delighted that man is dead. He was an evil, mean man that the world is better off without. Don't you worry about me. I would have killed him myself if I'd had the chance. I am glad he's gone so I don't ever have to fear him again."

Logan looked at her, afraid to ask the question that burned in his mind. With the words forming on his lips, he bit them back. It didn't matter if Marcel had raped her or not. He loved her. Nothing would change that if she had been. Asking her would forever make her wonder if it mattered, if he loved her enough.

Instead he said, "I suppose we should try to bury him. I hate to see anyone left for the animals."

"We have nothing to dig with and you are in no condition to do something like that. Just let me get you bandaged up and we'll see if we can find Evangeline. That is far more important than that dead man."

"Oh, good Lord. I purely forgot about Miss Evangeline with all that was going on here. What has he done with her?"

"He must have left her for dead. God only knows if she is or not, but I have to go back and find her."

"Do you know the way?"

"I'm not sure. I just know I have to try. Are you able to ride that far or should we find a house somewhere that will take you in?"

"Finish the bandaging. I'm riding if it kills me. I love that woman like a mother. There is no way I can just stop until I know she's safe."

Ryan Madison heard the two shots. He had sent his men back to New Berne, unwilling to take them deeper into Confederate controlled territory and he had gone on alone determined to find the two women if he could. Tying his horse, he cautiously approached on foot, his gun drawn, not knowing what he might run into. In the clearing ahead he could see Cissy and the man she was bandaging. Noting the body off to the side and the fact that the man she was tending had been wounded, told him the source of the two shots he had heard.

At least Cissy LaRoque was safe. The tenderness of her movements revealed that the man was no casual stranger but someone she both knew and cared for. When she had finished, the man reached up and gave her cheek a loving caress. Her smile lit the clearing and wedged into a crack in Ryan's heart. He suspected the man of being Cissy's lover, her contact, and probably a spy. He fully realized that his duty required that he arrest them both. He could not bring himself to do it. That would be his gift to the beautiful young woman he would have liked to call his own. The man had saved the girl and she cared for him, maybe even loved him. Glancing balefully at the dead man, he wanted to bury one of his own bullets in the corpse in repayment for the treatment he had dealt Cissy. Her torn clothing was a clear signal of what the Frenchman had been about. He could only hope that the wounded man had arrived in time.

Briefly Ryan wished that he were the one that had saved her and earned that smile. That he was the one she loved. But it was not to be. Wondering what had become of Mrs. LaRoque, Ryan walked with silent steps back to his waiting horse. He would trust them to find her if she was still alive. His duty lay in New Berne among the enemies of the southern cause.

Not far behind, Cissy and Logan were also on horseback and attempting to retrace her path to the clearing where she had left Evangeline. Numerous false turns frustrated their efforts. The trees and bushes, swampy hillocks, and indifferent wildlife gave no clue. By early afternoon, Logan was in real pain and still bleeding from his wound. He needed rest and healing. Cissy was on the point of broaching that suggestion, when horsemen on the path behind hailed them.

Turning in the saddle, Cissy saw her father leading a group of old men and young boys. With a joyous voice she returned the greeting. Logan and she reined in their horses and waited.

Graham flung himself from the saddle and ran to his daughter, pulling her into his arms. Tears filled his eyes and threatened to spill down his cheeks. He wanted to tell her how worried he had been, how much he loved her, and of his desperation to find her. He could not get the words past the lump in his throat.

Caleb introduced himself to Logan, "I see you been hurt. Let's git you on back to my cabin. My missus can fix you up."

"That'd be welcome. But we need to find Mr. LaRoque's wife first."

"That's already took care of. She found us and we got her tucked up in bed."

Chapter 24

Cissy stood beside the swirling waters of the Cape Fear River in Wilmington. In her hand she held the letter Logan had written. The message she had given him had not averted the attack on Goldsborough. The Confederate troops in Kinston had dug in and extended their breastworks, but on December 13th and 14th, the attacking Union forces had defeated them in a ferocious battle. After facing far more determined opposition than he had counted on, General Foster and his army had moved on towards Goldsborough and the all-important bridge. Their confidence broken, the rattled troops had gained a Pyrrhic victory. The bridge while damaged was quickly repaired and the whole exercise had done little more than kill a lot of soldiers: far more of them wearing the blue uniform than the gray.

Folding the letter, Cissy tucked it into her pocket. Her engagement ring glinted in the sunlight dancing off the water. Catching a bright beam in her eye, she smiled down at the golden circle. While she had not agreed to marry him until after the war, she had accepted his ring with a joyous heart.

A baby's cry broke the stillness of the morning. Although premature, her sturdy little brother was a hungry and demanding little fellow. She laughed at the sound and turned back toward the house they now called home. Evangeline was still bedridden but the doctor assured them she would be on her feet in a few more days.

When Cissy reached the top of the steps, her father was waiting.

"That is one beautiful racket. It takes me back to when you were a baby. I don't know which of you could cry the loudest." Graham and Cissy laughed together, their hearts glad for the joy that had come to them.

Cissy looked up at her father, "Papa, it is so good to know that in the midst of so much death and evil, life can go on."

"It always has, Cissy. Somehow, it always will."

Other titles by B.J. Vaughn

Title: *Muddy Waters*

- Paperback: 9780874260793
- Ebook: 9780874262506
- 236 pages
- Language: English

The War Between the States has come to eastern North Carolina, bringing hardships, pillaging, and fear to the local residents. For those left at home, the struggle to procure the needs of daily life is all-consuming; for those serving in the armies of both North and South, death is a daily companion. Against this backdrop, an unlikely and forbidden love affair between a local woman and a Union officer leads to difficult choices for them both—choices that will tear them apart and force them to deal with the abandonment of their dream of a life together.

Despite broken hearts, misunderstandings, and missed chances, Penny and Ryan strive to survive the dangers and ravages of war and make the best of their separate futures. With the surrender of the South at Appomattox, Penny realizes she has one last chance to either find the man she loves or settle for a life alone.

Title: ***Turbulent Waters***

- Hard Cover: 9781590951743
- Paperback: 9781590951750
- Ebook: 9781590951767
- 328 pages
- Language: English

Love is personal, war is not, especially in North Carolina, 1865-1867, during the reconstruction. With a love they are certain will transcend all else, southern belle Penny Kennedy marries Union Officer and attorney, Ryan Madison, despite the condemnation of those around them. The initial days of wedded bliss end abruptly when Marcus, the man who courted Penny for years in anticipation that she would marry him, is arrested for murder, and Ryan is assigned to prosecute him. As hard as this development is to tolerate for Penny, she will discover worse things await her before Ryan and she can attain the life they desire.

www.ingramcontent.com/pod-product-compliance
Lightning Source LLC
Chambersburg PA
CBHW020346120726
47904CB00002B/470

9781590956755